Having p[illegible]hotherapist, Caroline Dunford enjoyed many years helping other people shape their personal life stories before taking the plunge and writing her own stories. She has now published almost thirty books in genres ranging from historical crime to thrillers and romance, including her much-loved Euphemia Martins mysteries and a brand-new series set around WWII featuring Euphemia's perceptive daughter Hope Stapleford. Caroline also teaches creative writing courses part-time at the University of Edinburgh.

Praise for Caroline Dunford:

'A sparkling and witty crime debut with a female protagonist to challenge Miss Marple' Lin Anderson

'Impeccable historical detail with a light touch' Lesley Cookman

'Euphemia Martins is feisty, funny and completely adorable' Colette McCormick

'A rattlingly good dose of Edwardian country house intrigue with plenty of twists and turns and clues to puzzle through' *Booklore.co.uk*

'The sharp dialogue capture(s) the feel of the era . . . an engaging and entertaining read' *Portobello Book Blog*

*Also by Caroline Dunford*

*Euphemia Martins Mysteries:*

A Death in the Family
A Death in the Highlands
A Death in the Asylum
A Death in the Wedding Party
The Mistletoe Mystery (a short story)
A Death in the Pavilion
A Death in the Loch
A Death for King and Country
A Death for a Cause
A Death by Arson
A Death Overseas
A Death at Crystal Palace
A Death at a Gentleman's Club
A Death at the Church
A Death at the Races
A Death in the Hospital
A Death on Stage

*Hope Stapleford Series:*

Hope for the Innocent
Hope to Survive

*Others:*

Highland Inheritance
Playing for Love
Burke's Last Witness

# A DEATH ON STAGE

A EUPHEMIA MARTINS MYSTERY

CAROLINE DUNFORD

ACCENT

First published in 2021 by Headline Accent
An imprint of HEADLINE PUBLISHING GROUP

1



Cataloguing in Publication Data is available from the British Library

ISBN 978 1 7861 5798 0

Typeset in 10.5/13pt Bembo Std by Jouve (UK), Milton Keynes

Printed and bound in Great Britain by Clays Ltd, Elcograf S.p.A.

Headline's policy is to use papers that are natural, renewable and recyclable products and made from wood grown in well-managed forests and other controlled sources. The logging and manufacturing processes are expected to conform to the environmental regulations of the country of origin.

HEADLINE PUBLISHING GROUP
An Hachette UK Company
Carmelite House
50 Victoria Embankment
London
EC4Y 0DZ

www.headline.co.uk
www.hachette.co.uk

For Andrew Girdwood in thanks for all the help and support he has given along the way.

# Chapter One

## Driving to London

Fitzroy drove in a manner most unlike his usual style. No one could have called his progression slow. Even the descriptor 'carefully' would only be applied by the most tolerant. Yet he was not driving with his usual reckless abandonment. Instead, he appeared to be stretching out our journey to London for as long as his pre-emptive nature allowed. Every now and then he would take his eyes off the road for a good few seconds as he glanced over at me. This wasn't as worrying as it might sound. In general, it always seemed as if he paid next to no heed to what was ahead. A honk of the horn might be the only warning some poor Sunday motorist might get to whip himself to the side of the road or risk being run into a ditch by our passing.

I knew it had been a bad idea to let him drive in the Monte Carlo rally. He thought himself an even better driver now. And he'd hardly been modest about his driving ability before.

'For God's sake, Euphemia, tell me what you are thinking!'

The use of my real name, rather than my spy moniker Alice, got my attention. I blinked twice and tried to focus on what he was really asking. He wanted to know if he was forgiven. I didn't have an answer for him yet.

'I didn't lie,' he protested. 'I told you Bertram was safe, and he was.'

'Safe in hospital after undergoing a life-threatening operation,' I retorted.

'Yes, well,' said Fitzroy, his cheeks slightly tinged with red. 'Those were details you didn't need to know at the time.'

'Details I didn't need to know about my own husband?'

'Euphemia – Alice – you were mid-mission. A serious mission, the outcome of which would have a major impact on the war. Did you think I would divide your focus at such a crucial time? It wasn't as if there was anything you could have done to help him at that moment.'

'I could have gone to him.'

'And been shot for desertion? Leaving the villain uncaught? Bertram was unconscious and wouldn't have thanked you anyway. Or do you think your bond with your husband is so spiritual he would have somehow sensed your presence and come out of his coma?'

My head snapped round at that. 'He was in a coma? You never told me that!'

'I checked this morning before we left, he's out of it now. Well on the mend.'

'You are a swine!'

I saw him wince at that. I knew I was being unfair – to a degree at least. My husband had undertaken a mission Fitzroy was too ill to complete, and had masqueraded as the master spy. Unfortunately, the mission had been a blind, to capture Fitzroy and blackmail the British Secret Service. Bertram, who is only an asset, not an operative, never having completed the training I have, was hugely out of his depth and taken hostage. At this point, as they still had the real Fitzroy and all his knowledge and skills intact, the Service disavowed the mission and forbade a rescue attempt. All of which was quite in tune with my general image of them. I expected them to deal with their spies without mercy. It was implicit in our oath. But to desert a civilian asset, a loyal subject of the Crown – the very people we were meant to protect – struck me as unconscionable.

Fitzroy ignored the disavowal and went alone to rescue Bertram. He managed to do so, at severe physical cost to himself, but an even worse cost to my husband, who has a chronic heart condition. They returned with Bertram barely alive. Fitzroy got him to hospital and told me my husband was pulling – or had pulled – through.

'I don't ignore your courage in going to retrieve Bertram,' I said. 'Nor do I fail to understand why you lied to me. I was in the middle of a critical—'

'I didn't lie!' yelled Fitzroy, thumping his fist on the steering wheel and almost taking us into a ditch. He swerved back and forth, regaining control of the car. In earlier times I might have made a sound of distress – not a scream, but more of a gasping yelp. Now, however, I merely braced myself and held on to the sides of my seat until the car was once more firmly on the road.

Slightly breathless from his exertions, Fitzroy repeated, 'I didn't lie to you. I *don't* lie to you. I promised I would never lie to you.'

As he regularly lied to everyone else he knew, with the possible exception of his dog, Jack, this was a major undertaking for him.

'Perhaps you didn't lie, but you omitted details.'

Fitzroy made a soft grumbling sound. 'I always do that,' he said. 'It's my training.'

'I know,' I said. 'I'm not cross with you about you not telling me what was happening with Bertram.' The spy looked round with an unusual expression on his face: hopefulness. 'I don't *like* that you did that,' I said, 'but upon consideration I can see why you did it, for my sake as much as for the mission. If I had been preoccupied I could have come to harm.'

'You did,' said Fitzroy darkly. He hates it when I get hurt. This, despite him regularly getting stabbed, shot, or thrown off cliffs and gathering scars as if they are some kind of merit badge, of the sort awarded to children at Sunday school.

'Pah!' I said, quoting him. 'It's a scratch. Besides, that was my forgiving you.'

'Everything?'

'No,' I said. 'I don't think so. I am truly grateful and humbled that you disobeyed orders to fetch him back.'

'You would have done the same for me,' he said, suddenly staring intently at the road.

'You don't have a spouse,' I said. 'I'd go a long way for Jack, but I'm not entirely sure I'd risk my life to rescue him from behind enemy lines.'

'Alice! And Jack would rather lick your ankles than anyone else's.'

'I wish he didn't lick ankles at all,' I said, momentarily distracted, 'it gives one the most peculiar feeling.'

'So why are you at odds with me? And don't say you're not. I know you, and I can hear the cogs of your mind turning unkindly!'

Fitzroy is not usually given to imaginative flights of fantasy. On missions together, he is the master of practicality and ruthlessness. I am the one who looks for more gentle solutions. I sighed. 'I imagine I am no more cross with you than you are with yourself.'

'Ah,' said Fitzroy, who followed me with his normal uncanny accuracy. 'You mean because I didn't realise it was a trap?'

I nodded. 'It's not like you not to thoroughly scrutinise the details of any mission.'

There was silence for a few minutes, during which Fitzroy carefully drove around a squirrel. He might have no compunction about ridding the world of his fellow man, but he had otherwise an intense regard for life. Apparently, this even went as far as squirrels. Despite their tufty tails, I always saw them as vermin. Tree rats.

Eventually he said, 'You've only ever seen me prepare for missions that have involved the two of us.' He turned to look at me, his eyebrows lowered. 'I haven't always been so careful.'

'I see. Before I became an agent, I had always thought you erratic and reckless. Then when we began to work together, I was surprised at how professional you were. Was my first impression accurate?'

The spy looked back at the road and shrugged, the furred shoulders of his driving coat rippling. 'Reckless is fair. Although I always had reasons. I would not have described myself as erratic.'

'Method in your madness?'

'I wasn't especially concerned over my own safety, I suppose. I'd been in the game ten years, and was close to considering myself immortal!' He gave me a swift smile. 'I had no desire to shuffle off this mortal coil, but I was daring.'

'Humph!' I said, summing up what I thought about the male notion of being 'daring'.

'I admit I made mistakes, Alice. In those few weeks we had training Bertram to pass as me, I didn't think of mixing in any actual spycraft. I concentrated on the look of it. I thought the only danger to him would be if he was caught out as an imposter. I trained him, as best as I could in such a short time, to notice if things were going awry and how to extricate himself diplomatically. It never entered my head that the mission was a trap. That he needed to learn more physical skills.'

'I expect you thought if you did teach him things of that nature he might try using them again.'

Fitzroy gave an assenting grunt.

'My husband is nothing if not brave.'

'Too damn brave for his own good. And for your good too!' snarled the spy. 'You'd go to pieces if anything happened to him.'

For once, I didn't disown my weakness. Fitzroy made another grunting noise. This time more surly.

'What I should have done,' he continued, 'was sit down and go over the entire mission from an asset's point of view. It never entered my head it could be a trap, but if I'd been going and it had turned out to be a trap I'd have—'

'Winged it,' I said. 'You'd have made it up as you went along.'

'Well, you know now, Alice, how many plans are a bust within minutes of engagement.'

'Most,' I said. 'At least, most of yours.'

Fitzroy gave me a pained look, but let me take the point.

'I didn't think it through from your husband's point of view. For that, I wholeheartedly apologise.'

The spymaster looked at me with an expression closer to humble than I had ever thought possible. 'You were still knocked up from your previous mission,' I said.

'More than I realised,' said Fitzroy.

'I believe understanding one's own limitations is a necessary precursor to working with others.'

'Touché.'

'That really doesn't make it any better, you know.'

'I know,' said Fitzroy quietly. 'I was too . . .'

'Too busy being rude to me?'

'I admit I wasn't in the best of shape myself,' said Fitzroy. 'You know where I'd been and what I'd seen. I arrived at White Orchards barely able to stand. Only you saw how ill I was.'

I nodded. 'So why were you such a pig to me?'

Fitzroy's shoulders sagged. 'Do we have to go over old ground? It's in the past, isn't it?'

'You were the one who suggested we talk on the way to London,' I exclaimed. 'You said we needed to sort things out.'

'Well, I'm an idiot.'

'That's one thing we can agree on. Now, spill!'

'Oh, very well,' snapped the spy, 'if you must know, I thought we had got too close on that last mission and we needed more distance between us.'

I shook my head. 'I don't understand. You came to my home. How is that creating more distance?'

'Don't be wilfully blind, Alice! That's not the kind of distance I meant.'

I gasped as if hit in the solar plexus. 'You mean an emotional distance? You mean . . . you're fond of me?'

'You know I am,' said Fitzroy. 'You are the only person I count in this world as a friend. But, no, I didn't mean that. I meant that you were getting too fond of me!'

I turned in my seat at that. 'If you weren't driving, I'd slap you! I'll have you know I love my husband!'

'I could pull over if you wanted to slap me,' said Fitzroy, his tone reverting to his usual teasing manner. 'I'd rather you didn't make a habit of it, but the last time you slapped me, we did get on rather well afterwards. I could allow it one more time. Overlook the superior officer bit.'

'Senior,' I corrected automatically. 'You should have talked to me at White Orchards. Let me know what you were thinking. By pushing me away like that all you did was put me off kilter for my mission, as well as causing you to make mistakes – mistakes that involved my husband.'

'I wasn't myself,' said Fitzroy.

'No, I see that now. I knew you were unwell. I didn't realise you'd lost your mind.'

Fitzroy flashed me a grin. 'I've never been that big on sanity.'

I sat back in my seat, relaxing properly for the first time since we'd set out. 'So where are we going? Which hospital is Bertram in, and where am I staying? I suppose as you've got Griffin I could stay with you. He's a chaperon of sorts.'

Fitzroy snorted. 'You'd be better getting Jack to defend your honour. Which he would, by the way. He always tries to bite my lady friends. You're the only woman he's taken to.'

'Jack bites your paramours.'

'Clever dog,' said Fitzroy. 'We have to go into the office first. It seems we both have a new commanding officer. Ex-army man, invalided out of the regulars and into the SIS. Apparently rather clever, so they moved him sideways.'

'Oh,' I said. 'We don't have another mission yet, do we? I want to spend time with my recovering husband.'

'It will be fine,' said the spy. 'I expect he wants to assert his dominance by shouting at us a bit. You know what these higher-ups are like.'

But it didn't turn out to be like that at all.

# Chapter Two

## Introducing Colonel Morley

The name plate read *Col. J. Wilfred Morley.* Fitzroy sniffed in a sneering way, but he knocked on the heavy oak door. A firm, deep, masculine voice called, 'Enter!'

We went in to find a large comfortable office. Shelves on two sides of the room were packed with books. Worn spines mixed with brighter hues, suggesting the books were for more than show. I felt hopeful. The third side of the room had a large window which let light flood in. A scarlet, Indian rug dominated the centre of the floor. It looked like the real thing, brash and bold and not some pale English imitation. Across from us was a decent-sized old desk. In front of it were two most uncomfortable-looking chairs whose curly cane backs were barely the suggestion of support. Each had a single cushion. Behind the desk stood a tall, broad-shouldered man in uniform. He was looking down at the desk as his large hands shuffled papers into piles. His thick, dark hair had a faint sprinkling of white. I guessed him to be over forty years of age. His cap lay beside his swagger stick, both neatly placed to one side of his working area.

'Mrs Stapleford, I presume?' he said, still not looking up. 'Do come and take a seat. Close the door, please.'

'And Fitzroy,' said Fitzroy.

The Colonel did look up at that. He had classic English good looks, with a lantern jaw, pale rather piercing grey eyes, and the white line of a scar that ran from his left ear to the corner of his mouth, giving him a slightly rakish appearance which was at odds with everything else about him. He held himself like an army man, completely erect, shoulders well back, and with the kind of personality that filled the room. The air suddenly became rather close. This was clearly a man used to command. I tried hard not to be impressed.

'Ah, yes,' he said, studying Fitzroy in the manner of a man about to place a bet on a horse at the races, and not too sure of the pedigree of the one before him. 'I believe I'm seeing you after luncheon. My secretary will have the details. To your left on the way out, neat little thing with freckles and curls – Dorothy. Likes to be called Dotty. Goodness knows why.'

His voice was pleasant too. He was well-spoken, with mellow tones, and not the strident sound of your usual half-deaf army man. Clearly, he hadn't been placed too near the artillery.

Fitzroy froze at my side. The Colonel nodded at him.

'You may not be aware, sir, but Mrs Stapleford and I are partners.'

'Of the romantic sort?' asked the Colonel mildly.

At this point I think both Fitzroy and I blushed red. I'm not entirely sure, as I suddenly found the view out of the window fascinating.

'No, sir,' said Fitzroy, and I could hear him swallowing his anger at being asked this, 'professionally. I trained Alice.'

I managed to face the room again with this clear explanation.

'I am aware,' said the Colonel. He sat down and gestured to me to take a seat. Fitzroy pushed something into my hand. I pocketed it as I moved forward and sat down. Fitzroy, who hadn't been invited to sit, lingered. I could feel his presence like a warmth at my back.

'Was there something else?'

'No, sir.' I heard the rustle of fabric moving and realised Fitzroy must be saluting him. Shortly afterwards, the door closed. I wondered if the Colonel knew he had made an enemy for life.

'Excellent officer, Eric Danvers,' he said. 'Been on too loose a leash though.' He picked up an open file on his desk, lifted it and scanned the papers inside. 'For rather a long time, if these reports are correct. Needs to be brought back into the fold.'

There was an uncomfortable pause between us. The Colonel closed his file and put it down on the desk. I wondered what he was waiting for me to say. He'd called Fitzroy 'excellent', and I wasn't about to contradict that. How the Department had chosen to deploy him had never been my concern. I was more curious about his surname. He'd always refused to tell me it, but somehow it seemed familiar.

Eventually, I said, 'Is it an issue that he chose to train me? That he swore me in?'

The Colonel blinked once and gave a shrug. 'I shouldn't think so. It would have been more normal for him to consult his superiors, but I imagine he thought the project would be refused as you are female.'

'Is that your view, sir?'

He brightened perceptibly at this. 'Not at all. I couldn't care less if you were a dancing rhino, Mrs Stapleford, as long as you get the job done.'

'I'm glad to hear it, sir.'

The Colonel smiled for the first time. 'You were expecting some aged, white-bearded, be-monocled spy, who would blench at the sight of a woman, and demand you were removed from his presence?'

'Not quite, sir. But I am aware that there has been some resistance in the Department.'

He picked up another file. 'Ah, yes, Danvers punched out a senior officer.'

'I don't know, sir. I wasn't there.'

'But he mentioned it?'

'Only that there was some resistance,' I said loyally.

The Colonel sat back in his seat. 'Can you defend yourself?'

'Yes, sir. I can also shoot, ride, encrypt and decrypt code, analyse information, run an asset, perform dead drops, recover dead drops, drive a car, and, I believe, I am generally of basic competence in all activities that might be required in the field.'

'Are you indeed? That wasn't quite what I meant, but it will do.'

I kept silent.

'Do you enjoy working with Danvers?'

'We make a good team,' I said. 'I understand the way he thinks and he understands me.'

'Yes, I can see that would be an advantage in a partnership,' said the Colonel. 'Especially as no one else in the Department seems to have a clue about his methods.'

'As you said, sir, before he trained me he mostly worked solo.'

He picked up yet another file. 'Yes, the whole story of how you met, his assessment of you, and final recruitment, is most unorthodox, but makes excellent reading. Is it true?'

'Without seeing the report I can hardly say,' I said.

'So you're aware that Danvers is one of those agents who, er, edits their reports?'

'I have yet to read one of his reports, sir. We have discussed missions, and I believe my point of view has been included in some.'

'Yes, well, that's something you have to start doing at once. I need written reports from you on your activities. You might have been Danvers' trainee, but you sound and look as if you are able to stand on your own two feet.'

'You want me to be a solo agent?' I asked, forgetting to add 'sir', as I was so aghast.

'I want you to be capable of being one,' said the Colonel, folding shut this last report and putting it down.

He sat back in his chair. 'I am inclined to take your word that you and Danvers have a professional relationship. However, the two of you working exclusively together has provoked comment. In fact, I might say the pair of you are the talk of the Department. The gossip I've heard about you, Mrs Stapleford, would make a stablehand blush.'

'I had thought better of the British Intelligence Service, sir,' I said tightly.

'I have no idea how they normally behave. I'm ex-army. Lost part of my leg a few months ago.' He must have seen my surprise. 'Oh, I've got a thing to replace it. I can stand and walk, but riding is difficult and marching would be impossible. As I have more brains than the average army officer I've been promoted and dropped in here. The idea being, I presume, that I will bring a different, and more practical, angle to the shadowy game that you lot play.'

'I see, sir.'

He narrowed his eyes, slightly. 'I suspected you might. You've always been rather a fish out of water, haven't you? Makes for a good agent – the outsider perspective. But when it comes to Danvers, I'm torn between allowing you to work together and splitting you up to maximise my resources. I don't doubt he trained you to fit in with him—'

'We do argue,' I interrupted without thinking. 'I'm not some kind of lackey for him. He takes me seriously. We complement each other in the field.'

'I can imagine that. I can also imagine he might take fewer risks with you around. It's clear from his reports that he is both fond and watchful of you. And yet, his most stunning achievements, before you, have been when he is at his most reckless.'

'You mean I might be holding him back?' I said.

The Colonel leant forward over the table. 'Mrs Stapleford, would you mind terribly remembering to call me "sir". If we had met at a dinner party, I would never have expected that but as you are a serving junior officer I rather do expect it. If you'd been a man, I would have bollocked you several times already for your insubordination.'

I blushed a fiery red. 'My sincere apologies, sir. I haven't been into the Department often. I am still learning the protocols, sir.'

'And I can't bring myself to shout at a woman just because she is under my command. We must all strive to overcome our failings.'

'Indeed, sir.'

'So, I have a tricky little situation I think you might be just the man – er, woman – for. Don't know if you were ever into the theatre? Always enjoyed a good play, myself. Anyway, we have a number of French and Belgian theatre companies looking to flee here. Don't blame them, myself, but the Lord Chamberlain's office is getting a bit touchy that they might bring over the wrong kind of play, or suddenly surprise us with a pro-German song. Or wave the wrong flag. Sing the wrong anthem. You get the idea.'

'I can see those actions wouldn't be wanted, sir, but why is the Lord Chamberlain involved?'

Colonel Morley frowned. 'The Lord Chamberlain has to license any play that is performed on the British stage. We'd look a right lot of ding-dongs if he licensed something that proved to be a German revue, wouldn't we?' He wiped a hand across his forehead and murmured, 'Ding-dongs!'

'If it helps, sir, Fitzroy swears in front of me all the time. My vocabulary has been significantly enlarged since we first met.'

Morley looked up, eyes wide for a moment. 'Does he, by Jove? Well, I may be able to respect you as an agent – we'll have to see how things go – but I'm damn well not going to use the kind of language you'd find in the trenches in front of you. I'm surprised at Danvers.'

'So what is it you want me to do, sir?'

'How's your memory?'

'Good enough, I think, sir.'

'It'll need to be. I want you to go undercover as an understudy in a play that's rehearsing. There's a man, playing the character of Argent Foil. Calls himself Pierre Marron, says he's a Belgian. His real name is Dieter Braun – almost clever what he did with his name – and he's a mathematics genius. Says he's up for betraying the Kaiser if he can come and live here. In love with someone – another mathematician. A woman, as it turns out – named Mary Hill. Just as well really. Wouldn't have been able to help him otherwise.'

'I know Mary Hill,' I said. 'Not well, sir, but our paths have crossed.'

'Yes, I know you do. I hope it won't prejudice your judgement. Wouldn't do for your friend to get mixed up with a double agent, would it?'

'Not at all, sir. So you want me to check him out?'

'Exactly. Get me a report on him that covers his habits, his likes, where he goes when he's not at the theatre, what he does there . . . You know the kind of thing.'

'A full profile, sir,' I said, nodding.

'You know how to do that?'

'I've done character analysis before, sir. Fitzroy has trusted my judgement.'

'Really?' said Morley looking vaguely interested. 'I didn't think he trusted anyone, as a matter of principle. If that gets around no one will believe you're not lovers.'

'Sir! I have a husband.'

'Yes, I've read about him. A bit of the true blue. Seems a smart chap. Shame about that last outing. Pity about his dicky heart too. Could have used him. Still, he lets us have you.' He passed me a sheet of paper. 'This is where your digs will be while you're at the theatre. See Dotty on the way out and she'll get you over to the wardrobe people. What was it Danvers gave you as he left?'

I managed not to react. 'I haven't looked, sir, but I imagine it was an arrangement to meet up afterwards. Unless he is loitering in the corridor.'

'He might have tried, but I won't have loiterers. Could never abide them in the army either. So, yes, consider yourself in a Chinese box, my dear. You're not to tell your partner a word about this mission. Do you understand? This is an order.'

'He will be concerned if I don't contact him, sir.'

'You're under my command, not his.'

'Yes, sir.'

'I want to see what you're made of, Mrs Stapleford. What you can manage without your self-styled partner.'

'I see, sir. Are you forbidding me to have any contact with him at all?'

'I don't forbid, my dear. I order. I am ordering you not to involve him in your mission. If you feel you can't get by for a few weeks without seeing his pretty little face, I would ask you to consider if your relationship is strictly a professional one, and, if it is, is it likely to remain so?'

I stood. 'Understood, sir,' I said with as much dignity as I could muster.

'I'm aware you'd like to break the chair over my head,' said Morley unexpectedly. 'I'm not mercurial by nature. I like to line my ducks up all in a row. I need to understand what you're made of. Don't worry about Danvers, I'll find something to keep him occupied. I'll even turn a blind eye to him taking that dratted dog around with him.'

'Do I salute you, sir?'

'If you want. Nice smart way to end a meeting, I always think.'

I saluted him.

'Good God, woman, call that a salute? Never do that again. Dotty will show you how. She likes saluting everyone, even though she's a civilian. Let her do it because it keeps her happy and she does it with such style. Off you go. I'd say dismissed, but you'd only try to salute me again, and I don't think I could take that.'

# Chapter Three

## An afternoon in the park

Dotty, who we must have walked straight past when we arrived, proved to be a pretty little thing, a year or so younger than me. In front of her, she kept a huge diary and on either side were stacked neat files. Her curly hair was pinned back, but a few disobedient locks had crept out. Her young skin bloomed through her powder, and while she wore quite formidable spectacles they somehow made her seem all the sweeter. Altogether, she looked quite lovely, and hopelessly naive for handling a department full of duplicitous and disobedient spies.

However, she was both polite and clear as she described the somewhat tortuous route to Wardrobe. This transpired not to be the shabby old cupboard I was used to raking through, but an entire department in itself. Like most of the discreet departments I have ever visited it was subterranean. Frosted glass panels in the ceiling told me we were only just below street level, but the lack of cleanliness and the general gloom of the room made it feel far deeper underground. A number of women, all dressed in blue-skirted apron dresses, and a few very young men in khaki boiler suits scuttled around the room, talking in whispers to one another, like an infantry of mice.

One of these women, sporting bright yellow hair that could be described as neither natural nor advisable, with bad skin and a constant sniffle, took me behind a screen and dressed me from head to foot in suitable attire. She gave me a battered, blue suitcase. 'All your other bits,' she said, and handed me a large envelope. 'Your legend. Don't ask me anything about it. We only do the clothes down here.'

It took me a moment to realise that 'legend' must mean 'cover story', as Fitzroy and I had been wont to call it.

The girls were working like furies. I caught one biting off a thread rather than reaching for scissors. I saw baskets of shoes waiting stacked next to a bucket of mud and saw one young lad pulling at seams and waist bands as he aged clothes. He also seemed to be in charge of belts and buckles, which, by contrast, were shiny as new coins and hung on a peg board behind him.

'Where do I go now?' I asked.

'No idea,' said the taciturn woman who had dressed me. She must have seen how lost I felt, as she relented slightly. 'Doors are that way. Go down the steps and you're in the street. End of the street and turn left, there's a little park. I think a lot of them go there to read their legends. You're not meant to, but you're not allowed to read them in here, so what's a body to do?'

'What indeed?' I said and thanked her.

I used the door she gestured towards and found myself in a narrow, tiled corridor. There was barely room for a body to pass, and certainly nowhere I could discreetly sit and read my information. I went out of the back door, which closed on its hinge behind me with a final, sharp snap. A main street blazed in the sunlight. I waited a moment for my eyes to adjust, then I stepped out from under the inset entrance. I was immediately on the pavement in the middle of a busy street, lined with offices and shops, and with a congested two-lane road in the centre. I had to be somewhere near the banking district as there were still a lot of men on the street. Completely lost, I walked off in the direction the seamstress had suggested. Glancing in the reflection of the window of a car that was parked at the roadside, I saw the doorway stood deep enough to be no more than a shadow in the side of a rather ordinary-looking office block from this angle. That egress would never be used as an entrance. There was no going back.

A few minutes later I turned into a pretty little park. In the centre stood a small bandstand, empty, and although the flower-beds were bare of blooms, the pathway snaked in an interesting manner between short hedges and lawns. I could see a pond further across, no doubt with ducks. A small flotilla of nannies could be seen wheeling or towing their charges throughout the park. The male of the species appeared to have vanished from the planet. But then, even if it hadn't been wartime, I wouldn't have seen any men in the park at this time of day. My stomach grumbled, reminding me it wanted to be in the vicinity of luncheon. I only hoped I had been given some money. All my own possessions had been neatly boxed up, and, I was assured, would be sent on to my home.

I meandered along the path until I came to a park bench slightly off the path, under an elm tree. In the summer it would be a lovely shady place for a picnic. The wind nipped at my fingertips as I took off my gloves to open the envelope. I realised it was only a matter of eight weeks or so until Christmas. I hoped everything could be over by then and that Bertram and I would be back home.

Bertram. This bloody mission meant I couldn't go and see him. I began to read the first page. Alice Woodward was a young actress from Devon. (Good heavens, I hoped I wasn't expected to do the accent!) Her London-born parents (thank goodness!) had inherited a mid-sized villa when she was five and moved down to Devon. Alice had always longed to return to the bright lights of London, and after four successful seasons at home, her parents had reluctantly agreed for her to join the Golden Angel Theatre, which was recruiting for the winter season in London. I was to be the understudy to the leading lady and also play the part of Annie, the maid. I was expected to be line perfect in both parts when I arrived at the theatre tomorrow at eight a.m. sharp. The address of the theatre was given.

I turned the page. On the other side it said that digs had been rented for me by my agent, Lawrence, and that there was a telephone number should I need to reach him urgently. I interpreted that Lawrence was the code name of someone in the Department. I only hoped it was someone who had been prepared to inspect lowly digs and ensure they were clean, and not someone who had simply stuck a pin in a set of listings, as I knew a lot of men might.

At the bottom of the envelope, I found a small purse. The purse contained a very limited amount of money. I was looking into this and wondering about the uncertain relationship between my first wages and eating, when two pound notes, several shillings and some pennies slithered into my lap. I started, but instinctively clutched at the money so it didn't fall off my lap. Fitzroy sat down beside me.

'They're always bloody mean about petty cash,' he said. 'I should have thought of that before. That's the smallest I've got on me. I can't go giving you anything larger, you're clearly dressed as a respectable but less than wealthy young lady. What are you? A shop assistant? Not measuring men's inside legs, I hope? I hear there is a shocking lack of tailors and tailors' assistants now we're sending the men off to war.'

All hope that he might, in spite of what Morley had said, be Lawrence faded. He clearly had no idea of my mission. 'I've been ordered not to talk to you,' I said.

Fitzroy frowned. 'Not at all? Or not about the mission?'

'I'm not meant to be in contact.'

'But we're partners.'

'Apparently, the jury is out on that.'

'Is it, by Jove,' said Fitzroy. 'Well, I will have words with this Morley when I see him. I'm not having some jumped-up army squirt undoing all my good work. He's regular army, Alice. Regular army and he won't have a clue how to run a department like ours.'

'I found it a lot more organised than before.'

'Yes, well, damn it. The army is good at *organising* things. It's also good at polishing boots. That doesn't make them any good at what we do.'

'I don't think you should stay. I rather think this is a kind of a test. Colonel Morley is willing to give me the benefit of the doubt, but he wants me to prove I'm a decent member of the Department.'

Fitzroy said something extremely crude, then, 'It's because you're a woman, isn't it?'

'Who says you won't also be given a test?' I said with a cheeky grin.

Fitzroy's face went through a mixture of emotions. 'Are you being a cat?' he asked.

'I rather think I am.'

'Dash it all! I'll have to leave you to it. Take care, Euphemia, I'll see you once this is all over. You can help me give Jack a bath!'

He got up and then paused for a moment. 'If you take the exit straight across from us, there's a café where you'll get egg and chips for your lunch. Not the kind of place you're used to, but they might have a decent bun behind the counter.' Then he walked off. His coat was open and swung slightly from side to side as he clipped his cane smartly along the path. His shoulders tilted slightly with his swagger. I'd have known that gait anywhere.

He didn't look back.

Once he was gone, I distributed the various papers, play booklet, purse and keys about my person. Then I tore the plain envelope into strips and dropped the contents in a rubbish bin on my way across the park. Doubtless, Fitzroy would have set fire to the lot. For once, I felt like emulating him. Drat this rotten job.

# Chapter Four

## The Great Beryl Belairs

I thought through Fitzroy's closing remarks. It had all been a bit rushed, and thus confused. When he'd asked me if I was being a 'cat', he was asking if I had a tail he hadn't noticed. He's very good at noticing tails, and while I hadn't seen anything or anyone, it seemed a better idea to err on the side of caution. If nothing else it had been a good way of getting rid of him. His contrary nature meant he would want to defy Morley at any opportunity. However, he'd draw the line at actually getting me into trouble. He didn't care about himself, but, as Morley had said, he did look out for me. Perhaps too much.

The revelation that I might have a tail he hadn't spotted had caused him to rush what he'd said next. In talking of giving Jack a bath and not seeing me until it was all over, he had meant exactly the opposite. A long time ago, Fitzroy and I had decided that should we ever use our real names to each other on a mission, we meant the opposite of what we were saying from that moment on. It was only meant to be used for short comments and in bad situations, as it was all too easy to confuse.

Fitzroy would find another way of seeing me. My best way forward was to head him off at this particular pass and allow him to know I was safe. The only way I was going to get him to leave me alone would be to make him believe that contacting me would hurt me in some way.

In this case, I would cite Morley. The Colonel might have said he didn't mind me being a woman, but his use of the word *dear*, and talk of not being able to discipline me, had not passed me by. He clearly thought women were softer creatures than men. I suspected he would be content if I could do the job well, but that he anticipated that I would fall short of his expectations of what a spy should be. At this moment he was probably lining up some position like overseeing the wardrobe section for me. I jolly well wasn't having any of that. I could tell him that Mrs Wilson, a housekeeper I had once worked for, had said that my stitching was only good for sails.

Fitzroy's pause before mentioning the cafe, I assumed, was him switching back to normal speech. Which meant he wanted me to go there next. He'd left something there for me. At least that's what I thought he'd meant by 'a decent bun behind the counter'.

I had every intention of going to see Fitzroy at his flat, but it would require skill. I did not intend to discuss the mission with him, I didn't want him bludgeoning his way in. Knowing him as I did, I was almost certain that, unless I got him to promise to stay away, he wouldn't refrain from interfering. Even then it remained odds-on he wouldn't keep his nose out entirely. The best I could hope for was that he wouldn't make his involvement obvious.

Morley must know I could manage things. It must have occurred to him, as it had to me, that I had completed the majority of my last mission solo. I'd certainly handled all the critical parts by myself. Likewise, in the mission before that, I had separated from an injured Fitzroy to carry out a dangerous assignment with a double agent neither of us trusted. If Morley had read any of our recent reports, he would know how competent I was – not simply by my or Fitzroy's words, but by the results. Why was he questioning this? Something was off, and I wanted to discuss that with Fitzroy.

I hurried on towards the café, hoping he'd left more there for me than a decent bun.

The Reluctant Bride Café was clean, and that is the most I can say for it. There was a great deal of netting and broderie anglaise hung about the place. To be fair, this was bright white, startlingly so, and I could only imagine that the owner and staff spent most of their time and effort on keeping it that way. They certainly didn't spend it on the food.

My tea tasted like weak chicken stock, and the scone I had reluctantly opted for had the consistency of a pebble. So much so I briefly considered pocketing it for use as a weapon in extremis. I could not bring myself to try one of the many cream cakes on offer. The cream had a distinctly yellow tinge. The thought of sampling the egg and chips here I found repugnant. Fitzroy, as I well knew, could eat anything and everything without ill effect. However, when I enquired if there had been a package left for Alice, the woman serving me handed over a medium-sized parcel.

'Ooh, you know the fancy gent that left it?' she asked.

I nodded.

'Is 'e single?'

'I believe so,' I said, keeping my expression bland. The enquirer had a bad case of acne, but we must all have our dreams.

'Could you pass 'im a message? Say Doris at the Reluctant Bride would be most interested in seeing him again. I'd give him ham and chips on the house. I could even throw in a couple of extra eggs. Do you think he'd like that?'

'He is very fond of his food,' I said. Doris blushed a little and wandered off in a happy daze. I saw no reason not to pass on the message when I was able, and no reason at all to mention Doris's epidermis condition. Fitzroy was always up for a free meal and as there were three young women waiting hopefully to serve clients I doubted he would know which one Doris was.

I smiled slightly to myself. Fitzroy's proclivity for women had once annoyed me. Now, I rather delighted in teasing him about it. Not least because I had discovered that, like many single gentlemen, he was not above exaggerating his exploits. He was a born flirt. He was also rather soft-hearted where women were concerned.

I had chosen a seat behind a bamboo screen covered with white netting, which effectively screened me from the rest of the café. However, it soon became clear that I need not have concerned myself. Although the busy luncheon time was due, I was currently the only person seated at a table.

I pretended to sip at my tea. One taste had been more than enough. The knife I had been given would have been hard pushed to cut butter, let alone my scone. A pickaxe seemed the only thing likely to breach its sides. Or perhaps a small grenade.

I opened up my box and inside found a smaller neat parcel that would easily slip inside my suitcase. I peeked through a corner and confirmed it was much as I expected. I had just refastened my suitcase when Doris appeared with a plate of egg and chips.

'On the 'ouse,' she said. 'Seeing as you're doing me a favour like.'

I smiled and nodded my thanks. To my great surprise, the egg appeared well cooked and the crispness of the chips could only have been rivalled by the creases in a military uniform. Having added a modicum of salt, I tried the food. It was good. I should have listened more closely to what Fitzroy had told me. Not that I had any intention of relaying that to him.

Replete with luncheon, but still somewhat thirsty, I left The Reluctant Bride, and headed towards the address of the theatre the legend had given me. The afternoon light was already dimming, and somewhere in the park a keeper must have been burning leaves. That synonymous scent of autumn filling the air. Without my noticing, Britain had given up on summer, slipped most assuredly into autumn, and now cusped on winter. While Bertram had always thought of this as the dying part of the year, I loved this season. It was full of mellow colours, and prepared us gently for the coming of the winter chill. It was the end of harvesting, and time to pickle, preserve, and undertake other such arcane kitchen matters, as one began the preparations for Christmas.

I did not yet know, but I suspected, this mission being over, Fitzroy and I would arrange a house party at White Orchards. There would doubtless be many interested parties who were unable to converse, but who could be brought together either to aid the wretched war machine, or more hopefully, to find a way of stalling it at an innocuous Christmas gathering. We had spoken before about doing such a thing, but it had not yet transpired. Surely, now would be a good time to attempt it?

I confess the thought of spending Christmas in the Fens with no entertainment, working on the analysis of yet more intelligence from the Front, did not appeal. I was still in the early stages of understanding analysis, and my training had necessarily been patchy. What had stood out most for me was how sobering the work was – especially when one was forced to evaluate losses in a mission or now, I feared, in an advance. The little Fitzroy had spoken about the current plans for the war had not filled me with hope. He had spoken bitterly about a war of attrition but had refused to give me more details. It was as if he thought that voicing his darkest fears would make them more likely to come true. He was not a superstitious man, and this sudden volte-face about uttering these fears only added to my own worries of what was to come. Thank goodness my brother was far too young to join the army.

With an effort, I turned my mind to happier thoughts as I emerged from the park. Bertram would be recovered by Christmas. The strains on his heart had caused more than one episode in the past, but those had all been overcome with a few weeks of rest. A qualm assailed me that Bertram might be more unwell than Fitzroy had let on. The spy himself was far from being in the best of health. He was clever enough to disguise it from most, but I knew him too well. Plus, although my nursing training had been cut short, I now had a much better understanding of how the body functioned and how it recovered from injury and strain. I had seen in the hospital that the mind could be injured, as well as the body, by the harsh experiences of war. Fitzroy, I knew, would bottle things up until he broke apart at the seams. It would be my duty to ensure this did not happen, and I would get little thanks for it. Or at worst, to pick up the pieces and put him back together again. He certainly wouldn't allow anyone else to do so.

But how had Bertram fared? He was a passionate, caring man, but underneath it all he had a stoicism that few saw. Perhaps it was living with a potentially lethal condition that focused his mind on the present. Knowing I was safe and well was always his most pressing concern. Once assured of that, I hoped he would recover quickly. If I had a moment I might send him a note suggesting a New Year Duck Hunt, which he would adore. Whether or not we combined it with a spy-party was another matter. I should present it to Bertram as the one way I could be assured of being at home. Fitzroy would never let me go overseas now, nor anywhere near the front lines. I had yet to decide how I felt about that. I had no desire, nor any particular ability, to fight from a trench, but the thought that my gender should preclude me from defending my country made me both frustrated and angry. I could already fight hand-to-hand better than most men. They might be stronger, but I had learnt to be cunning, and to use their strength against them. I was also not a bad shot, although I generally refrained from handling a gun, not only because it was noisy and usually deadly, but because before he was tortured Fitzroy had been an Olympic marksman. I didn't like to remind him of what he had lost, and in some ways I still blamed myself for not rescuing him before . . .

I stopped suddenly, causing the gentleman behind me to almost trip. I heard the stutter of his cane. I had been watching out for the name of the street my 'digs', as I was to call them, were on. A tiny lane, dark and grimy, led off to my left. On the side I could barely make out a sign that read, 'Biblicott Street'. I knew I was looking for Biblicott Lane, but if this narrow vennel was the street, would I even be able to slip sideways into the lane? And as for taking my suitcase with me, I could forget that.

Taking a deep breath, I plunged into the gloomy passageway, telling myself I had nothing to be afraid of in the dark. Fitzroy, who I had learnt liked his little sayings when it came to my training, had often told me the way to get over any fears of shadows was to always be the most dangerous thing in the dark. I would rather not run into a London pick-pocket, or worse, but I was confident enough in my own abilities. As it was, I didn't meet anyone in what transpired to be a short street, which opened out into an unusual and thankfully broader lane.

It was one of those quaint London byways that were generally thought to have all been burnt down in the Great Fire. It didn't have the precarious leaning of the Shambles in the city of York, but the long, three-storey building I faced did bulge slightly at the sides. It rather looked as if the black beams that studded the fascia not only held it together, but held it in, rather like an old lady trussed up in corsets.

In the middle of the ground floor there stood a main door, but two separate sets of steep, wooden steps led up to balconies along on the first and second floors. These upper floors all had three separate doors opening on to the walkways. The upper doors were painted a ruby red. However, the main door was a deep, respectable navy. Outside it hung a bell. I rang it.

I knew immediately that the lady who opened the door had spent most of her career on the stage. Her make-up was highly decorative. The natural wrinkles from ageing broke what would have once been a lovely face into a myriad of crannies and creases; rather like a balled-up old sock. Her hair was clipped into a short, violently red mane. It might have been a wig, but it was bushy enough that it might also have been some small rare South American mammal.

She wore a blue cotton dress that bulged in all the right, and all the wrong, places. I diagnosed an addiction to cake, much like my sister-in-law Richenda had had. The necklace she wore sparkled even in the dim evening light. If it was anything other than paste it could buy the navy another dreadnought or two.

'Hello, ducks,' she said. 'You Miss Alice Woodward? Think I'd change that name if I was you. Dull. Dull as dull. Come on in for a minute and we'll have a cuppa. I like to know something of my tenants. Normally meet them for a good old chinwag before I let them into my home, but your pa booked these for you. Sounded a right proper gent, he did.'

I didn't attempt to get a word in edgeways, but obediently followed my landlady into her home. I found myself standing at once in a long and deep living room filled with vibrant, mismatched colour. Chintz armchairs and a dresser adorned with glittering Crown Derby china stood proud against a sea of little oak tables. Framed photographs of my landlady at various ages and in various states of dress, some minimal, were scattered about like leaves after a storm. The largest was of her as a slender long-haired beauty. Its dark sepia tones and blurry edges suggested the lady was older than she might care to admit. The other images charted her journey from vaudeville girl to mature actress. As her career progressed, her poses acquired more clothing.

'These are lovely,' I said.

She nodded regally. 'Thank you. Now, I'll just pop through the back and get our tea. I don't hold with having a maid hanging around the place. I like my privacy. Or as much as I can get of it with you lot on top of me, as it were!' She gave a throaty laugh. 'Make yourself as home, ducks. I know it's a funny old place, but I like it. Won't be a mo!'

I sat down gingerly on a chintz sofa and was immediately almost swallowed whole. After a bit of floundering I managed to surface. I found that if I balanced on the edge I avoided both indignity and the danger of suffocation.

The landlady returned carrying a tea tray. I stood up and took it from her. She gave a slightly breathless word of gratitude. 'Forget I'm getting on a bit, I do. Don't feel no different than when I first stepped onto the stage at five and I almost wee-ed meself in excitement. I knew there and then it was the life for me!' She must have misread the expression on my face, because she laughed again. 'Don't worry, dearie, I'm in no danger of that now. I ain't that old yet. All me pipes in working order. Lord love you, put the things on that table there. Ain't you polite waiting for me to tell you where. I bet you're as much of a lady as your father is a gent. I have to warn you, ducks, this is a hard living for a nicely brought-up girl. There's one on the level above yours, bit younger I reckon, hard as bleedin' nails, she is. Got what it takes to make it, she does. Be a trail of bodies behind her though.'

By now I had placed the tray down, and sat on the edge of my seat, but I almost bounced back up again. 'Bodies!' I said, my voice quivering slightly.

My landlady laughed. 'Don't you worry, ducks. I meant that metaforagable like. She's not some kind of murderess. Although, if looks could kill! The ones she gives me when I has to chase her for the rent.'

'If you don't like her . . .' I began, finally getting a word in edgeways, but it was not to last.

'Why did I take her on? Well, when she turned up she was as sweet as pie. Butter wouldn't melt. Big eyes. Blonde ringlets. Gawky as a fawn. She'd dressed down too, looked dowdy. No fool like an old fool. I let her have the place and at half rent. Talk her way out of the gates of hell that one would. Not once you're wise to her tricks, of course. I've put the rent up now. Won't be showing no favouritism ever again after that little madam. But while she pays she stays. I got to be fair. I've got my reputation to think of.'

'Madam, might I know what to call you?' I finally managed to say.

This sent my land lady off into another cackle of laughter. 'That's me, that is. Everyone round 'ere knows me, so I thinks, and you don't know me from a pigeon in a pie shop!' She held out her hand. 'Beryl Belairs, my ducks. Previously of the Theatre Royal, Lyceum and English Opera House. I trod the boards alongside Henry Irving, I did. Doesn't matter where you start, my dear, it's where you ends up. I took up the landladying profession when that Barrasford took over me cherished place. Rococo, would you believe. He did it up in the Rococo style, hoping to bring back music hall and variety. As if the best of us hadn't been doing our darnedest to leave that behind!'

She sighed deeply, causing the gems on her breast to sparkle and dazzle even in this dimly lit room. 'Those Melville boys are running a series of moany sad plays now. Melondramas, or whatever they're called. Who wants to see a sad play, I ask you? More than enough going wrong with the world. Things are not what they were.' Then she thrust her hand out at me, and said, 'Most pleased to make your acquaintance, Miss Woodward.'

The hand proffered towards me was held in a manner not unlike the Pope awaiting a cardinal's kiss on his ring. I took it gently and shook it.

'It's lovely to meet you too, Miss Belairs,' I said. I had no idea if she was married, but I'd read in my legend that the majority of actresses were addressed as if they were single. The taint of marriage being removed from their public image. At least while they were on stage, male audience members wished to think them virginal. Off stage would be another matter entirely.

It seemed I had done the right thing. She continued to talk to me about her past, her 'angels, apart from the cow what I mentioned before' that lived above – which had me confused for a moment until I realised she meant the upper storey and not celestial abodes. I got to say very little, but I did get to drink my tea. Gradually my thirst abated. As it did so, I learnt about 'the rules'. I could leave washing out on certain days, and, while she didn't cook, she had an arrangement with a pie-maker and a fish-fryer, who delivered supper on alternate nights. 'Always ending with fish on Friday. Proper like. Over the weekend they fend for themselves. You've only got a kettle and a single ring. I don't expect anyone to be cooking up a storm. Lots of nice little cafes round here that cater to our folks. You know, theatre people.'

I finally made my escape, learning as a parting blow that I was too late to join in tonight's pie run, as it had been 'made up on the Monday'.

I hauled my lumpy suitcase up the astoundingly steep stairs to the first floor and found lodging No. Two. My key opened the door into a neat little place. A sitting room with the promised gas ring for a kettle, a tiny hearth with some welcoming sticks in it and, further back, the minimal washing facilities and a small but tidy bedroom that looked out on to a courtyard below. The bed linen was simple, but clean and in good order, and the bed welcoming and firm. The walls were painted a light ochre in the front and a pale cream at the back. The only sign this place was for acting folk were the sturdy oak shelves waiting for books in the sitting room (bearing one dusty copy of Shakespeare's plays standing alone) and in the bedroom an extremely large mirror, in which it would be possible to examine yourself from all the usual and some of the more unusual angles.

What wasn't anywhere in sight was food.

I sat down on the bed and my stomach rumbled. I turned and opened the suitcase. None of the clothing given by the Department would be anything I would have normally worn, but I supposed this was the point. I ran my fingers through the clothes. It was odd suddenly having someone decide who I was pretending to be. Fitzroy and I were used to doing this for ourselves. There was no arguing the Department's way was more organised, but I felt resentment towards the process. I had to learn not only how to be a certain personage, decided for me, but also the lines of the ruddy play overnight. One thing was certain: I would not be doing any of this on an empty stomach. I opened the packet Fitzroy had left me and took out the contents.

# Chapter Five

## Night manoeuvres

I leant back, happily full of steak and onion pie, and stretched my feet out to the fire. Fitzroy passed me a glass of brandy. I couldn't help noticing that my helping was significantly smaller than this own.

'You almost frightened the life out of me when you knocked on the window,' he said. 'If Griffin had been in here, I swear he would have dropped dead on the spot. You have to be more careful, Alice.' However, his voice was teasing rather than angry.

'I'm sure in your sullied career you've had more than one woman knock on your window to be let in.'

'Yes, but not three storeys up. Seriously, Alice, promise me you won't try that when it's wet. I know the blocky structure makes it possible to find easy footholds, but that doesn't mean you have to climb it. I have an awfully nice front door downstairs. I've lived here over three years. It would take a lot to raise my porter's eyebrows. He's frightfully discreet. I give him a gift hamper at Christmas and the occasional racing tip.'

'I imagine he has to be,' I said, sipping the brandy. 'Is Griffin equally discreet?'

'Of course,' said Fitzroy. He gave a sigh. 'He's overly moral about it though.'

'You allow him to scold you?' I said, half laughing.

'Of course not,' said Fitzroy sitting down in the chair opposite by the fire, and raising his glass high so Jack, his white English Bull

Terrier, could jump unhindered onto his lap. 'But he gives me looks. Dark looks. I don't like 'em.'

'What do you think he might do? Leave the odd tract on your pillow?'

Fitzroy mock-shivered and Jack gave one of his odd whiffling barks. 'It's all right, boy,' he said, producing like a conjurer a dog treat out of his pocket. I couldn't help but smile to see the spymaster positively affectionate over a living being – of course, Jack had the advantage of not being human. In general, Fitzroy disliked his own species.

He looked up at me, and caught me watching him. He gave a surprisingly bashful grin, and pulled gently on one of Jack's ears. 'Shall we shock Griffin even further?' he said. 'Why don't you stay over? I have a spare room. I know it isn't the usual respectable behaviour one might expect of a lady, but we've both slept closer together before and in far from salubrious circumstances.'

'That boat,' I groaned. Fitzroy grinned.

'No one will ever make a sailor out of you, Alice.'

'I admit the idea of a comfortable bed after that wonderful supper . . .'

'Nonsense, it was no more than a bit of scratch.'

'I'd love to just fall asleep, but I've got lines to learn and more about . . . Oh, rats,' I said.

'Lines to learn?' asked Fitzroy, his head tilted and his most innocent look on his face.

'Damn you, Eric,' I said using his real name. 'That was a rotten trick.'

'I don't know what you mean.'

'I only turned up to tell you I was in no danger and the mission was one I could accomplish safely alone. I said categorically that I couldn't tell you anything about it, and that I wouldn't. Morley had given me orders. Then you fed me. You gave me brandy, and then you unsettled me with an improper suggestion.'

'I assure you, Euphemia, that was not an improper suggestion.

Believe me, when I make an improper suggestion a lady does not mistake it.'

I stood up, really angry now. 'I'd rather you had tried to kiss me than take advantage of my trust in you.'

'If only I'd known,' said Fitzroy playfully, carefully putting Jack down on the hearth rug and standing up. He broke off studying my face. 'You're angry, aren't you? You know I see it as my responsibility to look after you as my trainee, and now as my partner in espionage. Did you think I'd really let Morley send you off on your own without at least attempting to ensure your safety?'

'He was very clear, Eric, that if I cannot act without you I am no use as an agent. This was meant to be my chance to prove it. I came here to warn you off—' I broke off, feeling tears pricking behind my eyes. 'I'm tired,' I said. 'Tired through to my bones. I just conducted a supposedly solo mission, and I thought I had done a good job . . .'

'You had,' said Fitzroy.

'Apparently you turning up at the end removed all my credibility.'

'Morley said that? I'll thrash—'

'Not in so many words, but it was implied. So here I am, hours off another hard and testing mission, with my husband alone and seriously ill in hospital, and you're playing games, because as ever you want to be in control – and in control of me.'

Fitzroy didn't so much sit down as collapse back into his chair. 'I say, Alice, that's a bit harsh. I've never tried to control you. I've taken command in the field when I needed to, but I thought I'd given you as much free rein – more than is usual – as was possible for a new agent.'

Griffin came in bearing a tray of cheese, fruit, and crackers. 'I thought I heard shouting,' he said. 'Is everything all right?' He gave the merest glance at his master, and focussed on my face. From the hearth Jack growled.

I didn't answer him, but let Fitzroy speak. 'Everything is fine, isn't it, Euphemia?'

I gave a curt nod, and Jack gave a little whine. He squirmed towards me and rolled on his back.

Griffin looked down at the dog. 'He has been fed, sir. Contrary to appearances.'

Fitzroy shrugged. 'Make up the spare bedroom, will you, Griffin? Euphemia's staying over. It's started to rain and it's going to be a filthy night. Really not at all suitable for her to go climbing in and out of buildings.'

Griffin's facial expression contorted somewhat. I knew he liked me enough he would not wish me to come to harm, but I also knew he would consider it the height of impropriety for me to stay at a gentleman's flat when the man in question was present – and especially when that man was Fitzroy. Eventually, he managed to speak and with a fearful look at the spy said, 'Are you sure, madam?'

This did make the corners of my mouth lift. I saw the spy turn away to hide his expression. I hoped he was more amused than angry. 'It's fine, Griffin. We've had to share closer quarters on previous missions. We're both professionals.'

'Indeed,' said Griffin. He nodded stiffly and walked off.

'Anyone would else would be indignant at a servant questioning their morals,' I said. 'You appear proud.'

'Well, you know, Griffin is generally a dull kind of a chap. Smart, but dull. I have to make his life entertaining.'

A thought struck me. 'Tell me, you haven't had your spare room made up as a blind when you have had a lady stay here before, have you?'

Jack resumed his place by the fire, and Fitzroy settled back into his chair. 'I hope you brought the play with you. Can't learn the lines without 'em,' he said mildly.

I pulled the small book out of my pocket and handed it to him. 'I looked over my lines earlier. I was half hoping you'd help me with them. But you still haven't answered my question. Does Griffin have reason to think . . .' I stopped. 'I don't mean to be rude,' I said. 'It's entirely your own business, but I want to know if . . .'

'He'll still respect you in the morning?' quipped the spy. His eyes twinkled in the firelight. 'Wishing you'd kept hold of the book now . . .'

'To throw at you? I always have an eye out for things to throw at you. That candlestick, for instance, is a good option.'

'Please don't. It's rather ghastly, but it was my great-aunt's and apparently she was something of a renegade. Never met her, but I keep the candlestick in memory of her past wrongdoings.'

I sat back down in the opposite seat. 'Just tell me how things are?' I said wearily.

The humour in his face faded. 'Without details, I suppose Griffin may come to the wrong conclusions. I really don't want you out on a night like this. You're hardly dressed for it. You will be perfectly safe with me—'

'Oh, I didn't doubt that, 'I interrupted. 'You frequently infuriate me, but I will always trust you.'

Fitzroy gave a small seated bow. 'Thank you. I admit I may have over-reacted a little when Morley assigned you a position alone. I don't like him. I don't trust him. I was worried for you.'

'You think he's the traitor?' I said, referring to our past efforts to unmask a leak in the Department that had still not been plugged.

'What? No! He's a new arrival. Whoever's been acting against us has been around longer than him. No, he's a regular army man, do or die for the King and all that.'

'So?'

'I very much doubt he's up to the job. He'll have no idea of your capabilities.'

'Won't he have read your lengthy reports on my training?'

'Pass me some Stilton on a cracker, won't you, Alice? And a few grapes. Do you want to shift to port? I have a rather nice white port.'

'I see,' I said. 'Keeping all your cards against your chest as usual. I can assume my assessments were a masterpiece of brevity?'

Fitzroy popped a large piece of Stilton in his mouth, and nodded. He snapped the cracker in half and fed one part to Jack.

'I can assure you that the mission I have been given is something – well, something almost Jack could do.'

'He's an extremely clever dog,' said Fitzroy defensively.

I smiled. 'There is no reason to think I will be in any danger. You can leave this to me without worry. Trust me a little, please. You know I'd come to you if I needed you. Why, I've technically disobeyed orders even coming here.'

'Yes, I realised, but do you want to keep the mission to yourself? That way, if anyone ever finds out that you did visit me I can give my word that you didn't tell me anything except that you were acting in a play? Not sure that's a goer. Unlikely to trust my word.'

'They would be fools not to,' I said hotly.

Fitzroy smiled properly then. 'Alice, my giving my word to you and my giving my word to Morley are entirely different affairs.'

I sighed. 'Why do you have to be so difficult?'

'I phoned the hospital earlier. Bertram is doing very well. He's spending most of his time resting or asleep, but he has been told you are safe back on British soil and will visit as soon as he is up to it.'

'Oh, thank goodness,' I said. 'That is a huge weight off my mind. What happened?'

Fitzroy shook his head. 'I think it's up to Bertram to decide whether he wants to tell you. It got tricky. There was a fair bit of nastiness. No worse than I've had to do before, but . . .'

'You think he'd rather I didn't know what you had to do – what he had to do – to get away?'

Fitzroy shrugged. 'I don't know.'

'All right,' I said. 'I'll wait to see what he says. How are you?'

'I'm perfectly fine. No lingering moral qualms.'

'Obviously, but I meant physically.'

'As you see. Handsome as ever.'

'You haven't been given another mission, have you? You've been put on medical leave, haven't you.'

Fitzroy had been flicking idly through the play. 'What's your part?'

'The maid, and understudy to the fiancée.'

Fitzroy looked up, his colour slightly heightened. 'You do know that both of those roles involve being kissed on stage by the villain, don't you?'

'I'd noticed,' I said. 'I hope he doesn't have bad breath. What will you do with your leave? Torment Griffin.'

Fitzroy sniffed. 'That, and I think I might take in some shows. It's been ages since I've been to the theatre.'

# Chapter Six

## A tense breakfast

I had been relieved, though not altogether surprised, to find that Fitzroy had been able to produce appropriate attire for me to attend the theatre the next morning. He had made Griffin get up extra early to cook me a hearty breakfast. He presented this to me in a small dining room. There was no sign of the spy.

'Bacon, eggs, fried bread, sausages – please don't give any to the dog, madam. Contrary to his wistful appearance and low whining, he has already been copiously fed.'

I looked down at Jack, who wagged his stumpy tail hopefully. I winked at him. 'He does look a little stretched at the seams,' I said.

Griffin gave a deep sigh, such as only normally heard at a graveside. 'His master is most indulgent of him. I attempt to adjust his diet only to find it has been increased disproportionately by treats. I really wonder, madam, if the poor little dog won't one day simply pop!'

The poor little dog growled loudly as this. I strongly doubted he understood one word that Griffin had said, but he certainly viewed him as a barrier to my breakfast.

'Where is Fitzroy this morning?' I asked, making it as clear as I could that once we had said goodnight at the hearthside I had not seen the spy since.

'Still abed. I did look in on him, but he was sleeping soundly. I think it most wise of his superiors to have extended his medical leave. Of late, he has been pushing himself far too hard, and allowing no time for recovery.'

I raised my eyebrows at this. Griffin was not generally a one to share confidences, especially about Fitzroy. Jack pawed at my leg and looked meaningfully at Griffin.

'Was there something you wanted to ask me, Griffin?'

Griffin stepped back, straightened his spine, and let out a breath. It wasn't so much another sigh as a readying to speak. Clearly, he had something of import to relate.

'It is simply, madam, that the Major is over extending himself. If he doesn't rest properly, I fear he will never recover his full strength.'

'I know he can be difficult, but he is on medical leave. Without a mission, he needs must be less active,' I said sympathetically. I knew all too well that a bored Fitzroy was ripe for any mischief, and often near impossible to control.

'I am referring to his activities with you, madam,' said Griffin. His back grew straighter by the second. Any moment now his vertebrate would lock into place with a snap and never unfuse.

I frowned, slightly. 'We're not lovers, if that is what you are asking,' I said. 'But I am sure that cannot be what you mean. Firstly, it would be most impertinent to say such a thing to me, and secondly, you are aware I am a married woman.'

Griffin's face suffused with red, like a glowing coal. 'Indeed, madam. I own to some confusion on that point. However, as you point out, it is hardly my business, except . . .'

It was at this point I realised how my relationship with Fitzroy had changed me. I was more curious than offended by Griffin's remarks, while some ladies might have fainted at his bald talk of affairs, or at least pretended to do so to get out of an awkward situation. Personally, before working with Fitzroy I would have stood up and slapped Griffin's face.

'Except what?' I said with what I felt was admirable calm. It did of course help that even sitting at the breakfast table I could see opportunity and weapons enough that I could kill the man ten times over. I had no such intention, but the mere ability to defend oneself installs considerable confidence. Besides, the introduction of a fork into a man's physique need not be fatal but could still be acutely painful.

'I believe my master is in the habit of thinking of you and your safety more often than a commander might usually think of the men – people – in his charge. In short, he dwells on you.'

I raised an eyebrow. 'Rubbish!' I said. Griffin lifted his nose a little higher and gave a tiny sniff. My curt reply had not convinced him. I continued, while wondering if the man who was testing me so sorely was aware of all my abilities, 'We generally consider ourselves partners when we are working together. Perhaps Fitzroy using such terminology has confused you. But we are not doing so now. My visit here was merely to assure Fitzroy that he needn't worry about the mission I am undertaking alone.'

'Ah, so you too have noticed his obsession,' said Griffin.

At this I did need to quell an impulse to slap him. 'I sincerely doubt Fitzroy has ever been obsessed, as you so forcefully put it, with any woman at any time in his life. But I assure you, we are colleagues and nothing more.'

'I do not believe that is how he sees you,' said Griffin. 'Besides, I do believe he came close to obsession over Celeste.'

Of course, I immediately wanted to know who Celeste was, and how she knew Fitzroy. Or rather, how well he knew her. However, I knew my duty.

'I do not think it proper of you to speak of him like this,' I said. 'It is perilously close to gossip, and if you are . . .'

At this point, the man himself walked into the dining room. 'How homely,' he said, smiling at me and pulling out a chair. 'I'll have the same as Alice, Griffin, only twice as much.' He felt the side of the coffee pot. 'This is cold,' he said, handing it to his man. 'Make us some fresh, there's a good fellow. And better make it three times as much. I'm feeling a mite peckish this morning.'

As Griffin disappeared off to the pantry to get fresh supplies, Fitzroy turned to me. 'Now what has Griffin done to ruffle you? You look as mad as a wet hen!'

'I am certain I do not,' I said, smearing marmalade on my toast. 'I have been keeping my emotions under control.'

My partner raised both his eyebrows at that. 'Good heavens, he must really have upset you. He didn't try to kiss you or anything, did he? I'll punch him in the face if he has, and then send him to be shot!'

It was difficult to tell if Fitzroy was joking. But being serious about matters was not his strong suit. Although he could be inordinately bad-tempered when things weren't going his way. Already one of the veins at his temple was throbbing. 'If he had tried to assault me in such a manner,' I said. 'You would have found him laid out flat on your kitchen floor,' I said. 'Alive, but unconscious, and I would have tried not to break any of your crockery.'

Fitzroy's face split into a grin. 'I believe that,' he said. 'Especially the bit about the crockery.' He picked up one of the cups. 'They are rather lovely, aren't they? Apparently my mother's favourite breakfast service. I told Griffin to use them in your honour. They should be used by a lady.'

'Thank you.'

The grin mellowed to a smile. 'How has he annoyed you? Don't say he made the eggs wrong. He is a master of the herb omelette.'

I picked my words carefully. Fitzroy was all too ready for action. He had been inactive too long. He might have arrived in time to see the end of my previous project, but before that he had been on medical leave, hanging around my home, with my husband, for some time. Then he had had that short flurry of action rescuing Bertram. He was overwrought both physically and mentally. Fitzroy claimed never to experience guilt, but I knew he felt bad about Bertram. In such a mood he was ripe for action, and ripe for a fight – he wanted to be doing, not reflecting. But he was far from well. His eyes remained too bright, and he was far too thin. Morley had been right to pull him from active service. Even if he had gone about it in quite the wrong way.

'He's worried about you,' I said. Fitzroy started to make puffing noises, halfway between annoyance and rebuttal. 'Stop it,' I said.

'You know you are absolutely useless at resting. You must have been a truly awful child. Continually getting into mischief and causing trouble.'

The smile brightened. 'You know me so well.'

'Anyway, you know with your two trips almost back to back – and with both of them going sideways . . .'

He shrugged at that. 'You know how the work is.'

'Yes,' I said. 'But both of these were particularly bad. It was only your skill that got people back on both occasions.' My voice shook almost imperceptibly, but of course he noticed, and at once reached out a hand across the table to hold mine.

'I promise you, he has the best doctors, and he will be well soon.'

At this point, of course, Griffin came back into the room – catching us in the action of holding hands. Both Fitzroy and I knew nothing looked worse than trying to undo a seen action, so neither of us removed our hands.

'Ah, food,' said Fitzroy, letting me go to pick up his cutlery 'I was close to fainting from hunger. Did you have to wait for the chicken to grow into a hen to lay the eggs?'

'No, sir. We do not keep live chickens in the kitchen. Having one animal in there is bad enough. Most unhygienic.'

'Oh, I don't know. A little bit of dirt never hurt anyone,' responded Fitzroy. 'Now, what's this I hear about you annoying Euphemia with impertinent questions?'

I hadn't told him a thing, and I tried to catch Griffin's eye, but the trick, as it usually does, worked.

'I am merely concerned for your well-being, sir,' said Griffin. 'You are aware I have a better appreciation of the workings of the human anatomy than most. I felt I had no option but to speak out.'

At this point, I attempted to edge my chair a little closer to him.

'Look out,' said Fitzroy, 'she thinks you're saying too much, and she's about to kick you. And she kicks like a mule. I know.'

Griffin reddened, and looked at me, realising his error. 'I had no intention of offending ma'am. I offer my unreserved apologies.'

'Then that's that,' I said, standing. 'I need to get to the theatre.'

'Which one was it again?' said Fitzroy.

'I didn't tell you,' I said, shrugging myself into a coat that Griffin had brought out.

'That'll be all, Griffin,' said Fitzroy in a curt tone. 'Now!'

I only had one arm in a sleeve, so I was left flapping like a half-dressed child as Griffin abandoned his post. Fitzroy took over the job of helping me into it. 'Don't let Griffin bother you,' he said. 'He has a bit of an issue about men getting obsessed with women. Bit of a prior trauma. All in the past.'

'What did you do?' I said, turning to face him now both my arms were through the sleeves.

Fitzroy pulled a face, his mouth turned down in disapproval. 'Why does everything have to be my fault?'

I raised one eyebrow and lowered the other in my practised quizzical gaze.

'Oh, all right,' said Fitzroy. 'Maybe I am a bit of a catalyst, but this time everything happened before I turned up on the scene. I'm the angel for once in this little tale. I'll tell you all about it some other time. Now, which theatre did you say it was?'

'I didn't,' I said.

Fitzroy grinned. 'By the way, do you have something in your eye? Your face looks rather odd.'

I growled in a most unladylike fashion, making him laugh, and left the building. I took a hurried but circuitous route, checking that he wasn't following me. My partner might be very good at such things in the general way, but at present he didn't have the energy to keep up with me. By the time I arrived at the stage door, I was certain I had not been followed. It was at this point that I realised I had left the script behind. I would have to hope all the memory training skills Fitzroy have ever taught me would hold up. I'd fallen asleep muttering my lines to myself. With luck they had lodged in my brain.

I stepped through the little stage door and came face to face with a hobgoblin.

# Chapter Seven

## Les Joueurs D'Or

'Morning, miss!' said the hobgoblin. 'Miss Woodward, is it? Our new ingénue?'

'Yes, it is,' I said with what I hoped was a mixture of haughtiness and shyness. 'Mr . . . ?'

'Oh, everyone around here just calls me Dickens. It's me name all right, and it's also a bit of a laugh, see? Me surname being like that writerly fellow? Never read any myself, but a lot of people seem to rate him.'

'He's good,' I said. 'Do you know where I'm meant to go, Dickens? I don't want to be late my first morning.'

'I think they're all up on the apron doing some blocking. Door through there'll lead to you to the auditorium. Probably easiest way to get to them. If I try directing you through the back, you'll no doubt get lost. Lots of stuff knocking about while they work out what they're using, and the last lot have left a few odds and sods too. Very unprofessional and so I told the director.'

I nodded my thanks and hurried through the door. I had only followed half of what he said. I was gathering the theatre had its own language. It was something the now professional-looking Service had failed to provide a briefing on. Something Fitzroy and I would never have overlooked during our pre-mission research. I began to feel less impressed by the slick operation Morley was running.

I was going to have to destroy the reputation of my provincial theatre, the Sunlit Fields, by saying they hadn't gone in for professional jargon. It would be a real theatre or I'd have never been accepted by this one. However, if any of the other actors had played there then I was in trouble. It wasn't as if I could claim a bad memory – well, not without getting fired.

The door I had been directed through led me into an arcing corridor. I walked along plush blue carpet. On one side was a series of doors leading into the stalls, and the other side I suspected would open out at the midway point into a lobby with stairs to the other levels. Not wanting to get lost, I opened the nearest polished wooden door by its gleaming brass bar-like handle and stepped through into the auditorium.

I had come in about halfway down the right-hand side. At the top lay the stage, its floor opening out to cover the orchestra pit, and on this lounged various people, presumably actors by their louche deportment. One young woman lay on her back smoking a cigarette through a freakishly long-stemmed holder. A pile of curls surrounded her head. I doubted the curls were natural, but their colour was golden, like a cornfield in summer. For some reason I found this irritating. She wore a pink feather boa and the palest of rose dresses that skimmed her figure so tightly I was surprised she could breathe let alone move. Next to her a bored-looking man in a grey suit, with a suspiciously orange face, flicked through a manuscript. By the movement of his shoulders I saw he sighed frequently and deeply. A man in an evening suit sat at a baby grand piano on the stage, the lid closed, and scribbled frantically on something which I couldn't quite make out. Walking up and down the stage with what could only be described as a strutting manner was an exceptionally thin man in his shirtsleeves. He wore what must have been, when worn in its entirety, a very smart grey suit. The outfit was completed, and outclassed, by the vivid blue-with-silver stars waistcoat he had wrapped round his spindly chest.

No one paid the least attention to me. They were all intent on their internal worlds. I waited for a few minutes to be noticed, but the tableau in front of me did not change, the only exception being that the man with the orange face sighed so deeply I thought he was about to shrug his jacket off. Ash lengthened on the impossibly long cigarette, and trembled. A moment before it fell, the girl extended her arm very slightly and tapped with one long forefinger. The ash fell into a heap on the floor.

'You really were brought up in a slum, weren't you, Rosa?' said the orange-faced man. The phrasing was perfectly fine English, but the accent extremely French, which made it sound most odd.

The girl raised herself on one elbow and sneered at the man. 'At least I'm bloody English. Unlike you, *Henree*!' Her voice was pure working class London. 'Besides, I'm a star. I can do what I like.'

Henri stood up and glowered down at her. 'You are a dirty little *salope*! Why the director hired you I cannot think.'

'*Mes enfants! Tais-toi!*' said the strutting man, who had turned back on himself and finally noticed me. 'We have a visitor!' Although he had spoken French, unlike Henri, this man spoke it with a Cockney twang.

The thin man approached me. 'Welcome to Les Joueurs d'Or, mademoiselle! I am Yves d'Yves.' He bowed low, ending in a theatrical flourish. 'How can we help you?'

'I'm Alice Woodward,' I said. 'I'm to join you, I believe.' I knew people used made-up names in the theatre, but a Cockney-sounding Yves d'Yves bordered on the farcical.

'Oh, Lord,' said Rosa, 'it's my understudy. I mean, look at her! She's got reddy-brown hair. Even if you use a bottle on that it will come out all yellowy-green.' She gave me one of her sneers. 'Wrong face for theatre as well.'

Yves came rapidly towards me. 'Ah yes, Miss Woodward. I am the director of our little piece, and manager, for my sins, of Les Joueurs d'Or. My good friend Charles Lesington recommended you. I believe you come straight from a stint at the Tunbridge Wells Rep?'

I cast my mind back to the paper I'd been given. For a moment I couldn't recall it mentioning where I was from. 'The Sunlit

Fields,' I said politely as the name finally dropped, and hoping he wouldn't enquire further. I'd be dashed if they'd written anything about what I was meant to have been cast in. 'I am also to play the maid, am I not?'

'Yes,' said Yves, 'but she is more prop than part. On stage a great deal, but rarely says a line. No idea why Reggie wrote her in.'

The man at the piano ran a hand through his hair, making it stand up in short brown curls. He then stuck the pencil behind his ear and stood up. 'Because, dear chap,' he said. 'Rosa's understudy needs a part of her own, and because it's an easy way to get things from A to B across the stage.' He picked his way swiftly past the other two and came to shake hands with me. 'I'm Reginald Pierce,' he said, 'the writer. You may have heard of me.' He was of medium height, wearing a good tweed suit, but extremely rumpled. His tie knot seemed to have lodged behind one of his ears. He looked not long out of school, but closer to, the lines around his eyes suggested he was in his late twenties. He had the kind of weak chin that marks a certain unfortunate section of the upper classes. I felt Reginald had done well in deciding to adopt a role behind the scenes rather than among them.

I nodded enthusiastically. Then, suddenly, hoped he didn't do the same. I knew his face could not actually move, but still it remained a worry. I thought I should discourage him from rapid head movements.

'Excellent,' he said. His chest swelled with pride, and his jacket swung open displaying a rather shabby knitted waistcoat. It was an extraordinary thing of pink, mauve, yellow, and olive green. 'Excellent. I'm one of the Flemish Pierces,' he continued. 'Or that's what me father said to convince my mother to marry him. She's rather high up in the Belgian nobility, as you'll know. All bolted over here together. Father might not be the richest, but he has the pedigree. That counts, you know, in war time. Father's doing something behind a desk for the war office, and Mother is being the hostess with the mostest. Tried to enlist myself, but flat feet.' He turned up one of the soles of his feet and looked down at it sadly. 'Never have thought fallen arches would stand between me and serving my country. I mean, Father has the same and it didn't prevent him skewering a few of those Boers back in the day.' He heaved a sigh almost worthy of the orange-faced man. 'Anyway, doing my bit. Some of my old scribbles are being done over for the war effort. You probably saw *Kidnaps and Kissing* the first time round?'

'I know the play very well,' I said. I should do. I'd spent hours with Fitzroy last night learning lines. It was a dull, mediocre drawing room-type farce. I couldn't see how it could possibly connect with the war effort.

'Darlings, I'm bored,' said Rosa. 'I think I need my lunch I know you'll miss me, but I need to keep my strength up.' She rose languidly, but with great control. As someone who had only recently become aware of the possible strength of the female body, I recognised someone who had spent significant time training hers. Despite her apparent thinness, she must have a wiry strength. How odd for an actress, I thought. I had never seen it as a rigorous, active profession. So far it seemed to be all lolling about. Though even I could see that Rosa lolled to her advantage. I really wasn't taking to this female.

By now Rosa was floating over towards us. She placed a proprietorial hand on Reggie's arm. 'Don't worry, darling. I won't drag you away from your work. Maurice Attenbury is giving it to me today.'

I blinked at that.

'Lunch. Luncheon,' said Rosa, looking directly at me for the first time. 'He's giving me luncheon.'

'But, my beauteous Rosamunda!' said Yves. 'We must work on Reggie's new lines. Work! Work! Work!'

Rosa shrugged an elegant little shoulder. 'You have her to stand in for me. Use her. I will be word perfect tomorrow. You know Reggie will explain everything to me tonight. I will be perfect tomorrow. As always.'

Then she slunk – there was no other word for it – her way past us and through the door. From our position it was difficult to believe she was wearing a shred of underwear.

I waited for the door to close behind her. I knew from working with Fitzroy, who always had an eye for the female form, that I wouldn't get a word of sense out of these men until her derrière was out of sight.

'She's right, of course,' said Reggie. 'She will be perfect tomorrow. You have to admire her.'

Personally, I doubted this, but I kept my mouth shut. I thought I caught a glint in Yves' eye that suggested he felt much the same.

The orange-faced man came across to me and drew me slightly to one side, while Reggie and Yves seems to still be lost in thoughts about Rosa. 'I am Henri de la Cloche,' he said. His French accent was subtle. Clearly he had spent a long time trying to lose it. 'With a name such as that I really could be nothing other than an actor. These others, they make up their names, but I think mine, which is real, sounds sillier. But what can you do? Disrespect one's forebears? It is not to be thought of. I have the name of a clown. *Tant pis!*'

I smiled and shook his hand. Closer to I realised that the make-up, clearly done for the stage lighting, covered a wealth of lines. He was far older than the male lead would normally be. He noticed me looking. 'All the young men are keen for the war,' he said. 'I do not think they will like it much when they get there. But it means the good parts are finally given to the second-rate actors such as myself.'

My mind flashed back to the morning at the hospital by the coast I had so recently left, when I saw my first wave of wounded. I shook my head. 'One must do one's duty by one's country,' I said. 'But to think war romantic is imbecilic.'

'And yet, there will be some men who enjoy it,' said Henri. 'Me, I am glad I am too old to be recruited. But I suppose when they run out of the younger men I will have to go. *Tant pis!*'

'You're a curious character, Monsieur de la Cloche,' I said. 'I cannot tell when you are serious and when you are not.'

Henri gave a little chuckle. 'And I like you very much, Miss Alice. You would be much better as our lead. Rosa is . . .' he paused, then finished rather weakly, 'Not so very nice.'

'That bad?' I asked surprised. Was my irritation with her my intuition talking, and not because she reminded me of the kind of female Fitzroy often took up with for amusement? Experience had taught me that when he had a paramour he was more difficult than usual.

'Pah! Before her, the play was not a great work of art, but Reggie knows the basics of telling a story. But now, with the three new investors, it is all about attracting the troops when they are here on leave. We are duty bound to entertain them and inspire others, so Rosa, and now poor Reggie, are saying. But it is all about the money. All about the payments. And, *mon Dieu*, it is a review now!'

'A review?' I said, startled. 'The play I have learnt is not a review.'

'You must have been sent one of the older scripts.' He quickly sang the notes of half a scale in a surprisingly deep voice. 'Now,' he said. 'We have songs.'

'Dear God,' I said.

'You do sing, don't you, Miss Woodward?' said Yves suddenly. I realised he must be able to listen to two conversations at once. I would have to watch out for that.

'As it happens,' I said, 'I am able to carry a tune well enough.' I crossed my fingers behind my back when I said this. I could only hope my mission would be long over before the curtain was raised on the first performance. I wasn't entirely lying, but the thought of singing in front of a full auditorium of troops, probably already half drunk, had no appeal. In fact the whole damn thing had no appeal. Where on earth was the man I was meant to be accessing?

As if summoned by my thought, one of the doors to the stalls opened, and Mary Hill walked in. In her wake came a tall man with dark hair, dressed in a good but discreet grey suit. He looked about as out of place there as Mary did in her long black skirt, tucked white jacket, and neat straw hat. Mary looked like a mathematician, and so did her lover, down to his fingertips.

Mary's eyes met mine and I saw she recognised me. The mission was blown before it had even started.

# Chapter Eight

## A girl's best friend is her agent

Dieter Braun – Pierre – bent to kiss Mary swiftly and chastely on the cheek. Then with one hand at her back he ushered her out of the door again, closing it behind her. He paused briefly before coming forward to join the group. It took me a moment, but I realised he was restraining himself from clicking his heels and bowing. He was not hiding his nationality well.

However, the main question occupying my mind was, had Mary had a chance to warn him who I was? If not, I might be able to put a spoke in the works. As he approached, Braun looked no more than mildly curious when he registered my presence.

'I'm Rosa's new understudy,' I explained.

'Pierre Marron,' said Braun, 'I play the butler of evil. Argent Foil.' Again, I saw him struggle not to bow. 'Although Reggie talks of making him the hero. I could almost advise, Miss Woodward, not attempting to learn your lines until first night is in sight. They change so often.'

'I really must get a look at the new manuscript,' I said to Henri. 'I've learnt all the old lines. I am going to be so confused!'

'A good point, Miss Woodward,' said Reggie. 'Allow me to give you one of mine. Some of the notes are handwritten, but it is the most up to date, other than Yves', of course. He has to see everything first. Wait a mo, and I'll fetch it.'

He loped off up the aisle and hopped onto the stage.

'Be careful,' called Braun. 'I have not heard that the rigs are again fastened properly.'

Reggie bounded back to our sides again in a trice. He presented me with a rather dog-eared manuscript, and grinned. Immediately reminding me of a golden retriever my late father had owned when I was little. Hercules had been a friendly, fluffy creature, always eager to please, and with barely the brains of a cucumber. I shook the image of the dog out of my head. 'Thank you. I think perhaps I should find a nook somewhere and study.'

'Excellent dedication to your art,' said Braun. 'But your role is small if mobile. Rosa is not the kind who suffers sickness, I'm afraid. She is how do you say in English? A tough tart?'

Henri laughed so much at this he had to sit down in an auditorium chair. Tears leaked out of his eyes.

'I make a funny?' asked Braun, in the tones of a man who only ever encounters humour by misadventure. 'Henri, he tells me it is an affectionate to call a woman after a cake or sweet dish?'

Henri sat up wiping his eyes. 'I may have exaggerated a little,' he said. He looked at me. 'He heard me talking about what a tart Rosa is.'

'Who were you talking to?' I asked, glancing at the other men.

'Oh, just one of the stage hands. The one who can get cheap French cigarettes. Cutter?'

'Cutler, Ivor Cutler,' said Reggie. 'I'd watch it there if I were you, Henri. Chap's a dodgy one and no mistake. Not the kind of company I'd care to keep.'

'He also has the most excellent brandy – for a price.'

Reggie snorted. There was a lull in the conversation. I told myself there had to be a lot of Ivor Cutlers in England. And this couldn't possibly be the man I had recruited during my previous mission to help me infiltrate the black market. Unless, of course, he'd bolted – but surely Morley would have told me? That would be all I needed, Mary Hill recognising me and then my first asset absconding. I'd be on the first train back to the Fens by the evening.

'Places. Places!' said Yves suddenly, making me jump.

'The stage is again safe?' asked Braun.

'Safe as houses,' said Reggie. 'I've been working up there all morning.'

A pair of legs beneath one of the biggest aspidistras I have ever seen – and my mother used to be a county champion grower – appeared, and shuffled with some difficulty towards the middle of the stage.

'How can I work!' cried Yves, placing one hand on his forehead in what I felt was a rather overdone manner.

'I say, old bean,' said Reggie. 'We're only doing a bit of blocking today.'

'But don't you want to block around things – like this here plant? Ain't that the point of blocking?' The voice sounded horribly familiar.

'Oh, my giddy aunt, a stagehand who thinks he knows about theatre! What will the gods drop on us next,' said Reggie under his breath. 'Just leave it in the corner, dear boy. We'll get the ASM to deal with it.'

Meanwhile Yves was striding back and forth along a row of seats, his hands now clasped in front of him, now one on his forehead and one to his back. 'How? How? How?' he cried, sounding rather like a lost owl with a minor speech impediment. He stopped suddenly and cried out, rather loudly, 'How am I to work among these fools? I would rather the gods smite me than my art be so ignored!'

'Ah,' said Reggie quietly to me. 'I think Yves may be about to take a bit of a pet. He does that sometimes. All blow over with a cup of tea and some abject praise. But you're not needed now. Pop off, there's a good girl. There'll be a space for you somewhere. Pretty sure I heard Cutler talk about turning the broom cupboard into a dressing room for you.'

He said this as if it were a high treat for me. But with surprises coming at me from all angles, I decided my priority was to get Mary Hill off the scent. I walked quickly towards the door and, before anyone else suggested otherwise, made my escape into the lobby. It took me a moment to get my bearings, but I did. I found my way back to Dickens, my manuscript clutched tightly in my hand.

'Hello,' said the friendly goblin. 'You find them all right?' He leant forward. 'You ain't been fired already, have you?'

'Not yet,' I said. 'But something happened – nothing to do with me,' I said as I saw his eyes narrow, 'and Yves is having a bit of a pet.'

'Yves d'Yves,' said the goblin, huffing through his moustache. 'He was Danny Griggs when he was on the music hall. Comedy filler with water effects. That was his billing. Fancies himself a "director" now, he does. Couldn't direct a turd into a sewer, if you'll excuse me saying so.'

'If I must,' I said, trying my best to gain some moral high ground. 'But . . .'

'Why's he here? Those bloody Enfants Door, or whatever they are, are bleeding cursed if you ask me. More cast changes than a bakery sells buns. Can't get anyone else, can they? Friend of Reginald Pierce. I mean, he's not too bad, but bloody Griggs? Don't go making me laugh.'

'I won't,' I said.

'Yer what?' said Dickens, thrown off his game. Normally I'd have lapped up his gossip, but I had to call 'Lawrence, my agent' – my Department contact.

'Is there a telephone apparatus around here I could use?'

'Not touching mine,' said Dickens. 'Emergencies only. More than me job's worth.'

'Is there another?' I asked, wondering what kind of emergency I could make up, and what I could say that would make it sound believable to Dickens, who I was sure would listen in, and intelligible to my handler. If only it had been Fitzroy.

'There's one in the box office and an extension in the theatre manager's office. But he locks that.'

'But not the box office? That's not locked.'

'Couldn't tell you,' said Dickens. 'More than me job's worth.'

'Do you like toffees, Dickens? Or are you more of a mint humbugs sort of man?'

'I'm most partial to them lemon drops. The ones that have a bit of the fizz inside them.'

'Sherbet lemons,' I said. 'Would a pint be sufficient?'

Dickens drew a pencil from behind his ear and sketched a rough plan of the theatre with a big X marked in one room. 'If someone were looking for the box office, this would be where they'd head. If that someone had business there.'

'It will be empty?'

'None of the box office people come in before dinner time, and right now, we're dark, so doubt anyone's been in for a while. Thinking about it, you better take this.' He reached down beneath his desk and handed me a key. 'Dorothea what does the wages left it behind. Going a bit doo-lally, if you get my meaning. Leave it on one of the desks, she'll think she left it there.'

'Two pints it is,' I said, snatching up the key.

Of course the flaw with the plan was that I would have to go through the operator. I could only hope the theatre didn't have its own internal switchboard.

I scurried through the theatre to the box office, which lay at the far end of the lobby nearest the front entrance. It had one set of windows that opened out to the street, but these were shuttered. Likewise were the internal windows into the lobby. The door was locked, so checking behind me I slipped the key into the lock. There was enough resistance that at first I thought Dickens had given me the wrong key, when suddenly the tumblers turned and fell with a thunk. The lock hadn't been oiled in a very long time. I slipped through the door and shut it.

I quickly ascertained by means of touch that this room had no other obvious exits. The shutters would give out to small glassless spaces where tickets and money might be exchanged, but there would be no space for me to get through even if I managed to take down the boards.

The room was dark, but the shutters seemed tight enough I might risk a small light to use the telephone. This I had yet to find. A ledge ran around two sides by the shutters, complete with stools.

Feeling under the ledges I found two slide-able drawers. These were what convinced me to lock the door. I could not risk being caught here. I would be taken as a potential thief. My fingers had touched some coins, so while there wouldn't be a night's takings there, whoever set up the box office was lazy and had left the cash drawer open.

I crept back to the door, banging my shin painfully on the edge of one of the two desks that took up the middle of the floor. Fortunately my skirts muffled the sound of the impact and I managed to stuff my fist in my mouth rather than cry out.

I locked the door. It was as resistant as before. I felt my way over to the two desks until I found the telephone. There was a small electric light next to it, and now the room was secured I turned the lamp on.

Electricity was still new enough to me that I silently marvelled for a moment as the cool, circle of buttery light appeared instantaneously. Then I remembered my location, and tilted the lampshade, so the merest glimmer only fell onto the telephone. Fortunately Fitzroy had insisted I memorise my agent's number. I had thought to have left a copy back at my lodgings. The last thing I had wanted to do was ring up for help when I had already claimed to be so independent. However, pride could not get in the way of saving a mission.

I spoke softly into the receiver and requested the number from the operator. I then went through the normal round of security questions, before I was finally connected to 'Lawrence'.

'Good heavens, Alice,' said another familiar voice. 'Job done already? A written report would have done, unless you've discovered this chap is a German spy. He isn't, is he?'

'Colonel Morley?' I said his name aloud I was so shocked.

'Lawrence, my dear. You know the drill.'

'Of course,' I said. Even in the dark I could feel the heat come into my face. It was an elementary error. 'Unforgivable of me.'

A snort answered me.

'It's Mary Hill, sir. She came to the theatre. She saw me. I'm not sure if she recognised me or not. I mean, she wouldn't have expected to see me, so she might not recognise me. We met rarely enough, although we have also met unexpectedly abroad. Dieter Braun showed her out almost as soon as she came into the theatre. She was clearly escorting him, and I got the impression he was also late. I don't know why. And I don't know if, when her back was to me, she managed to tell Dieter – Pierre – who I was and what I was. I wasn't a spy when I met her, but I was working undercover as an asset. I think she always suspected I was some kind of agent.'

I stopped before I started stuttering. It felt both difficult and wrong to be reporting in to anyone other than Fitzroy.

'I do hope no one can overhear you, Alice.'

'I'm in a locked room, si—Lawrence. There are shutters on two sides, thick walls on the other two sides, with a single locked door. Beyond that is a tiled or marble-floored lobby. It is hard to walk across without making noise. I believe I would hear anyone coming.'

'And you want from me?'

I had been thinking about this. 'Could Mary be intercepted and sent to work on military matters? She is a first-class mathematician. She would understand the importance, and she would be allowed to send a note to her – to Dieter, saying she had been called away and would be back shortly. Hopefully she could phrase it in a way that wouldn't alarm him. She could even say that she was working on something of national importance and hoped it would improve his chances of being allowed to stay in the country.'

'Yes, I suppose that's possible. But not if she has already told him she knows you.'

'I'm afraid I will have to leave that to someone else to discover. Unless Dieter mentions it to me, I can hardly ask. I don't want to probe in any way. That would only arouse suspicion. I've only been here a few hours, but it is clear there is a lot wrong with this production and its company.' I heard a sharp intake of breath at the other end. 'I don't mean, Lawrence,' I said beginning to use the name where I might have said sir, 'that it has anything necessarily to do with our business. I mean that the cast are at odds, and some of them are very odd. And there have been a number of cast changes. The doorman told me the director is an ex-music hall performer named Danny Griggs.'

'Danny Griggs,' repeated Lawrence in the tone of someone writing something down.

'He goes by Yves d'Yves now . . .'

'Rather silly, isn't that?'

'They all have rather silly names, even the real ones – I mean real names. It does seem rather a good place to hide – I mean among a theatre. Everyone is already pretending to be someone they are not, so one more layer of deception hardly matters. And that leaves beside the whole issue of people reinventing themselves before or after the theatre.'

'Valets and butlers,' said Lawrence succinctly. 'I take it if you were talking to Fitzroy, you would have reported in a much shorter manner.'

'We have a shorthand, if that's what you mean, Lawrence.'

'Well, despite my failure to be him, I think I can take it from here. I have intellect enough to see what you need, even if neither of us quite know where you're heading.'

'There's another thing. Ivor Cutler . . .'

'Ah, I had hoped to broach that with you later. I take it he's passed through the theatre?'

'He's working here.'

'Ah.'

I waited a few moments. Then said, 'I'm afraid I am not sufficiently cognoscente with army terminology to understand what "Ah" means. Ivor Cutler was my asset. I left him with instructions at an entirely different location during my last mission. To my knowledge and understanding he was still working as my asset.'

'Ah,' said Lawrence again. 'Well, you were coming back to town, and we expected you to go straight to your husband's bedside.'

'Who is we?'

'That is beyond your pay grade, my dear. I rather thought we'd have you weeping and wailing in the hospital. We managed to contact Fitzroy in the field, and he said he thought that would be most unlike you. If anything he expected you to be angry, but to continue to do your duty. I regret to say, we all thought he was thinking of you rather too much as if you were a normal agent.'

'You mean a man?'

'Well, yes. He said you'd quickly see your husband was having the best care, and see no point being there while he was in a coma.'

'Naturally.'

'That's the thing, isn't it, Alice? That's not the way most wives would think – naturally.'

I took a deep breath. 'With respect, most wives haven't spent several years in this business. You develop a perspective.'

'You know, I can't make up my mind yet if Fitzroy has made an excellent agent of you, or simply ruined a good woman.'

'Probably both, sir,' I snapped.

'You can see how it seems as if you prefer the company of old Eric rather than your husband.'

'Can I say, again with respect, sir, this is not the time or place for me to discuss such things. We both have other matters to attend to.'

There was silence on the line. 'So how long would it have taken you to brief Fitzroy?'

'Under a minute,' I said, 'but we would have stuck to the business at hand.'

I hung up the telephone. I could always say later that I had heard someone coming. Morley obviously already thought little of me, and if we had continued the conversation I would have told him exactly what I thought of him.

It would have been a shame to lay waste to all of Fitzroy's efforts in training me. Besides, most of the time I liked my work, very much indeed. If only the wretched Morley would leave me and Fitzroy alone to get on with it.

Hell's teeth, but life would be easier if I was a man.

# Chapter Nine

## Once an asset . . .

I had no idea what had induced Morley to be my handler. His behaviour was as appalling as his code name. I stumped back towards the auditorium, and then had to retrace my steps to put the key in the box room. Surely, even an imbecile would realise it was not the thing to upset an agent during a mission. Especially if the details were entirely unrelated to what was happening at the time. 'Unnatural wife,' I murmured under my breath. 'How bloody dare he!'

I stopped outside the auditorium and took several deep breaths. I opened the door to see Braun and Henri on stage with Yves and Reggie sitting in the first row. To the left side of the stage stood three men of similar heights and indulgent girths. They were all dressed in matching lime-coloured suits and all had cheeks flushed a rosy red with embarrassment. The middle one was looking at the ceiling and the two end ones at their shoes. Not at the audience. Clearly unhappy, they looked as out of place as they obviously felt.

'Not manage to find your cupboard?' called Henri, spotting me from the stage. He and Braun were posed opposite each other. Braun leant forward, his manuscript clutched in his hand. The other hand he held aloft in a fist.

'Oh, for the sake of the dear *Dieu*,' Yves was shouting. 'You're meant to be preparing to punch him, not giving him a ruddy salute!' The director turned and looked at me. He raised his eyebrows in mock surprise.

It was only at that moment that remembered that I had been

meant to be finding my dressing room and learning my new lines. 'I must have got turned around,' I said feebly.

'Yes, indeed,' said Yves. 'The door to the auditorium clearly looks so like the door to the dressing room of the most junior cast member present.'

I started slightly at his sharpness. I put my hands behind my back. My fingers had already curled into fists. I really was emotionally out of order. I blinked rapidly, trying to make it look as if I might cry rather than that I wanted to tie the director's thin body into a reef knot. A flare of red hot anger shot through me. I wanted to tie him up so tight he'd squeal like a piglet.

'That's all right, governor,' said Ivor popping up from under a seat, a screwdriver in his hand. 'I'll show her where it is.'

He ushered me out of the west door of the auditorium. Instead of heading towards the lobby, he pushed on a section of the back wall, which was painted white and half panelled. A door swung open.

'Oh,' I said.

'Yeah,' said Ivor, 'it's pretty well hidden until you know where it is. Then it seems bleedin' obvious. Follow me. The dressing rooms and the green room are down this way. There's even a little kitchenette. We should go there first. It's where you get your tea.'

'Kitchenette' turned out to be something of an exaggeration. It was a tiny room with a two-ring stove, with a kettle, a bottle of milk, a teapot, and a tin full of tea leaves standing on a small shelf. Behind the shelf was a small, oddly shaped window that opened on a slant, hinging on a bar in the middle. You could just see a narrow side street below. There was also a small cupboard over a tiny sink that had clearly not been cleaned for a while. Ivor reached up and opened the cupboard, displaying a number of mugs.

'You'd better use one of the plain tin mugs,' he said. 'The others all have their favourites and Gawd knows the lot of them are more liable to bust your chops as soon as look at you.'

He spoke quickly, and avoided my gaze. He moved quickly. Taking down two mugs and putting milk and tea into them, before excusing himself to get past me and at the sink to fill the kettle. I was reminded of playing sardines at the rectory with little Joe. Being many years my junior, my brother had been especially good at getting into small spaces, and had once spent half an hour up the kitchen chimney before I gave in and called him out.

'So, Ivor, you've moved on in the world,' I said, choosing my words carefully.

Ivor gave me a frightened look, and scurried across, spilling water from his kettle in his haste to close the small door.

'It's easier to see if anyone is standing outside with it open,' I said.

'Whispers go a long way in this old building,' said Ivor. 'Marvel of modern architecture when it were built. Supposedly you could hear a pin dropped on the stage way up in the gods. Anyway, they mucked about with the inside of the building over the years, but sound still travels further than it should.' He filled the kettle and put it on the hob.

'I'll remember that.'

'You haven't asked me why I'm here yet,' said Ivor, and I saw sweat beading on his brow. 'It weren't my idea. I can tell you that.'

'What else can you tell me?'

'Not a lot. I know you're here to look into that Pierre fella. I was told I should provide you with physical back-up if asked. Otherwise I weren't to interfere.'

'Physical back-up?'

Ivor chuckled. 'I know. I laughed like a drain when they said that. I said have you seen 'er in action? She could snap me like a twig and not even have to redo her hair.' He shrugged. 'I'm not sure they believed me. Once they found out I didn't believe in fighting and killing and stuff like that . . . well, they treated me different. I said, no one has asked me to go to war yet. I haven't said no. I know my duty like any other bloke.'

'Would you go to war?' I asked.

'Rather be a miner – and I'm dead afraid of the dark. But you saw how those boys came back.'

'Alice Woodward has never been a nurse.'

Ivor cringed, and ran his right hand though his thin hair. 'This is all so bleedin' complicated. I'm just going to stick to me bit.' The kettle whistled and Ivor jumped a good two inches in the air.

'I think you better let me handle the boiling water,' I said, filling the two mugs. I found a rather disgustingly stained teaspoon on the shelf. I rinsed it over the sink with the dregs of the kettle, and did my best to extract the tea leaves from the two cups. There was no sign of a tea strainer. 'What do I do with the leaves?' I asked.

'Most of them open that little window and throw them out,' he said. 'It's better if you don't stir. Let it sit for a while and then they settle, like. You throw 'em out at the end.'

'Really,' I said looking astonished. 'Don't the local residents mind?'

'No idea. Never met any of 'em,' said Ivor. He took the teaspoon off me and flicked the leaves out the window. 'For all I know the pigeons eat them.'

'Birds don't eat tea leaves,' I said.

'Not country birds, no. But these city birds'll eat anything. I found a pair of them feasting on poor old Gus' eyes.'

I felt my jaw slacken. 'I sincerely hope you are about to tell me that Gus was not a person.'

'Theatre cat. Someone poisoned the poor bugger.' He gave me an askance look.

'This isn't a very happy place, is it?'

'Bit of an understatement of the year, miss.'

'I think we should sit down somewhere and drink our tea while you fill me in on what's been going on here.'

'I can do some of that, miss. The seats are a bit beyond me. There's a stool in your dressing room. But you wouldn't have been able to swing old Gus in there. If he'd lived, poor bugger.'

'Very well, we shall make do with leaning in here.'

Ivor accepted his tea from me, and leant back in a well practiced posture. I leant my shoulders against the wall in a rather more uncomfortable manner. I crossed my ankles and tipped up the toe of one of my lady-like shoes. I sighed. The truth was that although I loved a beautiful dress as much as the next woman, more often than not I wished I could dress like a man. Fitzroy had left me one of my undercover costumes at the café. It had been in the parcel I had picked up. However, I'd immediately got it soaked when I went to visit him. Griffin was presumably currently washing and drying it, while sniffing in near-terminal disapproval.

I realised Ivor had been speaking for the last few minutes. Damn Lawrence and his implications.

'I apologize, Ivor. I was somewhat lost in my own thoughts. Could you repeat what you just said?'

'Oh, I hadn't got to the important bit. I was just saying how I was kidnapped and bundled up 'ere, and told to keep an eye out for black market trading through the theatre lot – the backstage staff, even the stars. I was told to incinerate meself. Which I can't say I'm keen on.'

I smothered a smile. 'I think they meant insinuate, as in become known to the gang as a willing legman.'

'Right,' said Ivor, swilling down a gulp, 'I knew that.'

'Of course,' I said, managing to keep a straight face.

'Then they told me to provide yer with physical back-up if you needed it with whatever you were doing. I've already said that, haven't I? But just goes to show what a pile of bleedin' useless whatever-they-ares.'

'Really? Surely you've been trained fully in hand-to-hand combat in the short time we have been apart.'

'No, I bleedin' ain't,' said Ivor. 'I told them you were the expert in that area. Don't think the bugger believed me.' He gave a deep sigh. 'Poor old Gus.'

'You're not going to tell me the cat set you on this mission?'

'What? No, don't be daft. It's just that Gus always got under your feet like. I was always telling him to "get away, yer bugger" and "go to hell, yer bugger". He loved trying to trip me up, especially if I was carrying stuff. First time I met a cat with a sense of humour.'

'Do you think it was deliberately poisoned?' I found myself asking.

'Yes. Yes, I do, miss. He were a black cat and a good luck charm for the Golden Angel. It were like as soon as Gus were gone the whole thing started coming unravelled.'

'Explain,' I said, glad we were back on track. I couldn't see Braun being involved with poisoning a cat, but he might be involved in whatever was happening here. I already had a bad feeling.

'Apparently, Gus were a stray. It's the doorman's job to feed him. He come in on a rainy night some ten years ago, when the production weren't going very well, but that night it sold out. These theatre folk are a superstitious lot. To them a black cat is either very lucky or very unlucky. Gus fell on his paws when they decided he were lucky. Even got fresh fish on a Friday. Ate better than some of the stage hands from what I've seen. Old Dickens is getting a bit unsteady on his pegs, so I'd been feeding the little mite. Affectionate soul, more purr about him than body. Gave me the fright of me life when I came across him stiff as a board, all twisty up like. Arsenic. They put it down for the rats. But if you ask me Gus knew better than to eat from the rat bait. He'd been here ten years an' always avoided it. I reckon that someone poisoned him deliberate. Bastard. It's one thing to jam a bayonet in the guts of a Hun, but to hurt a little pussy cat? That ain't right.'

I finally managed to get a word in edgewards while Ivor took a slurp of his tea. 'You're suggesting the Germans poisoned the cat?'

'Nah, of course not. But someone who didn't like this lot did. Was after that Michael Keaton left. He were the first director for *Kidnaps and Kissing.* Had the rep of being bloody good. It'd all been going well, then Gus died and Keaton starts thinking his dressing room is haunted. Finally, ups and says he can't stay on a damned ship.' Ivor shook his head. 'Nutty, the lot of them. Of course an old building like this is going to have the odd ghost. Can't harm you though, can they? Being incorporation and all.'

'Disembodied, you mean?'

Ivor nodded. 'That's what I said. First of a string o' bad things. Mind you, nothing bad's happened for a week or so now. Cast are at each other's throats, but as far as I can make out that's not unusual with these actors. All rather egotasticallical.'

'They kept going on about the stage being safe?'

'Oh yeah, one of the last things I remember going sideways was some idiot up in the rigging not tying off a knot right. One of them big sandbags they use ter weigh down the sets came rattling down. Sent trepidations through the whole rig, a chimney came down as well. Smashed into the stage enough to make a decent dent.'

'Chimney?'

'Part of the set. Not a real one. But if anyone had been underneath it woulda made a nasty mess of them. Just like what happened to little Janice Hargreaves.'

'What?'

'The previous leading lady. Miss what's her face weren't always star of the show. She had your part. Janice had the lead. Small woman, big brown eyes, shy as mouse until she were on the stage and then, by Jove, she didn't half light your blood up. She had what they call presence.'

'She was killed here?'

'Nah, outside. Fell in front of one of them new-fangled buses. Going at a bit of clip it was.' He shook his head. 'Musta been a good twenty miles an hour. Tossed her up in the air like she were a paper doll. When she came down a number o' the other vehicles bumped her, but it were the drayman's horses that really messed her up. I only hope she was dead by then. Worse than an ambulance arriving at the hospital, it was.'

'What was Janice like?'

'Oh, a complete pet of a girl. We all doted on her. I'd been here barely a minute, and she already knew my name. She was like that. Thoughtful. Kind. Professional. A proper star.'

'I'm surprised they didn't close the show down.'

'Nah, miss. Too much money caught up in this one. Part of the reason I'm 'ere. This is one of the new patriot plays. Meant to inspire men to join up. And buoy up the ones on leave from the front. Lot of money tied up in that, you know. They poor buggers will laugh at anything. Anything that takes their mind off the fighting. What they're going back to. Don't know how the poor bleeders stand it.'

I opened my mouth to speak, but he carried on. 'Pay burning a hole in their pockets. It's not only tickets we sell, but treats and cigarettes. Chocolate when we got it. And this place has a deal with the ale house next door. We opened a door between the two buildings and send 'em through at the interval. There's a standing deal over sharing the money. Now, as far as I can tell most of it is above board, but you can see how the black market might like to get its sticky fingers in here. And it's my job to give 'em an 'elping hand, right up until we take 'em down.'

'How is that going to work?'

'No bleedin' idea,' said Ivor. 'If this were a chess board I'm a bleedin' prawn. You must be a bishop at least.'

It occurred to me to say 'no, but my mother is married to one'. The whole conversation had taken a decidedly odd turn. It seemed there was a whole host of potential shenanigans going on at the Golden Angel. Most of which had nothing to do with me.

But I couldn't shake the feeling that poor Janice Hargreaves might have been helped on her way. How horrible to die under a shire horse's hooves. It wasn't merely that I didn't like our new leading lady . . . I had a strong hunch bad things were happening here. Things that Morley would say were none of the Department's concern. He'd tell me to leave them alone. Fitzroy would think the same, but he knew me well enough to know that the only way to stop me investigating a potential murder would be to remove me from the scene.

# Chapter Ten

## Janice Hargreaves

The rest of the week went by in a blur. I was kept on my toes learning all the terminology of the theatre. Rosa also regularly tried to edge me off the stage for no apparent reason but spite. The days fell into a pattern. I came to the theatre, I went home. I saw no opportunity to catch Dieter Braun alone, and I was learning little more about him.

Attempts to learn his address failed. He was extremely careful of his personal possessions and my one attempt to steal his pocketbook to see if he had recorded it inside, almost got me caught.

I decided the best thing I could do was play for time. Morley might want his report yesterday, but this theatre group struck me already as so entangled with undercurrents, that if I wished to do a proper job, I would need to go more slowly than usual.

It was indeed all going terribly slowly, when I ended up having a quick luncheon with Henri at the local café that catered to actors on low incomes – The Masked Cat. The food was mediocre, and I didn't dare order anything other than the ubiquitous egg and chips. Firstly I suspected the 'croque monsieur' advertised on the menu was most likely to be a crock itself. It was bound to contain very low-quality meat, and worse yet, I doubted very much it had come from a pig at such prices. Besides, I was meant to be an aspiring actress. Fitzroy's pocket change was more than I was to earn in a month. I had to be careful.

The main impression the café gave was of age and dust. The dust wasn't actually on the tables, but you could see it lurking with its attendant spider webs in every corner. You could taste it, or that may have been the quality of the cooking. While we were waiting for our order a spider, from a slightly moth-eaten curtain, dropped onto the head of a white-haired man with more wrinkles than a turtle. His large spotted cravat proclaimed him as 'theatre folk'. He didn't appear to notice, and no one told him. This, despite the astonishing size of the creature, and the fact it was black against his snowy white hair. I assumed he was no longer someone of importance. Finally a waiter, in passing, conceded and flicked the creature off him and onto the floor.

'Hey, what?' said the old man.

'There was dust in your hair, sir,' said the waiter.

'Not surprised,' said the old man. 'As long as it isn't in my soup. Though dare say you'd charge me extra for that!'

The waiter walked off with his nose in the air. The old man chuckled to himself. Looked up at the customers in the room, who were watching, and loudly slurped his soup at us. I let my gaze drift away.

There were images everywhere of long-gone actors and actresses – all dusty. Old playbills, and a few black and white photographs, covered the walls. The table linen was very, very old ruby red damask with large paper napkins laid where there was any danger of a spillage. The furniture was a mismatch of dark wood tables, some single-legged, some gate-legged. The best seats were the round tables in the booths, but these appeared to be reserved for the well-known. At least that is the only reason I can ascribe to the single maitre d' bowing and scraping his way across the floor when any particularly well-clothed, but garish individuals arrived. Henri and I had to make do with a waitress, who clearly hadn't been in post very long, and had no idea the English language contained the letter H.

The windows were covered with tassel-edged ruby curtains, and the carpet, although it ran wall to wall, stuck slightly to one's shoes and was of a colour between red and brown. It reminded me of dried blood.

'It is not the nicest establishment,' said Henri. 'But it is near the theatre, cheap of price, and has never once made me ill. On occasion I have even enjoyed my food.'

I laughed. 'Now that is high praise indeed. I had not realised that London was so rife with these little eateries.'

'Perhaps not for so much longer,' said Henri with sigh. 'I wouldn't mind if they were to be replaced with the better places, but I fear that the war will bring about a sufficient lack of clients that many may close. We are fortunate that our play has been changed to support the war effort. It was a wise move on our writer's part.'

'I didn't realise.'

'Oh yes, the lines change often. But that is what happens if you allow a writer into the rehearsal room, *tant pis*! But this has been much more. Our play was once a melodrama such as the first customers of this place,' he gestured widely and un-embarrassedly about him. 'They must have been something to see. Not to the modern taste, but still rife with acting in the grand style. You can still sniff the smelling salts in the curtains.'

'Smells more like cat to me,' I said.

Henri's face fell at once. '*Le pauvre chat*. Gus, he was a magnificent cat! He could devour an entire fish head in the blink of an eye. I won many a bet on him. There was nothing he would not eat.'

'Sadly, it appears so.'

'*Mais non*. It was murder. He was killed.' He made a wringing gesture with his hands.

'I thought he was poisoned?'

'I did not see his *pauvre* little corpse, but I have heard he was poisoned, stabbed, and had his neck wrung. He was not easy to kill. He came from the streets, *comme moi*!'

Why, I thought, does everyone keep mentioning the cat and not Janice Hargreaves? However beloved a pet it was, surely a young woman's life is worth more consideration than that of a cat! 'I believe he was something of a lucky mascot for the Golden Angel!'

'Mascot! A mascot is a tawdry thing, a child's toy. Gus was the heart of the theatre. Everyone loved him. Why, on opening nights he would visit the dressing rooms of the actors who would be well received. Only if you had visit from old Gus would you do well on the stage!'

'And did he visit you?' I asked.

'This is my first play at the Golden Angel. He would have visited me on opening night, and I would have given the performance of my life. But without Gus? It is a disaster! The play will do nothing. They will riot in the aisles!'

'You think the death of the cat will make that much difference?'

'But everything is torn asunder since the passing of our Gus. Scenery tumbles from the sky. We acquire a leading lady of the most dubious character – you see *mon visage*!' He pointed to his face. 'I am orange! Orange! I use my crème that makes the skin so youthful, to help with the tiny creasings of age. And why should I not! The ladies, they do, and my skin is more important than most women's. Alas, I do not have a lot of money, so I must buy the crème in the biggest pot I can. I must be the handsome figure. The desirable man for the ladies to admire. It is why they come to the theatre, after all. To indulge in fantasy. I must live up to their fantasies, non? If my skin were not orange you would think I was a young man, would you not?'

'Of course,' I lied. 'So Rosa tampered with your crème. At the very least should not the director have words with her, if not the police?'

Henri reached out across the table to take my hand. Fortunately, I was in the midst of a tricky procedure to convey a very yolky and floppy bit of egg from the plate to my mouth. Even Henri realised this was not the time to lay hands upon me, and so contented himself with a clumsy, and rather sweaty caress. He was obviously a gentleman who sweats. It was repulsive. The room was not in the least warm. Could he be nervous about something?

'You are an angel to say so, my dear. But our Rosa is a sly little thing. I know it was her. She smirks when she sees me this morning, and says something about eating too many carrots. As if I, a Frenchman, would eat too much food of the rabbits! I see in her eyes, she knows. She did it. But how can I prove it? My instincts, they are excellent. I know it was her, but I can hardly show my guts to anyone! Of course I could throw the crème away, but it will be some time before I can afford more. So now, I use the smoothing crème that turns me orange, and hope by the time the show opens I will be able to afford a new pot.'

'But it makes you look orange!'

'I know. I know. If I do not use it my face will crease like a thrown-out paper bag.'

'How dreadful for you!' I said, inching my chair back very slightly. 'Should we not head back to the theatre? We have been gone a while.'

Henri shrugged. 'I suppose. We pay half each?'

Henri had had a glass of wine with his luncheon. I had not. I decided now was not the time to fuss about money. I did, however, take a while to scratch the coins out of my purse. I wanted to appear amiable, but not a free ticket to luncheon.

Henri nodded as I put my money on the table. 'You are a good girl. If you continue to be a good girl I will make you my mistress, if you like?'

I felt my eyebrows shoot up into my hairline so fast my eyelids stretched. 'Oh really, don't bother yourself,' I found myself saying. I stopped myself from adding 'I don't want to be any trouble,' just in time. It was the kind of denial I gave our tenants at White Orchards, when they invited me in to take a cup of tea. I either had to go in to all or none of the houses on a general visiting day, and other bodily functions aside, that much tea makes me sick. I had come, under Fitzroy's influence, to prefer coffee.

It was, in short, an entirely inadequate response. If I had not been under cover my response would have been more clear. And more painful for Henri.

'We shall see, *mon petit cadeau*,' said Henri. 'We shall see.' He seemed most off-hand about the whole business. It was as if we were discussing the weather more than a possible liaison. Perhaps this was his sense of humour. Or perhaps junior actresses did leap into the beds of their more successful peers. I decided the best thing to do was pretend it had happened. If he mentioned it again, I would pretend not to understand.

Then as I edged past him to get out I felt a light but definite pat on my bottom. I gritted my teeth, and told myself Alice Woodward would not counter with a strong attack. She would remain aloof, as if unaware of the impropriety, like a well-brought-up upper-middle class girl. She would not now be fantasising about jumping up and down on Henri's bloodied body.

As Henri joined me on the street outside and offered me his arm, I smiled sweetly, thinking of the many ways I could do him harm, and of which he was blissfully unaware. There was a little succour in this, but not much.

The streets were busy today. Or perhaps it was merely the bustle of luncheon. I had yet to accustom myself to how this part of London disported itself. This was an area that, unless I was visiting a show or working undercover, I would never visit. Truthfully, I wasn't entirely sure I would see a show here. Fitzroy, being a man, could go wherever he liked. However I suspected that in the normal way of things I would have been likely to go to the opera or the ballet. Shows, such as the one I was in, Bertram would have thought far beneath me.

It was only at this point I reflected on the wisdom of putting someone on stage who had never seen a play in a theatre. Of course, I had read some plays while growing up. My father had tutored me. I was familiar with most of the great Greek plays and all the Shakespearean tragedies and comedies. However, I had never actually seen someone produce a play. I could only imagine that Morley must be of a class that would attend plays. Usually I have no interest in the class system, having found my truest friends among the so-called working or lower middle classes, but for once I felt the loftiness of being an Earl's granddaughter, whose step-father was also a Bishop. Morley might speak nicely, but as Fitzroy would have put it, one would never have heard of the school the Colonel had attended.

'You are thinking of a seriousness?' said Henri, as he tapped my fingers with his free hand. 'It is not good for you. It will give you lines on the face. *Dit-moi, ma petite.* What troubles you?'

I seized this opening. 'I was thinking how busy it is today, and remembering poor Janice Hargreaves. What a tragic accident.'

'It was sad,' said Henri with a small sigh. 'She was most talented. We had luncheon together most often. I had been about to invite her to a supper a deux. I had been planning it for some time. I had even got the restaurant to order in her favourite wine. Though she was never to drink it I still had to pay for it. *Tant pis!* It was an investment. An investment that never had the chance to bear fruit.'

'A horrible way to die,' I said.

Henri shivered. 'I do not wish to think of it. I prefer to remember her as she was.'

'Quite right. Poor girl.'

'She was always rushing,' said Henri. 'We would have luncheon together. I would suggest a promenade in the park before we returned, to refresh ourselves, but always she would have to run off. I do not know where she always had to run to, but often after our little conversations it would be so. I think she had great worries. Why else would she so often flee my company?'

'Why indeed?'

'That must have been what happened that fateful day,' he said. 'She was doing her running, and she did not look properly. *La pauvre.* Still, we must all meet our fates one day. And as you say, "the show must go on". Even one like ours.' This time he gave a truly deep sigh.

'Was it her first time in London?' I asked. 'I find this area so busy and confusing.'

'Not at all,' said Henri. 'She had played many of the theatres around here. She was born backstage, so she claimed. The theatre was her life, and this was her world.'

Why, I thought, would a woman who had lived all her life around these streets suddenly lose her sense of how dangerous the roads could be? I decided I had talked enough about poor Janice, and more questions would only make me sound suspicious, yet I itched to know more. There was a mystery here, and I wanted to uncover it. But instead I said, 'Thank you for accompanying me to luncheon, Henri. You are opening my eyes to the Metropolis.'

This seemed to please him, and he began to make various suggestions about where else he might escort me. 'In a fatherly way, of course,' he said. Seeming to completely forget he had talked less than half an hour ago about making me his mistress. A very odd sort of man.

I decided to distract him by asking more about the revisions of the play. I had barely had time to flick through a few pages. Then he said the words that struck dread into my heart.

'No lines this *après-midi*. The singing master comes and we must all sing for our supper.'

# Chapter Eleven

## Billets *not* doux

The afternoon was quite as awful as I feared. The songs were dreadful. The tunes erratically insipid or overly grandiose. The worst were the comedy ones, and that was all I seemed to have to sing. My voice was clear enough that the singing master, a Signor Medici, who was about as Italian as jellied eels in my opinion, decided to work in parts for me with the comical trio whom I had previously seen dressed in lime green.

I feared that Reggie had been overly influenced by the idea of a Greek chorus at school. The trio popped up whenever any dramatic action had occurred and recapped the event in a little ditty. Whoever had penned the songs doubtless regarded 'Three Blind Mice' as a masterpiece. The little ditties were direly rhymed and had appalling melodies. Although melody was hardly the right word. When a song writer rhymes 'naughty' with 'salty' and moves on to 'nearly bought it', I think there is little to be done.

'They sing with their souls in their boots,' Medici said. 'You will give them all a good lift.'

'Goodness, I wonder why?' I said, all wide-eyed and innocent. The three males of the trio – Michael (tenor), Mathew (baritone), and Marmaduke (basso) – on completion of each song scuttled off into a corner together and refused to mix with the rest of the group. Instead they cast dark looks at us. However, each of them was thoroughly unprepossessing in the extreme. I rated them altogether as no more dangerous than a mousetrap. Braun, on the other hand, clearly found their attention unnerving.

Braun turned out to have a basso voice that seemed to come from the depths of the earth, and Henri had a pleasant, if weak, baritone. Of Rosa there was no sign. But the singing master assured me she had the voice of an angel. One of the best he had ever had the privilege of training. 'And no fear. No fear at all. She throws herself into the song and sings like a bird,' he told me after describing my own efforts as 'fair and passable'.

As soon as I was able I retreated to my tiny dressing room, which still had a broom in it, to sit on the one rickety stool, opposite a crookedly hung mirror, and look through Reggie's latest manuscript. I found that underneath it all it was still the play I had learnt lines from, but it had been so altered it was almost impossible to find the connection between the old play and the new one. In particular there was a long patriotic call to arms that Henri's character gave, extolling all male members of the audience to enlist to fight the 'dastardly Hun'. I found this rather uncomfortable reading. In my admittedly limited experience it had been politicians and senior soldiers who decided to fight wars, not the general populace. My brother-in-law, Hans Muller, was of German decent, and a more English gentleman it would be hard to find.

The thought of Hans and Richenda filled me with guilt. I had made few enquiries over Richenda's recovery. She had been savagely attacked by her now deceased sister-in-law and lain in a coma for many days – or was it weeks? I had no clear recollection. My time abroad, then undercover in a hospital, and with only a few weeks back at White Orchards, had very much taken up my attention and occupied my thoughts. I knew Hans worked in London occasionally, and I decided to write him a note to see if we could meet up for luncheon at some time.

The pair of them had not signed the Official Secrets Act, and no one had precisely told them what I, or Fitzroy, did, but I knew they suspected. They would have been quite dunderheaded not to, with the adventures I had dragged Richenda into. Especially as Fitzroy had muttered something about ensuring Hans and his family would not be interred for the duration of the war, if only Hans might do a little something for him.

This led on to the thought that really it was too much for Fitzroy to have insisted on knowing my mission. When he undertook a mission without me I never demanded to know the details. I should have asked what he was up to with Hans. My connection to this side of the family was through Bertram, but I regarded Richenda as the nearest I had to a real sister. I definitely had fallen down in my familial duties. I took some paper from the notebook in my reticule, and scribbled a note. Now all I had to find was an envelope and a stamp. Cutler should be able to help with that.

I opened the door to my little cupboard and started with fright. Like some genie summoned by thought, Cutler was there holding out an envelope to me. One quick look showed me that my powers of telepathy had not arisen overnight, but that the envelope was addressed to me. I took it, thanking him, and asking him to find me a fresh envelope and a stamp. I forestalled any complaints by pressing a couple of coins into his hand.

Then I retreated back into my cupboard. Oddly for a cupboard, there was a small window high up on the wall. It showed how much the theatre had been cut up and messed about with by various architects. The small window was also why it had been considered a possible dressing room. I thought it unlikely that even a junior player like Alice Woodward would have accepted being shut in an actual cupboard with no light. No one had thought to include a lamp, though, or maybe it was considered too much of a risk to have flames backstage. I had noticed that only the foyer and box office appeared to have been set up with electric light.

It was already dark outside, but the little illumination given off by the street lamps, and by which I had been reading, was enough to for me to recognise the lazy scrawl on the envelope. It was Fitzroy's hand. So much for not telling him which theatre I was at. It was even addressed to Alice Woodward. I doubted Morley had told him that. Most likely he had gone and flirted with the wardrobe girls. Or bribed one of the boys working there with a packet of cigarettes. Or taken poor Dotty out to dinner. It really was appalling how he managed to insinuate himself anywhere. It would also undoubtedly infuriate our new commanding officer, who wouldn't like to see his vessel pointed out quite as leaky as it appeared to be. Still, Fitzroy had always been a man more concerned with the final omelette than the breaking of a few eggs. I wondered if he had yet realised this approach wasn't going to wash with Morley.

Using a nail file I carefully slit open the envelope. There is always the faint chance that a missive may be fraudulent, and even contain a poisoned pin. Fitzroy had had one of these – although it turned out to be from a disgruntled ex-lover rather than an enemy of the state.

Inside was one sheet of paper, again written in Fitzroy's distinctive scrawl. The words were all bunched up in the middle of the paper. There were barely any gaps between the lines. No doubt an expert in such things could tell much of his character from the distinctiveness of his lettering. I mainly knew that there was no way I could read such a missive in this poor light. Upon brief consideration I decided to take it to the room laughably called a kitchen. The walls of this room had been painted white, and there was a single gas lamp. I would hardly call it well illuminated, but it was much better than here. Also, it had the added advantage of being a place where no one could sneak up on me.

I had only stepped out into the corridor when I almost tripped over Cutler again. 'I got what you wanted, Miss Woodward,' he said, looking up and down the corridor to see if we were being overheard. It was more than a touch melodramatic. I took the proffered envelope, sealed my note within, and leant against the wall to address it. Then I passed it back to Cutler. 'Please post this for me, will you, Ivor.'

'Miss,' said Cutler, lowering his voice to what I presume he thought was a conspiratorial whisper, 'it ain't normal for a stagehand to run errands for a junior member of the cast.' Even in the low light of the corridor I would see beads of sweat on his forehead. He wasn't shaking, but lines of tension were clear throughout his body. I wondered if dropping out of a tree onto him during our initial meeting had given him a fear of me, or if the whole undercover business was proving too much. However, I felt that he should have been made of slightly sterner stuff. Keeping a look out while working, well-paid, as a stagehand, and with presumably all the conditions we had agreed on his becoming an asset met, he had no reason to be so on edge. As we both knew, he was getting a far easier life than the poor souls fighting overseas.

I raised an eyebrow. 'And I thought you had been told to look after me?'

'Yes, miss, but I'm not meant to blow my cover either!'

'I hardly think one envelope will do that,' I said, relenting slightly. 'I do take your point, Ivor. It is not my intention to call on your services frequently, possibly ever again. You clearly have a new task master. I wish you all good luck with them.'

'The way things are going round here, I'm going to bleedin' need it. Begging your pardon, miss.'

He turned and left, disappearing into the gloom of the backstage corridors with ease. Really, the place was a labyrinth. I was going to have to spend some time scouting it out, or risk stumbling over others or being constantly surprised by them. The problem was that it was always badly lit. There was little natural light, and the electric light that had been introduced was sparse to say the least. Apart from the front of house there was the occasional fitting in a workshop area, but little more than that. Clearly the owners had not wanted to spend money modernising the theatre at this time.

This reminded me, if I was to wear stage make-up I would have to prevail on Ivor again to find me both the make-up and the lighting. I didn't know but suspected that most actors had their own. If Henri had been slightly less lecherous, I might have asked his advice. I had no intention of being shut in a confined space, such as my tiny dressing room, with him. Asking him for help procuring make-up was perilously akin to asking for a make-up lesson. I felt certain Henri would feel one should lead to the other. And yet, for all his commenting on perhaps making advances towards me, he never actually did anything. I shrugged mentally. I should forget the oddness and merely be grateful.

I tucked the letter into my pocket. Before I could decide upon my next action the silence was shattered by a piercing scream.

# Chapter Twelve

## Rosa and Gus

I ran as fast as I could towards the sound – and straight into a pillar. I rocked back on my heels, shaken and slightly stunned. The area was not so much a maze as a death trap. Whoever it was screamed again, but this time I felt it was more for effect. The first time, I had had no doubt, the vocalist was terrified. I proceeded with more caution.

It took me a several minutes of feeling my way, until I stumbled into a stage wing and the tender sight of Reggie on one knee holding the hand of a semi-prostrate Rosa. I stopped and leant on the wall, watching. They didn't appear to have noticed me.

'I am certain, my darling, that no one would do such a thing on purpose,' Reggie was saying. 'I'll speak to Dickens. He must be more careful when the stage door is opened.'

'Him! I wouldn't be surprised if he did it himself.'

'Good heavens, Rosa. Dickens has been one of the foundation stones of this theatre since I don't know when. He's the last person to want to . . .'

Rosa sat up straighter. Gracefully, and fluidly, but with a feminine liquidity I could never hope to emulate. She clung to Reggie's shoulder, dripping damsel in distress all over him as if she were a new range of cologne. Reggie's eyes opened very wide. The house lights were on in the auditorium, shedding light onto the stage. I and the rest of backstage remained in darkness. Naturally, the lighting seemed to flatter Rosa. She was very beautiful in a helpless kind of way.

However, the helpless sprite spoke with an unexpected malevolence. 'They all hate me, Reg. I'm younger, more beautiful. I'm going places and the rest of them are finishing up. They are one stage away from a retirement boarding house. Their jealousy consumes them. You mustn't listen to a word they say about me, Reg. Promise me you won't. Only you understand me. If it wasn't for you I'd be so alone.'

'Oh, my darling!'

I swallowed my bile. Surely the poor chump couldn't be falling for this? But then with his looks I doubted if he'd ever been the flavour de jour. From the angle I was standing at, his chin looked as weak as ever, but his Adam's apple threw a most unflattering shadow. Why was it that the majority of gentlemen I came across were so ill made?

'Oh, Reggie. You, only you.'

They were still cooing at each other in a sickening manner. I stepped back, and my foot rocked on a loop of rope. I didn't stumble, and made only the slightest sound. However, Rosa jumped to her feet, knocking Reggie backwards, so he floundered for his balance like a bad comic turn. 'I say, Rosa! Watch out!' he squeaked.

'There's someone there! I can hear them. Come out! I said come out, you damn trickster!'

The woman must have ears like a bat. Reggie was now on his feet and peering into the darkness. 'I say, are you sure? I can't see a bally thing.'

If I had already fulfilled my intention of getting to grips with the backstage layout I might have tried sneaking away. But I hadn't, and my encounter with the pillar had left me dizzy. It would be worse to be caught. I stepped forward. 'I heard you scream,' I said. 'I came to help.'

'Oh, really,' said Rosa, coming up to me and standing astride. She put her hands on her hips. 'Like you wouldn't do anything to get my part!'

'I don't want it,' I said with real honestly. 'I'm not prepared to do a big role. I'm here to watch, listen, and learn. I've heard nothing but praise about your performances.'

Any hopes that flattery would work on Rosa faded as she took another step forward and wagged an index finger in my face. I had to brace myself to stay where I was. All my instincts urged me to evade and counter. Ridiculous. She was a tiny slip of a thing.

'A likely bleedin' story. There might have been others who've been seen off, but not me!' She was close enough now that her spit reached my face. I decided that timid little Alice Woodward would step away from that.

'Not here one buggering day,' she said, her accent getting coarser by the minute, 'and you're up to your tricks. I know your type. Upper-class hussies who think that being born with a silver spoon up their arse makes them God's gift to the stage. You might think you've got Uncle Henri in your sights. Well, I could tell you a thing or two about him'

Reggie tried to intercede. 'I say, Rosa. This isn't the thing. You're terrifying the poor girl.' He turned to me. 'Miss Rosa is a little overwrought. She had a nasty surprise. A cat got into the theatre and surprised her. She hates cats.'

'Filthy, dirty creatures,' spat Rosa. 'I bet it was you that brought the wretched thing in.'

I shook my head. 'No, I haven't seen a cat. One of the stage hands told me about Gus, but he died, didn't he!'

'Oh, for—' (here she swore in words I will not write,) 'once and for all, I did not kill that bleedin' cat! I didn't like it, but it had the sense to stay clear of me. Unlike you, missy, creeping around and spying on me and Reginald.'

'I've explained—' I began. My words ended abruptly as she slapped me.

She was fast. I dodged back, but the nails on her right hand caught the side of my face.

'Ow!' I cried, pressing my hand to my face, and resisting the urge to tip her off the stage onto her bony little bottom.

At this point Reggie grabbed Rosa around the waist with both arms, and pulled her back. 'She's having a very trying day,' he said. 'Please forgive her. I'll send Henri to make you tea in the kitchen!'

I didn't bother to respond. I went to the kitchen anyway to read my letter. I reached it, after three wrong turns, in a violently angry mood. I was cross with myself for getting into the argument. I was furious with Rosa. My cheek stung, and I had no idea where to get some iodine. My forehead hurt from the accidental contact with the wall. I had been here for what was beginning to feel like forever and I had barely seen Pierre/Dieter. I had barely begun to even scratch the surface of profiling and assessing him. Worse still, I had no idea how to get into close enough contact with him to do so. The troupe was run in such a ramshackle manner I doubted anything would make it to the stage. Besides, I didn't want to be on the ruddy stage. The whole stupid mission was doubtless already blown by Mary spotting me on day one. Morley, supposedly my handler, was a first-class bungler when it came to supporting an agent in the field. He might do all right with front-line soldiers, but the concept of increasing the morale of, rather than emotionally disturbing, his agents appeared to completely elude him. And I did feel guilty about not being at Bertram's side. But what would be the point? I knew he'd rather that I made myself useful. Neither of us would see the point of my moping at his bedside like a wet dishrag. Besides, for all I knew he'd gone back into a coma. The thought knocked the wind out of me, and I leant more heavily on the cupboard.

Morley had utterly confused me. And underneath it all, I was aware of a strong pull to run to Fitzroy tonight and lay all my problems at his feet. I had no doubt he'd made quick work of it all. He'd undoubtedly cook me a fine meal as well. He wouldn't say a word about my turning to him. He'd like it. Clearly, this meant I was unfit to be an agent on my own. Incapable, and only able to do anything when I had a man to support me.

On this dire note, I covered my face with my hands and cried like a newborn. This was close to being the final straw. It was so utterly unlike me to weep, and in a public place, *and* on a mission. I knew something was badly wrong. I just wished I knew what it was. I sank down into a little ball on the floor, and buried my head under my arms.

I didn't stop crying until my head was lifted and a mug of tea thrust into my hand. '*Ma chère*, you need to drink this,' said Henri. 'Rosa is a spiteful little daughter of a dog! Do not take her nastiness to heart. If she thinks you are weak she will only torment you more. I have seen her kind before. She delights in stepping on the heads of others as she rises. Now, drink. It is sweet. It will help. We will not tell Yves of this contretemps, non?'

I sipped my tea and regarded him from reddened eyes as he crouched in front of me. I sniffed. 'Why do you all let her get away with being so unpleasant?' I said. Admittedly this sounded childish even to my own ears, but at least it was in line with how I thought Alice Woodward would act.

'She is beautiful,' said Henri, shrugging. 'She has talent.'

'She is horrible,' I said putting more feeling into that word than I ever remembered using before in my life.

'*Mais*, she will make the company a lot of money.' He took me by the elbows, and helped me stand. 'I will tell you a secret that not many know. Reggie, Yves, and I all have shares in the show. We stand to make money if this is a good run.'

'Rosa doesn't?'

'I think she may have an agreement with Reggie. I don't know. He is certainly all, how does one say it? All puppy dog over her. He is a decent chap, but Rosa twists him around her little finger. She says jump. He says, how high? It is sad when a man comes to that. Eventually the woman will no longer respect him.'

'But she started out as only the maid, didn't she?'

Henri nodded. 'I do not ask how she got the part. She is very beautiful, and not, I believe, overly troubled by morals.'

'But . . .' I said thinking of Janice and her accident.

'I need to apologise to you, *ma chère*. I am sadly very poor, and there will not be many more parts for one as old as I, even with the war. I might return as an aged gentleman, but for the present I enter the doldrums of the middle age, without having made my name. I need *La Rosa* to make the money. I am sympathetic, but if I must choose . . . I do not want to die alone in some rat-infested boarding house for aging theatricals. *Tiens!* I would rather be run down myself by an auto-bus.'

'You're saying I cannot complain about Rosa to anyone? I must put up with how she treats me?'

'I am saying, *ma pauvre*, that should it come to it, although I like you very much more than that harpy, I will back Rosa over you. *C'est le theatre! Tant pis!*'

'I see.'

'You are young, and I think perhaps not tough enough for the theatrical world. *Eh, bien*, you are too nice.'

So saying he kissed me briefly on the cheek, with what seemed more like genuine regret than salaciousness, and left me alone with my tea. As a child in the vicarage I had always imagined that actors, or 'players' as my mother referred to them with scorn, had rather a jolly time. After all, what did they do but play at make-believe like any schoolchild, and be paid for it? They didn't even write their own words. They swanned across the stage and repeated lines someone else had written and, hey presto, became stars. It was nothing like the acting Fitzroy and I had to do when we went undercover. Our lives, and others', often depended on our performance. Here, when the Joueurs d'Or had, as it seemed to me, a rather easy time of it, they filled up their lives with nothing but spite.

Give me a dozen enemy agents to deal with any day, I thought, rather than a pack of actors!

# Chapter Thirteen

## Invitation to an assignation

When I finally got to read Fitzroy's letter, it read,

*Dearest Sis,*

*Sorry to disturb you when you're making it big on the London stage – by the way, Mamma and Pa say save them tickets for opening night. Anyway, seems old Uncle Horace is on the mend. Pa wants you to go and see him in the hospital, but Mamma wants to ensure you're escorted. Something to do with all these soldiers being around. Pa thinks your pretty face will cheer up H no end. Mamma thinks you need someone with you in case H gets a bit too handy. Personally, I don't think he's up to any kind of that at the mo.*

*Anyway, I've been sent down (again), so I can partially raise my stock again with the mater and pater if I take you in, and defend your virtue from H. Meet me at our favourite café for luncheon tomorrow and we can thrash out the details. They do let you stop to eat, don't they?*

*Cheerio-ho*
*Your ever loving brother Billy*

I thought of reasons for such a meeting. Firstly, Fitzroy might merely be disobeying orders again. The letter gave me a sort of plausible deniability. I could always say I thought it was a genuine assignation. I also had a bad feeling Morley might pull me in. Despite his assurances he wasn't biased against my sex, he seemed to have rather an issue about my moral welfare. (All I could think on this was if he was going to take that attitude with all his field agents, he was going to be headed for a nervous breakdown within weeks. The most pleasant of the agents I had met could perhaps be generously described as politely amoral. If Morley had any ridiculous ideas of saving their immortal souls than he was flogging a dead horse.) The other possibility that occurred to me was that Bertram really had become worse, and was possibly dying. In that case I knew Fitzroy would move heaven and earth to get me to his side. Regardless of the repercussions to his own position.

Accordingly, imagining the worst, I slept very badly that night in my little bedroom. I was woken twice by commotions on the upper floor. However, as I knew Braun did not stay here – I had yet to discover where he had his luncheon, let alone where he lodged – I felt no need to interfere. Alice Woodward wasn't the kind of a girl to involve herself in the business of others. Especially if that business sounded rowdy. Short of them setting the house on fire, I had no intention of finding out what was going on. Instead I stuck my head under my pillow and tried, fruitlessly, to sleep.

The morning brought a running through of our lines on stage, and the realization that the maid's part was indeed little more than a creation to move props around the stage. On one occasion I was to be kissed by the dastardly Argent Foil, who it turned out was also hiding in plain sight as the butler, or was he now the hero? – really, the play made little sense. Braun was playing this part, and I did not feel at all comfortable with the idea of rehearsing that scene. Fortunately, the morning passed in the cast attempting and failing to get the first scene into good order. I wasn't due to be kissed until Act Five, and I began to entertain hopes that not only might I be gone before we reached production, but even before we reached that stage of rehearsal.

I left exactly on time for my luncheon meeting. No one appeared to care where I would be lunching. I didn't offer an explanation for my quick departure. I fancied Braun had given me more than one curious look over the morning, but that could be no more than someone summing up the new player in the pack. At least, that is what I told myself. I had given him no reason to pay extra attention to me.

I waved hello and goodbye to Dickens, who I already knew loved a bit of a chat, and stepped outside. The air again had a nip in it. Inside the theatre is was all too easy to forget that outside the theatre, life and time moved on. I had never before worked somewhere for so many hours that relied on man-made light. The stage area, the wings, and the auditorium had no windows. This made perfect sense, but among the brewing emotions of the cast, and their constant sniping and upstaging each other, left me feeling marooned on another planet with unfriendly inhabitants. At its worst I felt I was somehow under a sea, drowning in their animosity. This was fanciful, even for me. Fitzroy would have told me to pull myself together, and not eat cheese before bed.

I couldn't seem to get my fingers into my gloves. The heat inside the theatre must have made them swell. Either that or I was so tired I was fumbling. Each day I felt more and more drained. I stepped back to one side of the door to allow a passageway for anyone else wishing to leave. Then I dropped my glove. A gust of wind blew it slightly along the ground, towards the tiny passageway that went around the back of the theatre. I had yet to explore this path. It was exceedingly narrow and dark. It was, I imagined, a place where men were liable to relieve themselves after a night in the bar. Accordingly I had no interest in it, but I had even less desire to see my glove disappear down there. I scurried after it with no thought that I was entering a dark vennel on my own. Even with the noonday sun having passed not long overhead, the area was in deep shadow from the surrounding buildings. But, I told myself, Alice Woodward would not easily find the money for a new pair of gloves. I had no wish to go bare-handed in the coming weeks. It also, for reasons I could not fathom, seemed extremely important I retrieved my glove. In fact I felt almost tearful at the thought of losing it. What on earth was the matter with me? It was a glove, not a puppy!

Fortunately for my sudden over-sensibility to millinery, the glove had caught against a long forgotten rubbish bin. The container was overflowing, and extremely smelly. No doubt it would be a splendid hang-out for the local rats. I therefore took a little care inspecting the surroundings, and tapping my feet to frighten any long-tailed furry creatures away. Some of the soldiers I had tended to had suffered from ailments caused by rats in the trenches. I still shivered even thinking about that.

I can only think that it was this distracting thought that caused me to miss that someone else had left the building and had been met by another.

'Darling,' Rosa's voice broke over me in a harsh whisper, 'what have I said about being discreet. The newspaper reporters! They're watching me like a hawk. I told you I'm being considered for the movies. There's a Californian director who has booked out four boxes for his party on the opening night. If the press fill their nasty little gossip columns with hideous stories about me then it will all be over. Our dreams of you joining me in the New World vanished. Besides, your wife may read them.'

I drew back into the shadows, hoping that I would neither be noticed nor step on a rat. They must be standing not far from the stage door, I thought. The path to it was narrow enough that they were unlikely to be seen from the main street. Hopefully, it wouldn't occur to them that anyone would be in this rat-infested area during daytime.

'My wife is not a problem. If I give her enough money she will go away. In Hollywood, people will understand our relationship. Besides, when one has as much money as I, no one dare criticise.' The man speaking had a very English voice: light, clearly from the upper classes, and he spoke with the arrogance and assurance of a rich man.

'Maybe not you, my love, but I will be cast as the evil husband stealer.'

'At worst you will be a siren, my dear. A temptress. A goddess.'

'You won't give her too much money, will you, honey-boo. We

need a little something to live on until I am famous,' said Rosa in a voice of genuine concern.

'No more than pocket change,' reassured the man.

Was this the person Rosa had gaily announced to us one luncheon break she was going off to meet? It certainly wasn't Reggie, who she had been cooing over earlier. But above all, did it have anything to do with Braun?

I edged forward far enough to get a peek at the gentleman in question. Although it was the middle of the day, he was wearing tails and a top hat, and carrying a cane. He had on one of those short capes some men wear of an evening. It occurred to me that he might have been out all night. The most outstanding thing about him was his long, curly, bright red beard. Between it, his hat, and Rosa's face, which he now appeared somewhat entangled with, I couldn't get a clear look at his visage. From the way he carried himself, I guessed he was more than a youth but had yet to enter middle age. Hopefully the beard would be enough to identify him.

Behind me something clattered. I darted back into the deepest shadows, no longer caring if I encountered local wildlife. Even a rat would be preferable to a hissing Rosa.

The person in question squeaked some words in a high pitch. I couldn't make them out clearly, but I presume they were along the lines of 'What was that?' The man murmured something low and soothing. Rosa's voice became sharp with emotion.

'There's someone there, I tell you. We have a new girl in the cast. Not an ounce of talent. No doubt the press are paying her for a scoop. I've already caught her spying on me once. Go on! Look! Root her out. This is harassment!'

She wittered on like this, making it clear that there would be no kissing until the matter was dealt with. I squinted down into the dark. I didn't know for certain that there was another exit to this passageway. It seemed more of a rubbish-dumping area behind this section of the theatre. I could make out various blocks of deeper darkness, suggesting all kinds of obstacles lay in my way. It might be better for me to own up. I couldn't say I spent all this time looking for my glove . . . I needed a reason, a story. For once my brain refused to come up with an idea. Usually when the adrenaline starts going on a mission I am very creative, but I could come out with nothing. Then . . .

I barely managed to control myself as a furry length swept past my ankles.

I heard the man laugh. 'It's only a cat.'

'I hate cats!' said Rosa. There was the sound of a crash and a startled meow. Then I heard the voices of both Rosa and her beau moving away from me. I waited as long as I could bear before emerging into the alleyway.

No one else was about. I marched quickly down between the buildings and came out onto the open road. It wasn't far to the park, but I felt I had had enough trials for the day, and hailed a cab.

I must surely have chosen the most badly sprung cab in the whole of London for when I arrived at The Reluctant Bride Café, I was feeling extremely nauseous. I asked the driver to stop a short walk away on the other side of the park. I tipped the man, but not as much as I might have done if my journey had been more comfortable.

I took some bracing gulps of fresh air, and congratulated myself on having had merely coffee and toast for breakfast. Doubtless if I had had a *Griffin special* it would have been all over the pavement by now.

Head high, and thinking how I was looking forward to a decent cup of tea – and hoping that today someone in the café might know how to make one – I walked briskly through the park, breathing deeply. I had just about regained my equilibrium, when I rounded the corner to the café's location and saw Colonel Morley standing there, fiddling with his swagger stick. I had the awful sensation I was about to be sick on the spot.

# Chapter Fourteen

## Meeting Pa

'Ah, my dear!' Morley spotted me and came forward to take my arm. 'I thought you would likely come through the park, so I waited for you.' He looked down at me with affection. 'Your dear mother will be delighted you are looking so well. Positively blooming.'

Thoughts of my mother and Morley sitting down to tea and cakes chased themselves through my head. Then I realised he was playing the part of my father.

'Pa,' I said. 'You have taken me quite by surprise. I thought Billy was going to escort me to the hospital?'

Something almost like respect flickered in the Colonel's eye. 'Ah, yes, well, it did occur to me if you thought your old pa was coming to see you, you might plead pressure of work. If play-acting can be called work! A little subterfuge on my part, dear girl.' He opened the café door for me. 'But have no fear, I haven't come to spirit you back home. Your brother has quite pleaded your case.'

I waited until we were seated. Morley put his hat and stick down on the table next to him. Regrettably he had not steered the waitress towards one of the most discreet tables, and ours, although towards the back of the room, was in full view. I suspected it was also in full hearing of anyone else present.

He glanced at the menu, pulled a comical face at me behind the waitress' back for the sake of the two elderly ladies already seated at a nearby table, and ordered a scotch egg and lettuce for us both, with a large pot of tea. I didn't fancy this much, but I was relieved he'd passed over the speciality of the day, liver and onions. I asked the waitress for a glass of water. The two older ladies had the look of the lonely. They had clearly dressed up above and beyond what was necessary for a café. Their hair was neat, and they had brooches on their hats. Anywhere between forty and fifty-five, they had the look of well-off maiden aunts come down in the world, or governesses who had gone up in the world, as far as they could go. As I watched, they called for more hot water for the pot. This was clearly a special outing for them and they were going to get their pennies' worth from it. As I watched, one of them began to extol the use of lavender water to ward off moths among one's summer clothes.

'So, how are things in the theatre world?' asked my 'father', deflecting my attention back to him.

'Getting along,' I said. 'How is Uncle?'

'Oh, definitely perkier,' said Morley.

'Are we going to the hospital today?'

'Well, I'm only in town today and tomorrow, so I thought we'd go tomorrow at luncheon time. If your director will let you out.'

I pursed my lips. Was he trying to tell me that he'd arranged a visit for me to Bertram by way of an apology? Or was he preparing me for a husband in a worse state than I had anticipated? His manner was a studied mix of the mild and the amiable. It told me nothing. He clearly had no idea how to send subtle signs.

The sensible thing would have been to divert me at the door and take me to the hospital. I failed to see the point of this meeting. There was little we could say to each other. Those ladies were entrenched, and even as I pondered I heard the tinkle of the little bell above the door. Two women with two small children came in. Morley flinched.

'It is rather busy in here,' I said. 'What a pity we had already ordered. We could have moved on elsewhere.'

'Oh, no rush,' said Morley. 'It's nice to spend time with my grown-up daughter.'

I tried with my eyes to ask him what the devil he was playing at, but the waitress brought over our plates at this moment. He asked her if they had any sauce, and smiled broadly when she said yes. She returned in a moment with something red and viscous in a gravy boat. Whatever it was, Morley recognised it. He took up the small spoon sunk into the mess and ladled it with a free hand over his Scotch egg. The wretched things had been cut in two. They were cold, and a little grease oozed onto the plates from their patchily covered meat shells. I felt my stomach churn.

'Wonderful things, these,' said Morley. 'Created by Fortnum and Mason for the wealthy traveller in 1738, would you believe. Never had a sandwich to beat them.'

If someone had captured my likeness at that moment, I am uncertain whether it would have been surprise, confusion, utter bewilderment, or disgust that was the dominant expression on my face.

'Come on, dear girl. Eat up. Your mother worries you're not eating enough.'

I poked my fork at the boiled egg centre and cut up a bit of lettuce. Behind me a small child was demanding fried potatoes. I decided to take the goat by the horns. Metaphorically speaking.

'I'm not sure I see the point of this meeting, Pa. If we were going to see Uncle then . . .' I trailed off. 'It's not as if we have a lot to say to each other, under current circumstances.'

'I don't know about that, dear girl,' said my 'father' in voice that was considerably less fond. 'I think it's about time we talked about several things. You are aware I don't like you play-acting.'

I looked up, trying to give a quizzical look. All I could think was, he was referring to my activities for the Department. Was this going to be some dreadful kind of can-you-guess-what-I-really-mean game? Was this how he thought spies operated? Could he possibly have been reading novels? My blood chilled.

'What else might you suggest I do?' I threw at him. 'Be a good wife?'

He did redden faintly at that, so this had been intended as some kind of mild apology. 'I'm not suggesting you give up your independence all together. You're clearly an intelligent girl, and I do believe intelligence should be put to use. Maybe something in the training line. Keep you close to home and out of harm's way. You doubtless have excellent skills to pass on.'

'If I have excellent skills, why am I not to use them?' I was finding this double talk hard to follow. It seemed he was suggesting I start training younger spies. I couldn't see many of the Department's typical young male recruits being impressed by me. It would doubtless end with Fitzroy knocking out half a dozen of them. He took it as a personal insult should anyone question my abilities.

'That's always a hard decision,' said Morley. 'Do we risk losing our most capable agents in the field, or do we attempt to preserve their skills by passing them on to others. There is no good answer.'

I looked up alarmed. The older ladies had departed without my noticing. That was bad. I had been certain they would dither this way and that. In the reflection of the counter's glass-fronted shelves, I could see the other two women much occupied with their two charges. There was no one else around.

'You don't like having me in the field,' I said in a low voice.

'No, I don't. And not all my reasons are bound up in your unorthodox training and general waywardness. Goodness, Alice, you were trained by an excellent agent, but one who is rightly infamous for his independent activity. He's going to be hard enough to cope with without my having to oversee you. This is not a sudden decision. I have read your files and his in depth. I have also spoken to others who have worked with you. Overall it's not a pretty picture. You're effective enough, but you're renegades. I can't have that in my department.'

'So you're releasing him into the wild too.'

Morley shook his head. 'I can discipline your partner in ways I could never do to you. He'll have a very hard time of it, but we'll keep him.'

'So that job I'm on was just a blind to split us apart?'

'It does need doing,' said Morley. 'And I was prepared to rethink my attitude to you should that brilliance your trainer is always talking about have emerged. But you've been in quite a while, and I've had nothing but an overly emotional telephone call from you.'

'Because you hadn't checked to see if Braun had already made contact with Mary. That was the first thing whoever wrote up this mission should have assured! Whoever set this up has no idea how covert missions work!'

Of course it was only at that moment that I realised who had set this mission up. Morley himself. I had blown any chance of remaining a field agent. He'd clearly made up his mind before he even met me. I suspected what got under his collar was the gossip Fitzroy and I always inspired. He wanted his department clean and ship-shape. He still had no idea of the calibre of people he was working with. In my experience all agents had a sackful of secrets they lugged around with them. What we did was not an ordinary employment. We would, and most of us had, killed for our country. This usually took place in closer and more violent quarters than a soldier might see. There is a huge difference between shooting from a distance and sticking a knife in your victim's neck. I didn't doubt the trenches were hell on earth, and I had no wish to experience them. However, spies generally construct their own hells – even if it is no more than holding on to an enemy while you watch the light extinguish in his eyes.

'I have done things that put me outside the norm of women – of any class,' I said, a little unsteadily. 'I have sworn an oath to my country . . .'

'And I decide how your country needs you,' said Morley.

I had never stabbed someone in the eye with a fork. I had never had to resist the temptation to do so as much as I did now.

'I have turned my life upside down for the Department. I cannot go back,' I said. I allowed an undercurrent of the anger I was feeling into my voice.

'Of course you're bound to be a little upset,' said Morley. He paused to spoon some more sauce from the pot onto his scotch egg.

That he could think of such things at a time like this. I saw red. Regardless of who was present, I shot to my feet.

Immediately the room revolved around me. From a long way away I heard someone cry out in alarm, then I felt my legs go from beneath me. I went down, completely out of control. I tried to catch myself on the edge of the table. Instead I managed to bring the whole lot crashing down around me. I lay on the floor, and watched a saucer roll away on its side. So something survived, I thought, and then I was overtaken by darkness.

# Chapter Fifteen

## An awful lot of shouting and a startling surprise

I woke up on something comfortable. I looked up and saw a small, extremely sparkly chandelier. Definitely not a hospital fixture. I had a vague memory of having seen it before and thinking it a bit over-elaborate for its surroundings. Was I back at the theatre? I tried to remember what I had been doing. Gingerly I felt the back of my head. There was a lump brewing. I must have been hit over the head. How very unprofessional. I tried to call to mind who had done it.

The door opened, and I looked up. My vision was slightly blurry.

'Oh, that's why it looked so glittery,' I said.

The figure came into focus as he came closer. It was Griffin. He went over to the hearth and poked at the fire, before drawing up a chair to sit beside me. I was in Fitzroy's flat, lying on the sofa in his living room.

I struggled to sit up. Immediately Griffin stood and rearranged my pillows so I could do so. 'Where's Fitzroy?'

'He and the Colonel are currently yelling at each other in my lounge. In the service apartment attached to the main flat,' said Griffin. 'They didn't want to wake you.'

'So they're not actually fighting yet?'

Griffin gave me a slight smile. 'Not yet. I don't think Fitzroy feels up to a brawl. He's still in recovery.'

'Oh, that's going to annoy him,' I said. 'Poor thing. He always feels better when he's punched someone.'

'Perhaps not his senior officer?' said Griffin mildly. 'Although I do believe he's starting each shout with "with respect".'

'Normally, I'd agree,' I said, nodding my head and immediately feeling slightly sick. I sank back down on the cushions. 'But the Colonel is rather a pill.'

'How are you feeling now? You fainted in a café, do you remember? The Colonel bundled you into a taxi and brought you here.'

'Why?'

Griffin frowned. 'Why didn't he take you to a hospital? I have no idea. He certainly should have in my opinion. He brought you here because he is aware I used to be a general practitioner. Like a lot of people, he believes a degree in medicine gives you an instant insight into whatever is wrong with anyone. Ridiculous. It's a science. You need facilities to make a proper diagnosis.'

'Do you think there is something seriously wrong me with me?' I said, feeling a little worried.

Griffin put his head on one side and raised an eyebrow.

'You were a family doctor. You must have had to make analyses on the spot. Besides, you're not going to tell me Fitzroy hasn't got you trucked out with a medical kit here. He loathes hospitals.'

'Yes, I know. Says they're full of sick people.' Griffin sighed. 'Tell me how you have been feeling, if you will. Nothing about the mission. I'm not cleared for that. And you don't have to tell me anything. I'm not a doctor anymore.'

'If I don't?'

'I would have no option but to suggest – strongly – you were taken to a hospital either civilian or military.'

'That doesn't leave me an option.' I told him in detail how I had been feeling over the last few days. Finishing with, 'So do I need to see a mind doctor of some kind? Is Morley right, and I don't have the mental resilience to do this kind of work.'

'Is it a difficult mission?' asked Griffin.

'Not at all,' I said. 'No one is trying to kill anyone, and it's more observation than anything. It should be easy. I should have finished by now.'

'Hmm, I'm afraid I'm going to have to ask you some deeply personal questions.'

'Oh, please not about my relationship with Eric again. I've told you so many times we are partners in work, nothing more. Well, close friends. But not that kind of close friends.'

Griffin nodded. 'That said, may I ask if when you came back from the Continent with Fitzroy, if you had relations with your husband? And have your monthly courses been to schedule?'

'Those are not even questions Fitzroy would dare ask me!' I felt myself blush beetroot.

'I should think not,' said Griffin. 'I am asking them as your doctor.'

I took some deep breaths and reflected for a moment. 'Oh,' I said. Then, 'Oh! Oh! Oh!'

'In women as physically trained and healthy as yourself, there may be no physical signs other than the ones you are experiencing until much later on in the pregnancy.'

'But . . .'

'From what you have told me, I estimate you are between three and a half and four months pregnant. Your baby should be born in the spring or early summer.'

I sat up and counted the issues off on my fingers. 'Dizziness, nausea . . .'

'Excessive emotionalism,' added Griffin. 'Need I say, it is my advice you withdraw from this mission immediately.'

'I can't do that! Besides, now I know what is wrong with me I can be treated, can't I?'

'You can take ginger for nausea. Eat properly to ensure you keep your blood sugar up, and you need to rest.'

'Why? You said I'm fit.'

'Euphemia! Euphemia or Alice, which do you prefer I call you?'

I thought about saying 'Mrs Stapleford'. 'Euphemia,' I said. 'You're not part of the other stuff.'

Griffin nodded. 'Euphemia, regardless of your fitness, being with child has not been called "in a delicate situation" for no reason. You would need to limit your exercise, and more than anything limit your chances of harming the baby.'

'I'd never harm it!'

'A fall, a sudden shock, extreme exertion – all the kinds of things that may happen on your missions could compromise your pregnancy.'

'But this is an observation mission. Nothing like that is going to happen.'

Griffin sighed. 'I don't think you are taking me seriously.'

'If you're right, I was pregnant all the time I was at the military hospital – on my last mission. I climbed things, ran, fought with people, and none of this did me or the baby any harm – did it?'

'Not as far as I can tell. But it was very early days, Euphemia. We are talking about the welfare of your unborn child.'

I took a deep breath. 'I see. Morley wants to expel me from the Department as it is. I don't want to be a woman who doesn't get to use her brains or her gifts. I swore an oath . . .'

Griffin opened his mouth to speak. I held up my hand. 'I know. The welfare of the unborn baby must come first. Will you give me time to consider how I will reveal my situation to Fitzroy and Morley? It may be I can continue in some capacity with this mission. I assure you it is a passive mission. There is no danger to me – or as far as I know, anyone else. The worst I can say of the people I am watching is that they are self-centred and mildly lecherous. There is no violence.'

'Can I ask that you consider your situation most seriously? You are putting me in a very difficult position. I assume you don't want me to tell anyone that you are with child.'

'No, not yet,' I said. 'You've taken the Hippocratic Oath. I ask you to keep my secret – you said I was to treat you as my doctor. I trust you will treat me as your patient.'

Griffin stood up. 'You drive a hard bargain, Euphemia. I will give you a day's grace if you give me your word you will take what I have told you seriously.'

'Two days and I will,' I said.

He left me then. I sat there, confused and excited. Of course I was pleased I was to have a child with Bertram. I had always assumed I would have children. How it was to fit in with my career as a spy I had not known. However, it seemed the baby had made the decision for me. It would come when it wanted. I had to make the best of it.

I thought rapidly. I wanted to play a large part in my child's upbringing, which was at odds with those of my class, who generally gave the child away to the nursery then sent it to boarding school, barely seeing it in between. I would have to discuss the matter with Bertram, but my own opinion was that we could manage much better than that. Of course, Bertram would be resistant to my continuing as a spy. I would only need to remind him of my oath. At first it would be with him at home most of the time, a good nanny, an excellent governess, and both Bertram and I teaching the child. I would focus on improving my analysis work. Then I would start again with short missions – which frankly I thought there was all there was likely to be for me, during the war. That couldn't do any harm. I could do my bit, raise my child and be a reasonably attentive wife.

Fitzroy and I had agreed that the war would be long. We hoped to help shorten it in any way we could, but we both knew this was already more about attrition than advances. To my mind, then, some time would pass before the war was over and, as Fitzroy repeatedly assured me, we had won. I hoped we would, and would strive to make it so. By the time the war ended, my child would be of an age when I might responsibly leave them with Bertram and a nanny. Certainly they would no longer be a babe in arms. However you looked at it the child would have far more advantages than myself. I was educated solely by my father. My mother, though physically present, was always at length to me emotionally. I would ensure that I was home as often as my career allowed. But more importantly that I made every effort to be close to my child. I would leave him or her in no doubt that they were loved and wanted. It had taken me until I was an adult to understand the complex nature of my own mother – and that she did love me in her own way.

The only fly in this particular soup was Fitzroy, who had lost his own mother at a young age, and suffered greatly for it. But, really, as long as my husband, the father of my child, agreed, it was no business of his. Or, I could be more cunning, and ask him to be a godparent. I had no doubt if I managed to get him to agree he would prove to be an excellent one. The trick was to convince him, and once he was, why I could even involve him in the child-care plans!

Morley would also have to be handled carefully.

Hopefully, I would get to see Bertram tomorrow and we could figure out the matter together. As far as I was concerned, our opinions were the only two that mattered. Everyone else could be brought to see how good our reasoning was in time. Having Fitzroy on side would be an advantage. However, I knew my husband well. He would be furious if I revealed my condition to *that man* before I had told him all.

I patted my stomach thoughtfully. My life was going to change again, and in ways I had not foreseen so early in my lifetime. Perhaps Bertram and I would have scores of children? On a very brief consideration I decided that three or maybe four would be my limit.

The door opened again. Fitzroy poked his head around it, an expression of concern on his face. 'Are you all right, Alice?' he asked in what for him was a gentle, if slightly hoarse voice.

'I'm excellent,' I said with a smile. 'Couldn't possibly be better!'

# Chapter Sixteen

## Reading in Fitzroy

Fitzroy came in and sat down in the chair that Griffin had recently vacated. He leant in and looked rather too closely at my face. I could smell the oil he used on his moustache. It wasn't unpleasant, cloves and bay leaves, but I drew back slightly. He sat back at once. 'Well', to my untutored eye, you look extremely healthy. More bright-eyed and bushy-tailed than I've seen you in a long time. Acting must agree with you.'

'Oh, he told you?' I said.

'Morley? Yes. Griffin on the other hand has become remarkably close-mouthed and grumpy. What did you do to the man?'

'Not me. You. I don't think he likes you shouting in his living quarters.'

Fitzroy reached up and massaged his throat with his right hand. 'Might have over done that a bit. I mean, Morley turns up here out of the blue, with you in the arms of a cab driver. Apart from the sheer alarm I felt at seeing you passed out, there is also some resentment on my behalf of having my personal space, and safe house, invaded by cab drivers and colonels. He isn't meant to know this location. It's my private residence.'

I smiled slightly. 'It sounds like a play. *Cab Drivers and Colonels*,' I said. 'The fact that he knows where you live makes it more likely he does know his job, doesn't it? Besides, he clearly thought Griffin was the nearest help for me.'

'Yes, well, I suppose so. I didn't even know he knew about Griffin,' said Fitzroy looked slightly flustered. 'Looks like we're both slipping, Alice. You fainted on the job from exhaustion and I'm not the secretive mastermind I like to believe myself to be.'

'When you buy a property I believe there is a deed of ownership registered.'

'I registered it under my real name.'

'Oh, he knows that. He mentioned it the other day.'

Fitzroy's eyebrows shot up. 'Good God, and you said nothing?'

'Why should I? I admit it sounded vaguely familiar to me, but apart from that what difference does it make. You have to see that SIS needs to know who it is employing.'

'I suppose so,' said Fitzroy.

'You would if you were in charge.'

'That's different,' said Fitzroy. 'I know what I'm doing.'

'I think Morley may be slightly better than you credit at his job. Although if it's any solace, I can't stand the man.'

Fitzroy brightened considerably at that. 'Let's have some tea and cakes. Griffin has been baking the oddest-looking things, but they taste good.'

I struggled to sit up. 'I need to get back to the theatre.'

Fitzroy briefly placed a hand on my shoulder pushing me down. Griffin might think the spymaster had yet to recover his strength, but he seemed strong enough to me. I didn't even try struggling.

'Good girl,' said Fitzroy, in what I felt was an overly patronising tone. 'Your agent, Mr Lawrence, will be arranging with the theatre for you to have two days away. He has plans to send in an understudy as your understudy. Whole mission sounds a bit of a bust. I wouldn't worry about it. Mary Hill clocking you at the start should never have happened. That should have been sorted long before you came on board.'

He got up and went out briefly. I assumed he was cajoling Griffin into making us food. When he came back I had been thinking. 'Does this mean you're all read in on this mission?' I asked.

'Not exactly, I know that you're undercover as an actress to check out some German mathematician who wants to defect, and who is currently part of a Belgian troupe.'

'That's about it,' I said. 'I'm meant to watch him and profile him. See if he does anything suspicious or contacts anyone suspicious.'

'Hmm,' said Fitzroy, 'it's not much of a mission, is it? And, without being rude, it would have been much better done by a man.'

Because it was Fitzroy saying this I took a second to think before I opened my mouth. 'You mean a man could have got closer to him. Gone drinking or whatever?'

Fitzroy nodded. 'Exactly. The problem with going into semi-confined situations like rehearsals at a theatre, is that it's the bit when work is over that you actually want to know about. You've every excuse to be around the man during the day, but none to follow him about at night. If there is anything dodgy about him, he's hardly going to let the rest of the company see. Especially as I believe he's posing as being Belgian? Or is it French? What's his accent like?'

'It's slightly odd French. I think he's supposed to be French.'

Fitzroy frowned at me.

'It's not my fault I have a tin ear when it comes to accents!'

Fitzroy sighed and rolled his eyes. My inability with languages constantly irritated him. However, I found learning a new language as hard as did the next person, whereas he picked up languages as easily as he did enemies.

'Can you tell me how Bertram is?'

Fitzroy was in the process of taking a tray from Griffin, who had entered the room as I asked. The tray was piled high with sandwiches, steaming small (presumably savoury) pastries, biscuits, little cakes that did look odd, and a large pot of tea with the usual accessories. Fitzroy waited till he'd set this all down on a small table, and then started distributing its wares onto two plates. Griffin hovered in the doorway until Fitzroy looked at him. At the time his back was to me, so I didn't see the spy's expression, only the slight wince that crossed Griffin's face. As he closed the door, Jack bolted through at the last minute. Fitzroy handed him an entire sandwich.

'Good boy. Go and lie by the fire,' he said, and the animal obeyed. He turned and looked at me. 'You don't mind, do you?'

'You over-feeding Jack? That's nothing to do with me.'

'Him being in here?'

'Of course not, you know I like Jack very much. And besides, with my feet up on your sofa he can't get to my ankles.'

Fitzroy smirked before turning back to the tray. 'If I was a dog I'd lick your ankles,' he said. Then he passed me a plate. I was going to respond, but I suddenly realised how very hungry I was. I was just finishing the food when I looked up to see him sitting staring at me.

'What? I was hungry.'

'Clearly,' said Fitzroy, taking my plate and going to refill it.

'That was the funny thing about that last mission at the hospital,' I said. 'I kept eating, as well as getting grumpy. I had the sense I was turning into you. Couldn't sleep much either.'

Fitzroy handed me another filled plate, and set a cup of tea down beside me. 'Yes, well working alone brings its stresses.'

'I had Merry.'

'Who is, at best, an asset, not a trained agent.'

'So what happens with this mission?'

'Oh, you're going back in, and I'm coming with you.' He saw the look on my face. 'Now, don't get worked up. Even Griffin weighed in on this. The Department didn't give you the recovery time you needed, and it's taken its toll. You've also been set a mission that is hampered by your sex – and I don't think that was deliberate. I think Morley had some idea about women picking up more gossip than men. Idiot.'

'So what's the new plan?'

'Oh, much the same as the old. I reckon if I can get a night on the town with him, and you manage to talk to the others there, we should have the whole thing wrapped up by tomorrow night. No, make that the night after tomorrow or the following one. You're staying here tonight, and I'm taking you to see Bertram tomorrow. It'll take them that long to wangle me into the theatre. It'll also reassure me, at least, that you're up to going in again.'

'Oh, thank goodness. I didn't understand why Morley wouldn't let me see him today. Instead of inventing that ghastly luncheon.'

'He made you eat there? He told me that letter was a ruse to meet up to take you to your husband.' He paused. 'Cunning b—. What he said was the letter was a ruse to meet up to *arrange* to meet your husband. Yes, strictly speaking, he didn't lie.'

'But he was deceitful.'

'Hmmm. Should make me like him more, but it doesn't.'

'That's because you caught him out easily, and he put one over on you. It's plain rude,' I said indignantly.

Fitzroy filled his own plate. 'It's all very refreshing, exploring our mutual hatred of Morley, but if he is going to stay in post – and he probably will – then we will have to find a way of working with him. We'll have to pull out all the stops on our next mission, Alice. Do something ace. I'll start thinking about it.'

'How is Bertram?'

'Oh, as I said, awake, aware, recovering. No longer in a coma and reassured you're safe. I take it you don't want me to tell him about your little collapse?'

'No,' I said slowly. 'Not until he's fully recovered.' I was just starting to rethink whether or not I should tell Bertram about the pregnancy. It would be a shock, albeit a lovely one. He would undoubtedly start worrying about financing the estate again.

'Penny for them?'

I looked up blankly.

'Your thoughts? Penny for them. You seem somewhat distracted.'

'Oh, just thinking about what Morley must think of me.'

Fitzroy frowned slightly. 'If you say so. But I don't think there will be much of an issue. Griffin represented to him rather strongly how he couldn't expect us to be in any better state after what we've been through recently. He didn't go as far as to suggest we were overworked. He knows there is a war on, but he did make the point we'd both been badly overstretched, and had not had anywhere near enough recovery time. The old man seemed to accept that. Even in the front lines they rotate you off every couple of weeks. So as I said, after this parochial little nothing, we need an ace in the hole. Shall we kidnap the Kaiser?'

'I wish I could be sure you were joking,' I said smiling. 'But about this parochial little nothing. There is quite a lot going on in the theatre that simply isn't right.'

'Enemy spies?' said Fitzroy, hope sounding in his voice.

I shook my head. 'No, much more mundane than that. I think there is going to be a murder.'

# Chapter Seventeen

## The play's the thing

I caught Fitzroy mid-sip of tea, so he choked a bit. However, he managed to thump his own chest, signalling me to stay where I was. Eventually he managed to say, 'This isn't the old days, you know. I appreciate you had a habit of collecting murderers and they did fairly often coincide with threats to the realm. But a few actors getting wound up isn't in our purview.'

'I have a list.'

'You wrote it down,' said Fitzroy, frowning heavily.

'Don't do that,' I said, 'You'll look like a tortoise before you're forty.'

'I'll have you know I am a very long way off from forty,' said Fitzroy, as usual concentrating on what he found important.

'I meant I've been carrying a list in my head. I don't have anywhere safe to keep any documentation. I can't carry my reticule with me all the time. Especially when I'm on stage.'

'Hmmm. All right, then.' He passed me another two sandwiches in the manner of peace offerings.

I gave a little sigh. 'You do see the sandwich tongs on the tray that Griffin provided?'

'You don't usually have a problem with me passing you food.'

'Nowadays your fingers are liable to be covered in dog hair and dog slobber. And much as I love Jack . . .'

'Oh, very well,' said Fitzroy. 'I will remember my manners if you insist upon it. I thought you liked it when I treated you like an equal.'

I ignored this. 'First of all there was the death of Gus, the theatre cat. He'd been taken in as a stray and been around the theatre for eight or ten years, something like that. They've always had a problem with mice and rats, but for some reason he appears to have digested rat poison. The theory currently held by most is that someone mixed it in with his food.'

'Hmmm,' said Fitzroy. 'Anyone who'd poison a well-liked feline – I assume he was well liked?'

'By everyone but the leading lady, who is rather a pill.'

'Mystery solved,' said Fitzroy. 'Now all you have to decide is how to punish her.'

'I thought we weren't to get involved?'

'A cat's life, Euphemia! I've known far more good cats than I've known good people.'

Again I wasn't entirely sure how serious he was, so I pushed on. Sometimes trying to get Fitzroy to listen to something he didn't want to hear was not unakin to King Canute attempting to turn back the tide. I readjusted my mental crown and continued.

'Then the last director left because he thought the theatre was haunted.'

'Pah,' said Fitzroy. 'All theatres are haunted. It's part of their charm.'

'Some of the ropes and flying sets came crashing down on stage. It was lucky no one was killed.'

'We'll have to keep you away from that then.'

'I'm an actress. Acting on the stage.'

'Yes, well, as I said before we'll be out in a couple of days. Definitely inside the week.'

'The previous leading lady died under the hooves of a shire horse, having been knocked over by an omnibus.'

'Nasty,' said Fitzroy. 'Poor girl. Do people think she was pushed? Police investigation happen, that sort of thing?'

'No,' I said slowly. 'Apparently she was never very good with traffic.'

'I'm not hearing anything yet that's to do with us.'

'Janice's death led to Rosa being promoted from my part to the leading lady. Quite a leap.'

'The one that killed the cat? Well, then obviously if you can kill a defenceless creature, killing a rival is a piece of cake. But that doesn't mean she did it. Not having an affair with anyone important, is she?'

'I'll come to that,' I said. 'There's been a lot of cast changes. No one is very happy, and someone added dye to the leading man's make-up making his face go orange.'

Fitzroy barked with laughter. Jack raised his head from the hearth, and joined in with a couple of his odd whiffling barks.

'You'll be laughing on the other side of your face when someone puts itching powder in your moustache oil.'

'I don't use any,' said Fitzroy, stroking his right index finger along his upper lip. 'I'm naturally slick and bushy.'

'I can smell it,' I said. 'And Ivor Cutler has been picked up by someone and is working at the theatre looking into black marketeering. He was told to provide physical back-up for me too. The cheek!'

'This is the chap you fell out of a tree on?'

I nodded.

'Sounds like we have a lot of crossed wires to untangle, but I really can't see how any of this might be relevant to us or the Department. Except for the cat part. Gus needs to be avenged.'

'You're not going to kill her, are you?' I said slightly nervously.

Fitzroy stood up. 'Of course not. What do you take me for?' He piled the remains of our repast, such as they were, onto the tray. 'No, I shall have to think of a fate far worse than mere death for such a heinous crime,' he said, and carefully opening the door with his elbow carried the tray out.

I looked at Jack. 'Do you think he meant it?'

Jack whiffled at me and thumped his tail on the ground, but he stayed by the hearth.

'Much help you are!'

'Jack?' said Fitzroy returning. 'Oh, a sandwich and a warm

hearth and he's happy. Simple pleasures for my dog. Although I suppose I shall eventually have to find him a bitch.'

'Please,' I said. 'I don't want to know about your dog's amorous adventures any more than I want to hear about your own.'

'Ah, that reminds me, you said something about the proclivities of the leading lady? Is she very pretty?'

'An absolute beauty, if you like the blonde curls and wide blue eyes kind of a girl.'

'Hmm,' said Fitzroy wrinkling his nose, 'not usually my type. I'm more of a brunette man, myself. Besides, let's not forget she is a cat killer.'

'And she's in a relationship with the playwright, Reginald Pierce.'

'The Belgian Pierces?'

'Yes,' I said. 'How did you know?'

'I know the English side of the family. I read Debrett's nightly. Mine's all annotated with ticks on people I've met and crosses on people I've – well you get the idea.'

'Killed!' I said, horrified.

'Women I've known intimately,' said Fitzroy. 'For goodness' sake, I don't go around assassinating subjects of the Crown. It's our job to protect them. I know you're not feeling the thing right now, Euphemia, but get a grip, please!'

'Rosa also appears to be courting investors in the play. For all I know this may go only as far as dinners and a little light flirting. Still it seems a bit odd. I keep finding her professing her affections for different men.'

'And you're sure she's not a foreign spy? It's the kind of thing spies do.'

'Not all of us,' I said sharply. 'Anyway, so far I've discovered there are three different investors. All of whom may also be suitors. I can only imagine what would happen if they learnt of each other.'

'You're assuming they don't,' said Fitzroy. 'They might be quite comfortable with the current arrangement.'

'That's the kind of knowledge I rely on you knowing,' I said curtly. 'I wouldn't know.'

'I suppose we don't want the whole thing imploding before we get Braun out.'

'So the theatre *is* of interest to us?'

'Possibly,' said Fitzroy slumping down in one of the chairs by the fire. 'You win, Euphemia. I will pay attention to your motley band of would-be murderers. By the way who do you imagine is about to be murdered?'

'I have no idea. It's just a feeling I have.'

'Oh wonderful,' said Fitzroy. 'I am so going to enjoy our visit to the theatre. I can tell it will be fun and games from beginning to end. Lucky, lucky me.'

# Chapter Eighteen

## Bertram

To be fair, Fitzroy was most solicitous of my health for the remainder of the day. He provided me with light reading materials (Dickens and Austen). Griffin was summoned to fulfil my slightest culinary desires. Then after having talked briefly through all the cast and crew I had come to know, Fitzroy told me to forget about work. He, in his turn, either wrote at small desk or read by the fireside. At one point Griffin came in to take Jack for a walk. It was clear there still no love lost between them.

'If you want to go with him, Fitzroy, I wouldn't object,' I said. 'After all, Griffin is the doctor.'

'Was the doctor,' corrected Fitzroy. 'No, I have more than enough to do here. Off you go, Griffin, and enjoy yourself.'

Griffin made a grunting noise and Jack whiffled. Once the door had shut behind them, I said, 'That wasn't kind. Jack would have much preferred you to go.'

Fitzroy looked up, his eyes slightly hazy and distanced. 'I really do have a lot to do, and I also thought I might get a march on dinner before Griffin gets back. The man is tyrannical in his control over the kitchen. I rather fancy a beef wellington. Lots of red meat to build you up! And you know mine is a thing of beauty. I have a way with red meat. Griffin would cook it till it was brown all the way through.'

I shuddered.

'Precisely. Cheese, fruit, and port afterwards, do you?'

'That would be lovely. Thank you.'

'Nonsense, gets me a chance to get away from Griffin's wretched stews. He's always making them because they are so economical. Since when have I asked him to be economical! Goodness knows I've lived off the land, eating stewed rabbit and whatnot these last few months. Now I am home I intend to indulge my gastronomic desires to the hilt!

He poked and made up the fire. Then he left me to go to the kitchen. I found myself drifting off to sleep. I nestled down into the cushions. As I was losing consciousness I thought I heard vague snatches of opera. In my last few moments of wakefulness I realised Fitzroy was singing. I desperately wanted to stay awake and listen. More than anything to see if he could carry a tune. But Morpheus claimed me.

I was awoken by the delicious smell of roasting beef. Fitzroy had managed to keep Griffin out of the kitchen and supplied us with a marvellous dinner, of which I ate far too much. After a deep and restful sleep in Fitzroy's spare room, which I was beginning to think of as my home from home, I awoke in the early hours of the morning feeling awful. I managed to reach the bathroom before I was copiously sick. Morning sickness. I was undoubtedly pregnant.

When I told Griffin at breakfast before Fitzroy appeared, he said that perhaps as I wasn't as far along as he had first thought. We worked through the dates again, gaining a maximum and a minimum length of time. Oddly enough I wasn't in the least embarrassed, but far more interested in both the maths and Griffin's rough explanation of what the baby was like at various stages. It seemed likely it was bean-sized at present.

The conversation was curtailed by the arrival of my host, who, it turned out, had been running in the local park and was extremely hungry. To my surprise I managed to make a decent breakfast too. Griffin had slipped me a piece of ginger and I kept this with me in case of further feelings of sickness.

'Set off in half an hour, Alice?' said Fitzroy. 'Visiting hours technically start at eleven a.m., but we've got a bit of a pass, as long as we allow them time to clear the mid-morning biscuits, we're all right. Hospitals start at the crack of dawn. But then you'd know all about that . . . where is my head this morning?'

'In the park looking at the pretty nannies?' I suggested.

Fitzroy gave me a grin, and ran a finger along his moustache. 'The ladies do seem to like a good manly form, it's true, but I don't trifle with nannies.'

'Of course not,' I said. 'Did you take Jack?'

'No, he was looking so peaceful in his basket. Do you mind if I take a shower after I've eaten?'

'Good heavens, sir. You cannot sit down to breakfast with a lady in that attire,' said Griffin.

'Fitzroy was just saying that he couldn't bear to wake Jack to go with him,' I said, trying to divert the argument before it started.

'Ah, well,' said Griffin. 'That may have more to do with Jack's weight than his appearance. The creature is positively stretched at the seams.'

Fitzroy and Griffin continued to bicker, reminding me of an old married couple, and quite took my mind off worrying over the hospital visit. I admit this may have been their intention all along. I had gradually learnt that despite Griffin's over-fussy behaviour he was capable of being quite as devious as his employer.

We arrived at the hospital just after ten. A rather prim ward sister told us that the doctors would be doing their rounds shortly and she couldn't possibly admit us. Fitzroy immediately began his charming routine, and I admit this might have worked on any female who wasn't a professional nurse. I, on the other hand, as an ex-nurse, commented that my husband was in a single room, and we would be less of a disturbance visiting him than discussing the situation in the hall. Furthermore, as my husband's closest relative I had every right to speak with the doctor and did indeed intend to do so. Catching the man on his rounds would make his duties of the day that little bit lighter. I threw in a couple of technical terms, and relatively quickly had the sister regarding me with an almost respectful eye. Fitzroy faded apologetically into the background.

We took a seat in the corridor, and waited for a nurse to fetch us. 'I don't think you need me here at all,' said the spy. 'I thought, despite it being sanctioned, we'd have a bit of trouble, but you handled that sister easily. In fact I'd say you made more of an impression on her than I did. Which is remarkable. I was doing some of my best flirting.'

I smiled at him. 'Male patients try to flirt with nurses all the time. Anyone who has made it to sister is completely impervious to male charm while in uniform. A fellow competent female, as opposed to a watering pot, is always welcome.'

Fitzroy made a small, sad noise.

'Out of uniform I'm sure you'd have no difficulty charming her. At this moment she is all nurse . . .'

'But out of it she would be all woman?' finished Fitzroy, giving me a sly smile.

'And a woman who knows her way around anatomy.'

Fitzroy's lips twitched at that. 'You know, Alice, I think you're becoming rather a bad influence on me.'

I patted his knee as I might have done a naughty schoolboy. At that moment a nurse turned up looking for Mrs Stapleford. It was not quite how I would have liked to be found, touching another man's trousers while waiting to see my husband, but I believe I only blushed very faintly.

'I'll be here if you need me,' said Fitzroy. 'If Bertram wants to see me I'm at his disposal.'

I followed the nurse's brisk steps along the corridor and onto another wing. This wing had a series of personal rooms. She stopped by a door with a man standing outside. 'This is Mrs Stapleford,' she told him. The man nodded at me, and opened the door.

I recognised his type at once. He was one of the police-like officials we use for guard duties. Although privileged to have a security clearance, he was not a field agent, but rather someone who followed instructions and whose range of skills did not extend much beyond observation, detection, and elimination of threats. I smiled at him as I went through the door, and gave a slight nod. However, I now had a knot in the pit of my stomach. Why on earth should Bertram be considered in danger here? Fitzroy had let me think whatever had transpired in France was over, and all threat from it gone.

My husband was sitting up in bed wearing green paisley pyjamas. They were the kind with dark green, black, and white swirls that always made me giddy. They certainly hadn't come from home. Bertram saw me looking at them.

'Natty, aren't they? No idea who got them for me. Suspect it was that little girl they had running around after me. Hello, wife!'

He was pale, and the fine lines around his eyes were slightly deeper. His neck no longer puffed up over his collar. He'd lost weight, and while this was good, it also made me suddenly incredibly sad. Of all the things that might have happened to Bertram I dreaded to think of him alone and hungry. Which was silly, as there are far worse things that can happen to one in the field.

I went over to the bed, and sat down gingerly. One corner of his collar was folded over the wrong way, so I reached over and fixed it.

'Do I look so dreadful you can't speak?' said Bertram. 'And to think when I was shaved this morning I thought I was looking a whole lot better.'

'You look marvellous,' I said. I had to bite my bottom lip to stop it trembling. 'It is so good to see you. I'd been told you were safe, but I couldn't quite believe . . .'

'Do I get a kiss?'

I leant in and hugged him. He felt frail in my arms. I fancied I could feel his ribs, and only one arm of his returned my embrace. I drew back and looked at him.

'I did say kiss,' he said slightly plaintively. 'I was hoping you wouldn't notice the arm. They've got me doing all sorts of exercises to try and strengthen it back up. It's surprising what you can manage with one hand. Just as well I was always right-handed.'

'Your left side, your heart,' I managed to say.

'Yes, well. I'm sure Fizz-bang mentioned my ticker did a couple of turns when we were away. Not even sure if it didn't stop once. Certainly felt like it. But he did something or other and got me going again. Still can't stand the man, but he's certainly resourceful in the field. Mind you, does nag a bit. Kept saying how much you needed me, and how I had to get home for you. To be honest, my darling, there were times were I was ready to give up the ghost, but I couldn't stand him harping on at me so I kept going!'

'Fitzroy said you'd had a bad time. Not in those words. You know what he's like, but he said he wouldn't tell me anything. That it was down to you to decide what to say.'

'Those Frenchmen I was going to meet. They weren't. Actually Germans. All went a bit downhill after that. Then of course they wouldn't accept I wasn't Fitzroy. Spent quite a while trying to persuade me who I was. Nasty business.'

'You mean they tortured you!' I said, horrified.

'Well, I wouldn't say that. Besides, they thought I was that man. I mean, if I don't like him and he's on our side, imagine how they feel about him!'

'What did they do to you?'

Bertram waved it aside. 'Oh, not that much. Kept passing out. One good thing of having a dicky heart. They got rather annoyed about that.' He gave a slight chuckle. 'Spent ages talking to me in German too. Funny language. Blunt and a bit hissy. Absolutely convinced I could understand. Does he speak German?'

I nodded.

'I suppose I shouldn't speak badly of him. He did get me out.'

'He also got you in,' I said, my eyes pricking with tears. 'He promised me you wouldn't be in any danger.'

'Yes, well, we should both have known that posing as Spymaster Fitzroy would get people's backs up. The man breeds enemies like farmers breed rabbits.'

I refrained from saying that farmers don't breed rabbits, but made a mental note to check with our factor how things were progressing on the home farm. I had been letting Bertram do much of the running of the estate on his own. I realised this attempt to give him the full role of master of the house might have been mistaken. He was much happier in his libraries and doing his writing than he was outside among vegetables.

Almost as if he had picked up on my thoughts he said, 'By the way, Euphemia, the doc says I need to take it easy for a while. Gentle building back up, you know. They're being a bit on the Cassandra side.'

'They think you're dying?' A hand clasped tightly around my heart.

'No. No. Just over-doing the bit about me being an invalid. I've been told I was a bally invalid most of my life, and look at the scrapes we got up to! Besides, now I've been out in the field solo that man will have to give me my due.' Bertram must have seen the horror in my face. 'No, don't worry. I'm not clamouring to be a field agent. I've had quite enough of that. But they should up my security clearance. Then I'd be able to help you with the planning and analysis stuff.'

'I'll mention it to him,' I said.

'You'd like that, wouldn't you, sweetheart? Us working together like the old days? It's how we fell in love, isn't it?'

'Actually, it was trying to catch your father's murderer that did it. I was ready to marry you then.' I touched his hand lightly.

'I know. I was a damn fool. I was so worried about our difference in rank – you being a maid at the time. Could have knocked me down with a feather when I found out you were the granddaughter of an Earl. I mean, I'm the grandson of a banker! When did *he* find out?'

'Fitzroy? Oh, he always knew who I was.'

'You told him?'

I shook my head. 'Apparently he knew my father.'

'Well,' said Bertram. 'Well. Well. Well. I really don't like the fellow, you know, Euphemia. Are you sure you couldn't find someone else to work with later on? What about Merry? She could be trained up, couldn't she? Always been a game girl.'

'Fitzroy didn't think Merrit would let her.'

Bertram frowned. 'Yes, he is a bit of a stiff-rumped fellow. Think she rather hurried into that one. Not who I would have chosen for her.'

I smiled. 'I don't know. There might be some who would think us an odd match, but I think we're perfect.' I reached out to take his right hand and held it tight.

Bertram gave me a big soppy grin. 'Definitely soul mates,' he said. 'Are you going to speak to the doctor?'

I nodded. He hurried on, 'I don't want you to take them too literally. I've learnt, being here, they present the worst case scenario, so that when it all turns out better everyone can see how brilliant they are. Egos as big as a whale, most of them.'

There was a thin sheen of sweat forming on his forehead. 'Are you feeling well enough?' I asked. I put the back of my hand against his forehead. 'You feel rather cold.'

'Goodness, quite the professional touch,' said Bertram.

I opened my mouth to tell him about my last mission, but I realised he hadn't asked. He'd known where I was going, but I understood he must still think I was simply training as a nurse. By "later on", he'd meant after the war. He had no idea I remained active in the field. If you could call a little light investigation active.

'Yes,' I said, 'I do feel I am getting the hang of nursing.'

'Jolly good,' said Bertram. 'Helping the injured seems like an excellent use of your time. It's a nice feminine skill too.'

I did start at this, but Bertram didn't appear to notice. 'I can imagine you in your uniform, a sort of modern Florence Nightingale – only far more beautiful. Do they let you have lanterns on night duty where you are? I can just see you emerging from the darkness, surrounded in a halo of light, to mop some fortunate chap's brow.' He lowered his voice. 'I must say the nurses they have here are built like bruisers. No, you'll be a credit to the profession, I know it.'

I should, at this point, have told him that I was no longer nursing, that I had no intention of sitting out the war mopping brows, and on that point, I should have told him that nurses weren't so much mopping brows as helping patch up butchered bodies, and sitting with men crying as they died. However, he looked so frail – frail, and not as familiar.

When you come off a mission there is always a sense of disconnection. You've been operating in one world and now you're back in another. I've always thought half of the ridiculous things Fitzroy gets up to, including the women, is because he doesn't know how be to a normal person. I, on the other hand, have always had a role to return to. As Bertram's wife.

Just then, though, I knew it must be the pregnancy putting me off colour, but it didn't feel as if we were connecting. I was concerned for him, of course. I loathed what had happened to him, but he seemed to have drifted away from me, from us. I had a fanciful image of us on a lake, rowing keenly towards each other in our little boats, but no matter how hard we tried the tide, which had no business being in a lake, kept pulling us apart.

'If that's what you want to do, of course,' said Bertram abruptly. 'I mean, I know it's all very well for me to lay out how I want things to be, but you'll always steer your own course. Quite extraordinary in a woman, but one of the reasons I love you. Even if it is bloody inconvenient at times.'

This finally made me laugh. I saw Bertram's face relax. 'Ah, that's better. I thought the doctors might have put you off me!'

'Good gracious,' I said. 'How on earth could they do that? We're married. Bound together by a sacred vow. I realise some doctors think themselves akin to gods, but they're not, no matter how hard they starch their white coats.'

'Yes, well, you know things won't be the same after I get home. Not how we might have wanted them, anyway.'

'Oh, you needn't worry,' I said, seeing a neat trick ahead of me.

'I know they are posting some nurses overseas.' Bertram gasped at this, but I carried on. 'But I've asked to move back into analysis and counter-intelligence here. I'm staying put on British soil. I thought you'd prefer that, and honestly, there are other girls that are much better at nursing that I. I'm good enough to give Merry a hand in the planning and administration if we do set up a convalescent home at White Orchards.'

Bertram panted a bit. I handed him a glass of water from beside his bed. 'I haven't upset you, have I?'

'And to think I thought being a nurse would keep you safe. Deploying women to a battlefront – it's unheard of!'

'No, they will keep the front line medical staff male, but there is such a deluge of casualties expected that they are setting up overseas hospitals. In reach of transportation, but well behind the lines.'

'Still be bloody dangerous,' said Bertram. 'God, how could I be so naive as to think it would be over by Christmas?'

'We were all hoping it would be,' I said. 'Or even that the Kaiser would make it up with the King. They're family, for heaven's sake, but it is not to be. It looks like it will be a war of attrition, like . . .' I broke off.

'Like that man said,' grumbled my husband. 'Tell me he's wrong sometimes, Euphemia. I'd hate to think of that arrogant . . . arrogant . . . dash it, I can't think of a word I can use in your company that sums him up well enough.'

'He is arrogant,' I said. 'It's one of the ways he copes with stress, but he does get things wrong. Everyone does. Fitzroy's just rather good at covering his tracks.'

'He doesn't endanger you, does he, with all his nonsense and peacock ways?'

'Actually, I might not be working with him any more. We have a new commanding officer who thinks I'm holding him back.'

'What!' roared Bertram, leaning forward and reddening, only to collapse back quickly on the pillows. 'You're ten times the agent he is!'

'I think probably only six times,' I said with a straight face. 'But he actually meant Fitzroy won't take risks when I'm around.'

'I expect he doesn't fancy explaining things to me if you get injured again. I gave him a right ticking off last time you were hurt.'

I blinked and tried to think back. I couldn't recall what I had done to myself or when this argument might have been. But then there were so many injuries I'd never told my husband about.

'But the good news is I'll be in Britain. I expect even at home a lot,' I said, thinking of the baby growing inside of me. 'It'll be lovely to spend time with you at White Orchards. We've haven't had a chance to settle in yet, have we?'

'Thursday night crumpets!' said Bertram. 'Kippers for breakfast on Sundays. Early evening walks.' He reached out and grasped my hand. 'We'll do all right, won't we, Euphemia? I mean, despite . . . ? I do so want to share my life with you.'

'And you will,' I said smiling. 'I think I should go. You're beginning to look tired. I will try and come back before you're sent home. But if I don't, I'll be back at White Orchards within a week, two at most, and I think I'll be spending quite a few more months based there. That man might have to visit. I'll put him in an attic room, so you won't have to see him unless you want to.'

'I say, Euphemia. That's a bit much, isn't it. Still a guest and all that. Might be bats up there!'

'Actually I had a bit of a wander around while he was training you. We can make a set of rather nice rooms up there. I've got McArthur looking into getting some plans drawn up. We'll need somewhere for a nursery,' I said. I held my breath to see if he caught my implication. His reaction was not what I expected.

'Er, yes, I suppose Richenda and her brood will visit us eventually.' He looked crestfallen. 'Hans has dropped me a line or two while I've been in. Found out I was ill. Probably that man told him. Anyway, he says Richenda has been talking about us a lot. He thinks she's improving. Not sure if he can visit. Has some kind of curfew in place. Didn't quite follow that bit. Anyway you must do what you think best, my dear. I'll leave it in your hands. Now, I think I must rest.' He turned on his side, away from me. 'Be careful, Euphemia. I'll see you back at home.'

I waited a moment, thinking this was some kind of joke. I had at least intended to kiss his cheek before I left. But he didn't turn round again, and as I watched his breathing grew deeper and slower. He had fallen asleep.

I left the room quietly and went looking for a doctor.

# Chapter Nineteen

## The truth about Bertram's condition

I found two doctors hanging around the nurses' kitchen, drinking tea and angling for someone to make them a bacon sandwich. As I had thought I might. 'If I could have a word,' I said to the man in the white coat. I checked his tag. It said doctor and not consultant. But then he was, I gauged, far too young to have seniority. Pity. But then you had to balance experience against new knowledge. I was prepared to give him the benefit of the doubt.

'I'm Mrs Stapleford,' I said. 'My husband has been with you following a heart attack. I was hoping you could tell me more about his condition.'

'Bertram Stapleford? Ah, well, yes, perhaps we should find somewhere you can sit down.'

'I was led to believe his life was not in danger!' I said. 'Has this changed?'

The doctor, who I gauged was around my age, placed a hand gently over the small of my back and guided me towards an unused consulting room. I quelled my reaction to break his fingers. He was trying to be kind, I told myself, but why?

I sat down, gripping my hands in my lap. The doctor took a seat in a chair behind a desk. He looked stupidly young, with brown hair, quite short, but still curling. He had freckles, for heaven's sake. He was composing his face into a serious expression.

'I should tell you I have done some army nursing,' I said. 'I would never promote myself as an expert, but I am accustomed to dealing with severe and life-changing injuries.'

The doctor's shoulders, which I now saw had been hunched up around his shoulders, dropped. 'That will make things easier,' he said. 'You both being a nurse and in the army.' I didn't correct him, but waited.

'You won't know this, Mrs Stapleford, and I shouldn't be telling you, but I think under the circumstances you have a right to know.'

Would he ever get to the point? I gripped my hands together more tightly. I could feel the seams of my gloves beginning to give at the knuckle. I forced myself to take some deep breaths. It wouldn't help Bertram if I threw this young man against a wall and demanded answers with my fingers clamped around his trachea.

'The thing is, Mrs Stapleford. The thing is . . .'

I was pretty sure I was screaming inside my head now. Any moment now the noise would leak out of my skull.

'Your husband was doing something rather hush-hush for his country. I can't tell you much more, but it put him through the wringer in a bad way. I don't think you'll ever be able to imagine what he went through, and don't be surprised if he never tells you. Those kinds of men,' he seemed to focus on some noble idea far in the distance behind my head, 'well, strong and silent is pretty much their watch word.'

'Words,' I said.

'Yes, exactly,' he said and his eyes focused back on me. 'So when I tell you the following I hope you will understand that the repercussions of his actions on his physical form were for the sake of his country. You will have to live with these, and it might be difficult at times, but we marry for better or worse, don't we?'

'Have you amputated a leg or something?' I said. I knew it was a silly thing to say, but I had to break the tension building up inside me.

'No, that might have been easier for most couples to deal with.'

'Doctor, please,' I said from between gritted teeth, 'put me out of my misery and tell me what is wrong with my husband.'

So he told me.

*

It must have been a good hour later that I stumbled back out to find Fitzroy. He was reading a newspaper and sneering. He got up, scrumpling the paper as he did so.

'What a rag,' he said. 'The modern reporter is as entertaining as a bad head cold and about as informed as a bowl of fruit.' He stopped and tilted his head slightly. 'What's wrong, Alice? All the reports I've had have said Bertram is doing splendidly. What's changed?'

'Do you think we could go somewhere discreet for a cup of tea?' I said. I heard the waver in my voice, and knew I was on the edge of tears. Damn my condition. Fitzroy took two quick strides towards me, and took my arm.

'My dear girl, whatever you need.'

I don't have a distinct recollection of how we ended up in the tea shop or even of where it was. We were seated at a corner table, and Fitzroy was drawing horrified looks from people all through the shop by pouring me tea from a huge teapot. I looked down. It was clear and slightly tinged with green. 'It smells odd,' I said.

'Jasmine tea. Only place I know in London that currently serves it. Refreshing and mentally stimulating. Now tell me what's wrong.'

I took the cup, sniffed at it and took a sip. It tasted a little like stewed paper with a hint of lemon as an after taste. Not unpleasant and somehow strangely enticing. Over the rim of my cup I saw the spymaster starting at me. 'You're looking at me like you look at Jack,' I said, making a discovery.

'Really? How is that?'

'In a soft sort of way. Soppy.'

Fitzroy blinked, and shook his head. 'No, you're not drawing me into an argument to avoid the subject. You were clearly very shaken when we left the hospital. In fact you've been decidedly strange since you started this mission. Tell me what is wrong.'

I sighed. It wasn't any business of Fitzroy to know the details of Bertram's problems. But then again it was. As his partner, what was about to happen to our marriage would have repercussions on me, and how I felt about life. Which right now was decidedly bitter. Above all I didn't want Fitzroy looking at either Bertram or me with pity. I also knew he would be like a terrier with a bone until I told him something.

The tea was helping. I could feel myself becoming calmer. My breathing had almost slowed to normal, and tears were further from me than they had been all day. I decided on a compromise. I said, 'Although Bertram is not in any actual danger, he is weaker. He will not be able to do all that he could before—'

'That's good, isn't it,' said Fitzroy rushing to interrupt. 'He was getting rather too keen on joining you in the field, and you know he wasn't fit enough to become a full agent. Morley would never have him. This way he can bow out of that sort of thing without feeling he's letting the side down. I mean, he's only getting confirmation of what we already knew. He's not a fit man.'

'I don't think you know my husband very well. Once he knows there are things afoot, unless he is in the thick of things he will always think he's letting the side down. Letting me down. I don't think you are listening to me.'

'Then we don't let on things are happening,' ran on Fitzroy. 'Be awkward, but we can work it out.'

I held out my cup for more tea. This time an elderly lady at the back of the room tutted at us. I ignored her. If a gentleman pouring tea for a lady was the most improper thing she ever saw then she could consider herself lucky. Although that sounded like a truly dull life. I wouldn't wish that on anyone.

Fitzroy, more than aware of her disapproval, poured the tea with an extravagant flourish and winked at her. That, I thought uncharitably, was probably the biggest thrill she had had in decades.

'Besides, that isn't what I meant. Bertram half believes that exercise and healthy eating will allow him to get back to where he was.'

'Oh dear,' said Fitzroy. I scowled. The spy shrugged. 'He's not keen on either, but I expect you can jolly him on.'

'His doctor was clear that any improvement will be minor and for the sake of his health there are things we should avoid.'

'Is this my cue to apologize again? I had no idea that mission was an ambush. If I'd had even an inkling things weren't above board I'd never have let him go. What can I do to make things up to you?'

'I know that.'

'Yes, well, I wouldn't blame you if you were angry with me. I should have known. It's my business to know that sort of thing. It was just . . .' Fitzroy looked down at the table. 'Damn it, Alice. You know I bitterly regret what happened. I should have . . . I should have looked into things more deeply. I had no reason . . . I'm not trying to excuse myself. I am in your debt.'

'In Bertram's, surely?'

'I meant if there is anything Bertram can no longer do then I am only too happy to take up the slack. Talk to your factor. Attend to matters of business—' He broke off as I gave a crack of a laugh. I heard the sound as if from a long way away. It was harsh, like the call of a crow.

Fitzroy paled slightly. 'Just tell me.'

'He is no longer allowed to over-exert himself. The doctor advised against us resuming marital relations.' I watched with perverse pleasure as the meaning of my words washed over my partner. Already pale, he went white, as if all the blood had spilled out of him. Then it rushed back, leaving him pink in the face with only a white ring remaining around his mouth.

'I don't know what to say,' he managed to croak.

'You always said I could tell you anything,' I replied. Being cruel to him helped me forget the pain I was feeling. 'Besides, you're always telling me about your stream of conquests, you'll hardly notice adding another woman to your harem, will you?'

'Alice, no. You know I don't think of you like that.' His sounded as if his throat was full of sand. He hurriedly drank down a cup of tea. I watched his discomfort without words.

'I had no idea,' he said. 'I never imagined. You can't possibly mean . . .' I had never seen him at such a loss for words.

Eventually, I had had enough. 'Stop it,' I said. 'There is no way you could ever replace my husband in any of his roles. Your suggestion that you could was offensive.'

'I didn't know what you were talking about,' said Fitzroy.

'It doesn't matter. You're a fraction of the man he is.'

'I've always said that,' said the spy defensively. 'I've always said Bertram is a good man.'

'You've—' I paused. 'My married life has been ruined,' I said. 'I know it's not fair to blame you, but you must see that the changes I must now embrace will require a great deal of adjustment. I am hurt and I am angry. You know my life has not always taken the easiest path, but I had thought finding Bertram, becoming an agent, I finally had everything I could wish for. It seems however I am not destined for the kind of happiness I momentarily enjoyed.' I swallowed. 'But I still have him. It is simply that things must change and I will accustom myself. I would prefer it if you would not tell him that you know about this . . . this trouble.'

'I don't know what to say, Alice. I would understand if you hated me.'

'I don't,' I said. 'You risked your own life and your career to bring him back. I assume you defied orders to do so.' Fitzroy nodded slightly. 'But,' I continued, 'I think it will be some time before I can look at you again and see a friend I can trust. I will always respect you as a professional but, on a personal level, I am sure I can be civil.'

Grim-faced, Fitzroy gave me a curt nod. We finished the pot without speaking another word to each other.

# Chapter Twenty

## Rosa outdoes herself

It was even more awkward when we returned to the spy's flat. Fitzroy had Griffin pack up my things before I even asked, and called me a cab to take me back to my own lodgings. I found I had nothing to say to him, so we parted wordlessly. If he still intended to join me on the mission then he would appear and I, as Alice Woodward, would regard him as a stranger.

In the cab on the way back the sky shifted to grey and the heavens opened. From the warm mellow tones of autumn light, the city suddenly wreathed itself in shawls of shadow. The world had become as melancholy as my thoughts.

I leant my forehead against the cold glass of the window. Rain ran like tears on the pane. Like I had as a child, I watched the drops run into one another and streak away. For a morbid moment I thought of all of us coursing through life, attempting what mattered to us, but in the end being washed away by time. In the end how much did anything matter? I had always tried to do what I had been taught was morally right. I had edged over the boundaries of normal morality in the Service, but always I had strived to do what was best for my country. Now, I stood on the bittersweet edge of knowing I carried a child within me, which would realistically end my career as a spy. It would be assumed if I took time out of my work for a child once, then I would do it again. Not even mentioning the atrophying of essential skills and necessity of regaining my full health and strength after the birth. On the other hand, this gift from God would in all likelihood be my only child. Bertram was not incapable of fathering further children, but any attempt would put his heart under potentially fatal strain. I would not ask him to risk his life for the sake of our union nor for the furtherance of our family.

At the back of my mind was the knowledge that I would never forgive Fitzroy for what had happened to my husband. I knew intellectually that we had both been pushed hard, and how it had been all too easy for him to miss any warning signs about that mission. It happened to the best of the Department. I had seen and heard it before. Both from Fitzroy telling me about other agents, during training, and, rarely, when I was in the Department myself. None of us were infallible, and we were in the midst of war. It was all understandable and I would never forgive him.

The cab pulled up outside my lodgings. I got out and the driver handed me my bag. It wasn't heavy, but I immediately wished I had someone to carry it for me. I had flights of stairs to negotiate. Automatically my eyes went to assess how slippery they had become in the rain. Ordinarily I would be thinking that way in case I had to make a quick exit or if I was likely to be accosted on treacherous ground. Now I was thinking of the precious cargo within me. I could not risk falling. For the first time I felt a pitch of fear. Should I have told Morley and had myself withdrawn from this mission? Was I being selfish? Or was I merely trying to occupy myself rather than face my new reality?

'Miss Woodward?' In her open doorway stood my landlady, holding an umbrella and swaddled in numerous shawls against the weather. 'Could I have a word, please, my dear?'

I trotted over to her and edged under the umbrella. Her body language was such that I knew she had no intention of inviting me in. Something was wrong. I stood closer to her than I wished, but this was the coat I would be wearing tomorrow. I did not wish my small room to be steaming with drying clothes tonight. Nor did I wish to become chilled, while she told me whatever had upset her. I already knew she was not a woman to use fewer words. Close to, she smelt oddly of cloves. Protection against moths no doubt.

'My dear Miss Woodward, have you been away?'

'My uncle,' I said. 'He had a turn and my mother called me home for support.'

'I trust your speedy return means he has recovered?'

'Not entirely,' I said, 'but enough for the doctor to think he is out of danger.'

'You're a very dutiful daughter.' Was that a note of disbelief I heard in her voice? 'You certainly chose the right time to be away . . .'

'Really?'

'Indeed, your Miss Rosa has excelled herself this time!'

'Rosa de la Croix? The leading lady of my troupe?'

'She lives above you. I believe I mentioned her on our initial meeting. She is a friend of yours?'

I could feel myself beginning to shiver. 'No,' I said. 'There is no love lost between us.' I saw Beryl clearly relax when I admitted this. The tension went from her shoulders and they settled lower. She shifted her weight onto her back foot.

'I am glad for your sake,' she said with overplayed graciousness. 'As I mentioned, she's a little cow,' her pronunciation began to slip. 'Convinced me she couldn't afford my full rates and what do I see yesterday but her swanning around in a brand new mink coat. Poor my backside! I'm barely able to clothe myself, I'm so generous in my rates, and miss is walking around with her nose in the air, dressed as fine as a Christmas goose.'

'Yes,' I agreed. 'That seems most unfair.' My bag was growing heavy in my hand. I did not wish to set it down. If I did I would have to exert myself to retrieve it. Worse yet, my landlady might think it a signal of an intention to stay a moment longer. 'Perhaps you can raise the issue with her when she next orders her dinners?'

'Ha!' said my landlady. From behind me I felt a blast of warmth. It would take me a while to stoke my fire to such a degree. If only she would ask me in? At this moment I'd put up with her moaning to keep stop the cold creeping into my bones.

I realised Beryl was still talking. 'Keeping us up to all hours with her banshee wailing.'

'Is she ill?' Then I remembered the night before my meeting with Morley. I had heard a great deal of noise from the upstairs lodgings I now knew to be Rosa's.

'No such luck,' said Beryl, pouting. 'The first time I think it was more,' and she stole a look askance at me, 'shall we say an excess of passion.'

I began to dislike Rosa even more. 'How uncouth,' I said.

'Well, sound carries more than one might imagine through these old walls. I was young once. I might have overlooked that occasion, but last night . . . unbelievable!'

'The same again?' I had not thought I could dislike Rosa more, and yet I found myself doing so now.

'No, this time a right royal row. Screaming she was, at some poor sod. Mind you, he gave her what for. Ended with the sound of a ringing slap – who slapped who hard to know, I hope she was on the wrong end of a palm – and slamming of the door at past three a.m. And the man, stalking off without even a hat.'

'Did you see who it was?'

'I happened to be straightening my photographs by the window. That wretched cat does a deal of damage with its tail. But you've got to love them, haven't you?'

'Who was it? Did you recognise them?'

Beryl shook her head. 'Tall, broad-shouldered chap, hair a bit on the long side. But I couldn't see clearly. I was going to ask you to have a word with her.'

'I suppose I should check if she is uninjured,' I said with a sigh. Another flight of stairs.

'Ha! I couldn't care less about that. I just want her to keep her shenanigans down. Some of us decent folk need our beauty sleep. But it sounds as if you would have as much luck as I. I should have known a nice girl like you wouldn't have been friends with *her*.' The last statement was said with more disapproval than approval. I was not about to prove useful.

'I'll try and mention it to her at the theatre tomorrow. I'm understudying her.' My landlady gave me a pitying look. I could not decide if this was because I was understudying such a wretched girl or if I was a poor understudy for an annoying, but beautiful and accomplished actress.

However, the pitying look was my cue to escape. I hefted by my bag higher and walked at a fast pace towards the stairs. I didn't exactly trot my way up, but I went at a quick enough pace that once I closed the door to my small flat I felt quite out of breath.

I took my suitcase through to the bedroom and unpacked it swiftly, before I became too tired to care. I lit the fire, which I had built before I left, took off my coat and shoes, and put the kettle on. After the past several weeks of constantly living alongside others I found the small flat restful. I sat down in my chair by the fire, intending to watch the pictures in the flames while the kettle boiled. I nodded off almost at once, and was awoken by the screaming kettle.

I hastened to the kitchenette before Beryl could start accusing me of screaming in passion. It did make me wonder what she had really heard. There could be no possible way she would have heard a slap from the ground floor. She might have heard a body fall, but that was quite a different affair. She had seen a man leave the place. In fact, I suspected that the comings and goings of her tenants, and the small insight such things offered into their lives, was all spice to Beryl's existence.

I did consider going to check on Rosa, but if she had been the one who was felled last night, then frankly she was either recovering or dead. The thought of discovering either did not fill me with joy. Should she be alive, I would end up having an unwanted conversation. Possibly a cold one, too. I wouldn't put it past her not to invite me in even on a filthy night like this. If she was dead, then there was nothing I could do for her. Discovery tonight would entail going to find a telephone to call the police, and staying around to answer idiotic questions.

I sat back down, putting my tea on the hearth to keep it warm. No one had ever told me how I was meant to deal with the regular police. I should ask Fitzroy at some point, when I felt able to look him in the face without wanting to kick him. Failing that, the best thing would be to drop the entire situation in Morley's lap and let him sort it out. I found myself smiling. The idea of dropping things on Morley was most appealing.

With that last pleasant thought I drifted off to sleep in my chair.

# Chapter Twenty-one

## Fitzroy takes centre stage

I awoke, stiff and cold, to a burnt out fire. The grey light of morning was slipping in under my curtains. I got up slowly only to find my back was sore and in spasm. The clock on the bookcase told me I had a little time before I had to get to the theatre. If I skipped breakfast, which had no appeal, I could try for a quick bath in the hope hot water would help.

But I had been spoiled by staying at Fitzroy's flat. Even the hospital had been able to supply hot water on demand. Not so my lodgings. The best I could get was a few tepid inches. At least I felt clean. I clambered into my clothes still damp. I hadn't had the time to clear out the ashes to light a new fire. Wedged between two floors, the flat was not completely cold, but it was uncomfortable. Still, a brisk walk to the theatre would do me good.

I had barely set foot on the street when Beryl erupted out of her flat. 'I forgot this came for you,' she said, handing me a letter.

I recognised my brother-in-law Hans' rather florid handwriting. I took it, but she held on to the other edge. 'You will remember to speak to Rosa de la Croix, won't you?' she said earnestly. 'It's important that she knows the walls are thin. Perhaps you might suggest she comes to see me?'

'I'll do my best,' I said. 'I must hurry or I'll be late.' A sharp tug and the letter was mine. Beryl tried to put a good face on it, but she was far from pleased. I shoved the letter in my coat pocket and hurried off. She neither followed nor called after me. I reflected on her request and her behaviour. Could it be that Beryl had a side income in the form of blackmail? Had she really not seen who it was coming out from Rosa's flat after the argument? I should remember to check if my letter had been steamed open. Not that I thought Hans would say anything odd. I could always claim that Alice was my stage name to Beryl, if she *had* read it. Goodness, but this way of life made you suspect everyone.

I entered the stage door and nodded to Dickens, who tipped his cap at me. I made my way to my little cupboard, by way of the kitchen where I got myself a cup of hot water. Into this I grated a little of the ginger Griffin had given me. Just smelling this quelled the nausea that threatened to rise from my belly. I opened Hans' note, and found it to be little more than a reassurance that Richenda was improving and that he himself was rarely in London, otherwise he would have been delighted to see me. I breathed a sigh of relief. It had been a silly idea to write to him. Suppose he had caught a whiff of my acting? What would he have thought? That I had run away from Bertram for a life on the stage? I realised now that my desire to write to him was really a desire to clutch on to my old life. Although there had been murders then, circumstances had somehow been more comforting.

I sat in my dressing room accustoming myself to the temperature of the theatre and sipping my tea. I had removed my coat. The heating backstage was running full steam. Every now and then the pipes creaked and uttered gurgles. This, I thought, was no doubt the ghost the previous director had heard. The power of suggestion was a mighty thing.

After ten minutes I made my way to the auditorium only to find that Fitzroy was strutting across the stage. He wore a smart suit that wasn't wholly out of tune with his usual sartorial style. It was the oversized and floppy lavender cravat at this throat that drew the attention. I watched from the edge of the door, half hidden by one of the pillars. He also carried a cane which he flourished from time to time. 'I can see how this must have been a great theatre once,' he was saying in an accent I couldn't immediately place. 'The original acoustics must have been delightful. Then to my surprise he sang a perfect scale in a pleasant baritone. 'Yes, very nice. It will doubtless do for your little musical.'

'Glad you agree,' said Reggie. He sounded rather subdued.

'Who is this peacock?' demanded Henri's voice in a loud and angry tone.

I slipped round the side of the pillar and into a seat. As far as I was concerned the second act had just started, and with a new and controversial character ready to stir up the plot.

Fitzroy paused dramatically mid-stage. 'I am your new assistant director, and understudy to the male lead. Julius Cantori. Previously of the Rome Grand Theatre.' Although he used good English, he added a strong accent I now realised was Italian. 'This is a great step down for me, but it is wartime and we must all do our bit. I understand you will be singing the many patriotic songs? I have been sent by my government as a token of good will.'

'German lover!' muttered a male voice behind me. I turned to see Braun sitting in the preceding row. This is going to go well, I thought. Fitzroy's target already seemed determined to despise him. Still, the spy had nigh on a lifetime of bending people to his will. Braun did not strike me as socially accomplished, and I did not find it inconceivable that he might still end up spending the night on the town with Fitzroy.

At this point Yves d'Yves entered. He had a fixed smile on his face, so fixed it could have been a death mask. Fitzroy jumped down from the stage, demonstrating his fitness, and rushed up to the director. 'The man himself. It is an honour to meet you, sir,' he said, shaking Yves' hand. Yves, somewhat surprised, was caught in the act of taking off his gloves and returned the handshake while clasping his glove in his hand. Fitzroy ignored this and smiled broadly. 'Even in Italy, we have heard of your *Hamlet*,' he said. 'Using foliage to represent the court was an idea extraordinary. We Italians applaud the unusualness. Especially from one working in British theatre. As we both know, it is all too often too hidebound, and its critics incapable of recognising true genius.'

Before my eyes Yves positively melted under Fitzroy's well-judged flattery. His little speech had made me feel sick, but it had been the right note to hit with Yves. After that Fitzroy came down off the stage and began greeting the others, Henri, Braun, and Reggie. He oozed flattery over each of them, and they opened like flowers in the sun. He asked Reggie who I was and learning I was only an understudy, merely gave me a kind smile and said he was sure I would learn a great deal from this distinguished troupe.

At this point I noticed a small blonde girl seated at the back of the theatre. 'The one who has been taking your place,' said Henri, sitting down beside me, while Fitzroy and Yves walked through the blocking of the first act. 'She has been playing the maid with all the imagination of a piece of wood. But she is obedient and makes excellent tea. She is keeping her tea duties and being allowed to watch us rehearse. She wants to be an actress. *Mon Dieu!* She can barely remember which side of the stage she is meant to stand on, but she is eager to please. She has already been fluttering her eyelashes at Reggie. But he only has eyes for *La Rosa*.'

'What do you think of the new assistant director?'

'He is very good,' said Henri. 'I have heard of him. Apparently his Antigone had people sobbing *au coeur* in La Roma two years ago. *Le Pays de France* described it as a tour de force.'

'Goodness,' I said.

'Indeed,' said Henri. 'We have much to learn from him.'

The small blonde girl, whose name I finally learnt was Aggie, disappeared and returned with tea and biscuits. Yves got Henri and Braun up on stage to demonstrate how he thought the first two scenes of Act Two should go. I focused my attention on Braun, who was playing Argent Foil, now changed to the hero of the plot who was intent on wooing Rosa's character. He moved stiffly, clearly self-conscious of every move he made. I could not imagine anything further from a dashing hero, and wondered if Yves intended his part be played for laughs. Initially I had assumed that Braun, who was no actor, would have some kind of background duty; to find him the star had startled me. But then the more I had seen the group playing the more I had realised that the actors were the bottom of the barrel. No doubt Yves had given Braun the part on account of his age and height. He had no other qualifying virtue that I had seen. Overall I suspected the whole thing was going to be rather awful.

Henri played the father determined to separate the young lovers. Act One centred mainly around Argent Foil declaring his love for Rosa and Rosa being dutiful to her father. Act Two was based around Rosa's kidnapping and the machinations of the Evil Butler, no longer a dual character, who was the terrible villain and mastermind of all that went wrong.

'Who is playing the butler?' asked Fitzroy.

A very obvious question. In Act One the character had had no more than a few incidental lines in the background, which Reggie had read in.

'Pal of mine,' said Reggie. 'Michael Bills. He's been a bit held up, but he knows the play and he's a fine professional.'

Fitzroy looked at Yves. 'That must be most worrying for you, Monsieur Yves. It does not seem right at a man of your reputation should be forced to rehearse with only part of your cast.'

'I could read in for him,' suggested Reggie. 'I'm sure he'll be here any day.'

'Your pardon,' said Fitzroy, 'but that is hardly the same.'

Yves shrugged. 'It is not. It is a grave trial to me and gives me the *megrimes*. But what can I do?'

'Would you permit me to stand in for now,' said Fitzroy. 'It would at least give you a better sense of what you are doing. You know of my experience as a player, of course.'

Yves' face went somewhat blank. Fitzroy jumped up onto the stage, and looked down waiting for approval with casual confidence. 'Of course,' said Yves after a moment. 'We would be honoured.'

'And if Michael continues to be held up, I could, if I were forced to, stand in for him on opening night. However, it seems most unlikely such a thing could happen.'

'Let us see how you do?' suggested Yves.

Within twenty minutes of Fitzroy being on stage it was clear he had missed his vocation. He was a natural. Totally at his ease on display, he made the butler's evil asides alternatively funny and threatening. The villain became charming, fascinating, and yet at the bottom of it all a rather nasty fellow. It was doubtless how Fitzroy saw himself.

They came to the end of Act One, Scene Two, and it was time for the butler to spring his trap on the unsuspecting heroine. It was at this point we discovered Rosa was not present.

'Where is she?' asked Fitzroy. 'I was rather looking forward to my kissing scene.'

'She needs a lot of sleep,' said Reggie defensively. 'So she often only comes when she knows she'll be needed.'

'But we're doing Act Two today,' said Fitzroy. 'Of course, she is needed.'

'Er, my landlady did say she'd been burning the midnight oil recently,' I spoke up, doing my best to sound bashful.

'Hen's teeth,' said Henri, 'she is a silly little girl. Parties are for the last night. Not mid-rehearsals.'

'But she's terribly talented,' said Reggie to Fitzroy.

'She is beautiful. If you call that talent,' said Henri. 'That is undeniable.'

Braun shuffled from foot to foot, concentrating on the stage boards beneath his feet.

'Reggie, if you still want her to play the part, you must fetch her at lunchtime,' said Yves. 'In the meantime Alice can stand in. Up you go, Alice. You're off book, aren't you? We'll take it from the start of Scene Three. Remember, the butler repulses you. You'd rather die than let him kiss you, and yet he is strong and cunning. You are like a hare trapped in a snare. Perhaps a tiny part of you is fascinated by him, but as his bewhiskered face comes closer you struggle but cannot escape. You are preparing to experience a fate worse than death. He manages to kiss you ruthlessly, and then we hear the sounds of the car arriving, so he locks you in the chest. That is the cue for the trio to come and sing their ditty about protecting

English maidens. At that point, you take centre stage, Henri, and give the speech about protecting our damsels from the curse of the Germans.'

'I'm not meant to be German, am I? asked Fitzroy in a light tone. I could see under the harsh glare of the lights he had gone somewhat pale.

'No,' said Reggie. 'But it's been a bit of struggle getting in all the songs the investors wanted. We did talk about making you German, but as you don't get hanged at the end in the latest version, we thought it was better to keep you English.'

'Well, thank goodness for that,' said Fitzroy. 'But shouldn't we wait for Miss de la Croix? We could move on to the police chase scenes. There's a number of songs there, and it all seems a bit complicated.'

'Oh, the trio already have that down pat,' said Yves. 'It was the first section we blocked. I didn't want anyone chasing anyone else off the stage, but they got it quickly. They're used to doing a tumbling act, so it was a piece of cake for them. It's the only section of the play I have any confidence in so far. Now, come on, Alice, up you go. Scene Three.'

I took my time getting onto the stage although I could have jumped up easily by pushing off with one hand. I went and found the steps and walked up. I was hoping that Rosa would burst through the door any minute. But she didn't.

Fitzroy and I found ourselves facing off alone on stage. We had to block out a quick chase scene before he caught me in his arms and ruthlessly kissed me, or so the playbook said. 'Bit of a disappoint, not waiting for Rosa,' he said in an aside to Henri, who gave a smiling shrug.

'But think,' said Henri in a slightly louder voice, 'what an adventure for little Alice. If I hadn't known she had trodden the boards before I would have thought she had never been kissed. It will be a thrill for her to be kissed by an experienced man of the world. She is such a sweet thing. So innocent.'

'Shall we block it first?' asked Fitzroy. The others might have missed it, but I heard the note of desperation in his voice. It might be that he hated the idea of kissing me, but I rather thought it more that he knew how keen I would be on the idea myself. If he understood that then he knew how much I would make him suffer if his lips came anywhere near mine. I threw him a glowering look from the other side of the stage, out of eye line from the others. I clearly signalled, you try and kiss me and it will be the worse for you.

Considering the current stage of our partnership, it was really too annoying of Fitzroy to have got himself in on the act when he knew I was an understudy. Meanwhile Yves was blethering on about doing some acting. 'Alice, remember this is a big theatre,' he was saying. 'You will need to summon your emotions strongly. We need to feel your loathing of this man. Your hatred. Your fear, and then finally your unwilling surrender. We want every woman in the audience to be breathless with sympathy, and every man barely able to stop himself from running onto the stage to defend you.'

I nodded.

'First of all,' continued the director, 'let us see what you are made of. Cantori, you will need to provide the foil to Alice's innocence. You are the baddest of men. A villain. I want you to feel the part. I want evil to ooze from your soul.'

'That shouldn't be a problem,' I muttered under my breath.

Fitzroy's slight tilt of the head showed he had heard me, but instead of looking affronted he grinned. 'Do you want us to see what we can up with ourselves? A little warm-up exercise for young Alice?'

'Excellent idea,' said Yves.

I glared at Fitzroy. 'Remember,' he said, 'you are a beautiful, innocent English rose.'

'Roses have thorns,' I said.

'Ah no, Alice, your character is sweet and innocent. Not thorny. She has an instinct to self-protect, but is all too easily overcome by the predatory male.'

'Sweet and innocent,' Fitzroy said softly to me. 'Let's see how well you can act.'

Out of the corner of my eye I saw Henri rubbing his hands together and smiling. Reggie sat sucking on the end of an unlit cigarette in a pose almost like that of *The Thinker.* Yves had stayed on his feet. He had shifted his weight forward like a man on edge, waiting to see the start of a race. Aggie, in the background, clashed together the used cups.

'Aha,' said Fitzroy dramatically, 'At last I have you alone, my sweet. It is time for you to realise that you need a real man to make you a woman!' He paced forward slowly. His head lowered slightly like a prowling wolf's.

'What do you mean, Evans?' I said my line, hearing the annoyance in my voice. 'How dare you address me thus.'

Yves clapped his hands. 'No! No! No! You are perfect, Cantori, but, Alice, you are more petulant fishwife than soft English rose. Again. Again. Use your feminine emotions.'

Fitzroy cocked an eyebrow at me, then returned to his starting position. I knew he was being Cantori, not my partner, but I could not shift the feeling he was deliberately winding me up. Last night I had been too hard on him, I knew. I thought he understood where I was emotionally with all that was going on? Or was he trying to suggest that women were always the prey where lovemaking was concerned, and I was well out of it? That seems unlikely. Fitzroy had always shown his softer side where women were concerned. Sometimes coming within a whiff of being compromised as an agent.

I darted around another chair. It fell with a crash that made me jump.

'Yes, that is it!' said Yves. 'You are afraid. Afraid and vulnerable.' Goodness, these men and their idea of fragile women. Where on earth was Rosa? She would undoubtedly enjoy being preyed upon by the spy.

Fitzroy cornered me by the side of a table. He leered at me rather too effectively. I kicked him hard in the shin and slipped from his clutches. The spy hopped on one leg and cast a mournful look at the director. 'Not what I was expecting,' he said. 'I didn't realise this role involved stage fighting.'

'No! No! No!' cried Yves. Fitzroy rubbed his shin and hopped back to his starting point.

We began again, only for Yves to stop us once more. 'You are not feeling the right things, Alice. The girl, she is weak. She is mild. She is fragile. She is without protection. She is not a she-wolf standing off against her mate. You are too strong. Cantori, you cannot hop. I regret you must work through the pain. Alice, do not injure your fellow actor again!'

This time the look Fitzroy gave me was one of annoyance. 'What's the matter, Alice?' he said. 'Do you need a break?'

'We have no time for breaks,' said Yves. 'Alice, you must act. Do you best. Rosa will take over later, but for now I need you to perform. I must get a sense of how Cantori can fill this role. I am thinking Reggie's friend may not be needed.'

At this moment something within me snapped. Trust Fitzroy to storm into my mission, know exactly and easily how to get the information we needed, and bloody well steal a starring part in the show. While I was bullied and had to sit in a cupboard. Usually when I reach the stage of being at my last straw it is because I am about to fight, to take on the world either physically or verbally. This change within me heralds disobedience, a disregard for orders and even law, but not so today. What I felt instead was a tidal wave of tears rising within me. I felt bullied by Fitzroy, even though I knew he was only playing a part. It didn't help that the other men in the theatre were enjoying themselves as if I was some sporting show. This was meant to be a comedy. My character was ultimately saved in the nick of time, but I did not like the way the gentlemen present were enjoying the hunt.

By the time I said, 'how dare you address me thus?' I was quivering holding back the tears. Fitzroy chased me around the stage, as I clung to the set furniture or tried to hide behind a chair. Finally, he pulled me out by the arm from behind a table.

Then he pulled me roughly into his arms. Very quietly, he said in my ear, 'Sorry about this.' He lowered his face to towards mine. I shrank back in his hold. For some reason my vision focused on his moustache as he lowered it towards my lips. Had it always been quite so bristly? I could have used it to scrub floors. I really didn't fancy that touching my face. I would have admitted, if asked, that it did smell pleasant enough; of bay leaves with a faint hint of citrus.

Oh, Lord! The wretched hairy red caterpillar was almost upon me. I closed my eyes. There had to be a way out of this.

'Now,' he cried, 'you will learn what it is like to be kissed by a real man!'

At this point he was supposed to kiss me while I feebly attempted to push him away. Inspired by the moment, I pretended to drop into a dead faint. With me supposedly unconscious in his arms, Fitzroy was able to close down on my limp form and appear to kiss me without doing so. 'Very clever,' he said quietly. 'I really thought you had fainted for a moment.'

'Your breath is terrible,' I said. 'Also, I rather think Rosa has been murdered.'

'What?' said the spy, still pretending to embrace me. 'What a time to tell me!'

# Chapter Twenty-two

## An informative luncheon with Henri

Before I had the chance to explain further we were both startled by a round of applause coming from our small audience. Fitzroy raised me back to my feet and bowed dramatically. I stood there feeling awkward, and doubtless looking so.

'Well done, Alice,' said Yves. 'It took you time to find yourself, but that was excellent. The faint at the end – perfect. I don't believe *La Rosa* could have done better herself. Everyone take five!'

'Indeed so,' said Henri. 'You were wonderful, Alice.'

From my vantage point on the stage I saw Rosa enter the room in time to hear their comments.

Reggie came forward to help me down from the stage, 'Not bad at all, old girl,' he said.

Fitzroy, who had spotted Rosa, jumped down and moved towards her.

'Why the hell is she taking my role!' said Rosa loudly. Everyone but Fitzroy and I started. Aggie broke a couple of cups. As usual everyone ignored her.

Fitzroy moved suavely towards her. He didn't have his cane to flourish, but he exaggerated the normal tilt of his shoulders that gave him his usual swaggering gait. He lifted his chin slightly higher than usual. 'Ah, bella!' he said in a voice that projected perfectly without being raised. 'It is *La Rosa*. I had heard of your beauty, but the reality is even more breathtaking.' He possessed himself of one of her hands and kissed her fingers.

Rosa, who had been all set to throw a tantrum, was thrown off guard. 'Who are you?'

'I am Julius Cantori, late of the Roma Grand Theatre. I am to be the assistant director, courtesy of my government. And the understudy for the role of Evans until Reggie's friend appears. But now, indeed, I hope he never will.' He kissed her fingers again.

Rosa changed before our eyes from feral wildcat to purring kitten. I felt nauseous. Everyone's attention was now on Rosa. All of them hoping she had successfully been calmed.

'We need to get to know one another,' said Fitzroy. 'I know we must sing a duet. I will hear your voice and you will hear mine. The voice is the sound of the soul. You know that, do you not, my rose? Reggie, play the song she sings with Pierre in Act One. The one where she dreams of coral seas and misty isles. You see, I know all the parts, my rose. We must sing.'

He hadn't let go of her hand, so he was able to lead her to the piano. Reggie was fumbling through papers frantically to find the script. Yves looked torn between annoyance and relief. Reggie struck up the tune, and Fitzroy sung the opening line. He really was remarkably good. I felt a tap on my shoulder.

'Do you wish to come to luncheon with me, *ma petite*?' said Henri. 'I will pay. I do not think we will be needed for some time.'

I nodded, and went to fetch my coat. In the background I could hear the voices of the spy and the actress combining in a way that made Reggie's rather lacklustre score sound quite lovely. The spy leant into the actress in an adoring manner that was on the edge of being far too intimate. They were within a hair's breadth of touching, and somehow this made the obvious attraction that sparked between them all the more inappropriate. Fitzroy was doubtlessly enjoying himself enormously.

If I thought there was any chance Henri was going to take me for a good luncheon, this hope was dashed when I realised we were walking towards the small theatrical cafe restaurant with all the dust, where he had made me pay before.

He had offered me his arm, and while I didn't want to encourage him, I was finding that my pregnancy made me more tired than usual. I have never in my life, since I was a baby, had a pre-luncheon nap, but the thought of such now was like the thought of water to a man in the desert. I had never felt such an intense drain on my vital functions. Still, a good intake of food would doubtless perk me up. At least here, the special was unlikely to be egg and chips.

Minutes later I lost my appetite entirely. I had thoughtlessly ordered a lamb chop, vegetables of the season, and gravy. The chop was an unappealing grey, but not the worst I had ever been offered. However, the gravy was full of oil; a foul brown congealing spill that covered the entire plate. I noticed that they had left the bone marrow between the bone ends of the chop. A grey, mushy substance that my father had always assured me was full of protein. Staring at my meal I also now saw that much of the fat on the chop remained white. It had not been rendered down sufficiently. I must have been thoroughly deluded to think the cook here could cope with something as sophisticated as a chop. I felt appalled that anyone could eat such horrors.

'Ah, *ma petite*, has *La Rosa* put you off your food? Do not allow yourself to be troubled. Today you showed us all that you are the stuff that stars are made of.'

I smiled. 'You are very kind.'

'Indeed, I am not,' said Henri. 'The more you come to know me the more you will know this is the truth. Today you displayed such passion, such empathy. The emotions, they flowed from you like water – we, the watchers, were all drenched in your talent.'

I wondered if that would sound less odd in Henri's native tongue. I doubted it. There was an undercurrent of lewdness to his speech that made me regret having agreed to eat with him. However, apart from the occasional warm glance, he did not overstep the mark. Indeed, as I had struggled with my main course, he insisted on buying me a pudding, *Iles de Flottant*, soft meringues floating in cream patisserie, which was rather excellent.

'See, you have such taste,' joked Henri. 'You prefer your food a la Française. When I am next with funds I will take you to a proper French restaurant and you will see what France has to offer you!'

'I thought you were Belgian?' I said.

'Ah . . . Mixed ancestry. My mother was Belgian, but she said my father was most likely French.'

'She didn't know?'

'Ah, *ma petite*, the theatrical world was more, how would you say it? More passionate then. My mother was an actress herself. A very fine one, adored.'

'I see,' I said, somewhat surprised by this confidence. 'I wonder what Rosa's antecedents are?'

'An alley cat?' suggested Henri, sipping from his glass of red wine. 'She has no history in our world. She is an interloper. I believe she was a servant of some kind.'

'My parents were not actors,' I said.

'Ah, you are the supreme kind of star. You are as gracious as you are talented. Rosa is beautiful. Much of her talent is her beauty. Her temper is foul. She will become no more than an aged harpy. You, on the other hand, will always have grace and charm, and will be the beloved of the theatre for a lifetime. I see a grand career ahead of you. Would that I were a young man to play opposite your lead. But alas, I am an old man.' He dropped his head, then looked up through his eyelashes, not unlike a coquette, clearly waiting for me to cry out that he was not old.

Instead I glanced at my watch. 'Should we not be getting back?'

He shrugged. 'There is no need. Yves will have kept them rehearsing for a while after we left. He will only just have departed for his own meal. Can you believe he enjoys Italian food? Gloops of tomatoes and noodles!'

'Has Rosa always had such a temper?' I asked. 'Only my landlady mentioned there had been a few incidents while I was away.'

'Romantic disputes?'

'I don't exactly know. At least one argument with a man leaving in anger. At least that's what my landlady said.' I frowned down at my plate. 'I shouldn't gossip. For all I know she imagined the whole thing.'

'If you are talking about Beryl Belairs, I wouldn't put it past her to fall asleep after a few gins and have a fantastic dream which she believed was true. Never could admit to her drinking problem, *la pauvre.*'

'Oh, dear. I had no idea. That cannot be safe in a boarding house.' I felt this was something Alice Woodward would say, but I genuinely felt some concern. The old house was as dry as a bone, and one over-looked candle would send the whole thing up like a tinderbox.

'I do hope, ma cherie, that you are not anywhere above the ground floor. Whereabouts is your flat?'

'My landlady has asked me to request her to be less . . . less noisy. Do you think that is a good idea?' I said, trying to divert this line of enquiry. It was bad enough he already knew where I lived.

'The fact that you are asking suggests you already know the answer, *ma petite.*'

'I suppose so. She is difficult.'

Henri nodded. 'She is indeed. Unlike you, *ma petite*. You were inspired today. It seems you have been hiding your torch under bushes, n'est pas?'

'Under bushes? Oh, hiding my light under a bushel. I don't know about that. I think you are being very kind. I found acting opposite Cantori intimidating.'

'Pah! He is a flibbertigibbet! I have seen his kind a thousand times. He uses youth and energy rather than talent. He charms the director and sleeps with the leading lady. Ah, your saying, "all mouth and no trousers", fits nicely!'

'I thought you said you had heard of him?'

'Eh, well, people will always speak well of that type, but now I see him *dans son peau* – he is nothing. He will pass, *tant pis*! He, like *La Rosa*, is only good for one thing.'

I felt it would be asking for trouble to enquire further, but I couldn't be entirely sure what he was getting at. Henri had adopted an expression I couldn't quite fathom. It was an intense expression, with a frown and glittering eyes. A vein near his temple throbbed. I paused before answering to see if he would say more.

Henri leant forward and snapped his fingers near my face, 'Gathering the monies from the angels. Both of them, they will charm investors for the play. This war will see a lot of companies making money. Those two will lure in the investors and before you know it we will be touring the country, appearing in the drab and dingy little places to drum up sacrifices for the armies. Why, *La Rosa*, she has three of them on a string right now. I say to her, telling all of them you adore them, while you make the love with the writer, it will end badly. Very badly.'

'Goodness, three gentlemen suitors or investors?'

'Ha! Both, if you are asking me. And each of them she bleeds. Reggie, he doesn't give her the money, but he makes her the leading lady. I would not be surprised if he has given her some of his shares in the play. There is Maurice Attenbury. They call him the boot king. He is the main manufacturer of boots in the Empire. At only forty he is a most successful businessman, a louche kind of man. Rosa will only have got him to invest one way. Then there is the Pleasant fellow, some kind of government person. Most unwise. If she displeases him, I tell her, he will make her disappear.'

'Surely not! This is England!'

'Ah, ma petit chou. And then there is the flame-haired lord, Frake, no real rank, but of riches rare, and with a temper to match his hair. She is having the sex with all of them!'

I decided to allow Alice to be shocked by this, and managed to do so in such a flustered manner that Henri agreed to take me back to the theatre. He was as good as his word, and he did pay for luncheon. This worried me. I had been promoted from someone to sponge from to someone with whom he wanted to curry favour. As the most junior member of the players, what on earth could he want from me?

# Chapter Twenty-three

## I forgive Fitzroy a little

The afternoon at the theatre passed in rehearsals, during which Rosa alternated between acting, even I had to admit, divinely, and behaving, as Fitzroy managed to whisper to me in passing, like a devil in a dress. She was alternatively charming to Cantori, spiteful to Henri, rude to Reggie, and whinging to Yves. She spent most of the time ignoring me, though once almost physically forcing me off the stage.

Fitzroy, as Cantori, kept up a show of being charming and practically obsequious to her. Yet I knew him well enough to know he was losing patience with her. Normally, he is a man quite affected by beauty. While I have no doubts he would never raise his hand to a woman, I had the feeling that by the end of the day, he would happily have locked her in a cupboard for a few hours.

We were having a cup of tea provided by Aggie before a final run through of the second act, when he took my arm and led me slightly to one side. Rosa was lying on top of the piano smoking, while Reggie ran through some of the songs, still attempting to tweak the score.

'Look adoringly at me,' commanded the spy.

'Why on earth would I do that?'

'Because I am an exciting, charming foreign actor and you're overwhelmed with desire for me.'

I shook my head. 'Alice isn't that gullible or that immoral.'

Fitzroy shrugged, 'Well, just look admiring then. As if I'm giving you the benefit of my acting advice.'

'And?'

'I've managed to get Braun to agree to go out for a drink with me tonight. Seems the poor fish is at a bit of a loose end. Apparently, his girl has disappeared off to do something patriotic. Your idea, I presume?'

I nodded.

'Anyway, I've yet to get his address, but when I do I'll pass it to you. Break in tonight while we're out, will you? Have a good look around for incriminating material evidence, while I attempt to drink him under the table and get him to reveal his true self. With luck we'll have this wrapped up by tomorrow. I'll drop round and pick you up for breakfast and we can compare notes?'

He had at least the courtesy to finish off as if it was a request rather than an order.

'Quick work,' I said.

'The rest of the cast are foul enough even I seem like a good companion for a lost mathematician.'

'Sounds like you will have an exciting evening,' I said. 'At least there will be alcohol.'

Fitzroy shook his head. 'I'll be buying more than my fair share. Surprising how much water looks like vodka, or grenadine syrup in water can pass for wine. I really don't know which one I hate most.' He put on a mournful face that made me smile.

'You look like Jack watching Griffin walk away with the biscuit tin,' I said quietly. Fitzroy grinned back at me.

'Flirting, Alice? How very unlike you!' said Rosa's voice from behind me. At some point during our conversation she'd slunk off the piano and slithered her way up behind me. She directed her attention at Fitzroy, 'You won't get anywhere with this one. Quite the country mouse. First time in the big city, and runs home at the slightest thing.'

'My uncle was seriously ill,' I said.

'If I had done that when I was playing the maid I would have been sacked on the spot. You must have some influence. Have I underrated you? Are you more than . . .'

'Rosa,' interrupted Fitzroy. 'It has been a long day. I am tired or I would invite you to dine with me. Perhaps we could enjoy tomorrow evening in each other's company. Unless you have somewhere else you need to be?'

'I always have somewhere else I need to be, dear boy,' she said, and flicked the end of Fitzroy's cravat in his face. She walked off with an exaggerated sashay of her hips. I could have told her this was pointless. Fitzroy was still counting under his breath. While he wouldn't have hurt her, I was fairly sure his code would have allowed him to pick her up and put her over his knee to spank her. I noticed he had even closed his eyes, he was fighting so hard to control his temper.

'She's not your type, is she? I'll go to dinner with you,' I said quietly, 'and I won't pull your tail.'

Fitzroy's eyes opened wide and he raised an eyebrow.

'I don't think Rosa suspected she had a tiger by the tail,' I explained.

'No, these people are a constant irritant, aren't they? I completely understand why Morley on top of all this would send you a bit ratty.'

'Is that what he said?' I asked, feeling my own temper rise.

Fitzroy grimaced. 'The word he used was hysterical.' He was standing very close to me now, watching my face intently. 'I told him that he had to be mistaken. You were not the kind of woman to go into hysterics. Tore quite a strip off him in fact. Didn't do much for relations between us.'

'Thank you,' I said. I saw the tension leave Fitzroy's shoulders.

'Does this mean I'm forgiven for everything?' he said with a cheeky smile.

'Oh, why not,' I said. 'I'm too tired to stay angry with you. Anyway you're bound to do something else to annoy me before the day is out. We can start with a clean slate.'

'I'd shake your hand but it would look odd. We should move apart. Give me another adoring look, there's a good girl. I'll do a brush past with the address later. You remember how?'

'Yes, of course.'

'Adoration, remember!'

I looked up at him and imagined he was Bertram, home safe, happy, and healthy. I might have overdone it a bit as Fitzroy's head started back slightly. 'I'm sure we'll get a chance to talk later, Miss Woodward,' he said audibly enough for the others to hear.

Yves clapped his hands loudly. 'I have decided this is enough for today. Tomorrow we start early and we do not leave until we have run through all three acts. Opening night approaches. We need to work harder and work better. Go home. Sleep well, for this will be the last long night's rest you will have. I am warning you.'

I caught Fitzroy's eye. He gave the tiniest of nods and headed over to Braun. Henri, coat over his arm, passed me on his way out. He had been the quickest to gather his possessions. 'Yves, he has to stop. We could go no further without Rosa, and again she is . . . pfff!' He gestured like a magician. 'At least this time it was less of a storm. But it grows to be a bore. She is not good enough to keep doing this. We cannot allow the play to fail. Too much is at stake.'

'I expect he will telephone her tonight and explain the new rehearsal schedule. She cannot want the play to fail either.'

'Hubris,' said Henri darkly. 'Besides, how will he know which bedroom she is in to telephone?'

I gave a shocked little gasp. 'I believe messages can be left with the landlady, who has a telephone.'

Henri nodded, clearly enjoying my shock, and made his way past me to the exit. In truth I wasn't in the least surprised. Fitzroy, a long time ago, had intimated to me that there were women who used their – er – charms to their own personal gain. They would not think of themselves as prostitutes, as I might. As I recall, this being a time before he recruited me, he had been trying to goad me. I cannot remember why he did that – and still does it so often. But the moment I had seen Rosa I saw her for what she was: desperate, insecure, and ready to do anything to secure her place in a world she saw as being run by men. I didn't doubt that her personal history would be a tragic one and go a long way to explaining why she was as she was today. I also knew that only another woman could appreciate her predicament. I did not approve of her choices, but I felt sorry for her. I had no doubt she would be horrified by this, and scorn any friendly approach I made. For women like Rosa, the only person in the world they would ever trust was themselves. I only hoped that Janice Hargreaves' death really had been an accident. Once Rosa crossed that line there would be no turning back as she headed for the hangman's noose. Her squires and suitors would vanish into the distance at the first sign of any real scandal.

Fitzroy bumped into me, and pressed something into my palm.

'Goodness, Mr Cantori,' I said. 'Are you inebriated? I could make you some coffee if you wished.' It galled me, but I did my best to sound sycophantic. Fitzroy gave a noise remarkably close to a snort and pushed past me. Our undercover relationships were now quite established in the eyes of the others

Braun followed him, and doffed his hat to me politely. I moved back into an aisle, out of the way. He seemed a nice enough fellow, but extremely quiet until he was cued to speak on stage. There, he bellowed his lines without intonation or feeling. His choices of clothing were equally dull. I would have given much to be a fly on the wall when Fitzroy managed to get him drunk. I had no doubt the spy would do so. Even if he had to add substances to his drink to get him to talk.

I felt eyes on me and realised Yves was watching me. I hurried to help Aggie clear up the cups and tea things. She was cheerily grateful and nattered on about how her mother couldn't find the wool match she wanted. 'Every time she goes into a shop she forgets the exact colour and comes out with the wrong shade. Oh, how Dad and me laugh. She's making him multicoloured socks, but he says he'll never wear them.'

I stacked the final cup on the tray. 'Couldn't she take some of the wool with her?' I said.

Aggie stopped in her tracks as if struck by lightning. 'Well, ain't that the most clever of ideas.' She laughed. 'We must be a family of right idiots not to think of that!'

Not knowing what to say, I headed for the kitchen. Ivor Cutler was there, and proceeded to flirt with Aggie. I washed a few cups and left Aggie to the rest. 'You'll be better off without me,' I said, winking at Cutler. Aggie frowned in puzzlement and I made my escape.

Outside, I opened the paper Fitzroy had given me. I thought I had a good idea of the fashionable parts of London, but this was nowhere I knew.

# Chapter Twenty-four

## Night-time manoeuvres redux

Doubtless Fitzroy had a London street atlas in his flat. Failing that, he could always drop by his club and get the porter to find an address for him. I, on the other hand, had limited resources. I decided the best thing to do was take a cab. Braun had to live reasonably near the theatre.

I could have visited Griffin at the flat, but I didn't want to climb now I knew my condition. Of course, it might be that this could not be avoided. This wasn't a case of talking myself into Braun's place and getting past a lazy concierge or landlady, I had to be careful no one saw me. Sometimes working abroad where you are unknown is so much easier. Doubtless that was why Fitzroy preferred it. One could take enormous risks and no one at home would ever know unless you told them.

I settled on wearing a cloak, and under this a boy's attire and sensible shoes. I'd dressed as a boy many times before. I was used to changing my gait and the way I held myself. The question was, did I have suitable enough clothes provided to be convincing? I certainly couldn't do without a cap or scarf for my hair. It was shoulder-length now, and thick and curly enough that no boy would put up with it. There was no question of dyeing it, as I had to look exactly as I did today, tomorrow at the theatre.

As for transport, I would have to hail a cab and deal with the cost. If Fitzroy was right and we would be getting out of there in two days, it would not be a problem.

I did find a cap among my possessions, and decided to hail a cab as a female, but transform into a boy before approaching Braun's address. It was far from being a good disguise, but it was the best I could do at this time. I didn't know whether to blame Fitzroy for assigning me the night-time excursion or be flattered that he had no doubts in my ability. Certainly, I couldn't have gone out drinking with Braun. Fitzroy had said there were women like Rosa used as assets within the Service, but he had been immovable that I was never to learn any of those skills.

The night was clear and bright with diamond stars. London smelt better than usual. There was a very faint tang hovering on the breeze. Autumn had clearly said her farewells and the sharp scent of winter was in the air.

I hailed a cab and gave the driver the address. It was too dark to see his face clearly, but there seemed to be no reaction to my request. At least Braun must be living in a respectable part of town. However, the ride was taking some time. My purse was going to be seriously depleted from the fare, and I was beginning to wonder if I would be able to afford the ride back. It was clear it would be too far to walk, and while I occasionally took five-mile runs, to keep myself fit, I wasn't at all sure I was up to it at the moment, let alone what I might look like. Usually, Fitzroy and I went on our long runs in the countryside and not through populated areas.

As we went further and further away from the heart of London, there was less and less noise from outside the cab. The light level lowered as the street lamps grew fewer, and more old-fashioned, in lieu of the bright electric ones in central London. When the driver finally pulled up we were, by my reckoning, deep into the suburbs. Somewhere clerks, bankers, and reasonably well-to-do working men might live. I paid my fare. It was a little more than half the money I had. At least I would be able to get a cab most of the way back.

As the cab drove away, I took proper stock of my surroundings. What I saw surprised me. I also realised that the chances of finding a cab to take me back were remote. I would have to deal with this later.

I was on a tree-lined street with detached houses on either side. A green verge ran down both sides of the street and down the middle. The trees were young and spindly, suggesting the entire street had been built or rebuilt recently. The houses all had white wooden features that strongly suggested the influence of the Arts and Crafts movement. I drew back into the shadow of a wall at the end of the street, and observed the properties further. The only light offered came from the houses themselves, peeking between shutters and under doorways. I could not see well, but then, I was hopeful, neither would any occupant looking out easily see me.

On the right side of each of the houses was a five-paned bay window on the lower floor. Above its red-tiled upper slope was a jutting rectangular window. Every effort had been made to bring light into the buildings. Also on the right side, the houses rose to a point that had been picked out in white and Tudor-style black beams. Then on the left side of each building, the entrance door, half-paned with coloured glass, was slightly recessed to form a small porch. Along the top of the porch ran a detailed fretwork decoration. Above this another jutting window, a much smaller version of the other on this level, poked out from amid white stucco which ended in a flat roof.

The houses stood in awkward pairs. Between each pair of houses ran a small driveway. Each pair huddled apart like guilty lovers at a dance, but on the other side of each ran back a small gravel path that ended in a garage. Presumably behind each house also lay a garden. Even I, who had grown up in a poor vicarage, thought them small and poky. I didn't doubt they were meant to be family homes, but goodness how the people must be on top of one another.

Clearly these were houses of the new age. My mother would not have known what to make of them. Great Houses she understood, and workers' cottages. Anything in between was lost on her. At White Orchards we had a few Georgian-style buildings in the nearby town, where richer local merchants and widows of wealth lived. But these houses were something else. Wherever I had imagined Braun might be staying, it was nothing like this.

These house Braun was meant to be at, number nineteen, was in excellent order with a neatly mown front lawn, and rose bushes planted under the windows. If this was his address. The possibility that Fitzroy had been given a false one did not escape me. He must be staying with a family. A lone actor could never afford such extravagance as renting a house for himself. As far as I knew Mary Hill lived in University lodgings. It was the norm for female tutors to be required to live at the college.

In short, this was most unlikely to be Mary's house. So who lived here? And why on earth had Morley not got his men to do a proper background check on Braun? Could it be that he had only thought of checking his connections in Germany?

More to the point, how was I to sneak into such a place? Even small London flats or lodgings generally had useful stairs or corridors. This small packaged house had nothing. Why, opening the front door, one must almost fall directly into the living area.

However, standing there and thinking could get me no further. Light glimmered from the edges of the bay window of number nineteen. Any entrance I made into the building would either have to be from the rear or directly into an upper floor.

I crouched down in the shadows and scurried to the house, and up to the gravel path. I made myself look in outline as least like myself as possible. People often catch sight of movement in the dark, but if it isn't human-shaped they tend not to focus on it.

I stopped at the end of the gravel path. How on earth was I to deal with this? I was confident I could walk along it more quietly than most, but I was so close to the house. Also, while I didn't know what lay beneath the white stucco, I suspected it was not stone, and therefore noise must carry too easily.

With a sinking heart I realised that my way into the house must be up the lawn and up the side of the house. If I covered my hair with my cap, and moved carefully . . .

Bending double, I slunk up the short lawn and made it easily into the porch. Looking up and down the street, I could see no open curtains. I reached up and grabbed hold of the wooden fretwork. It gave slightly under my weight, but I managed to pull myself up and onto a small ledge by the side of the smaller square window. I didn't even consider trying this window. I again checked the street to ensure no one was visible, then used the side and top of this window as leverage to gain the roof.

I lay flat on the roof, catching my breath. It had been a long day, and I was feeling extremely tired. A chimney beside me belched grey plumes into the air. I could feel the heat coming off the brick-work, and was glad of it. The night sky above had now partly clouded over, but was a soft dark blue you rarely see in the city. I was grateful the night had not turned to ice, but it was cold enough that my fingers felt numb. I curled up and looked around the roof. It was bare and unhelpful. I would need to check out the side and rear of the house. I ruled out climbing over the Tudor apex. Either I would find a way in on this side of the building or I would give up. I wasn't going to risk falling simply because I hadn't been briefed properly.

The rear of the property had windows, as you might expect, but they all appeared tightly closed. There was also no decent ledge to use as a halfway point down to the back door. However, on the side of the house a round window had been left open on what appeared to be the uppermost floor. It was a single window and it was dark.

It was this or nothing. Now, whatever I might protest, there was no way I was going to leave this mission without trying. Carefully, and with aching muscles, I managed to lower myself down the side of the building, catching the window open with my foot so I could get a purchase on the ledge. No one screamed at the sight of my foot inching in, so I followed through quickly with the rest of me.

I had intended to land with a soft thump and a roll. I hadn't counted on landing on the edge of the water closet, or lavatory as it was more often called now. Fortunately the bathroom was incredibly small, and I was able to throw out my arms and wedge myself between the wall and various facilities without coming to harm. In fact it was so tight I don't think I even got a bruise.

I extracted myself as quickly and quietly as I could from the room and found myself on an upper landing that could have been no more than ten feet long. A light shone up the odd little staircase from the lower floor, but here everything was in darkness. With luck no one was on this floor. I had thought to bring my Eveready military torch, a recent present from Fitzroy. But the light was too bright to use in the hall. I looked away from the stairs and waited for my eyes to adjust. From downstairs I heard someone playing softly on the piano. I had to assume they were trying not to wake someone on this floor. Perhaps children.

There were a further three doors off the narrow landing – although describing it as a landing is making it sound overly grandiose. It was no bigger than a medium-sized rug. One door I marked as being the master bedroom. Now I had to decide which one was the child's or children's and which the guest room.

I guessed wrong, but fortunately the twins, in matching cots, were deeply asleep. I tiptoed out thinking how I would feel if a stranger got into my child's nursery. Finally, I knew which was Braun's room.

I closed the door softly behind me. The curtains were already drawn, so I risked lighting my torch. I kept it as low as I could to avoid light leaking onto the street. The room was incredibly neat. A single bed stood next to a tiny nightstand with a framed picture of Mary, and the smallest wardrobe I had ever seen. In the window area, the small jutting-out window, stood a small desk.

I went for the wardrobe first. Nothing of any note. Clean well-pressed clothes of average cost, and a spare pair of shoes, well-polished. Empty pockets. The nightstand had a small lower cupboard which held underwear, socks, and a toilet bag. In the latter was nothing unusual. I searched the bed and found nothing, except a rather racy British novel. I flicked through it, but none of the pages had been marked in any way to suggest it was being used as a code book. All the same I memorised the title just in case. The desk was my last stop. I'd already spent more time in here than I wanted.

It was more difficult to shield the light here, but I had to use it. Papers were spread out across the top. I dared not pick them up and risk disordering them. I did my best to hide the light behind my hand as I inspected them. All of it was in mathematical notation. I chose one line to memorise. I have never studied mathematics in any depth, so it was meaningless to me as a whole. I opened the one drawer, expecting to find nothing but rulers, compasses, and other odd mathematical bits and pieces. I found these plus some pencils and a signet ring with a crest.

I cursed inwardly. I couldn't take the ring, and it would be hard to describe. After a few moments, which felt like hours, I found a piece of blank paper and a pencil. I quickly made a sketch of the ring, extinguished my torch, and slipped out of the room. The piano had stopped, and instead I could hear the murmur of a male and a female voice downstairs deep in conversation.

In an ideal world they would have gone to bed, and to sleep, while I was in their guest room. The only way I could think of getting out was the way I had come in. Perhaps this time I could manage it in a more gainly manner.

It was then that I saw that the bathroom was occupied. My head swam. I hadn't heard anyone come in, and I couldn't imagine either of the two infants I had seen being able to climb out of their cots, let alone walk to the bathroom. All I could do was duck back into Braun's room and wait for whoever it was to leave.

I left the door open a crack, and saw a small child of around five eventually emerge from the bathroom. It was difficult to tell if it was a boy or girl. The hair was mussed and much of the child's face was obscured by a large pink rabbit that was adhered to it. The eyes were half-closed, and a thumb firmly wedged into the mouth. It tottered out, about as steady on its legs as an old tar after a bottle of rum. I willed it to carry on to its bed. I could only think there was another small bed in the twins' room I had missed in the dark. But where on earth did the nanny sleep? Were there further rooms in the attic? I could see no way up except for a small hatch in the hallway. Surely that couldn't be . . .

As I watched, the tot stumbled slightly and the rabbit slipped. For a stuffed animal it had some bounce in it, and after hitting the floor it bounced down the stairs. The tot, who was obviously of an adventurous nature, if not an intelligent one, went after the rabbit.

I only had a second or two to make a decision.

I couldn't let the child fall.

I leapt out of my hiding place and caught the end of its nightgown. I managed to sweep the small creature out of danger, and into my arms. 'Shhh,' I said, trying my best to sound like a stern nanny. 'Rabbit has gone on an adventure. Mummy will bring him back later.'

The child appeared stunned into silence at my appearance. I hurriedly put it down and shooed it back into the babies' room. 'Quiet now,' I said, feeling inspired. 'I work for Father Christmas, and he'll want you to go back to bed right now.' I gave it a small push inwards and closed the door. Then I bolted for the bathroom.

I wasn't going to be able to make a song and dance about this. I climbed over the lavatory and hung from my finger tips from the window. I dropped and rolled. The gravel was rough against my skin, and the ground as hard as ground often is, but I managed it.

It was at this point that I heard the tinny sound of a police car's bell. Forgetting about stealth, I pelted across the gravel to gain some shadows in a garden opposite that had a large, untidy hydrangea. The tinny tinkle got louder. I had a sudden irrational thought that Father Christmas wanted me arrested for impersonating an elf. I really had been on active duty too long. My nerves were frayed.

I crouched down in the shadow of the bush. I could hear the sound of the engine now. No, I could hear two engines.

This was getting serious. I had no choice. I climbed quickly over the wall and into the middle of the hydrangea bush. Inside, it was pointy. The drying winter ends of a number of branches found resting places in me that I felt were hardly appropriate after such a short acquaintance.

The bells grew louder and louder, and mercifully swept past the end of the road. I began to climb out of the bush only for a different car to swing into the street. I launched myself backwards. This time I ended up in the embrace of a fir. A much gentler, but even more invasive experience.

The car pulled up opposite number nineteen. A man got out, someone else remained inside.

'Night, old fellow!' I heard Fitzroy's voice call loudly. He had clearly forgotten his accent. 'Must do this again sometime. Awfully jolly. Sure, I can't tempt you back to mine for a nightcap?'

I heard Braun make a murmured response. I guessed this was along the lines of 'keep your voice down, and why would I head all the way back into London after coming all the way out here?' I realised as Fitzroy called him back to the car for the fourth time that he was trying to give me notice of Braun's arrival and time to get out of the house. Braun was trying to get away from this madman and get to bed, before the entire street was roused. Fitzroy had to be enjoying himself enormously. When slightly drunk, he delighted in being annoying to others.

Eventually Braun broke away and went up to the house. He opened the front door and went in. There was no rush of exclamation, so as yet no one had realised I had been in the house. The chances the child wouldn't tell anyone were remote. It was whether or not it was believed. I had done my best to leave no trace, but my exit had been hasty.

I extricated myself from the fir only to see the cab drive off. I found myself swearing under my breath in language Fitzroy himself would have used. But I had done the spy an injustice. The cab turned round at the top of the street, where the verge ended, and started coming slowly back down the street. I ran out towards it, and Fitzroy opened the door. I jumped in and we drove off. The interior reeked of brandy.

'That seems to have gone rather well,' said Fitzroy.

'Perhaps not as well as you might think,' I said, and told him what had happened.

# Chapter Twenty-five

## A most unexpected arrival and a murder

'Oh, come on, Euphemia! Don't be such a prude!' The spy was sitting at his ease in front of his own hearth with a brandy in his hand. 'You've been running around London in the middle of the night, dressed as a boy, and you won't pretend to be my mistress.' He held up a hand. 'Wait, not even my mistress. A one-night fling! Call yourself an actress!'

'I realise it would give us both alibis for the break-in,' I said. 'But I really don't think Alice Woodward would fall for your charms.'

'Nonsense,' said Fitzroy. 'Why, he's almost as charming as I am. Women simply fall into his arms.'

'Trips them up, does he?'

Fitzroy looked pained. 'Most agents after successful manoeuvres tend to be upbeat. You're being rather wet.'

Griffin came in. 'Will you be staying, Mrs Stapleford? Shall I make up the spare room?'

I sighed. 'I didn't intend to, but I must say I am extremely tired. Would you mind, Griffin? I know it's extra work for you.'

'Oh, Griffin lives for extra work,' said Fitzroy.

'Anything else, ma'am?' asked Griffin, ignoring the spy.

'I would love a cup of tea,' I said, 'and maybe some toast. I didn't get the chance to eat tonight.'

'I shall make something appropriate,' said Griffin. 'And it is no trouble at all.'

'Never calls me ma'am,' said Fitzroy as Griffin walked out.

'Would you want him to?'

'I meant sir, dammit.'

'Yes, he does,' I said.

'Well, if he does, he doesn't mean it.' Fitzroy pouted.

'How much did you have to drink tonight?'

'More than I wanted,' said Fitzroy. 'Who would have thought the blasted Braun would have a cast iron constitution? Took positively vats of brandy to get him to open up, and even then he was cagey. If I didn't know better I'd think he'd been trained as a spy.'

'How drunk are you?'

'Well, I wouldn't drive you anywhere. It's all a bit fuzzy.'

'And yet, you're drinking more?'

'Ah, this,' said Fitzroy, holding up his glass. 'This is a trick some chemistry chap told me about. Means you don't get a hangover.'

'If you're talking about the trick of a "hair of the dog", I believe you drink it in the morning.'

Fitzroy regarded his glass in disgust. 'Should have known it was some silly navy idea. It's only making me feel worse. I should go to bed. You really should be my mistress, you know. It would save an awful lot of bother.'

'Go to bed,' I said. 'We can talk about alibis in the morning.'

'Gods,' muttered Fitzroy. 'You sound more like my wife.' He gave a dramatic shudder and staggered out of the room.

After a loud argument over breakfast, we arrived at the theatre together. Fitzroy was in a foul mood. He described his headache as a gun repeatedly firing inside his skull. He blamed the quality of the brandy. I blamed the quantity. I hadn't been sick this morning, but I had felt like it. The nausea had now more or less abated. Griffin had slipped me a fresh supply of ginger. I was taking the nausea as a good sign that last night's escapades had done the baby no harm.

In the cold light of day I was shocked at what I had done. How could I have thought that it was no problem to go climbing over roofs in my condition? Admittedly my plan had been to let myself in by picking a window or door lock. I had assumed Braun was in lodgings. If I'd known he was living in a small house I would have done things differently. Or would I? I wanted to complete this mission very much. After the baby my career as a spy was hazy, and I didn't want to leave with things half done.

I felt a tiny twinge in my stomach. No, it wasn't on. I had someone else to think of now. I would avoid all physically strenuous acts, and if that meant I had to reveal my condition to Fitzroy, so be it.

'C'mon, Alice,' Fitzroy called. 'You're lagging behind. Catch up, there's a good little thing.' I caught up, giving him a look of loathing. His lifted his index finger and pressed lightly against the end of my nose. 'We're lovers, remember. You adore me.'

'We are not . . .' I began

'Hello, that's odd,' said the spy. 'There's no one here.'

'Where's Dickens?' I said peering past him.

'Dickens,' said Fitzroy. 'Isn't that what your in-laws called their puppy?'

I nodded. 'I'd forgotten that. I guess it's a popular name.'

'For puppies and doormen,' said Fitzroy grumpily.' Where is everyone? The place is silent as a tomb.'

We walked through the little antechamber that functioned as the stage door entrance. The lights were on in the small lobby, but when we opened the door to the auditorium we found it dark and empty. 'Hellooo!' called Fitzroy, stepping fearlessly into the dark chamber. I hesitated. The place seemed overwhelmingly large unlit. The light from the door showed me some of the edges of the seats, the stage, and some of the boxes, but they were no more than faint blue lines in the darkness. Having been on the stage, I also knew that behind it yawned the massive maw of the backstage with its ropes, sets, and props. I had a sudden fantastic image of the backstage opening like a giant mouth to swallow us.

I tugged on Fitzroy's sleeve. 'Leave it. There's no one there. We could try the main lobby or the box office.' I shivered. The spy looked at me askance.

'If you say you're getting a bad feeling about this I will shake you. Once we've got that insignia you copied checked we can be on our way. I have a date with some serious rest and relaxation and I don't want anything spoiling that. I'm coming to yours, by the way.'

'You're what?' I managed to say, before we opened the door to the lobby and found everyone.

Reggie leant against a pillar, his head in his hands. Henri stood looking out of a window and smoking. Yves was talking animatedly with a man who stood with his back to us, and who I couldn't place. Braun proved to be at the far end, pacing back and forth. Each turn was executed with military precision. Aggie rushed up to us with two mugs of tea. She thrust one at each of us.

'Tea!' She said urgently. 'With sugar. You should drink it now.'

Fitzroy wrinkled his nose. 'I don't take sugar or milk. I take lemon.'

'I'm sorry, sir,' said Aggie, 'but my mum's a nurse and if she were here she'd say you have to drink that.' She looked at me. 'She can be right formidable, my mum, when she's being medical.'

'What are you wittering about, girl?' said Fitzroy, shifting his accent more into Cantori's voice.

'For shock, sir,' said Aggie. 'Seeing how Miss Rosa's been murdered.'

I dropped my cup. It smashed on the marble floor. Pieces scattered everywhere. The tea spread out like a multi-pointed milky star. I felt myself sway slightly. Fitzroy thrust his cup back at Aggie and caught me around the waist in the nick of time.

'Sorry,' I murmured. 'I don't feel quite the thing.'

The next thing I recall with any degree of clarity was that someone had opened up the box office, and I was seated by one of the desks, sipping a glass of water. I heard Fitzroy behind me. 'Good God, man, don't you think she's had more than enough shocks for one day?'

I turned to see him talking to another man, slightly taller than himself. That was unusual. Fitzroy was a good six foot. However, the man he was addressing had his hat pulled down towards his eyes and I couldn't see his face.

It seemed the three of us were alone in the box office, and that whoever was on the other end of Fitzroy's temper was someone he knew.

'I don't have a lot of choice,' said a man with a faintly Scottish accent. 'There's been a murder and the two of you are potential suspects.'

'You know better than anyone we're agents of the Crown and above such pettiness,' said Fitzroy, his voice sharp with annoyance.

'Look, even if I wanted to, and I don't, I'm only an acting sergeant. This is a trial for the police force, bringing in ex-soldiers. I'm not three days into post and I run across you pair. I need this like I need shrapnel in my other leg.'

'Rory?' I said. 'Rory McLeod?'

'Aye,' said Rory. His tone was gentler when he addressed me. 'Are you feeling more the thing, Euphemia? It's not like you to be squeamish over a bit of murdering.'

'That's unfair,' I said. 'Rosa was far from being my favourite person, but I've had a bad feeling about . . .'

'And ye said nothing?'

'Oh yes, Rory,' I said, sitting up. 'I thought it would be an excellent idea while undercover in the service of my country to walk into the nearest police station and say, "I've a feeling there is going to be a murder. I have no evidence, but I'm sure that won't stop you investigating."' I put my hand to my head. It was swimming and I felt sick.

'I meant to the young lady herself?'

'Ah, no . . .' I said, doing my best to pull myself together. 'She rarely let me get a word in between the insults she flung at me. However, I don't think this had any real meaning. She despised other women in principle. I couldn't think of a way of expressing my fears to her in a way that meant she would have listened.'

'You have no evidence?'

'I was fairly sure someone had tried to sabotage the play, but it had become quieter of late. In Rosa's case it was more that she treated men badly. She pushed them to the edge with the rivalries she fostered. She seemed to enjoy playing them off one against the other.'

'I see, you recognised yourself in her. I assume you felt some sympathy?'

'Excuse me?'

'Is it not fair to say that you ran rings around Bertram and myself? You even had Hans Muller hanging on a string for a while. Maybe you still do. And now I find you, instead of by the side of your ailing husband – Merry has been most informative – hanging out with yon mannie.' He jerked his head towards Fitzroy.

I couldn't help but notice the spy did not leap to my defence. 'I'm sorry you still feel that way,' I said. 'Rosa and I were quite unalike. Rosa was a most unpleasant person, but I imagine she became the way she did because life had treated her badly. I doubt anyone ever looked out for her, so she looked out for herself. Everyone else was only there for her to use. If ever someone acted as if they wanted to be murdered, it was her!'

'My acquaintanceship with her was shorter,' admitted Fitzroy. 'But long enough to determine she was a certain type of woman. While she didn't charge money, she expected to be paid favours for her favours.'

'That's nasty,' I said. 'Did you say Merry was here, Rory?'

Fitzroy shrugged. 'You're far more generous than me, Alice.'

'Was she one of your conquests – or,' Rory ignored my question and referred to his notes, 'one of Cantori's?'

Fitzroy shivered melodramatically. 'I have some standards,' he said. 'Besides, she had nothing to offer for our mission.'

'Which is?' said Rory.

'Sorry,' said Fitzroy, not sounding it in the slightest bit sorry, 'but that's need to know.'

'What happened to Rosa?' I asked. 'How did she die?'

'I'm sorry,' said Rory, 'but that's need to know.'

I lifted my head from my hand and elbowed Fitzroy in the ribs. 'See what you've done?'

Fitzroy shook his head. 'Don't flatter yourself, Alice. He dislikes you even more than he dislikes me. You can read it in his body language if you pay attention.'

'He is still here, and would like your alibis for last night – for both of your personas.'

'Oh, that's easy,' said Fitzroy before I could open my mouth. 'We were together all night. Except for the hours of five till eight in the evening, when Braun and I went for a drink. I picked Alice up from her lodgings after that and took her home. I have a flat in London, and a servant, who can confirm we were there all night if you wish to check. Or you could ask my dog. He's extremely honest. Although I suspect his loyalty might be swayed for a few sausages.'

I watched the clouds gather in Rory's face. 'I was under the impression that "Alice" was married now.'

'Oh, she is,' said Fitzroy casually. 'But other people's marriages never bother me. It's quite their own affair.'

Rory looked down at me. 'Euphemia?' he asked quietly. I knew Fitzroy was doing his best to annoy and deflect Rory. As some sort of experimental trainee policeman I doubted he had any real power, and his superiors wouldn't yet have learnt what an intelligent man he was. But I had worked hard during my stint at the hospital to mend bridges between us. We had, after all, once been engaged. 'It's not what you think, Rory,' I began.

'It's exactly what he thinks, Alice,' said Fitzroy curtly. 'There will be enough fallout from trying to untangle this mess without our adding to it. What you choose to do is no business of this man. He only needs to know that you didn't murder Rosa. Which in itself is absurd.'

'Thank you,' said Rory stonily. 'It's good to know where we all stand.' He looked at me. 'Merry told me much of what had been happening while I was at the hospital. She may be your best friend, but she has no idea who you've become,' he said. Then he turned smartly on his good leg and stalked off.

'I'll punch him later, Alice. When the mission is done.'

'That wasn't fair of you,' I said.

'I know,' said Fitzroy. 'But I'm afraid you need to put aside your finer feelings for the sake of the mission. We need to be clearly without suspicion and able to continue. If we're lucky Braun will find being around a murder stressful and possibly let something useful slip. In the meantime we need you free enough to get that sketch off to the Department and not banged up in some cell. I'd have thought you'd have had your fill of police cells.'

'How do I do that?' I said.

'There's a dead drop ten minutes walk from here. You can leave it with a note there. Once we're away from this lot I'll explain fully. I'd go myself, but Cantori's clothes are designed to attract attention. Yours aren't. It's better if you do it.'

'I could ask Cutler if he knows what happened.' I said.

'Leave it alone, Alice. We're not here to solve a murder. That's beneath our pay grade. Leave it to the little people who worry about such things. Our concern is the fate of the nation. Now, we should join the others, and see if we can get anything out of Braun. Remember, look at me adoringly and gush from time to time. You're in the first blush of love with me. And I am quite glorious. Why, I might even have taken your virginity last night. You doubtless think I'm a god!'

# Chapter Twenty-six

## Dead drop

There are times when it is only the knowledge that you are an agent of the Crown that prevents you from attempting to murder your partner. The rest of the morning was embarrassing enough that I wanted to claw my own skin off. Fitzroy smugly intimated to the other men that I was his latest conquest. He treated me in turns with affection, mild annoyance that I was following him around, and contempt for my adoration of him. I played the part he had cast me in. I hated every single minute, and I was already thinking of ways I could pay him back. These included watering down his best brandy the next time I was at his flat. That, I determined, would be only the beginning. I knew Jack loved chewing leather, and I knew Fitzroy had some favourite, and extremely expensive, handmade shoes. I had every intention of making these an early Christmas present to the dog.

It was petty of me. I knew it. I also knew why Fitzroy was acting the way he did. Where we parted company in ideals was that I felt a moral imperative to help the police solve the murder. I had various bits and pieces of information I wanted to share. I doubted Rory would listen to me, but this new Inspector might be more open. If I could help bring a murderer to justice then I would do so, Fitzroy or no Fitzroy. I would have to work out how to do so without endangering our mission. I did agree with Fitzroy, that must come first.

Yves was working himself into a terrible state. Throwing his arms about and saying loudly how everything was, 'Ruined!

Ruined! Ruined!' He made such a nuisance of himself that we were all moved back to the auditorium. The box office was set up for interviews.

'It is monstrous that we are left waiting around,' said Henri to Fitzroy. 'They have even interviewed the utility staff before us!'

Fitzroy raised an eyebrow. 'You mean the backstage people, cleaners and the like?'

Henri nodded. 'For some reason they must feel they are in the clear. It is us they focus on.'

'Perhaps they want to spend more time with the people who knew her best?' I suggested.

Henri looked down at me, and his face softened. 'It will at least be a great thing for you, *ma petite*. You will inherit Rosa's role.'

My jaw slackened. 'No, I couldn't,' I said, and I meant not only would I be unavailable for numerous reasons, but I had no ambition to star in a stage show for even a short period.

Henri placed a hand on my shoulder. Fitzroy took the opportunity to slope off. 'You will be wonderful. You showed your true acting ability yesterday. You will be a star. You are a star.' I couldn't help glancing towards Fitzroy. Henri nodded. 'I understand. He is dazzling to one so young. But he is nothing. A passing fancy. You will see that there are better men in this world. Men who would care for you much better.' He didn't then, as I feared, grab my hand and kiss it, but merely nodded and moved off to speak with Reggie, who was moping over the piano. On the way he paused and tapped Yves. The director was half sitting, half lying in one of the red plush seats. The tap seemed gentle enough, but Yves shot up out of his dramatic pose into a squiggle of ungainly arms and legs. Henri bent down to say something. Yves looked over at me, and nodded. Henri moved on to Reggie. Yves struggled out. of his seat and came over to me.

'You will, of course, take over Rosa's part,' he said. 'I think you. will do very well.' Then he turned his back and walked off before I could say a word. The matter as far as the cast were concerned was settled. With the exception of Reggie, they all seemed to have put Rosa behind them. She was gone and the play must go on. It was rather chilling.

We were told that an inspector would arrive after luncheon, and when fully briefed would interview us all again.

Cantori made a show of having to take me to luncheon. 'Can't ignore the girl, can I?' he said to Braun. 'Maybe we can catch up later, old man. Have another snifter. I rather think I'm going to need one by the end of this day.' He kept his English near perfect, but the Italian accent was back.

To my surprise Braun nodded. He ignored me by simply looking over my head. 'We can go, can't we, Mr Policeman?' said Fitzroy. 'I mean, unless the police force is intending to bring us in luncheon, we need sustenance. And I must warn you we are used to a certain standard. A lot better than that your police canteen might rustle up.'

Rory, to his credit, did not react as if in the slightest bit intimidated by Cantori's rather brash man-of-the-world character. Instead he said, 'You may all go and find your own lunch. However, a reminder that we have all your names and addresses. I expect you to be back here within the hour or we will come and find you. I can assure that making your own way back will be a much more favourable experience than our retrieving you.'

'Well, that was rude,' said Henri loudly. 'Is this the way the British generally treat their citizens?'

Reggie took his elbow. 'Come on, old man. Let's pop next door to the theatre bar. They will do us some decent nosh and we'll have a drink or two.'

Rory, overhearing them said, 'I'm afraid The Jester's Jug is closed and will remain so until at least the end of today.'

'It is intolerable!' cried Henri. Reggie shepherded him out the door making soothing noises. I was watching Yves, when I felt an arm around my waist and I was almost swung off my feet.

'C'mon Alice. I'll take you for a slap-up luncheon!'

Within moments we were outside and my feet had barely

touched the ground. Fitzroy paused, looking up and down the street.

'The troupe usually goes to the Masked Cat,' I said. 'It's not far.'

'I prefer not to get food poisoning today, Alice.' He hailed a cab. 'We'll go to the Savoy. I think Cantori would favour that over the Ritz. There's no accounting for taste.' He opened the cab door and ushered me in. 'Now, while I have you alone. The drop box is about ten minutes walk along the road perpendicular to the theatre. You'll see three elm trees on the corner. The remnant of something or other. Turn left there and you'll find yourself in an alleyway. On your right-hand side there's a brick slightly above my eyesight, approximately seven feet into the alley. Use your nail file and you'll see it will come out easily enough.'

'I don't have a nail file,' I said.

Fitzroy shook his head, and took a small rolled-up leather case from his inside pocket. He opened it to reveal a silver toothpick, a cocktail swizzler, a nail file, a beard comb, and several assorted lock picks. He passed me the nail file. 'Don't lose it. It's part of the set.' He put the kit back inside his jacket. 'Now, place the sketch inside with the request for information. You did write one, didn't you?'

I nodded.

'Put the brick back in, and as you leave the alley you'll see a bakery opposite. Go in and buy a loaf of rye bread, and ask them to keep it for Mr Baker to collect. Then leave and come back to the theatre in a roundabout way. I'll say that you had some female business to attend to, and that's why you're late back from luncheon.' He glanced at his pocket watch. 'If this chap keeps up the pace we should get there in time for two courses. What say you, appetiser and main course, or main course and a dessert? It's all so terribly rushed and not at all like good food should be enjoyed.'

'I'm not especially hungry.'

'It's going to be a long day. You need to eat. You used to have an appetite almost as good as mine. Are you unwell?'

For once this seemed to be said with genuine concern. 'I'm not at my best,' I admitted.

'A good meal will set you up. Anyway, I need your attention. It'll be a working meal, so I'll put it on expenses. No need to trouble yourself with the bill. There's something up with that troupe and I'm damned if I can work out what it is.'

He expounded on this over the meal at the Savoy. The maître d' of which took in his overblown cravat, rose pink today, and raised his eyebrows. Without blinking Fitzroy shifted one leg, edging his foot forward to reveal his shoe.

'Ah, this way, sir,' said the maître d', and gave us a particularly fine table.

'Shoes,' said Fitzroy, sitting down. 'By such things are a gentleman judged. Far too many people have access to decent tailors today.' He nodded at the waiter, who flipped a napkin out over his lap. 'Bring us the steaks au fou de la reine. The lady's medium rare and mine rare but not blue. The usual vegetables, and a good burgundy. Nothing too heavy. A 1905 would suit.'

With a deep bow the man departed. Fitzroy continued, 'The thing is, Braun is in some ways extremely reserved, but once he has enough brandy he starts singing. But he sang English songs. It's the kind of thing I would do if I was in Germany, but in German obviously.'

'You mean you think he's a spy?'

'He smells like one,' said Fitzroy, downing a glass of soft red burgundy. The waiter had delivered it so carefully that it had appeared on the table as if by magic. 'And then there's Aggie. Appears to be dull and dutiful, but she's always where the interesting conversations are, and she only makes mistakes after she's done something thoughtful.'

'You think she's a spy as well?'

'No, that would be ridiculous. Reggie is frightened. Probably because he killed Rosa, but I have the feeling it's not as straightforward as that. And Yves is too flamboyant to be real. Henri's French is off, too, but that could be because he's Belgian.'

'I thought you said all this was none of our concern?' I asked.

'It's not, which is why I wanted to talk to you about it. I agree your instincts are spot on and this is a very odd lot. I thought if we had a chat . . .'

'I'd get it out of my system?'

Fitzroy nodded. 'And we are having a very fine luncheon, aren't we?'

'Yes, but it's making me very sleepy.'

'Nonsense. You haven't even had any wine. What is the matter with you? You're not yourself.'

'So you keep saying, but last time I checked in the mirror the same face looked back. Do you honestly think that seeing the cause of justice done is not part of our duty?'

'It's why we have a police force, Alice. They will discover all on their own that Rosa had rows at her lodgings – I know you well enough to know you're itching to tell this police inspector that. Please don't. Don't get involved. I got a lot out of Braun, and you got that sketch. Most of what I learnt was harmless enough. I suspect the signet ring will be simply a family crest, but knowing which family is important.'

'You mean for or against the Kaiser?'

'No one in Germany is officially against the Kaiser,' said Fitzroy with a slight smile. 'But some are more for him than others.'

'So what do I do?'

'Apart from not getting into trouble? See if you can find out how the others see Braun. I read your initial thoughts, but see if you can get a little deeper under their skin. Henri seems fond of you, and now you're a fallen woman, he'll doubtless think he's in with a chance.'

'You have a very low opinion of your fellow man.'

'You think it unjustified?' said Fitzroy, refilling his glass. 'Because I don't. Given the choice between spending time in a man's company and spending it with my dog . . .'

'You'd choose Jack, I know. Aren't you even curious where

Rosa was murdered? If it's at the lodgings I'm not sure I want to go back.'

Fitzroy frowned. 'Again, most unlike you, but I shouldn't worry. I thought it was pretty clear she had been found dead in the Jester's Jug. Let's hope it wasn't in the cellar. That would be so cold it would mess all the timings up.'

# Chapter Twenty-seven

## Inspector Morris gets in the way

I was hastening in to the lobby after successfully completing the dead drop without issue, when I heard the man standing at the far end, wearing a cheap but well-pressed suit, say clearly, 'So you see, Miss de la Croix being found in the cellar means we have an unusually wide range of times that we must question you on. I'm afraid you will be here the rest of the afternoon. We will be with you as soon as is possible. Sterling work by Sgt McLeod has ensured I have the basics down. I suggest you convene in the auditorium, and that we allow Miss Aggie to bring you all refreshments. Once you have been interviewed, you are free to leave, but we would ask you to not return to the auditorium, but rather make your own way home. I trust this is all clear. And again, I offer my condolences for your loss. I understand that as well as being a fine actress, and a loss to the theatrical world, Rosa de la Croix was also your friend.'

I slipped into the small crowd next to Fitzroy. 'All good?' he asked quietly.

'All good,' I responded.

The group was now breaking up to head to the auditorium. Fitzroy slipped my arm through his. 'This Inspector gives a pretty speech. I imagine we will be here for a long time. Hopefully that will mean the others will be unsettled.'

'More unsettled than potentially having a murderer in the their midst?'

'Oh, they won't believe any one of them is guilty. I can tell that by looking at them. If you're interviewed before me, get a cab to the flat and wait for me.'

'I'm almost out of money,' I said. 'I don't have enough.'

'I'll pass you some as we sit down. Really, Morley's lot didn't think anything through properly.' He opened one of the doors to the auditorium for me, and I went through.

We all congregated near the middle on either side of the central aisle. Fitzroy slipped me both notes and coins as we sat down. Fortunately, I managed to keep them in my hand. He'd passed me the contents of his pocket, which knowing him would be more than enough. He'd also paid for luncheon. I was more aware than most that the spy was comfortably situated financially, but for all our squabbles he took care never to make me feel small about accepting anything from him. He always said he'd claim it back on expenses, but now I was a full agent myself I knew the reality was that Department expenses were exceedingly small. They certainly didn't stretch to a midday meal at the Savoy.

'Away with the fairies?' asked Henri. He was sitting in the row in front, but had turned himself to face me.

I started slightly. Fitzroy had turned in his seat and was chatting, or rather flirting, with Aggie, who was taking orders for tea.

'Thinking,' I said. 'It's so sad that Rosa is gone. All that beauty and talent.'

Henri shrugged. '*Tant pis!* We all get a lifetime. No more. No less. She was a girl made for a bad end. You know that as well as I.' He glanced over towards Reggie, who was sitting a few seats along, staring into the distance. 'He thinks his heart is breaking, but it will mend. Sooner than he thinks. No doubt he will learn more about her other suitors as the day wears on. More than one secret will be exposed, I expect.' He smiled kindly at me. 'What of you, *ma petite*? What secrets do you hide?'

'I suppose we all have some secrets,' I said. 'But don't you think that generally the things we think of as secret matter little to others? That's what I have found. People hang on so dearly to their mysteries, but seen by the light of day they are nothing but cobwebs.'

'How poetic, Miss Woodward,' said an unfamiliar voice.

I turned to see the Inspector. Closer to, I could see my first impression was correct. He was cheaply dressed, but with great care. But then, I spent time with Fitzroy, whose shoes, the ones I had earmarked for Jack, probably cost more than a month's salary for a Detective Inspector. Maybe two. Bertram, also, whatever other retrenchments he had to make, still had his suits made up in Savile Row.

'Do you have some experience at ferreting out secrets?' he continued. Fitzroy, without turning round, slyly pinched the top of my thigh through my skirt. Two pairs of shoes, I thought, two.

'No, not really, Inspector,' I said. 'There was a small fuss in the village where I grew up once. Someone sending nasty letters, but when it all came out none of the secrets people were trying to hide were that important.'

'A blackmailer? Rather rare. Where was this?'

I heard Fitzroy sigh under his breath.

'I don't exactly remember,' I said. 'It happened when I was very little, and we had moved on before my mother told me the story. It was a lesson about truthfulness.' I smiled up at the Inspector. He had gentle brown eyes, and a few locks of hair were curling under the brim of his hat, which he had chosen not to remove. I estimated he had to be around Fitzroy's age or slightly older. He had a square jaw that suggested tenacity, but the expression in his eyes was kind. A curious mixture for a police officer.

'Indeed,' he said. 'And did it work?'

'Excuse me?'

'Are you a truthful person?'

'I like to think so,' I said.

The Inspector offered me a hand. 'Then I suggest I start with you, Miss Woodward. It will be a refreshing change to interview a suspect who is completely open. You'd be surprised the things people don't like to admit, and it's often the little things that make all the difference to an investigation.'

'You mean the devil is in the details?' I said.

'Your words, not mine,' said the Inspector. He released my hand once I was out of the stalls. Fitzroy had had to rise to let me by, and he'd given me a fearsome look that I interpreted as an order to keep things simple.

I walked in silence with him to the box office. Once inside, he gestured to a seat in front of one of the desks and closed the door firmly behind us. Rory was sitting to one side, an open notebook on his lap and a pencil poised in his hand. His eyes flickered up and over me momentarily, but with no more than a look any man might pay a pretty woman. He gave no sign of recognition. This was certainly going to make things easier. I spent a moment re-arranging my skirt, so I was as neat as Miss Woodward liked to be. Then, once settled, I looked up at the Inspector, who was now sitting opposite, with a quiet and interested expression – or so I hoped.

'Does your boyfriend often pinch your leg?' said the Inspector.

Caught entirely off guard, I gave a half truth. 'No, but he is concerned I might pass on gossip and delay your investigation, and put the opening of the play in danger.'

'Are you a gossip then, Miss Woodward? Or may I call you Alice?'

'I'd rather you didn't,' answered my mother's daughter, before I had considered how the actress might react.

The Inspector nodded. 'In that case you may address me as Inspector Morris. This is Acting Sergeant McLeod. He will be taking notes. Do you require a chaperon present?'

'No, that won't be necessary, Inspector.'

'I see. You don't wish me to use your first name, but you are quite happy to sit with two strange men in a dark little office.'

'Firstly,' I said, 'you are officers of the law and it does not seem unreasonable that I should assume a certain level of behaviour from you. Secondly, this is a large office. Although I admit it is a little dim. Thirdly, and most importantly, I am well within screaming distance of the rest of the troupe and you left the door unlocked.'

'Screaming distance,' said the Inspector. 'I haven't heard that before. I rather like it. So, I can take it, Miss Woodward, that you are of above average intelligence and hopefully reasonably observant. What can you tell me?'

I looked at him blankly.

'What was Rosa like?' he said.

'Quite horrible,' I said. 'Beautiful and talented, but a most self-obsessed girl. I imagine life had treated her unkindly, and that the only person she was prepared to trust was herself.'

Inspector Morris took off his hat and ran his fingers through his hair, which appeared to be slightly longer than regulations would usually allow. It also curled delightfully under his administrations.

'I'm glad you don't feel you must speak well of the dead,' he said.

'If you are to catch her killer, then you need to know the truth,' I said. 'Platitudes will not find you a murderer.'

'You speak almost as if you know how a murder investigation must be run. Have you been involved in one before, Miss Woodward?'

'No, of course not,' I lied. 'But I have read stories. Such as the ones by Mr Conan Doyle.'

The Inspector closed his eyes in pain. 'I see. Well, please confine your answers to the basic facts. You are Miss de la Croix's understudy?'

'Yes.'

'So you will now take her role as lead in the play?'

'I have been asked to,' I said.

'Which gives you a strong motive for murder, does it not?'

I thought of bouncing out of my chair with indignation, but decided I was too tired to keep that act up. I decided to go with candour. 'For some it might,' I said. 'But not I. As I said, I had no liking for Rosa, but taking a life is a far more serious matter than dislike or even detestation. Besides, if you wish a plainer answer, I was most lucky to get the role as understudy. I have never been on the London stage, and this is my opportunity to learn. I do not believe I am good enough to take the star role. It is too early in my career.'

'But it is yours now, isn't it?'

'It has been offered to me, certainly,' I said. 'But I hope when the initial shock has worn off that the director may be prevailed upon to find another actress. A more experienced one. I have no wish to make a fool of myself in front of a London audience.'

The Inspector put his hands together and interlaced his fingers. He leant forward slightly. 'I understand you are a friend of Mr Cutler, the stage hand?'

'Friend is putting it a little strongly,' I said. 'He was asked to show me round when I first arrived. He showed me where I could make tea.'

'Most important,' said the Inspector. 'He told us that he is most impressed by your acting ability.'

'How kind,' I said, wondering what on earth had prompted Ivor to say that. 'But he isn't exactly a theatre critic.'

'Oh, I don't know,' said the Inspector. 'A stage hand sees at first hand the actors and actresses. Perhaps even knows their secrets. He was the one to find the body.'

'Did he raise the alarm?' I asked.

The Inspector frowned but nodded.

'In which case he would have to be a most reckless individual to be involved in the murder with me, as you seem to be suggesting.'

'What was the name of the theatre where you previously played?'

'The Sunlit Fields.'

'Acting Sergeant, put a telephone call through to the theatre as soon as we finish the interview and—'

'Check I was ever there?' I finished for him, sounding affronted.

'You understand we have to check everything. Would it surprise you to know that some time before her death Miss de la Croix had been engaged in fornication?'

'It surprises me that you would tell me that,' I said bluntly, 'but no, not really. She was known to have a number of suitors. How intimate she was with any or all of them was none of my concern.'

'Not the type to be saving herself for marriage?'

'As I said, Inspector, she was not a happy girl. She used her beauty and talent to get on in the world. In many ways one cannot blame her.'

Rory cleared his throat. I looked over and caught a flicker of anger in his eyes.

'My Acting Sergeant does not approve of that way of living.'

'I don't blame him,' I said. 'Neither do I.'

'And yet, I have it from more than one member of the cast that you are now embroiled with Mr Cantori?'

I felt myself blush. 'I appreciate you must ask this question, but I resent your implication that I am no better than Rosa. To my knowledge Rosa was involved with the director Reggie Pierce as well as, by rumour at least, three other men.'

'Indeed. You can vouch for these affairs as being true?'

'I believe I said by rumour,' I glanced at McLeod. 'Did I not, Acting Sergeant?'

Rory nodded and made an odd sort of noise, which I took as a gruff affirmative. 'I can vouch for her being involved with Reggie and with one other man. I was unfortunate enough to encounter her during two apparently amorous encounters.'

'These were?'

'In the theatre, and by the stage door,' I said. 'We also shared a landlady, Beryl Belairs, whose lodgings are on Biblicott Lane. She has complained to me about the noise from Rosa's flat, and asked me to speak to her about it. I did not get the chance. I believe Miss Belairs may be able to provide you with further information about who Rosa's visitors were and how frequently they visited.'

'That is very helpful,' said the Inspector. 'It also throws suspicion away from you.'

'I do not care to throw suspicion in anyone's direction,' I said tartly. 'I have no idea who harmed Rosa and I do not wish to accuse an innocent person.'

'Even if it saves your own neck?'

'If you do your job properly my neck will not need saving,' I snapped. 'I had nothing to do with Rosa's death.'

'Where were you when she was killed?'

'I have no idea,' I said.

'You mean you do not recall what you did yesterday?'

'No,' I said coldly. 'I mean I have no idea when Rosa was killed. I do not appreciate these obvious little traps, Inspector.'

'Most people don't notice them,' said the Inspector mildly.

'Then they must be fools,' I said.

'Generally, they merely ask, "what time was that?" If they are innocent, of course. You, on the other hand, seem to have more than a cursory understanding of police interview techniques. Have you been interviewed by the police before, or even several times before, Miss Woodward?'

'No, I have not. When did Rosa die?'

'We believe around eight p.m. last night.'

'Well, then I was with Mr Cantori, as you well know.'

The Inspector shook his head. 'Mr Cantori was somewhat imprecise in his timings. He suggested that he drank with Mr Marron until eight p.m. and also picked you up at eight p.m. Obviously, unless he is capable of being in two places at once this is not possible.'

I mentally damned Fitzroy's arrogance. 'He was certainly meant to collect me at eight p.m.,' I said. 'I was not watching the clock.'

'Awaiting your first assignation with the man and not watching the clock?' said the Inspector. 'Hardly the romantic type then, Miss Woodward.'

'I was praying,' I said. 'I was unsure if I was doing the right thing.'

The Inspector stood up. 'Oh, I think your parents taught you right from wrong, Miss Woodward,' he said. 'That will be all for now. Please do not leave the city. If I wish to contact you at which address will I find you?'

'I really have no idea,' I said. 'You may have to try both. I will, however, be at the theatre tomorrow to convince the director to find another leading lady.'

'Very well. You may go.'

# Chapter Twenty-eight

## I horrify Fitzroy almost beyond reason

'It sounds as if you made a right mess of that,' said Fitzroy, stroking Jack's ear as he lounged in his chair by the fire. 'A complete and utter mess.'

'Oh, please,' I said. 'Tell me what you really think! I suppose you did much better.'

Fitzroy released the dog, who snuggled up to his leg and looked up adoringly at him. 'Could I have done much worse?' he asked.

To my horror I burst into tears.

'Good Lord,' said Fitzroy leaping out of his seat to offer me his handkerchief. 'What is the matter with you?'

'I know I didn't do well,' I sobbed. 'I lost control of the conversation completely. Not only were the man's questions ruthless – he saw you pinch my leg, by the way, he's acute – but I had Rory sitting there disapproving silently all the time. It was horrible.'

'For heaven's sake, Euphemia, why should you care what McLeod thinks? You're not still carrying a torch for him, are you?'

'I'm married to Bertram,' I said, and found myself convulsed with weeping. I hid my face in the cloth, quite unable to say anything between sobs.

I heard the clink of a decanter being unstoppered, and a gentle nudge at my side proved to be a glass of brandy. I took a deep breath and looked up. Fitzroy nudged me again with the glass.

'Is this your answer to everything?' I said.

Fitzroy shook his head, 'Not usually, but I can't think what else to do, Euphemia. Bertram is safe. He has the best doctors. You wanted to continue on this mission, but you are clearly out of sorts and very emotional. Over-emotional.'

He put all the stress of a gentleman rather rattled at the situation he found himself in on the last two words. 'What can I do? If you tell me how to help you I'll do it at once. I'm not used to seeing you weeping, and I don't like it one bit. It makes me sad and uncomfortable – and it upsets Jack. Look at the way the poor dog is holding his ears.'

Hearing his name, Jack crawled forward on his belly towards me. He stuck his nose under my skirt and offered my ankle a single lick, before coming out and looking up at me. His expression was so comical that I had to smile.

'Well done, Jack,' said Fitzroy. He pulled his chair nearer to mine. 'You know you can tell me anything, don't you, Alice? If someone is distressing you, give me a name and I'll have the rotter dealt with. No questions asked. It isn't Rory, is it?' He added, a hopeful note in his voice, 'I'd quite like to give him a thrashing.'

'It's not him,' I said. 'Besides, you're not up to that.'

'Rubbish,' said Fitzroy. 'Both of my legs work perfectly well. That has to count for something.'

'You are an awful man,' I said.

Fitzroy grinned at me. 'Haven't I been telling you that for years?'

'I'm sorry,' I said. 'I'm worn out with everything that's been happening. I was foolish to take this mission on so soon after the last. I'm run down. If there was a way for me to exit gracefully I would.'

'What, and prove old Morley's point?'

I sighed. 'I admit I have been trying to prove a point, but that was mostly that I could manage the mission solo. That, I clearly haven't done. He also wanted me to stay away from you to prove we weren't romantically involved, and here am I staying overnight at your flat again.'

'I could tell him that we continue to have doubts over Braun and get him to pull us from the scene. As agents of the Crown the police would have to let us go.'

I shook my head. Fitzroy gave an earth-rending sigh. 'Oh, very well, Alice. You win. We'll solve this bloody murder.'

'Why would you agree to that?'

Fitzroy sighed again. 'Firstly, it will make you happier, and that does matter to me. I don't want a partner who's a watering can. Secondly, if we push Rory in the right way we'll have the police out of our hair, and be able to finish this mission properly. If we're extremely lucky it will be Braun who killed her, and then the whole question about whether he is fit to defect is nicely dealt with. While he's in prison we can still get him to do work for us as well. That would be neat. I don't suppose there is any chance he's guilty?'

'I can't see why.'

'Starved of female company now his beloved Mary has been sent away?' suggested Fitzroy.

'So he strangles an actress? I don't see it.'

'Maybe she learnt he was German?'

'I think you're heading down the wrong avenue,' I said. 'I agree not to rule Braun out, but it isn't likely. We need to look at who might have wanted Rosa dead because of what she had done, or because of what they had done.'

'Or because of what her death means for them,' said Fitzroy. 'Morris had a good point. If you really were an actress you'd be singing in the streets now she's dead. You are suddenly the lead in a London play. That's the kind of thing a small-town actress would give almost anything for – or do almost anything.'

'Yes, I know,' I said. 'It's most inconvenient. I do hope whoever set up my . . . "legend" is it they're now calling it?'

Fitzroy nodded. 'Stupid label. It'll give younger spies a big head.'

I refrained from saying I'd never met a spy who didn't have an oversized ego and continued, 'I hope they have got me listed as working there or some such thing?'

'Oh, I expect Alice Woodward did,' said Fitzroy, getting up and fetching himself another brandy. 'I expect she's dead. Using the identities of dead people is an easy solution. You were never meant to get to the stage of – er – getting on stage, so I expect they hoped no one who knew her would notice.'

'But the people at the theatre will know she's dead! My legend will be over!'

Fitzroy shook his head. 'I don't know the details, but I expect she died abroad or some such thing. Anyway, it'll be covered.'

'Like they covered where Braun was living. I was all set to break into lodgings and I ended up in a suburb breaking into a family home.'

'I agree that was a mess – not yours, of course. I managed a word with him today. Apparently, he's staying with another mathematician he's been corresponding with. I passed that on up the line. If he does have some theory that will be useful to us, we might be able to fall back on this chap. If Braun fails to pass.'

'You wouldn't betray your country for love, would you?'

Fitzroy stopped in the middle of raising his glass to his lips. 'When I signed on to work for the Crown, I gave a commitment to my work above all else,' he said slowly. 'I've never been tested in the way you describe. I've had to do things that went strongly against the grain with me, but I haven't wavered. But I wouldn't say that I've ever been that challenged by my work. I don't generally let people get that close to me – or if I do, it's with the understanding that our affections are a transitory affair. I have lived my life in a way to consciously avoid the situation you describe.'

'Even Celeste?'

Fitzroy's eyebrows shot into his hairline. 'If you know about her, then you'll know there was never any possibility of our legally formalising our relationship. I remember her fondly, and wish her well, but yes, if I had to I would sacrifice her for the sake of our country. I'd be bloody upset about doing it, and if I could I'd take down those who put me in that position with painful finality. But at the end of the day, the country comes first.'

Fitzroy took a big slug of whisky. He sat back down near me. The lines around his lines deepened. I could see him trying not to frown. I realised he was wondering if I was about to ask him if he would put me above a mission. I suddenly wanted very much to ask him exactly that, but instead, I said. 'I'm trying to get into Braun's head. He's supposedly giving everything up for his love of Mary.'

Fitzroy visibly relaxed, the lines on his face vanished. 'It's a little different,' he said. 'The Kaiser, according to our sources, is seen as something of a warmonger by even his own people. The majority of the upper classes and maybe even middle classes of the German population have some connection to Britain. Through marriage. Through education. It rather seems as though the Kaiser's desire for war with Britain has surprised many of his subjects. Of course, the families most closely connected to him will stay loyal, as will many of his subjects. However, Braun is an academic. He is more likely to think about the bigger questions. He may even have an inkling of how many lives this war will cost. I wouldn't think of him as someone who set out to be a traitor, but rather someone whose weaker bonds of loyalty have been too tested by his sovereign's actions.'

'What if our Sover—'

'Don't be silly, Euphemia. The British royal family are above criticism. They always have the welfare of their subjects as their main concern. Besides which, our country, and everything we have built, is founded on the dual powers of Parliament and the Crown.'

I didn't push further. Fitzroy didn't actually say he believed in the divine right of British kings and queens, but it often seemed he came close to that. I rather suspected if his idols ever let him down his wrath would be impressive. Obviously, I said nothing of this to him.

'So, you're saying, Braun's desire to defect shouldn't prejudice me against him?'

'Sadly not,' said Fitzroy. 'As I said earlier, it would all be very neat if he was the killer, but frankly I don't think he has the imagination for it. I suspect this is more a crime passionelle.'

'Rosa was definitely involved with Reggie. I caught them embracing backstage. They seemed very, er, keen on each other.'

'My poor Alice, did they make you blush?'

'Yes,' I said. 'Unlike you I am not so familiar with seeking out others in such positions.'

'Touché.'

'Ivor Cutler told me she was also involved with Maurice Attenbury, Louis Frake, and Arnold Pleasant.'

Fitzroy gave a low whistle. 'All people of interest. I do hope Pleasant has nothing to do with this. He's the lynchpin of that department. His minister is next to useless. His loss through imprisonment would be catastrophic. It seems like you were right. It is our business to look into this. Is Cutler reliable?'

'I'd only recently engaged him as my asset, and then he was assigned to someone else. I haven't had the time to work with him. I offered him benefits to becoming an asset that were meaningful to him.'

'You mean you blackmailed him?'

'I got his mother decent care and got him out from under his debts in return for working for me. I'm not happy—'

'Yes, yes,' said Fitzroy. 'I'll get that sorted when we get back. He's yours and I'll get him returned. Morley doesn't understand the protocol.'

'I know Frake is a minor, but extremely rich lord, but what about the other man?'

'Attenbury? He's the Boot King. Makes most of the men's boots in Britain.'

'He must be very busy.'

Fitzroy wrinkled his nose at me. 'You know what I mean.'

I nodded, 'And in a time of war the army needs a lot of boots? I take it they will be coming from his factories?'

'Almost certainly. I'll telephone through the names to the night switchboard and get them to have some information for us on these chaps tomorrow. Anything pertinent. Any idea how she came into contact with them all? Did she work at an upper-class bordello or some such?'

'I hadn't thought of that,' I admitted. 'But from what Henri said they were all investors in the theatre. Angels, they call them. It would be worth finding out if they had invested in any other productions. Would we have information on that?'

'Yes,' said Fitzroy. 'Not because we have people watching theatres, but because we keep tabs on people of interest. You will become familiar with all these departments, Alice. You haven't been working as long as I have, or for that matter in the country of late. Plus with the war, it's all a bit trickier.'

'I'm glad to hear it,' I said. 'You always seem much more in the loop than I.'

'Mea culpa,' said Fitzroy. 'It's what happens when you have a notoriously solo operator as a trainer.'

'Why,' I said as a thought struck me, 'didn't we – or you – call for someone to come and get the sketch? Wouldn't that have been safer than leaving it in the drop box? I mean, those can always become compromised.'

'They can,' admitted Fitzroy. 'It was the quickest way.'

'No, it wasn't. The box wouldn't have been checked immediately.'

Fitzroy seemed to have been fascinated by Jack, and was stroking the dog's ears again. Jack whiffled in protest. He had been sleeping.

'Fitzroy,' I said. 'You're not meant to be using this as a base, are you?'

'I don't know what you mean,' said the spy. 'This is my home.'

'I mean, they put Cantori up in lodgings, didn't they, and you didn't fancy living in them. Honestly, when I think of the places you made me stay in France I can't see why you've suddenly become so fussy.'

Fitzroy looked at me with his head tilted, and out of the sides of his eyes, rather like a little boy who had been caught with his hand in the cookie jar and was wondering what excuse he could get away with.

'The truth , Eric,' I demanded.

'Oh, very well. It wasn't particularly pleasant, and when I had a flat nearby it seemed silly. I've sent Griffin around a few times. I think the landlord thinks *he's* Cantori, so it's all all right.'

'You are terrible.'

'But you love me anyway?'

'No, I don't.'

'You're just saying that because you are cross and tired. A good night's sleep and tomorrow you'll be transformed into an adoring acolyte again.'

I threw a cushion at him.

# Chapter Twenty-nine

## Setting things right over breakfast

Over breakfast Fitzroy quizzed me further. 'So, what else have you got? And did I say I would go for a drink with Braun tonight or last night? Never mind. I'll simply say I got engaged with your company. He'll know what I mean by that.'

I didn't rise to the bait, but cracked the top of my boiled egg with feeling. 'The whole production has been troubled almost from the start. Janice Hargreaves, the initial female lead, was killed under the hooves of a brewery horse outside the theatre. She tried to get out of the way of an omnibus and instead . . .'

'Earned herself a nastier death. Any suggestion she was pushed?'

'Cutler didn't know. He did say she was a nice girl and well liked. He also said that the traffic in the street is unpredictable and she wasn't the first fatal accident. But it did give Rosa her role.'

'Hmmm,' said Fitzroy. 'Obviously the police are working on the idea that the theatrical world works on dead men's or women's shoes.'

'Talking to Henri—'

'Henri de la Cloche?'

'He claims it is his real name. He says that parts are hard-won, and that anyone who gets any success will hold on tooth and nail till the end. He has a morbid dread of ending up in a home for old theatricals.'

'Sounds nasty.'

'But if Cutler has it right, then even before Janice's death, there were troubles. One director left, convinced his office, or whatever they have, was haunted. Other members of the cast moved on. The theatre cat unaccountably ate poison even though it had been around the stuff for years and never tried it before. And the finale, as it were, was a chunk of scenery falling onto the stage. Fortunately no one was hurt, but if there had been anyone up there at the time their chances wouldn't have been good.'

'Hmm,' said Fitzroy again. 'Griffin, we need more toast, more eggs, and a decent amount of bacon. We're not mice, you know,' he called out loudly. He sat back in his chair. 'Honestly, that man has these ridiculous notions about healthy eating. Would you believe it but he thinks bacon is bad for you? Poppycock. It will be some fad he's read about in a journal.'

'He's a doctor.'

'Struck off, as I am sure I told you. Griffin's story is his own. You're perfectly safe around him, and that's all you need to know. Although I have to watch my back occasionally.'

'I'm not surprised, if you're always this rude to him.'

Fitzroy shrugged 'I saved his life. By the way, I got some answers early this morning. The office knows I keep early hours rather than wasting my time sleeping.'

I didn't respond.

'Anyway, at present none of the men you mentioned have any particular black marks against them. You were right in thinking they do all share a love of the theatre. All of them have invested in productions before. None of them make a living from it. It appears to be a kind of passion project that yields first-night tickets, special seating, and invitations to cast parties, et cetera. Presumably it was at one of those parties during a different production that Rosa ran into them. I'm told the theatrical circles in London are rather small. Smaller still now many of the men are going off to join the war. Interestingly, they all invested after Rosa got the lead, not before. I assume they are either besotted or betting on her to bring the audience in. Or both,' said Fitzroy.

'That reminds me,' I said. 'Cutler made it sound as if all those problems stopped when Rosa got the lead. I need to check the timings with him. Everything seemed to revolve around her.'

'You mean she was causing them? Was she clever enough?'

'I don't think she was present when the first director left, at least. But I suppose the rumours could have given her ideas. I don't see why, though. Unless it was to get her the role, and ghosts and changing other members of the cast – how does that help her? As for being clever, she appears to have been capable of keeping four men on a string without them going for each other's throats,' I said. 'That must mean something.

Fitzroy shrugged. 'Her legs were rather nice. Not my type, but perhaps she is especially gifted between the sheets.'

'Could you take Reggie out for a drink too and see if he will reminisce? You're quite capable of getting that kind of information from other men.' I said. 'It's hardly the kind of thing any gentleman would mention to me.'

'And touché again,' said Fitzroy. 'You know, sometimes it feels to me as if we're married, but without any of the fun bits.'

I did feel myself redden at this. 'I'll try and check with Cutler about the timings of events.'

'The cat's death is interesting too,' said Fitzroy. 'I'd like to know more about that if you can get it.'

'Are you thinking the cat's death might have been a trial run for poisoning Rosa? She always said she didn't do it. I didn't say before but she hated cats. A lot of people thought she had killed it.'

'That's useful,' said Fitzroy.

'It means they all thought her capable of killing the animal.'

'Probably old and incontinent, and peed in her shoes,' said Fitzroy. 'Doesn't excuse killing the poor creature. But equally it could have been someone trying out how poison takes effect. How long. How much. That sort of thing. Not that we know yet how Rosa was killed. I hope it's poison. At least that would make some of the dots start to connect.'

He wiped his moustache with his napkin. 'Right, the plan is you're still head over heels about me. Your job is to pin Cutler down, and see if he knows anything else that's useful. You'd better have a sniff around the singing trio as well. I noticed they weren't grouped with the rest of us. If the police turn up again, you'll need to charm it out of Rory or Morris how she died. I don't mind which, just try not to lead either of them on too much. Rory's still carrying a torch for you, and Morris doesn't know you're married. In fact, considering you're known to be sleeping with me, he might find you fair game.'

'He's investigating the case!'

'He's still a man. I saw the way he looked at you.'

'He did what?'

'Oh, come on, Alice. You must have seen it. Half the men there are making eyes at you. Henri, Rory, Morris. In his debrief at HQ even Cutler spoke about how impressive you were.'

'Cutler's debrief?'

'Didn't I mention I got the intelligence on that this morning, too? He's been purloined by Ferris-Carter. He's running an investigation into the London black market. He's worried about some connections with the army. I couldn't get much more than that.'

I stood up, brushing crumbs off my lap. 'Do you know how unpleasant you're being of late?'

Fitzroy started as if I'd slapped him. 'I tried my very best to be supportive last night when you went all tearful. I can tell you women don't normally cry in my presence. It's not a situation I'm familiar with. For half a crown I would have bolted out the door to the nearest alcoholic beverage retailer. But no, I thought, Alice needs me. I must man up and I did. Wouldn't have done it for any other female.'

'Not even Celeste?'

'I wish you would stop mentioning her name,' said the spy testily. 'You never met her and I doubt you ever will. She's nothing to do with our work, and quite my own private affair. I don't care to have her name dragged up every five minutes. It's as if you're jealous of her.'

I gave a small snort. I tried not to, but I couldn't help it.

'Anyway, I'm being Cantori most of the time. And he's a cad. Bit of a theatrical genius, but a cad nonetheless. You know how hard it is to drop in and out of character. You could hardly have spent all those weeks acting as my younger brother if you were changing into a dress and waltzing around the room every night.'

'And what will you be doing?'

'You're on duty during the day. I'm on the town with Braun, Reggie, and even Henri tonight. I shall laze around rehearsals and try not to do very much. Between us we should root out the culprit in short order. Then all we have to do is point Rory in the right direction.'

'We don't have anything on the sketch yet?'

'Not yet. I'm taking that as a good sign. If it was a family well known for being close to the Kaiser I'm sure we would have heard by now. It's doubtless some old family line that's more or less dried up. His mother's or grandmother's or some such thing. Probably holds on to it to remind him of old Germany.'

'Old Germany?'

'The English don't hold the prerogative on self-indulgent, and fantastical, nostalgia.' He got up and shrugged himself into his coat. 'Have you never noticed that the golden age is always a decade or two behind the present? Your children might well consider your youth the golden age.'

Fitzroy realised what he had said and paled. He started forward and touched my forearm briefly. 'Euphemia, I didn't mean anything by that. I do think Bertram and you will find a way past your difficulties. You will make a wonderful mother – and I speak as someone who had one, albeit too briefly.' He gave me a hopeful smile.

'I know you didn't mean anything by it,' I said, reaching down to pat Jack, who was scrounging for food as usual. 'You may be unpleasant to me, but you're never cruel.'

I fed Jack my last piece of toast, rather than letting Fitzroy see how much his comment had unsettled me. Which made me even more sad, as I had really wanted that piece of toast.

'Well, that's something, I suppose,' said Fitzroy, unaware of my sacrifice. 'Let us away to the theatre, my dear, and be gay all day!'

# Chapter Thirty

## Everyone wants me to be a star

The atmosphere at the theatre was understandably subdued. Yves took a moment to stand on the stage and quieten everyone else down. 'I have to tell you,' he said, 'that there is to be an investors' meeting tomorrow. The theatre is keen for the play to go on. They will lose money if they go unexpectedly dark. We have also already sold a number of tickets for first night. Many of the boxes are taken. We will have to see if poor Rosa's death means people will return their tickets. The theatre manager has an idea of sending newspaper reporters to visit our rehearsals, and do some stories on the production. I would hope something along the lines of "tragedy brings country girl to stardom", but we have all had our run-ins with the press. We know that they want the most dramatic headlines to sell their papers. The death of Rosa, beautiful as she was, could lend itself to some very unpleasant headlines.'

Fitzroy spoke up. He was lazing in a seat, twirling his cane idly against the floor. 'My dear Yves de Yves, you seem to be saying a great deal, but failing to come to the point. What exactly is it you fear?'

Yves clasped his hands together. He didn't quite wring them, but he came close. I remembered how Dickens had told me the director used a false name and came a from base vaudeville background. I must remember to tell Fitzroy. As I looked around at the small group assembled, Reggie, Henri, Braun/Marron, Fitzroy/Cantori, the singing trio, Aggie amid her teacups, and Yves, I wondered if all companies were such an odd lot.

'Well,' said Yves, 'we must look past this tragedy, and soldier on. We need to have some scenes to display to the investors to ensure they will continue to back the play. Without their funds we will have to renege on our arrangement with the theatre. This would be financially damaging for Reggie and myself. Some others of you also have minor investments, but even without that I don't need to tell you how badly it would affect our reputations and future prospects.'

'It's not a tragedy,' said Reggie suddenly. 'Rosa was killed! Murdered!'

'Reggie, darling Reggie, we all feel for you so deeply,' said Yves. 'However, I had myself a long telephone conversation with the inspector this morning, and I managed to confirm that it is not absolutely murder. Apparently the circumstances are such that there is a suggestion of accidental or deliberate self-harm.'

'Nonsense!' said Reggie, rising to his feet. 'Rosa had everything to live for.' He turned to face the rest of us. 'One of you killed Rosa. You want to rehearse, Yves, and yet there is a murderer amongst us!' He gave a harsh laugh. 'Is that dramatic enough for everyone!'

'You should sit down, mon ami,' said Henri. 'I will find some brandy. You are understandably upset.'

'Upset! Upset! The love of my life lies dead. Foully murdered. I will not act as if nothing has happened. I will not betray her memory.' With that he stormed from the auditorium, slamming one of the doors behind him. As these door were designed to close softly and quietly, that was quite a feat.

'I say,' said Fitzroy. 'Has he ever thought of going on the stage? That was a fine display of passion.'

'If it requires the death of a cast member to inspire such passion I do not think he would find many companies willing to employ him,' said Henri, languidly.

Braun stood up, looked awkward and sat down again. 'I'll go after him,' said Aggie. 'You don't need me, and what he needs is a nice cup of tea, whether he knows it or not.' She spoke with surprising confidence for someone who had been more a shadow than a person amongst us. We all watched her go in silence.

Yves sat down on the stage, drooping like a maiden aunt. 'No music,' he said, each word dropping like a stone.

Fitzroy stood up and stretched in a most ungentlemanly manner. 'Oh, don't worry about that. I can pick out a tune, and Alice here knows how to play a bit. We can manage enough between us to keep going until Reggie gets his gumption back!' He made his way to the piano and began flicking through the score. 'Where do you want to start, Yves?'

Yves remained where he was, a puddle of dejection.

'Buck up, old man,' said Fitzroy. 'It's awful about Rosa, but the show must go on, what?'

These words seemed to bring Yves to his senses, and within moments. He had the trio and Braun singing one of their big songs. Fitzroy tinkled away at the piano. No one would have said he was a wonderful pianist, but he was good enough to pick out the tune for the others to follow.

Henri came to sit beside me. 'Maybe I should rethink my opinion of Cantori,' he said.

'I wouldn't go that far,' I said.

'The shine of love already fading?' said Henri.

Watching Fitzroy and thinking about how many faults he displayed in his attempt at the ivories and how much my mother would have scolded him, I'd quite forgotten I was meant to be in love.

'He does like being the centre of attention,' I said.

'Do not we all?' said Henri. 'I would not fear, *ma petite.* You will greatly outshine him in the play. He is the kind of man who makes a great show of himself for his company, but in front of masses he fades into oblivion. A small light against a great void. Whereas you, *mon choux*, will glow like a shooting star.'

'You seem very sure of me,' I said.

'I am,' said Henri fervently. 'As I am sure that you will leave behind Cantori and move on to a man much more worthy of you. A man who understands your true worth.'

This was getting uncomfortably close to a declaration for me. 'Have you learnt how Rosa died?' I asked.

Henri shook his head. 'The utility staff are being very closed-mouthed about it. I believe the stagehand Cutler found her, but he is saying nothing.'

I made a moue. 'How very inconsiderate of him,' I said.

'Do you care so much about her?' asked Henri.

'I would feel safer if I knew it was an accident that had killed her. There have been too many instances of bad luck around this production for me to feel safe.'

Henri sucked on his teeth. 'It is true there have been troubles, but that was at the beginning. Before we had our investors. As long as they are happy then we are all happy. It will all be good.'

'So you don't think there is a murderer in our midst.'

'I do not think there is anyone here who would harm you, *ma petite*. It is upon your pretty shoulders that all our careers must rest.'

'Goodness,' I said. 'I wish you wouldn't put it like that. It makes me feel sick.'

'All the best actresses have stage fright,' said Henri. 'They have too much emotion in them. It spills out when they are on stage like moonbeams. Rosa, she could keep herself under control. She could fake a good temper tantrum, but on the stage, she was like Cantori, no brighter than the rest. Although he is a trouper, I will give him that. He's quite buoyed Yves up. Perhaps I will go drinking with him one night. It will give you a rest if nothing else!'

I smiled, unable to think of anything else to say. I excused myself on the grounds of a call of nature, and went off to find Cutler. If he really had found they body then it was a stroke of luck for me.

I found him beyond the rear of the stage, in the more ramshackle areas of the theatre that served as workshops. He was carefully painting daisies on to a low piece of setting, meant to conjure up an image of a summer lawn.

'Bleeding 'ell,' he said when I came up to say hello. 'Don't do that to a body.'

'You seem on edge,' I said.

'You'd be bleedin' on edge if you'd found a dead body yesterday.'

I found a rather paint-splattered, but dry, stool and drew it over to sit on. 'I'm not sure I would be,' I said. 'It's happened to me more than once.'

'Of course it bleedin' has!' said Cutler. 'Well, it hasn't happened to me before. It gave me a right turn, it did. Specially seeing how what I was doing.'

'Which was?'

'I was opening the back of the public bar for a few gents to come and get a couple of kegs quiet like. Oh, don't worry, I've cleared it with my glover.'

'Do you mean handler?'

'That's the fellow. Snooty toff with a beet-red face and blond moustache. By the looks of him had terrible acne when he was a lad.'

'Sounds a most attractive gentleman,' I said.

'Oh, he's all right, once you get used to the fact he can't help speaking with pebbles in his mouth. Problem is I think he's a bit new on the job, unlike you. I didn't know what to say to the police. I didn't want to head straight to jail or cop to a job I wasn't really doing like. In the end I told 'em everything.'

'About me as well?'

'Nah, I'm not stupid. You're not part of my operation, are you? I have to say that's all a bit much seeing 'ow it was you I agreed to work for. You seem much more on the ball than that Ferris-Carter.'

'You agreed to work for the Crown,' I said. Although I felt a degree of sympathy. He should have been left with a contact and instructions in case of – well, not murder, that was unforeseeable, but Ferris-Carter must always have known there was a chance he might get caught by the police while infiltrating the black market.

However, I knew better than to side with an asset against another agent no matter how incompetent he appeared.

'Yeah, well, I didn't have no back-up like. So I told the cops everything. Again, not about you, but about how I was undercover. Laughed in my face, they did. But then this sergeant comes along, and says how I might be telling the truth. Next minute, they're all listening to him, and I'm in the middle of a fracas about how me handler shouldn't have been working on police business without telling them. I throw my hands up and say how I knows nothing about all that.' He took a deep breath. 'Anyway, someone somewhere vouched for me, which I suppose was kind of handy. Otherwise they might have been thinking that as I found her, I might have killed her. I had a few marks on me character – F-C had put them there to make me seem believable to the racketeers. But it could 'ave really sunk me.'

'So you're in the clear?' I said.

'I think so,' said Cutler. 'I'm keepin' my head down and stayin' out of everyone's way. I don't want to answer no questions from no one.'

'That's a pity,' I said. 'That's exactly why I'm here.'

'Oh well, you, miss. That's different. Always happy to talk to you. Me mum's getting her medicine regular now, and I don't have that other lot on my back. Always happy to help you out. What can I do?'

'I need to know how Rosa was murdered,' I said.

'You don't know?'

'I'm undercover too,' I said, 'so my sources of information are not exactly accessible. At least not without me potentially damaging my cover.'

'Right you are, miss. I keep forgetting that it's not like a police station or sumfink. There's actually quite a lot of you, aren't there?'

I nodded. I had no idea how many agents the Crown employed. Fitzroy had a habit of suddenly mentioning this or that person who I'd never heard of before. Working with him often felt like being out on the limb of a tree. He remained close enough to the tree to be in contact, but being beyond him, my understanding was greatly limited. Not that I intended to share any of this with Cutler.

'Right, well, I came down, about midnight, to open up the back doors. The others were coming around one a.m. It was the first thing I was doing for them, so I wanted to make sure everything was well in order.

'Anyways, I goes down to the cellar, to fetch up the kegs, and what should I see but someone lyin' on the floor. Me heart turns over. I think it's one of the gang got in to do me over, or maybe, I thinks, it's a tramp or some other lowlife hiding out. It were dark. I only had a little lantern. I didn't want anyone spotting lights on. So I creeps over to have a peek. I'm thinking he'll notice me when I start moving the kegs so I'd better get the jump on him – only it's not a fella, it's a bleedin' woman. So I says, "Miss, miss, you can't sleep here." But she doesn't move, like, and I can't think how she got down 'ere. I know I was being a bit slow, but it never occurred to me she'd be dead. Not until I shone the lantern in her face – then I screamed like a maiden aunt in a brothel I did. Excuse me language. But Gawd it didn't half give me a turn. I had to sit down to get me breath. I mean, soon as I saw her face I were pretty sure it was all over for her, but you never can tell. It's not like I'm a medically trained person or nothing, but I'd been around the hospital long enough to know that people can look dead when they're not. So I set my lantern down near her head and felt for a pulse. She were as cold as ice. No pulse. Not a flicker. I did the old trick of pinching the top of her nose real hard. Still nothing. Then I gave her a quick slap. Nothing. By that point I were fairly certain she were dead.'

'Do you know how she died?'

'There was this white stuff dried all around her mouth, but there were marks on her neck too. I think she were both strangled and given the same stuff as did for Gus. Whoever did her in wanted to be sure she were completely dead.'

'Not only a little dead, you mean?' I said.

'It's not funny, miss. I saw enough of death by violence in the military hospital, but to find that young and beautiful girl done in – what a waste. Not that she were a nice person, mind. Bit of a cow really. But she was awfully pretty. Not when I found her, though. Looked like a scrag end the cat had dragged in. Must have been quite the tussle. Least she still had her clothes on, so there hadn't been any funny stuff. That were a mercy for the poor cow.'

# Chapter Thirty-one

## I meet the ghost and horrify Fitzroy again

After he'd told me his story I suggested we went to the tiny kitchen to get some tea. 'I'd rather stay here, miss,' he said. 'I don't want to run into anyone. Wouldn't say no to a cuppa, though?'

I took pity on him and said I'd fetch him one.

I hadn't visited the workshops often and on the way back I took a wrong turn in the maze of passageways that had built up over the years. Now, I am not the kind of person to get frightened by strange noises. Even before my career in finding dead bodies began I had lived in my father's vicarage in a rural setting. Death was part of life then. I frequently saw the dead, laid out peacefully, awaiting interment, and I never came across any unfriendly ghosts. I need to make it clear that the dead do not frighten me. Even having to take part in seances at others' insistence has never bothered me, except that I feel disturbing someone's eternal slumber is very rude.

So when the wailing began I was surprised at my reaction. I was in a small corridor with a few doors right and left, leading to offices or possibly dressing rooms. The area was not well cared for, but that is not unusual backstage. Theatres, I had learnt were charlatans at heart. All painted and glitzy at the front, but areas behind the scenes were the very last to ever have money spent on them. After all, they were only for the actors.

Old posters had been stuck up on the walls, some with scrawled signatures. None of them were in good order, all peeling or torn, but clearly once some of the theatre's proudest moments. The ceiling was low here and painted black. I got the impression it was false, perhaps installed to help preserve the heat or to prevent sound from echoing back here. Certainly it felt oppressive. I was midway along this passage, hoping because there were rooms, it would lead to a concourse or even an outside door, and I would be able to re-orientate myself, when the wailing began.

It started as a low moan, so low I thought at first my mind was playing tricks on me. Then there came a strange drub-drub-drub sound that grew faster and faster as the low moan grew progressively louder. It reached a crescendo, a howl that had me with my hands over my ears. Then came what I can only describe as a clap of thunder. At this point I dropped to my knees. I am not frightened of thunder in the usual way of things, but then it does not normally come from inside a building. I was convinced that the noise emanated from the rooms around me. The sound was funnelling into the odd corridor, which made it louder and nearer, but it was not outside the building, of that I was sure.

My only other thought was that the sound of a shot being fired can sound like thunder when it happens at close range. So I dropped to the ground, throwing myself to one side and scrabbling for the handle of the nearest door. It was locked.

Of course it was.

Silence. Silence now came as loud as the noise before. I sat with my back against the locked door, waiting. Nothing. Then, as I put my left hand down to push myself up, the moaning began again. Now that I knew what was coming. I curled myself into a ball and put my hands over my ears. All rational thought had fled, and all that remained in my head was an overpowering primal fear. Again that final crash, and then silence. I should get up and run out of there, I knew it, but I found I couldn't move.

'What on earth are you doing down there?' said Fitzroy's voice.

I looked up to see him standing above me. I knew he could move quietly, but it still startled me. He must have seen something in my face, because pulling up the legs of his trousers slightly, he squatted down beside me. 'What's wrong?' he asked in a gentler tone.

Words flooded through my mind, but I couldn't seem to form a coherent response. Then the noise began again, and I covered my head with my arms. I felt Fitzroy's hand on my shoulder. 'It's fine, Alice. It's only noise.'

His voice was gentler still. I recognised it as the tone he used with Jack. I lifted my head, and spoke in his ear. 'I'm behaving like a frightened animal, aren't I? Rather than a rational being.'

He nodded. 'It is admittedly an unpleasant sound.' As before the sounds ended with a crash. For a moment he tightened his hand on my shoulder.

'I thought it was a shot first time I heard it,' I said.

Fitzroy stood up. He offered me a hand and I took it. The low moan was beginning once more. He moved from door to door listening. He stopped at the third door he tried. Attempting to open it, and finding it shut, he kicked the door in. He stood in the doorway for a moment, and then smiled. He reached out his hand and pulled me into the room with him.

In front of us was the most bizarre mechanism. There were two windows opposite. From the upper panes I could see these had been whitewashed. In front of the lower half of one window was a series of wooden boards of various thicknesses, and hanging above that connected by string and chain was suspended a thin sheet of metal. The whole structure was vibrating faster and faster. My head rang like a bell with the clamour it was making.

Fitzroy let go of my hand, went over, and looked behind the boards. Then he took hold of one of them and pulled hard, bracing himself with a foot against the wall. There was the sound of small nails popping and it came away in his hands. He staggered back slightly, but quickly regained his balance. He put the board behind by the window. The noise and movement stopped at once.

'Some little horror has taken out one of the panes back here with a catapult or a stone,' said Fitzroy.

'You mean one of the cast?'

Fitzroy laughed, and suddenly I felt a lot less tense. 'I meant a street urchin, but I can see how you would make that mistake. Do you know what this is?'

I shook my head.

'It's for creating the sound effect for a storm backstage. Modified, I admit. Did you not realise the sound had a relationship with the draughts blowing through the corridor?'

I shook my head again.

'Did you not think that there must be windows in these rooms as there is no other light in the corridor? If these had been windowless rooms you would have been wandering around in pitch black.'

'I've been rather stupid,' I said.

Fitzroy came over frowning. 'I wish you would tell me what's wrong,' he said. I didn't respond. 'But if you won't, allow me to remark you are acting far outside character. I am concerned your apparent lack of rational thought may lead you to unwittingly put yourself in danger. I think it's best if I tell Morley you're unwell and have you removed from the mission. Go back to my flat and Griffin will look after you.'

'But the play? The mission?'

'Alice, you're in no fit state to deal with either.'

'I'm sorry,' I said. 'I'm really sorry, Eric.'

Fitzroy put a hand on each of my shoulders. I couldn't meet his gaze. 'I only wish you trusted me enough to tell me what was wrong,' he said, sounding sad rather than angry. 'Please, Alice.'

I shook my head.

'At least tell me it's nothing to do with Braun?'

'It isn't.'

'Or Rosa?'

'No,' I said slowly. I looked directly into his eyes. 'I know what this is!'

He smiled slightly. 'I told you, it's . . .'

'It's a ghost,' I said. I saw him frown and continued, 'No, I'm not mad. I'm sure I told you a previous director left because he thought the place was haunted and couldn't deal with it.'

'You think it was this?'

'Yes,' I said. 'I haven't had a chance to ask Cutler yet, but I got the impression this happened before Janice Hargreaves' death. I mean, theatre folk are a superstitious lot. Wouldn't they have jumped to the conclusion that it was her?'

'Perhaps,' said Fitzroy. 'You're making one too many leaps ahead for my comfort. But I do agree this could have been set up to scare off a director. I also see that was a time when someone was trying to stop this production – possibly with this and the stuff falling on the stage, and possibly even Janice' death. But it all stopped when Rosa got the lead.'

'It doesn't all fit, does it?'

'No, either that or we're still missing pieces of the puzzle.'

'Do you still want me to go back to your flat?'

Fitzroy reached inside his jacket and pulled out a key. 'I got Griffin to get this cut for you. I'll request you only use it in emergencies or when I ask you to do so. It is my home.'

'Thank you,' I said. 'I appreciate your trust. I won't abuse it.'

Fitzroy laughed. 'I don't expect you to steal from me, Alice. I'm just warning you not to turn up unannounced, as I might be otherwise engaged. In an emergency, of course, I would put up with that – but it would have to be a serious emergency.'

I felt myself redden slightly. 'I did get what you were unsubtly hinting at,' I said. I quickly apologised. 'I'm sorry that was ungracious, but sometimes you seem to delight in telling me about your – er – adventures. As you have said more than once, it is none of my business.'

He gave a wry smile. 'Yet, of late, it has been you asking about Celeste.'

I bowed my head, accepting the criticism. 'And, as you have noted, I'm not exactly being myself.'

'If it's Bertram that concerns you,' said Fitzroy, 'we can arrange visits for you. More doctors. More opinions. Whatever you or he need.'

'I think the estate doesn't have the resources to be quite that liberal. I am satisfied his doctors have done their best, and we will meet their bills as soon as possible.'

'Oh, the Department will pay. He suffered his injuries on duty. You must let them pay.'

'Is it the Department who is paying?' I asked.

'Who else,' said Fitzroy with a shrug. 'Now, go home, Alice – or rather, go to my home. Put your feet up and let Griffin look you over. We'll discuss tonight if you're well enough to continue depending on what Griffin says.'

'Are you sure you can handle—'

'My dear, this is a storm in a teacup compared to what both of us are used to – and a dark and dreary time though it was, I did manage to do my job for an entire decade before you came on the scene.'

'How do I get out?'

'Go straight along and you'll find a red door. It's the entrance to the lobby. It was locked, but somehow it recently became unlocked.' He pulled a lock-pick from his pocket. 'I'll square your absence with our director, but don't expect me home until late. If I'm fortunate I'll get the whole situation sorted over dinner and drinks tonight. Then we can go to Morley together and report. We might even get out of writing the wretched thing up.'

'We always have to write a report up,' I said, knowing how much Fitzroy hated sitting down and writing.

'Yes, well, there's a war on. Maybe that will make it of less import.'

'Hardly,' I said. 'It means some of us are more liable than usual to be killed, so we need a written history of actions.'

Fitzroy grinned. 'Now you sound more like my Alice. Berating me as usual.'

'I do not berate you,' I said.

'You said I was unpleasant to you only this morning.'

'But you're not. You're being nothing but kind to me!' And then quite without warning to him or myself I burst into tears.

'Oh gods, Alice! Don't start this again!'

'I'm sorry,' I said. 'I'm feeling rather vulnerable today. You go ahead with whatever you're doing. I'll take a couple of minutes to calm down.' I said all this with my hands over my eyes. The next thing I knew I was being enveloped in a bear hug, both gentle and supportive.'

'Don't you dare go telling Bertram I've hugged you. And as for Rory, if he gets just as much as a glimpse of an idea of this he'll have me in jail so fast I won't even be able to sock him in the jaw.'

I lowered my head onto his shoulder, and did my best to stop sobbing. Fitzroy didn't say another word. He held me carefully, solidly, and supportively until I managed to get myself under control. I stepped away out of the embrace. He took a handkerchief out of his pocket. 'Thank goodness you're not one of these women who covers themselves in paint,' he said, as he wiped away the remnants of my tears. Now, promise me you'll go straight home. If I could come with you, I would, but . . .'

'I know. I promise.'

'And please, Alice, think about telling me whatever it is. You can trust me with anything, you know. I'm always on your side.' He gave me a cheeky grin. 'Even if I shouldn't be.'

'It's nothing terrible,' I said. 'It really isn't.'

'Then why are you so damn upset?' He sighed. 'Go on, go. I'll see you tonight. Griffin will take care of you until I get home. Jack too. He has impeccable taste in ankles.'

I smiled at him, but decided not to voice my thanks in case I started crying again. All I could think of was my tears were down to my pregnancy and the impending stalling of my espionage career. Or could it be the baby? Did a child influence its mother? Was my baby going to be a sad person? I knew this was a silly thought, but my rationality wasn't faring well today.

I found the red door and crept out into the lobby beyond. I had no desire to run into any of the cast, and as far as I could see there was nothing I could do here for the mission. Carrying on the charade of being an actress had come to a natural end. There were still leads I could follow, but they could wait until tomorrow. They were also actions as easily done by Fitzroy as myself. It was time to take myself out of the field for all our sakes.

I crossed the empty lobby only for the outer door to open in front of me.

'Ah, Euphemia,' said Rory, 'I've been looking for you. I need your help.'

# Chapter Thirty-two

## Helping the police

'I'm not feeling quite the thing,' I said. 'I was on my way home.'

'Oh, this won't take long,' said Rory. 'Besides, I know how resilient you are. One more murder isn't going to upset you.' He stood in the doorway blocking my exit.

I gave a deep sigh. 'It's not that, Rory,' I said. 'I've been on missions back to back for several months, with only a few days of leave. I'm worn out. I've done my part here and I'm out. I'm heading home.'

'Which is Beryl Belairs' lodgings, isn't it?' said Rory.

'I have been staying there, yes,' I said carefully.

'I've been tasked with looking through Rosa's possessions and packing them up. Lowly sergeant that I am. I would like your help.'

'Why me?'

'Oh come on, Euphemia. We both know you have an eye for these kind of things. Besides, the landlady will talk more to you than to me. You already have a relationship with her. I take it you aren't behind with the rent?'

I shook my head. 'Why not take one of your colleagues?'

'I don't have any,' said Rory. 'The Inspector isn't keen on this idea of the army to palm unfit soldiers onto them. I overheard his saying how the last thing London needs is a bunch of wrecked men on its police force.'

'I'm sure he didn't mean you to hear that. He'll see what a good officer you'll make.'

'Yes, I'm so good your Department wouldn't have me back in their police force. I'm being turfed out by everyone. Because of a limp. A limp I'll have the rest of my life. As well as the unending nightmares of seeing my comrades blown to bits. I've seen more of the insides of a man than your average surgeon sees in a lifetime.'

'This bitterness doesn't suit you, Rory,' I said. 'You're a better man than this. Of course your experiences will affect you. Of course a limp is a handicap. But you're alive. You're whole. The boys I saw in the hospital, some of them barely more than children, without eyes or without limbs. Some of them afflicted in the mind, terrified of every living thing, others convinced they were still fighting in the war, unable to truly see what was around them . . .'

'You're saying I am one of the lucky ones?'

'Compared to some you are,' I said. I moved forward as if to push past him. He held out a hand.

'I need to succeed. I need to show Morris that I'm more than capable of doing this job.'

'And you are,' I said.

'I'd be even better at it if you helped me. Give me the rest of the day, Euphemia. Just that, to help me crack this case. I won't ask for more. For old times' sake?'

'I promised I'd go straight back to the flat,' I said.

'That's where I'm taking – wait a minute, to the flat? Not your lodgings? You are staying with *that man*?'

'Why does everyone call him *that man*,' I said. 'He does have a name. And no, not that it's any of your business, but I am not Fitzroy's lover. He lives in a large flat with a servant. I've been chaperoned every moment I've been there. When you see Belairs' place you'll realise it isn't the place one would choose to relax,' I said. 'It's small and poky and cold.'

'Does . . .' Rory stopped.

'If you were going to say does my husband know, then it was a wise decision to stop where you did,' I said in a low voice. 'Blackmail doesn't suit you.'

'I wouldn't,' he said. 'I stopped. Please help me, Euphemia. I want to do this job. We both believe in justice. Help me get that for Rosa. She might have been disliked by the whole world, but she didn't deserve to be murdered. I know you think that.'

'Oh, fine,' I said, exasperated. 'I'll help you go through her things. Do you even know what you're looking for?'

Rory moved aside to let me through the door. 'Whatever the others missed.'

At least they had given Rory a car. Not that it was much of a car. It had clearly seen much better days. I was also uncertain that making someone with a bad leg drive was much better than making him walk.

'Shall I drive?' I offered. 'I know the way.'

'You can drive?' said Rory. 'I mean – more than driving around the estate?'

'I've driven halfway across Europe,' I said. 'I'm not a bad driver, and some of the places I've driven make London look like a sleepy village.'

Rory shrugged. 'Fine, show me what you can do.'

He helped me into the driver's seat. Admittedly this older, cantankerous beast was a lot harder to drive than one of Fitzroy's top-of-the-line models, but I got us to the lodgings without major incident. I pulled up and put on the brakes.

'I didn't even understand half of what that cab driver said,' I commented.

'Just as well,' said Rory. 'It wasn't fit for your ears.'

I shrugged. 'I had right of way.'

'Aye, you did,' said Rory. 'Reckon he thought you'd give in to him as you're female.'

'Well, he was wrong.'

'Aye, he knows that now. I doubt he'll forget it.'

'The ditch wasn't that deep. A couple of friends will be able to push him out. If he has any.'

Rory smiled for the first time since we'd met at the theatre. 'I enjoyed your driving. I admit I'm getting used to it again. Or rather it's taking time for my leg to adjust. I'll get there, but it was good to take a break. Thank you for also providing entertainment.'

'Come on,' I said. 'I'll take you to meet Beryl. She'll fawn all over you. Tall, handsome, and green eyed.'

'Until I tell her I'm a copper. How old is this siren?'

'Oh, I should say late sixties,' I said. 'We could always say we've come to clear out Rosa's things. She'd like that. All the time the flat is full of Rosa's stuff she can't let it out again.'

'Aye, well, you can do things like that, but we regular police need to tell the truth.'

'Oh, hard luck,' I said. And I meant it.

The meeting with Beryl went much as expected. She gushed over Rory until she learnt he was with the police force. I explained that through my sorting through Rosa's things we were moving everything along. 'The Sergeant can take her possessions into evidence, and as the other officers have already checked the scene that should mean it will be available for you to re-let.'

Rory didn't correct me, and a few moments later we were walking up the creaky stairs to Rosa's rooms.

'I hope she has a suitcase,' said Rory darkly. 'I don't fancy carrying a lot of women's clothing out to the car.'

'Embarrassed by undergarments, are you?'

'Yes,' said Rory flatly.

Rosa's lodgings were the mirror image of mine, but laid out quite differently. The whole of the living area was filled with a large, ornate, but worn dressing table with a triple mirror. The tiny kitchenette was filled with luggage. Shoes sat on the hob, and stockings hung from the cupboards. Rosa clearly never cooked. The washing area was clean enough, and the soaps luxurious.

In the bedroom I found silk sheets and embroidered covers. Lanterns with candles, unlit, hung from the ceiling. The room smelt of stale perfume.

'More like a playroom than a bedroom,' said Rory succinctly, peering over my shoulder.

A small chest at the end of the bed proved to hold her clothes, all neatly pressed and folded in tissue paper. There were fewer items than I expected, and the solitary set of pink silk underwear I found folded in a triple layer of tissue paper struck me as sad and pitiful. Her other underthings were cotton and worn. I had the strong sense of a woman who loved nice things, and cherished them. In what had been both a short and a hard life Rosa had sought beauty as much as she had sought fame. I had a sudden mental image of her as the rose she was named for seeking out the sun. I gave a sniff and shut the lid of the chest.

'Nothing at the bottom,' I said. 'Nor under the mattresses, the bed, the pillows, or their coverings. This is nothing more than it seems.'

We went back into the living area. Expensive cosmetics covered the table. Brushes and powder pads, kohl and compacts of mascara, glass bottles of several perfumes, and hair ornaments were all laid out in neat rows. I looked over them.

'Lipstick is missing, but she might only have the one, and she'd carry that with her.' I glanced at Rory, 'To touch up her lips.'

'Aye, I do ken how some women like to paint themselves,' he said, much as a horse breeder might refer to the doping of horses.

'You disapprove.'

'Personally, I like to know what a woman actually looks like. Some of these pieces you see in London, not even their nearest and dearest would recognise them without their war paint.'

She had fewer possessions than I had expected. Her best piece, a fur coat of indeterminate origin, still hung on a hanger over the edge of her bedroom door. 'So whoever she was out meeting that night didn't merit the fur coat,' I said. 'It doesn't appear it was one of her main beaus.'

'I wanted to ask you about them as well,' said Rory. 'Who—'

'I expect she had an address book. If you didn't find it in her reticule, I expect she would have kept it in her dressing table drawer.' The drawer was locked. I didn't bother looking for a key. It would have been tiny, and she probably had it with her. Instead I opened my own reticule and took out a simple pick. It was the work of seconds to open the drawer. Rory rather obviously turned round while I opened it.

Inside lay a small blue book. The entries inside were few and sparing. Mum, Sis, Reggie, AP, MA, and LF. There were a couple of other names who appeared to be friends. One was scored out. But the saddest was *Dad* with *last known* scrawled beside it. *Mum* and *Sis* didn't have a telephone number, only an address. The others all had telephone numbers. With both addresses and numbers I really couldn't see the point of her putting only initials and not actual names. But then perhaps it gave her a feeling of security.

'So we need to find out who these initials belong to,' said Rory.

'Oh, I know who they are,' I said, and told him.

'Right, we'll head back to the station and set up some interviews,' he said.

'Would you mind very much leaving me in a nice café? We can meet up there later and have a good cup of tea. I can help you work on the questions you'll need to ask people tomorrow.'

'Who said anything about tomorrow?' said Rory. 'This is a murder enquiry. They'll agree to see us today or risk having their good names dragged into the mud. Besides, I've only got your help for today, and, begging your pardon, Euphemia, I damn well mean to make use of it.'

# Chapter Thirty-three

## A civil gentleman

At least I got my visit to the café. I had become aware that I needed to visit the facilities rather badly. This was not a matter I cared to raise with Rory, and I doubted the police station would have suitable lavatories for ladies. I was also both tired and hungry. I hoped that some good cake and a decent cup of tea would go a long way to revitalizing me. As it was now around luncheon time I ordered myself a plate of egg and chips. It was so good I ordered a second. Then I had a slice of sponge cake, extremely light with a filling of excellent home-made jam, and the better part of a pot of tea. This necessitated another trip to the facilities. By the time Rory came back I was delicately nibbling an Empire biscuit, and sipping at the first cup of a second pot of tea. I had ordered him a cup, and as soon as he sat down I poured for him, and told the waitress to bring him some egg and chips.

Rory swept his hand across his forehead. His bright blond hair had grown in hospital, so it flopped over his forehead. No one had yet made him cut it. Being on the plain clothes side of the police force had advantages. Presumably, his short employment with the SIS's own police had allowed him straight into his position without having to go on the beat. Either that, or someone had been pulling strings. I didn't begrudge him any advantage he'd been given. He'd more than proved his worth on a myriad of cases we had solved together, when we had been friends. It all felt so very long ago now. At the time his recompense had typically been no more than Fitzroy's scorn plus various abrasions.

Rory took a sip of his tea, and I caught his gaze over the rim of the cup. His eyes had lines around them now. More, I suspected, from what he had seen in battle than due to age. But his eyes were still the bright green, glowing with almost an inner luminosity, that I had noticed on our first meeting. His gaze had caught me so much by surprise then I had dropped a dish at his feet. He'd been rather nice about it, considering I had only been a maid at the time, and he the new butler.

Rory put down his cup. 'What are you thinking?' he asked. 'You're looking at me awful funny.'

'I was wondering if you had managed to set up any interviews this afternoon.'

'I have,' said Rory, 'and would you know it, but two out of the three men are married!'

Fitzroy hadn't mentioned this to me when we had discussed Rosa's beaus. But then he had had a low opinion of Rosa, and he generally had an even lower opinion of his own sex, so he may not have found it in the least remarkable.

Rory's meal arrived, and he ate it quickly. His manners remained those of a butler, well above his station, but he no longer seemed to bother much about his accent, and I remarked on this.

'Aye, well, I reckon if I sound Scottish they'll all think I come from Scotland Yard. It's a bit more intimidating than being only an Acting Sergeant.'

'But Scotland Yard—' I began.

'Aye, I know. But you'd be surprised how many people don't, or simply make the association without thinking it through.'

'You know this from your vast experience of three days on the job?' I said.

'And from working as police to you lot. Not all your Department are as smart as you, Euphemia. They have fodder like any other organisation. Men to do the heavy lifting and not think too much about what they're doing.'

'Who are we visiting first?'

'Arnold Pleasant. Works in one of the ministries. Fish and Agriculture. Some kind of pen-pushing civil servant. Must be quite a high-up. Had to go through three secretaries to speak to him, and the last one was male. You know what that means? He's got a senior assistant.'

'Do you want me to drive?'

'No, I'd better do it,' said Rory. 'Makes us look more formal.'

'How are you going to explain my presence?'

'I'm not,' said Rory. 'If they press it, I'll say you're from another ministry department that is assisting. That should shut them up. Just make sure you ask insightful questions and help me keep them on the back foot.'

Sir Arnold Pleasant had an oak-panelled office with a large red leather chair to sit on behind his enormous expanse of desk, the surface of which was mostly clear of papers. Two thin piles sat to one side, and a very modern-looking telephone machine stood on the other. Sir Arnold, himself, was rather less imposing than his surroundings, proving to be an overweight middle-aged gentleman, who was losing his greying hair. He had a round face, rather like a balloon. It looked as greasy as a badly cooked mutton chop.

He blustered at Rory's first questions, claiming he had 'hardly known the girl' and that he was a 'respectable married man.' That he was 'critically busy on crucial government matters.' That he could barely spare us 'a moment' and of course, the inevitable 'did we know who he was?' The loud dismissals became quieter when he learnt of Rosa's death. Clearly Rory had not mentioned this in his call to the man's secretary. He and Rory faced off like a couple of dogs vying for superiority. The interview was going nowhere.

I broke in on their discussion. 'Sir Arnold,' I said, 'if you barely knew this girl *and* you had no idea she was dead, why on earth did you agree to this interview when you are in the middle of crucial government work?'

He started a bit at my interruption. I had sat quietly enough, observing, for him to have ruled me out as a threat. He opened and shut his mouth a few times. He reminded me of those clowns you see at the fair, into whose mouths you attempt to lob a ball to win a prize.

'One wants to do one's part to help the police,' he said finally. Then he followed this up with an aggressive, 'What do you mean, if I didn't know she was dead? Are you suggesting I had something to do with her death? How dare you! *Do* you know who I am?'

'I know precisely who you are,' I said, when his bluster had run out of puff. 'In much the same way as I know this is not your first investment in a theatrical production. I also know that you frequent theatrical parties put on to attract investors. It was at one of these that you met Miss de la Croix.' The last part was a bit of a guess, but by the paling of his face, I knew I had hit the mark.

'I believe there is a Lady Pleasant,' I continued. 'Does she share your love of the theatre? Did she also meet Miss de la Croix? Perhaps she would have more time to answer our questions?'

'No. No,' The man fairly bounced in his seat. 'That won't be necessary. It's as you said, I met Miss de la Croix at a theatrical party. She suggested I might want to back her play. She'd heard about my previous successes, so I agreed to meet her and that writer fellow, Reginald Pierce. I thought him rather a clever chap. I liked what he was doing with the work to bring it up to date. Bring in the army lads. I thought it was a bit of a sure bet.'

'But it hasn't been?'

'Oh, no,' said Pleasant, settling down at once. 'There were some initial issues before Rosa came on board, but now she is the lead I believe the entire thing is going splendidly. We were to meet this week to discuss whether or not we should invest in a second cast to tour the regions, and continue the original cast in London. It would involve more investment, but Rosa has quite a head for figures. I mean had. Poor girl.'

'Was your relationship with Miss de la Croix entirely professional?' asked Rory.

The man went red, reached to loosen his tie, and blustered loudly about being a married man.

'I think we can take that as a no,' I said calmly. 'Can we also take it that in your own way you were fond of the girl?'

'Do you mind if I get myself a drink?' said Pleasant. 'I don't normally drink at this time of the day, but this is all rather rough. Would either of you like one?'

Rory and I both shook our heads. Pleasant went over to a panelled cupboard and opened it to reveal a gleaming set of decanters and rows of glasses. He selected one of each and poured himself a large drink. He immediately took a large pull from the glass, and then after a slight shiver came back to his seat.

'Yes, I was. I won't do you the discourtesy of pretending I was in love with her or that my wife doesn't understand me. Rosa was beautiful and talented. Genuine stage talent. She had that star quality that transcends age. I believe she would have gone on to be one of our greatest actresses.' He took another pull at his glass. This time a smaller sip. 'I admired that. People joke about civil servants being the men in grey suits, dull and dutiful, filing our papers with dedication with our sole extravagance being our food and drink. It's not the entire truth, but I find in general we are a dull lot. Including myself. Rosa was exotic and glorious. She brought excitement and flamboyance into my life. Much as the theatre does when I attend a play, but on a far greater scale.'

He put his glass down. 'But I am at heart a dull fellow. I know that. No matter what I spent, Rosa would move on in time. I knew that. In some ways it was something of a relief. I'm not a young man, and I doubted I would be able to deliver my side of the bargain in a way she might enjoy for much longer. I didn't take advantage of her. We had an agreement. An agreement that I believe she enjoyed. I'm not a monster, you know. The dying embers of my middle age spent in the arms of a rising star? There are worse ways to spend your time and your money.'

'Did your wife know?' asked Rory. 'Might she not have been a wee bit upset about this.'

'I married above my station. The class my wife comes from accepts liaisons are part of a successful marriage. She has certainly always had hers. The key is to be discreet. Any scandal and she would . . . well, I don't know what she would do, but it wouldn't be pleasant. Probably cut me off from the children and bar me from the country estate, so I had to live a bachelor life in London in my declining years.'

He pulled a handkerchief from his pocket and wiped his forehead. 'It doesn't bear thinking about! But you will see that neither my wife nor I would harm Rosa. It would cause quite the very thing we wish to avoid.'

'So she wouldnae care about your frittering the money away?'

'We have always kept our incomes separate. She has no cause for complaint.'

'Can I ask you how you spent your day and night the day before yesterday?' I said.

'I was here until eight in the evening. Working late. My secretary and other staff can vouch for that. Then it being far too late to drive home I went to my club for dinner, and took a bed there for the night. If you must confirm it with them I would be glad of your discretion. There will have been a number of members who also saw me.' He looked at Rory. 'You know the place? The Worcester? Mostly civil servants who frequent it?'

'Aye, I think I know the one you mean. I can make my enquiries discreet. However, Sir Arnold, if things do not add up, then I will be back with a vengeance.'

'What about the activities of your wife?' I said.

Pleasant blinked and frowned. 'I have no idea. She generally has house guests. If I'm staying there I leave before breakfast and I return late. I don't tend to involve myself with her visitors. I accept you could send a copper from the local constabulary to take statements on where she was. I wouldn't go myself, if I were you, Sergeant McLeod. She's bound to be unhappy about all this, and she has a formidable manner combined with a cruel tongue.'

'I've come from the war, Sir Arnold. If I can cope with what the Boche threw at me I can cope with your wife's disposition.'

'Well, it's your funeral,' said the civil servant, standing. 'Now, if you will excuse me, I do have a great deal to do. There *is* a war on.'

# Chapter Thirty-four

## No further on

'Aye well, I dinnae fancy him for it, do you?' said Rory as we climbed back into the car.

'He's a weak, worn-down, and frightened man,' I said. 'The worm can turn, but I don't think he's reached that stage.'

'Or he's past it,' said Rory putting the car into gear. 'As for the wife, it sounds like they're living separate lives. All very upper crust. You'd know about that.'

I shook my head. 'My grandfather might belong to that set, and live by those rules, but I assure you, as the daughter of a vicar I do not.'

'But you recognise the truth o' what he said?'

'Yes, I suppose there are some who live like that. Sounds horrible.'

'Each to their own,' said Rory with a shrug. 'It's not for me, but the only time I'm liable to be among the upper echelons is when I'm interviewing them about a crime. Your mannie would know all about that way of life, I expect.'

'Why not ask him?' I said tartly.

'I'll check on the alibis, of course, but my gut feeling is Pleasant is a wash-out.'

'He did confirm that all the weird things that happened at the theatre stopped when Rosa got the lead. Do you think she was behind them?'

Rory signalled right and shook his head. 'No, the cast changes and the director being scared away all happened before she came along. Even the stuff falling on the stage was before she got the lead.'

'Odd,' I said. 'Who do you think was behind it?'

'No idea. Unless it's relevant to this murder I think I will leave that mystery alone.'

'But it could be,' I said. 'Janice Hargreaves might have been pushed.'

'I'm sorry to say that had occurred to me,' said Rory. 'I've got someone digging out the newspaper clippings about the incident, but it would be hard to prove whether it was murder now. We have no leads on that at all.'

'You're hoping it was an accident?'

'Aye,' said Rory. 'Now we've got an interview with Maurice Attenbury. He's going to be a very different kind of a fish.'

'The Boot Maker,' I said.

'Yes,' answered Rory as he took a road that started us towards the outskirts of the city. 'He's a self-made man. Father was a coal miner. His mother took in laundry. He knows his own worth. Especially in these times, and he makes a show of despising the gentry. I don't imagine he'll have much time for you. However, whatever he thinks of the upper classes this doesn't stop him dining with ministers and civil servants. I've heard there's no better man at lobbying parliament for business.'

'Are you allowed to lobby ministers for business?'

Rory gave a slight chuckle. 'I doubt it. But I'd also be surprised if that wasn't how it worked. Whatever he does, Attenbury has gone from nothing to being a powerful man. He chooses to live away from the fashionable areas of the city, and yet I'm told his home is comparable to Buckingham Palace in gold plate and possibly size.'

'I doubt that's possible.'

'It'll be a generalisation, no doubt,' said Rory, 'but I'd prepare yourself for something grand, and, well, lacking in taste.'

'How do you know all this?' I asked.

'I've had a wee bit of time to look into matters. Scope out

sources and all that. I've a couple of contacts in the press. Men I knew in the trenches, who were invalided out before me. We kept in touch. Going through that sort of thing . . . I ken I wasnae there that long, but it felt like a lifetime passed each time you were switched back to the front.

'Did Morris leave you to your own devices?' I asked, changing the subject. 'You said he isn't too keen on an intake from the army.'

'I don't think it's personal,' said Rory. 'I think he's purely interested in results.'

'And if you give him some you won't be an acting sergeant much longer?'

'I want to be an inspector,' said Rory. 'As far as I can see you only get to start making a difference from that rank. Besides, I was an officer in your Department's police.'

'I haven't had anything to do with them,' I said. 'I wouldn't even know what they do.'

'Your commanding officer seems to like keeping you isolated even more so than mine,' said Rory, looking at me askance. 'A word of advice, Euphemia, I wouldn't trust Fitzroy's motives. He'll always put himself before anyone else.'

I shrugged. 'He puts his duty to his country before all else. That's the oath we take. I know he values me as a partner.'

'Aye, but a partner in what?'

I chose to ignore him as he turned the car through some large wrought iron gates and up a short drive. We were definitely in the suburbs, but the house that emerged as we turned into the last bend of the drive, would have been better situated in the country. It was very large. Larger than Stapleford Hall, and larger than the low sprawling mess of White Orchards. It was nowhere near as big as Buckingham Palace, but looked to my maid's eye as if it might hold thirty bedrooms. Then there would be the attics and lower accommodation for kitchen staff and servants involved with the general running of the house. I wondered how many people would be in residence. More than I could quickly count up certainly.

Rory parked the car neatly to one side. Not in front of the

house, but not round by the tradesman's entrance either. It was nicely done. It also gave me a chance to examine the house. It was a strange mix of styles with Georgian windows, Ionic columns, and a touch of the Gothic in its studded wooden door. As we approached on foot I became certain that although the house was recently built some of the building materials had been taken from older properties. There was a Grecian frieze above the Gothic door that was both distinctly out of place and very beautiful. Expertly sculpted, it showed the transformation of seven women into swans on a lake graced with lily pads. The women were in various stages, from clothed in loose toga-like robes, to nakedness, to part swan, and finally full swan.

'That's rather lovely,' I said pointing it out to Rory. 'Evidence of very good taste.'

'Not what I would have above my front door,' he said curtly. 'Oh, he's a widower with two daughters. The rumour is he regularly auditions for wives, but no one has yet made the grade. I heard there have been a lot of aspirants.'

'You think Rosa was one of those?'

'I don't know,' said Rory. 'The man is meant to be a "rough diamond", but his daughters, with their large potential inheritance and well educated manners are thought to be a prime matrimonial match.'

'Maybe one of them will take your fancy,' I teased.

Rory knocked at the door. A butler, who was almost too much a butler, took our names and, ascertaining we had an appointment, left us in an ante-chamber. I liked this too. The plaster walls had been hand-painted with exotic botanical sketches of flowers that were certainly not British. I loved the colour and flow of the design. I sat on a bench and admired the effect. Rory paced. He kept his gaze on the floor and appeared lost in thought. I was beginning to feel both hungry and tired again. After this I knew there was one more suitor to visit. However, to my mind, the most likely suspect remained Reginald Pierce. He would, of course, have been damning his play. But if he was as taken with Rosa as I suspected, then should he have discovered the true nature of the relationships with her three angels, it might have been enough to drive him to dramatic action. He was, after all, a writer.

I knew better than to voice my ideas here, so I saw and imagined the birds that might fly between such exotic flowers. Apart from my pregnancy malaise it was no discomfort to wait here. In each of the corners stood what at first appeared a ceramic stool, but was actually a small stove with a lattice-work ceramic top. With the doors closed the room was pleasantly warm without being stuffy. I wouldn't have minded more padding on the bench I had chosen, but I didn't think our host was trying to discomfort us.

Just as I was thinking this the door burst open and a portly gentleman in a well-cut suit with a purple waistcoat and thick gold fob chain erupted into the room. I took him to be in his late forties. His dark hair had only a trace of grey, and you could still make out that before he had started enlarging his proportions, he had once been a handsome man. Possibly a very handsome man.

'Good gods,' he bellowed in tones that would easily have been heard across a factory floor. 'A woman.'

Rory came forward offering his hand. 'Hello, sir, I made an appointment earlier today . . .'

'Yes. Yes. Rosa.' Attenbury fairly batted him out of the way as if he were a fly. 'My dear, I am so sorry. If I had known a member of the gentler sex was waiting for me then I would have had refreshments provided and had Smythe place you somewhere more comfortable.'

I went forward to meet him. 'Lord Attenbury, how nice to meet you. I have been most comfortable. This room is quite delightful. I have been imagining what birds might fly among such exotic plants.'

Attenbury seized my extended hand and kissed it. 'Not Lord yet, me dear. I'm awaiting the New Year's honours list. Nothing announced so far. Forgive me for describing you as a woman – you are most clearly a lady.'

He tucked my arm through his. 'Come,' he said. 'Let me show

you my house. Next time you visit I will have had birds painted on the walls of the garden room for you. You will come again, won't you?'

'Sir!' said Rory, clearly struggling to be polite. 'I must insist that we move directly to the interview.'

'All in good time,' said Attenbury calmly and amiably. 'As my friend the Chief Inspector of Scotland Yard likes to say, all things in the goodness of time. Now, my dear come. We shall begin our tour.'

I threw Rory a helpless look. The last I saw of him he was pacing the garden room like a caged tiger that hadn't been fed for a long time.

# Chapter Thirty-five

## The boot king

The house was simply glorious. I told Attenbury so on several occasions during my tour. I was glad he kept the pace slow. He appeared to think females were all fragile things, and as I did not feel at my best I did not enlighten him. In fact, when we had seen the oval music room, the roman atrium, the library, and the summer room, I was more than willing to accept his offer of tea, cucumber sandwiches, and what he deliciously described as 'a little light caking'.

Certainly the style of the house was eclectic, and Attenbury had no fear of strong colours. However, from the deep masculine crimsons and browns of the library with its railed ladders to the pale grace and statutory of the Romanesque music room, everything in each of the rooms was perfectly in balance. None of the rooms matched each other, but in themselves they were perfect. The house was like a cask of jewels and so I told Attenbury as we sat down for tea.

'I'm glad you like it,' he said. 'Not everyone sees it that way. Conformity is often mistaken for fashion. The policeman with you isn't your husband, is he?'

I shook my head. 'I am assisting him.'

Attenbury raised an eyebrow. 'Interesting. You must be with one of these new-fangled ministry departments. I am able to admit that a female brain can function better than a male one, but I always think it a great pity when women choose to work. You are generally so lovely, I want to give you everything including a life of ease. Although, I have to say, both my daughters are most accomplished. Either of them could run my factories if I let them. Fortunately Elouise has decided to embrace the social side of things, and is busy building schools and fostering content communities among the workers. Serena on the other hand longs to manage a vast estate and have a great many children. Being only fourteen, she has not yet realised that a husband will be necessary for the children production at least!'

I laughed. Attenbury passed me a cup of tea he poured himself. 'So what have you learnt about our poor Rosa?' he asked me.

'That she had extraordinary taste in men, for the most part.'

'The most part being Reginald,' said Attenbury, helping himself to a cup. 'Who, incidentally, is the only one of us she loved.'

'Did you love her?'

'I enjoyed having her as my mistress, and she liked visiting my lifestyle,' said Attenbury. 'But I think it's widely known I am looking for a second wife. Rosa, with her ambitions, could never have been that. I need a political hostess. A gracious and intelligent lady who will arrange dinners, and galas and charity balls, and who will, on rare occasions, overlook it when I temporarily fall for another actress. They are my weakness rather like other men have brandy or cigars.'

'You are being direct,' I said. 'Did Rosa understand her position?'

'You mean did she hope for more? I don't believe so. I was clear on all matters with her, and I did my best to explain that being my wife would be nowhere near as much fun as being an actress and my mistress.'

'You both got something out of your arrangement, then?'

He nodded. 'We were quite content for now.' He sat back in the over-padded settle and sighed. 'I am glad I decided to talk to you and not your colleague. I feel he might have been somewhat over-Calvinist with me. You, on the other hand, clearly live by higher principles than myself, yet you do not judge me.'

'I don't have the right, and besides, Mr Attenbury, you haven't yet mentioned anything of which I might disapprove.'

He twirled an imaginary moustache and said, 'Mistresses, and planned adultery, and over-educated daughters who have their own minds.'

'Well, I cannot say I am an advocate for adultery, but I have known men do far worse.'

'Not to you, I hope,' he said in a voice of genuine alarm.

'Not to me. I consider my husband perfect.'

'He's a lucky bastard,' said Attenbury. 'I could tell when I first saw you you were happily married. You have a glow.'

'Did you love Rosa?'

'I was fond of her, and I think even without the inducement of my finances, she was fond of me too. The girl had had a hard life, so I rather think anyone who showed her affection and kindness rather had her onside rather quickly.'

'Not if you were female,' I said.

'Oh no, you would have been the enemy! Apart for the obvious struggles to succeed I did wonder why she hated women so much. Her mother must have died early, or perhaps treated her badly in some way. What do you think?'

'I think Rosa has taken most of her secrets with her,' I said.

'Did she suffer?'

'I think so, yes. There seems to have been a combination of poison and an attempt to strangle her. I imagine her last moments were ones of intense fear. But I do not think they would have lasted long.'

'Thank you for telling me the truth,' he said. 'I suppose you need to know where I was? My alibi is concrete. I only came back from Yorkshire this morning. I was visiting some of the factories, and Elouise wanted to show me her latest school. I got back shortly before breakfast. Smythe can dig up a slew of witnesses for your chap.'

'And you didn't tell him during the telephone conversation . . .'

'Because I wanted to know what happened to the poor little thing. I also wanted to know the right people were looking into it.'

'I'm only helping Sergeant McLeod today, and as a man shortly invalided out of the hospital and tipped into the London Police force, I can't say he is getting much in the way of help. We knew one another before, so when he asked for my help – and I do have experience in these areas – I could give him today. The lead officer is an Inspector Morris. I don't know anything about him. He may be excellent at his job.'

'But he doesn't rate McLeod and you do?'

'Yes, I do.' I smiled. 'His father was a greengrocer, and before he went to war he was in service. He has shrapnel lodged in his right leg. He'll always limp, so he will always be a civilian now.'

Attenbury nodded. 'Unlike yourself, I'd warrant.' He looked over my head for a few moments, clearly thinking hard. Then he said, 'My dear, would you mind very much if we continued this house tour another time. I would very much like to show you my home, so this is not an idle invitation. However, I feel the need to light some fires under people. Rosa was a great gift to the stage. She would have brought joy to thousands. Her murder is a terrible crime.'

'Most murders are,' I said.

He nodded. 'Of course, you are right. As a young woman she deserves justice for herself.' He stood up. 'You're sure this McLeod chap has the right stuff?'

I nodded. 'He wants to be an Inspector. He has a strong sense of right and wrong, and he won't let rank deter him from his course.'

'Excellent,' said Attenbury. 'Allow me to escort you back to him. I'll get Smythe to sort out my alibi with him while you refresh yourself. I do believe the downstairs facility has recently been filled with lilies. I'm not entirely sure what my housekeeper is trying to tell me.'

When Rory and I were back together in the car, I gave him a summary of my conversation with Attenbury.

'Aye, he's right about me disapproving of his lifestyle,' said Rory. 'But it looks like the alibi his butler has passed me is solid. I'll have it checked. I'll send a telegram to the local constabulary tomorrow morning, and get them out and about. At least I hope I will. I'll have to present all this to Morris in the morning.'

I yawned. 'I am getting extremely tired,' I said.

'Day's not over yet, Mrs Stapleford. We've still Lord Frake to see.'

'I must insist this is the last interview,' I said. 'If it comes to dinner time and Fitzroy cannot find me I will be in a lot of trouble.'

'I thought you said he was taking the cast out to dine?' said Rory.

'I meant when he comes back to change for dinner. He'll expect me to be there. We could all meet up tomorrow and talk over what we know?' I suggested.

McLeod shook his head. 'I've no love for your mannie and no reason to trust what he says.'

'Very well, but he will have been studying the cast all day. It seems to me that if nothing else arises it must be Reginald.'

'Aye, he's the one I would bet on,' said Rory. 'But I dinnae have a scrap of evidence against the man. You saw him kissing the girl once, and that's it. Love might be a motive for murder, but an embrace on a deserted stage hardly makes them Romeo and Juliet. Looks to me like Rosa was quite free with her kissing.'

'Don't you think that could have upset him?'

Rory shrugged. 'Who knows. Once she appeared the play settled down, she was doing a grand job, and she was pulling in investors. Yes, she had other lovers, but she didn't go out last week and get them. From what we've heard they were all settled situations. Odd time to murder her, don't you think?'

'Yes,' I said. 'It doesn't seem to make any sense at all.'

# Chapter Thirty–six

## The would-be bigamist

I nodded off in the car on the way to see Louis Frake. Rory had the sense not to wake me. I dreamed of being chased through a theatre by a howling ghost only for Fitzroy to ride in on a white horse, holding a very long lance.

'Look at the length of my lance,' he said. 'Isn't it grand?'

'Kill the monster,' I screamed at him.

'Oh, very well,' he said. 'But honestly, Alice, you need to buck up and get on with the job.'

'That's all very well for you to say,' I said, but he was busy turning into the Cheshire Cat and didn't hear me. The ghost turned out to be Bertram, sitting on a large mushroom and smoking a pipe.

'I do wish you'd be more careful, Euphemia,' he said. 'All this having luncheon with murderers isn't the thing at all. You should come home and bake cakes.' Then Rosa appeared as the Red Queen and told me earnestly how it was always the older retainers she had to watch at court. She produced a jam tart from somewhere and choked on it.

Fortunately, I jerked myself awake before I had to witness her die.

'That sounded like some dream you were having, lassie. No clues as to what was going on, was there?'

I shook my head. 'It was all nonsense.' The last vestiges of the winter daylight had submitted to the dark while I slept. 'Where are we?'

'We're about to park in front of Lord Frake's club. The only time he had to meet us was for a few moments before dinner with his friends. Before you ask, he does know she is dead. He's offered up alibis of being out most nights gambling and visiting friends. Can't quite remember where he was when, but his secretary gave me a list of people to talk to.'

'That sounds like a lot of work,' I said.

Rory nodded. 'That's why I left him to last. I was hoping we'd have a result before him.'

'It has been a day of ruling people out,' I said. 'But that isn't a bad thing. Have you seriously considered the singing trio? I know nothing about them.'

Rory shrugged. 'I will have to investigate them soon. I don't know much about them either, but I couldn't find any connection with Rosa yet. They seem to stay much to themselves. They were a music hall act, right at the end of its popularity. As far as I can see the play turning into a musical was a Godsend for them. The last thing they would want to do is stop it. It's their big break.'

'Can I come into this club? I presume it's a gentlemen's one?'

'He's hardly going to belong to one of them new ladies' ones, is he?'

'So can I?'

'I did telephone them, and I was told there are rooms where ladies are allowed into to meet members. I'm hoping he will opt to take us into one these.'

'So you're hoping that this gentleman, who I've been told is rather fabulously rich, and who you've been told is a gambler and a ladies' man, will show some decency and hospitality towards us?'

'Och, Euphemia. The pair of us can handle it if he comes at us with a knife. A bit of rudeness isn't going to bother either of us. We've both been in service.'

I was about to open my mouth and comment obliquely that I had been somewhat emotional of late. That the long run of work had left me on the frail side of things, when I realised I hadn't felt once like weeping in Rory's company. It was rather an odd reflection for me to understand I was only emotional in Fitzroy's company. Apart from when he was grouchy, he was generally a man who displayed no emotion whatsoever.

Instead I said, 'Did I tell you what Beryl said about late night visitors to Rosa recently?'

Rory's head whipped round. 'No,' he said.

So I told him. He frowned during my story and seemed to make an effort to master himself afterwards. 'Are you annoyed?' I asked. 'I simply forgot to mention this. It's all circumstantial. No clear identifications.'

'Yes, but these are more dates for which we need an alibi.' He twisted in the seat to face me. The streetlight cast a pale beam across his face. 'Don't you see, whoever was angry with her might have caused her death at a later date, or even, these are wealthy men we are talking about, arranged for someone to harm her. It matters who it was.'

'Yes, but it doesn't need to have been any of them. It could be someone else entirely.'

'That glorious fact had not escaped me,' said Rory.

'You do know you are sounding more and more English?'

'Och well, all the better for talking to this Frake. But, Euphemia, what if the thumping noise was when she died? What if her body was brought to the theatre after she was killed?'

'I think a more likely explanation would be that she was poisoned there and passed out. The killer brought her body back to the theatre for whatever reason. She regained consciousness and he strangled her. Of course we've always assumed it was a he. Maybe Aggie is the killer.'

Rory smacked the heel of his hand against the steering wheel. 'Dinnae say that. We're getting nowhere.'

'Well, lets go and get somewhere inside where it's warmer,' I said.

Our reception at the club's desk was not all we could have hoped for. The porter confirmed that ladies were allowed in certain rooms and that Lord Frake was present tonight with a group of friends. However, he didn't feel he could take it upon himself to disturb his lordship. At first both Rory and I thought he was looking for a tip, so Rory displayed his police badge.

'I'm afraid, sir, I cannot allow you to enter without a warrant.'

Rory repeated, yet again, that we had an appointment with Lord Frake. Up until now I had let him deal with the man, thinking that as a porter of a men's club he would respond better to men than the occasional lady visitor. I was by now beginning to think I was wrong. I could also see from the way Rory's shoulders were rising towards his eyes, he was getting very tense indeed.

'My good man,' I said in an attempt to imitate my mother who can quell dukes, 'has it not occurred to you that if Lord Frake is expecting us, and if we depart without seeing him, he may be disappointed in your actions?'

This made the porter pause. He audibly swallowed. I was certain now Frake must have been the man outside the lodging house. 'He has been here for some time, miss,' said the Porter.

'He made the appointment,' I leant forward to read his badge, 'Williamson, and if he chooses to attend it while inebriated then who are you to stop him?' Then I turned to Rory. 'This is a waste of our time. I will send someone from the Ministry to his home first thing tomorrow. He will have to deal with the issue then.'

'No, ma'am, I'll fetch him for you,' said Williamson. 'If you care to wait in the little saloon opposite I will instruct a man to bring you refreshments.'

'That wo—' began Rory, but I kicked him hard in the shin and he stopped speaking. We went into the room he had indicated and found it rather a floral affair in decoration. However the seats were the usual club ones and quite comfortable.

'I'm not meant to take anything that could be considered a bribe,' said Rory.

'So don't have anything,' I said.

'I don't remember you being either this hungry or this difficult,' said Rory.

I smiled at him. 'Age and marriage,' I said. 'Did you see how I was elevated from miss to ma'am within a very short time. I think if I'd had longer I might have risen to ladyship. What do you think?'

'I think if you'd carried on like that you could have got him calling you your majesty. Do you have people to call on Frake?'

I shrugged. 'I could ask Fitzroy to do it, I suppose. But it was a bluff.'

Rory say back into his seat. 'I don't get to do that either,' he said.

'Your job isn't a lot of fun, is it?'

Rory threw me a filthy look and opened his mouth to respond when the door opened and a man in his mid-thirties, carrying a bottle of champagne, rolled in. When he wasn't red in the face from drink I imagine he was a handsome man. He wore an extremely expensive evening suit, but his bow tie was undone. He'd lost a few studs from the front. His cummerbund sagged as much as his jawline. Clearly, here was a man intent on disintegration by indulgence.

'So you're the buggers who want to see me?' He peered blearily at me. 'A woman? Hmm. So what am I supposed to have done now?'

'We are here to ask you about your relationship with Miss Rosa de la Croix,' began Rory.

'Oh, yes, poor little bitch was found dead, wasn't she? Stunning looks, a bit of nous, but a bit too free with her favours. I suppose someone was bound to get a bit jealous in the end. After all, a filly can only have so many runs before she goes to seed, can't she?'

He swayed on his feet, and took a slurp from the bottle. 'You're quite a looker,' he said to me. 'I've an opening for a mistress if you're free. I pay well if you're a good sport. Generous to a fault in fact. Like to share my good fortune with my friends, if you know what I mean.'

'The lady is working with me,' said Rory. 'I am Sergeant McLeod. I spoke to your man earlier. We arranged to meet. Perhaps you could take a seat, sir, and I could arrange some coffee for you?' He sounded reasonable and polite, but I saw the clenched fists at this sides.

'Don't use big words the poor man won't understand,' I said.

Rory shot me a glance.

'I mean like "work",' he's clearly never done a day in his life. And either he has powerful relatives or some personal disability, or he'd be away at war. As you were. We have to treat such shortcomings with understanding,' I said in a voice that was anything but understanding. Rory gave me a look of awe out of sight of Frake.

'I have fallen arches,' he stammered. Suddenly sounding more sober.

'How convenient,' I said.

'I could show you!'

'Please don't. I'd rather you explained what the rows you had with Rosa at her lodgings were about, and what terms you parted on.'

'You think I killed her,' he said, narrowing his eyes and rising slightly on the balls of his feet to intimidate me.

I remained seated. 'Would you like me to put my question in simpler terms? Or are you being wilfully uncooperative?' I raised my eyebrows slightly and looked down my nose at him while I remained seated. This is not an easy thing to do, but I managed it. The minor lord wilted.

'You're not a normal policewoman, are you?'

'I don't believe they have policewomen, do you, Sergeant McLeod? If you're asking about my pedigree, which I assume you are, my grandfather is an Earl. Now, will you kindly answer my questions.'

Frake dumped his bottle on the table that bore our refreshments, sloshing champagne over everything. He threw himself down in a chair.

'If you really must know, I wanted her to marry me.'

'And she was disinclined to do so?' I asked.

'She said I drank too much, and had an empty life.'

'How unusually perspicacious of Rosa,' I said glancing at Rory. 'I may have underestimated her intelligence after all.'

'So when she said no, you killed her? Or was it when you found out about her other lovers?'

'Oh, I knew about them,' said Frake. 'I'm hardly lily white myself. Besides, the civil servant and the cobbler were too old to bother her much. She only wanted money from them. I told her I had plenty. She said she wanted to make her own. That the money she was getting from others was a temporary thing. Once the play took off, she'd be her own woman. She said she never wanted to be anyone's wife.'

'That seems quite decisive,' I said. 'How did it make you feel?'

'How do you think it made me feel? I'd offered the little trollop my hand and half my fortune and she turned me down. I could give her status, a place in society . . .'

'Most ungrateful. Maybe you being already married discouraged her?' I said. 'Was this when you killed her, or the time you punched her?'

'It wasn't a punch. It was more of a slap, and I didn't mean to hit her so hard. At least I didn't touch her face, that would have upset her more than anything. As for my wife. I'd have sorted that.'

'Another murder?'

'No. I would have sent her to the country. I told Rosa all this. Rosa would have lived as my wife. My friends would have understood. These things in my class are understood. She would have been as good as my wife!'

'Instead she sent you away, but you went back again, didn't you?'

'I came with a diamond necklace and an apology. She wouldn't even let me in.'

'Is that when you killed her?' asked Rory.

'Are you deaf? I said she wouldn't let me in. Bolted the door and pulled her bloody dressing table behind it. I was well and truly shut out.'

'So when did you kill her?' asked Rory.

'You don't get it, do you? I loved her. I can't bear it that she's dead.'

Then he burst into loud and messy sobs.

# Chapter Thirty-seven

## The theatre after dark

Rory sat wordlessly at the wheel of the parked car. I didn't speak. Dealing with Frake had been rough enough on me. Rory, who prided himself on remaining calm, had found the man's display of raw emotion distasteful in the extreme. I could almost feel him vibrating disquiet as he sat next to me. Finally, when I was beginning to think he might not speak again that evening, he said, 'So where's mannie's house so I can drive you home.'

He put an emphasis on the last word that was far from pleasant. Frake had rattled him so much, he was clearly willing to take it out on all and sundry. 'What will you do next?' I asked.

'Write up my report. Formulate my actions for the morning,' he said. 'I release you from you duty to me today. I need to be alone to think it all through.'

'You think we're missing something?'

'Aye, the puzzle's not all in place. We may be looking at it wrong.'

'How?'

'If I knew that I wouldn't have a problem. So where to, Euphemia? Where does Fitzroy live?'

I had already realised that I could not tell him the answer to this. The spy had given me the key to his flat in a gesture of generosity, but with a polite plea not to abuse the privilege. Telling Rory McLeod, a man who despised him, the address was simply not good enough.

'Actually, do you think you could drop me at the theatre?' I said. 'I've left some things there I will need tonight.'

'How—'

'I'll get a cab. It's what I would do most nights. You know I can look after myself.'

Rory tensed ready to argue. Then his shoulders slumped. 'Whatever you want, Euphemia. I've got more than enough work to be getting on with.'

He didn't speak to me again until we reached the theatre. As I reached to open the door, he said, 'You're sure you'll be all right by yourself.'

'If I run into the murderer I'll bring him in for you,' I said.

'It's not funny, Euphemia. It is more than likely someone from the theatre.'

'My money is on Reginald,' I said. 'But it's hard to imagine him doing it. He doesn't strike me as a strong-hearted sort of man.'

'Aye, I can't see him having the stomach for murder either, but we've ruled so many out. It has to be one of the theatre people.'

'I have no intention of going into a dark cellar with anyone. I will be fine,' I said getting out. 'It was an interesting day, Rory. Quite like old times.'

I closed the door. Rory tipped his hat to me and drove away. I was unimpressed. Fitzroy, who knew more than most that I was capable of defending myself, would never have left me to go into a dark theatre alone. I had wanted Rory to leave, but at the same time I did not relish being alone. I looked about for a cab. Typically, the street was quieter than usual. Rather than wait around on the street I decided I would go into the theatre, but I would avoid the auditorium and go via the workshop to the small kitchen. What I needed was a cup of tea. More than likely Cutler would be working late, and having him nearby, although he was a dyed in the wool pacifist, would make me feel a little safer. Not that I thought anyone wanted to kill me. I was irrelevant to Rosa's killer.

The stage door was open again, but there was no sign of Dickens. I assumed he would be nearby. Then I heard a noise from the alley outside. I stepped out, but could see no one. It probably came from the vennel that continued past the box office. Local wildlife? Or possibly Dickens answering a call of nature? The day had been grim enough. I stepped smartly back through the box office door. I had no desire to see what might be happening under the cover of darkness outside. I made my way into the theatre. I hoped someone had left some heating on. I was feeling chilled.

There came more faint sounds from the alley. Perhaps the alley cats were competing to become the new theatre cat. My mind was definitely wandering. It had been a very long day, and I was looking forward to getting back to Fitzroy's flat. He would be out with the other men of the cast and Yves. Doubtless Griffin would make me something light and delicious for my supper. Jack would also be there, and the thought of cuddling a warm dog was most appealing.

The day had been useful in ruling people out, but it felt that we were no nearer identifying Rosa' murderer. Although Reginald now appeared the prime suspect. His motive could have been jealousy over her other lovers. But those lovers had been funding his plays. There was a connection there I was missing. Besides, Reginald didn't strike me as a killer. It wasn't more than a gut feeling – I'd met a number of murderers during my short career, and I couldn't see Reginald being one.

Who had we not considered? I wondered if Dickens had had some connection to Rosa we didn't know about. Father? Uncle? Certainly not a romantic one. He had nothing she wanted. Of course, it wasn't unknown for men to have a desperate crush on a beautiful woman. Although if Rosa was in the habit of attending theatrical parties, then a good proportion of London's gentlemen could fall into that category.

I walked across the lobby and around the auditorium. It was quiet and gloomy. I was wearing soft shoes and I knew how to make use of the shadows. I had discovered there is something almost magical about a theatre that is dark. The building struck me as waiting, the stories, the plays, brewing within it.

Once I had had no fear of the dark. Living in the country, the dark is nothing but a precursor to sleep. Then after meeting Fitzroy I learnt that there were monsters in the dark; men of his ilk and worse. I knew there was a common belief that the killer returned to the scene of the crime, but I had never seen it happen nor put any store in it. Although I did believe that after the first murder subsequent killings became much easier for the murderer.

At this point in my thoughts I heard footsteps. I drew back into a shadow. I had no doubt I could normally deal effectively with any member of the cast, but carrying a child made me wary of engaging physically. I assumed that this early on my body would protect the child. Griffin had told me that I was not as well-rounded as other women, not because the baby was unusually small, but because my body was strongly muscled and was protecting the child within a cage of strength. Still, I had no intention of throwing myself around.

There was enough light for me to see it was a man, and he was holding a handkerchief to his face. As he grew closer to where I was sheltering, I realised it was Henri and he was hurt.

'Goodness, Henri,' I said, stepping out of my hiding place. 'What has happened?'

I suppose I could hardly blame the man when he shot up in the air and cried out.

'I'm so sorry,' I said. 'It's Alice. I needn't mean to startle you.'

'*Mon Dieu*, Alice! What are you doing here?'

'There are no cabs outside, and I thought I would come in and warm up with a cup tea, before I went out to try again. It is getting so cold. What happened to you?'

'I tripped in the dark. Foolish. I am not used to the dark coming so early. En France it is not so dark so early.'

'Well, come through to the kitchen and I will patch you up. Unless Dickens has a first aid kit?'

'I doubt it,' said Henri. 'But you will excuse if we perhaps go to the bar next door? I could do with something stronger?'

'You have a key?' I asked in surprise.

'Dickens wanted away early tonight, so I said I would lock up for him. I've done it before. He's an old man, and the stage door box gets most of the cold. *Tant pis* for the bones old, *n'est pas*?'

'Yes, I can quite see how he would want away. Doesn't he have a small flue?'

Henri shook his head. He patted his forehead once more and rather fastidiously folded his handkerchief and put it in his pocket. 'Come, let us have un Cognac. It is all that will keep out the bitter British winter chill.'

I hesitated. Did I want to go near the cellar where Rosa had been found? My instincts told me to refuse. But I had no reason to say no, so I went with Henri

The bar connected to the theatre through a wide set of double doors, white with gilt scrolls along the edges. The masques of tragedy and comedy adorned the left and right doors. I knew on the other side were images of Bacchus. Whoever had decorated this section hadn't needed to stretch their imagination. However, it was excellently drawn. The doors were large, with a sizeable lock as well as bolt. They needed to be big enough to let an audience in and out during interval time. And of course, strong enough that the bar guests could not join the theatre without tickets. The theatre was connected through one of the newer parts of the building. A series of window panes had been built into the ceiling of the new corridor. The starlight gave faint illumination. The doors reflected what little light there was, giving off a faint, and in my fanciful mood, I thought, eerie glow.

Henri took a ring of keys from his pocket, inserted the largest in the lock, and opened the doors. The bolts had not been shot.

'Are you all meeting in here before dinner?' I asked Henri.

'No, ma belle. After what happened we are not dressing for dinner. We are engaged to meet at a local chop house. Cantori had business to attend to, so we agreed to meet there. Afterwards we may go on, but a damper on the evening has been cast.'

I followed him through into the bar. The chairs had been put on the tables, so I sat down in one of the booths. I lent back against the cushioning and felt weariness flow through me. Henri went behind the bar. He turned on some of the lights. Electric light. The prices on the drinks here must be very high.

Henri came over with a bottle of brandy and two glasses. He sat down opposite me and poured us both stiff drinks. 'A voter Sante!' he said, raising his glass and drinking it down in one. I sipped mine. Warmth flowed down my throat into my stomach. It was better than the brandy Bertram kept, but not as good as Fitzroy's. I managed not to choke.

'You are not used to drinking the brandy?'

I shook my head.

'You are the innocent you seem to be, are you not?' said Henri, pouring himself another measure. 'Is even your relationship with Cantori what it seems to be?'

'I fell asleep on his sofa,' I said. 'We agreed to pretend we were involved. He said he didn't want to damage his reputation as a ladies' man, and that it would also keep the other actors away. I think he was slightly scared of Rosa.'

Henri laughed. 'Gentlemen should have been. She was a force of nature, that one. The morals of an alley cat, but the formidable determination of a general. It was a shame it came to what it did.'

He gazed down into his glass, lost in thought.

'But wait, you said something happened today. Did Morris arrest her killer?'

'*Peut-être, peut-être pas*. He arrested Pierre Marron.'

'What!' I said, barely restraining myself from leaping up. 'Pierre! Why?'

'He is a German spy,' said Henri. He was watching me closely now. I didn't need to feign my astonishment.

'I don't understand.'

'Well, when he was injured he swore in German.'

I shook my head. 'He was injured?'

'When the scenery fell on him.'

'How? Why? You've lost me.'

'Not long after you left a large section of scenery fell onto the stage. Cantori –'

'Cantori was hurt?'

'A moment, *petite*. I will tell all. Your Cantori is fine. He has quick reflexes. He pushed Marron out of the way, and rolled away himself. However, it clipped Marron. Broke his arm. But better a broken arm than a broken head.' He smiled. 'Your Cantori fairly flew across the stage. He took a sort of running leap, and rolled like a gymnast. Never seen anything like it – and I've seen some good tumblers in my time. Anyway, he saved Marron's neck.'

'But who did it?'

'You immediately jump to the conclusion it was not an accident?'

'I thought it had happened before,' I said. 'I thought . . .'

'I can see you have been doing a lot of thinking,' said Henri. 'So it was not you who set the trap?'

'No, of course not,' I said. 'How on earth would I have ensured it didn't fall on you or Cantori? I neither like or dislike the others. I certainly wish them no harm, but I wouldn't have wanted to harm you two.'

Henri raised his glass and took a long pull. 'That is of a kindness, *ma petite*. I am glad. I had feared it was you had done that. Now, I see that it must have been Reginald all along.'

'But wait, how does a broken arm make Marron a German spy?'

'Because he swore like a trooper in German when it happened. Any of us who have come from the continent of late might not speak the language, but we can all recognise the swear words. Yves phoned the Inspector, and he and his men arrived most promptly. Marron was taken away.'

'At least he won't be hard to replace,' I said. 'His acting was nothing special. Even a stage hand would have been less wooden. Hopefully we can get someone better.'

'I am most pleased to hear you say so,' said Henri. 'I have enough investment in the show it is important to me that it does on.'

'What did you mean . . . it must have been Reggie all along?'

'Ah, you did hear me. I mean, my dear, that he has been our phantom. All that has gone wrong can be laid at his door.'

'Why on earth would he sabotage his own play?'

Henri smiled. 'Why, *ma petite*? Because he never wanted it to be staged.'

# Chapter Thirty-eight

## A deadly confrontation

I had by now managed to sip my way through my brandy. Henri poured me some more. 'You are looking much better,' he said. 'There is colour coming back into your cheeks. Good. I do believe that all our misfortunes are over. Cantori, for all his annoying ways, is good enough for his part. Reggie's friend will hopefully make it across to us, and take up Marron's role. Or perhaps I will take it and he will take mine. Reggie may end up in prison, or perhaps the fact we know what he did will be enough to make him stop.'

'You mean we should blackmail him?' I said.

'Would you do that?' asked Henri.

'I'd rather not, but if it was a choice between him going to prison or not, I'd hope we could persuade him to change his ways, and carry on with the show.'

'Nicely put,' said Henri. 'I thought when I first saw you there was a great deal of intelligence behind your eyes. I can tell that with women and dogs. Neither are necessarily gifted with an intelligence by nature, but some are. Very much so.'

'Like Rosa?'

'No, Rosa had a slyness and a cunning, she had learnt from her life. Did you know her mother turned her out of the house at thirteen? She went on the street, selling her body. She told her customers she was older, and inside she was. Her father had been abusing her since she was ten years old. Her mother, when she found out, blamed Rosa for being too pretty. But Rosa made her way up to the richer and more genteel clients. Then one of them suggested she try for the stage. Of course, by that time she was spending her whole life acting, to be whatever her client wanted. She could have been great. *Peut-être*, one of the greatest actresses of her age. She had, you see, quite lost the ability to tell truth from fantasy.'

'You mean she was mad?'

'No, but she had come to believe in fairy tale endings. That was her undoing. You, *ma petite*, have your head firmly screwed onto your shoulders. You will understand the business, and you will do well.'

'I'm sorry. I still don't understand why Reggie sabotaged his own play.'

'Ah, the hubris of the creator. Reggie had had a few plays produced and he thought he was going to be a great writer. He thought *Kisses and Kidnapping* was one of his very best. It was, in truth, no more than an average farce. There was nothing special about it. Then we were approached by a representative of the government, who asked if we would be prepared to support our troops. Of course we said yes to a man. Even Yves. We were men who could not fight for our countries, but if we could help, we would.'

'Yes, I see you would have been eager to help,' I said. 'But how were you to do so—' Then I saw it. 'Oh, the changes to the play, the songs, the patriot moments to stir the men, the bawdy humour . . .'

'Exactly,' said Henri. 'The rest of us did not mind. We knew that the play had the opportunity to be a great success. Many of us had shares. We had a new audience of soldiers on leave, with their pay burning a hole in their pocket. It was good for all of us.'

'But Reggie didn't want to change his play.'

'No, he thought it would ruin his art.' Henri laughed. 'He is still young enough to think that there is great art and there is popular art. The truth is more complex. But for a theatre, the good art is the one that puts derrières on the seats, and money in our pockets.'

'So Reggie tried to wreck the play. I'm assuming he had a contract that he couldn't get out of, but he tried to scare off directors with ghosts, he rigged the scenery, and also killed the theatre cat, who was a good omen. Did he kill Janice Hargreaves too?'

'No,' said Henri. 'Reggie is not a killer, I think. He is too weak.'

'No,' I said relieved. 'I don't believe he would kill anyone. But what an idiot. Why did he change his mind?' Then it hit me. 'Rosa. Rosa convinced him to carry on.'

Henri nodded. 'Rosa saw how good this could be for her, and for him. It could be the first of his plays to really make money, and to garner the attention he craved. She told him she would find him angels to invest in this and others of his works. She said the war plays would make them both rich. He only had to trust her.'

'Rosa did have a history of bending men to her will.'

Henri smiled. 'Most men, indeed.'

'She disliked you,' I said. 'I didn't see why.'

Henri shrugged. 'Despite my little joke about making you my mistress I am not a man much tempted by women. I flirt a little now and then. Of necessity, you understand.'

'Ah,' I said. 'I see.'

Henri's eyes flickered wide with interest. 'It seems you do. I did not expect that. The theatre has a history of welcoming men, like myself, who are not so welcome in society.'

Without thinking I repeated something Fitzroy had said to me, 'Oh, it's not as unusual as one might expect. Really, it shouldn't be anyone else's business.'

Henri smiled. 'Thank you. I would prefer to be a legally accepted member of society, but for now I will content myself with your silent approval.' He smiled when he said this, but I heard the bitterness in his voice.

'It must be hard having to hide who you are all the time,' I said.

'You think you understand?' he asked, anger in his voice.

'No, I can't, obviously. But I am sorry.'

Henri reached over to top up my drink. 'Now we must have the discussion proper. You will be our star.'

I didn't immediately contradict him. He said it so forcefully, and coming on the back of his very personal comments, I didn't think it wise. There was still something I was missing. The hair on the back of my neck was up.

'Good, you have the sense not to disagree. I will agree with Reggie that you will have shares in subsequent plays.'

'That's very kind,' I said. 'Why would you do that?'

Henri looked steadily at me and waited.

And then like a key turning in a lock, the tumblers turned and the door opened. I knew why Rosa disliked Henri so much. I knew why he knew so much about her. I met Henri's gaze. He pulled out a sheathed knife from his pocket and put it on the table. His fingers hovered over the end of the handle. 'I have kept this sharp. It has always been my intention should anyone realise what I was that I would kill myself. I would do that rather than endure the contempt of my public.'

'I have no intention of telling anyone.'

'I know that, *ma petite*. You strike me as a fundamentally decent person. I fear that will prove the problem, but I hope your desire to be famous is stronger than your desire to be good.'

'You're right. It was Reggie who set the trap tonight, wasn't it? Without Rosa he doesn't want to go ahead. But I don't believe either he or Marron meant Rosa harm,' I said slowly. I was a third of the way round into the booth. It was one of those awkward ones that meant you had to half crouch to get out. Not an exit I could make with any speed. Besides I was over tired. The adrenaline now coursing through me would help, but Henri was a tall man with long arms. My best chance was to agree to work with him. If I could get away . . .

'I could not do what Rosa did,' I said. There was no point lying about that.

'Ah, you have realised Rosa did not manage all herself? We were partners, Rosa and I. We planned it all together. Her conquests. Her conversion of Reggie. But . . .'

'She began to believe in fairy tales. She fell in love . . . with Reggie?' I said.

Henri slammed his hand down on the table making me jump. 'The foolishness of it. She has four men wrapped around her fingers and she chooses the one without the money. Three choices out of four I could have accepted, but not Reggie.'

'But the investors are all gone now, aren't they?'

'*Mais non*, they are continuing to fund the play in her memory.'

'Or because they don't want their association with her known? That's a dangerous game, Henri. These are powerful men.'

Henri shrugged. 'They are mainly fools. Rosa and I chose well.'

'I don't understand why Rosa worked with you,' I said. 'She had got herself off the streets and . . .'

'And then I became her pimp? That is what you are thinking. You are correct. But then I know who pushed poor Janice under the bus.'

It hit me like a punch in the solar plexus. 'Rosa.'

'Oh, she never meant to kill her. She hoped the girl would break an arm or a leg. What she couldn't have known was when poor Janice tumbled away from colliding with the vehicle the brewery cart would be coming by.'

'You saw what happened.'

'I did. There was nothing to be done for Janice. Rosa went into shock. I brought her in here. Gave her brandy. I could see how upset she was. We agreed that I would not go to the police. We came up with the plan to make us both rich.'

'You used her. You blackmailed her.' I felt fury for poor Rosa. She had pushed Janice, but her whole life people had used her. She hadn't meant to kill the other woman. It was all a tragedy.

'She and I came to an agreement. As will we.'

'I can see you're a dangerous man, Henri.' In the distance I heard the faint sounds of footsteps. I prayed it was Fitzroy having come to look for me. That when he had said he had something to do, it had been to find me, rather than to get Braun released. But it didn't matter who it was. Anyone finding us would give me a chance to get away.

'I am glad you see that. It will make things easier.'

'I am prepared to go along with your plan as long as no one else is harmed.'

'You understand that I killed Rosa?'

'She wanted out. You didn't have any other option. As you said, with her dead the investors can be persuaded to continue to help in her memory – or because of their liaisons. I will not make the mistake of underestimating you as she did. I do not like any of this, but I do not want to be your next victim.'

'No, I thought you would understand. That quickness of yours. I was concerned you were too naive. But now . . . but now I think you learn quickly. Almost too quickly,' said Henri. 'I have to be sure. You know too much. This is why you will come and help me finish Dickens. Once we are co-conspirators I will be content. No one else need be harmed.'

'Dickens?'

'I paid him to lend me the keys now and then. I have brought more than one *friend* here. He realised that my friends were . . . unusual.'

'You mean men,' I said bluntly.

Henri didn't respond. 'He began to realise what I was. He blackmailed me and when he realised I had killed Rosa, he set his price too high. That's the problem with blackmailers.'

'It was you and him I heard in the vennel.'

Henri indicated the scabbing wound on his face. 'For an old man he fought like a devil. I left him gagged and bound. We will finish him together.'

Behind him in the bar doorway I saw Fitzroy. I felt relief wash through me. The nightmare was almost over.

'I don't know that I can do it,' I said. 'He's an old man.'

'He's dying anyway, *ma petite*. It will be a kindness to shorten his suffering.'

I shook my head. Fitzroy crept into the room. He made no sound. I kept looking at Henri. I could see the spy from the corner of my eye. I daren't look straight at him. A few moments more and he would be behind Henri.

'Is it the only way to ensure his silence?' I said.

'He is a greedy man, *ma petite*. He will bleed me dry, and I have not done all of this only for one old man to be my downfall.'

'Do I have to do more than be there?' I asked. 'That would make me an accomplice, wouldn't it? I mean even if I closed my eyes while you did . . . the deed.' I needed to keep him talking, and I knew although he wanted my acceptance, if it was too easy he wouldn't believe it.

Henri watched me closely. Fitzroy was almost there. Some sense made Henri turn. He saw the spy. I tried to get out of the booth, but Henri grabbed me and slid across to my side. His long legs allowing him to propel his body instantly to my side. I felt the sharp prick of a knife at my waist.

'So you are her lover,' he said.

'He has a knife at my side,' I said to Fitzroy.

The spy had frozen. 'Ah, so you are our killer,' he said. 'I had begun to wonder. Of all of them you had no motive. The German was a gift for you, wasn't he?'

Henri nodded, his eyes not leaving Fitzroy. I glanced down at the knife. If I shoved him back hard enough in the space would I be able to get away. He wouldn't expect it, but . . . there was so little space. I couldn't think what to do. All that kept going through my mind was that the knife was above my womb.

'His guilt has already been accepted. He will hang for it. He is a German, who cares.'

'I imagine he will,' said Fitzroy lightly. 'Let the girl go and we can talk about the situation. Find a way that benefits us both?'

'We could be partners,' said Henri, 'but I cannot trust the girl. I had a task for her. Then she would have been safe, but you have arrived too early. Now, I am thinking about a lover's quarrel and that I was never here.'

'Dickens,' I said.

'A complication, but I will solve it. You two are the most pressing of my problems. I think I will be able to kill the girl before you reach me. I am stronger than I look. A fop like you I will make short work of.'

'You have no idea of what I am capable,' said Fitzroy in a low voice. His manner changed entirely as he readied his body to fight.

He came up on to the balls of his feet, leaning forward like a tiger ready to pounce. But what was most noticeable was that all the affability he had worn as Cantori dropped like the mask it was, and in its place came the cold, merciless look of an assassin.

Henri leant back slightly. 'You are not what you appear to be,' he said. He tried to keep his tone light, but I heard the fear in it.

'Neither is she,' said Fitzroy. 'If you wish to live, put down the knife and surrender.'

He flicked his gaze at me, and I realised with growing horror that he did plan to attack. He was giving me as much warning as he could. He was counting on me to get myself away from the knife. I should be able to do this. I should be able to counter. To force Henri back. I could strike him a rising blow to the throat as I pushed his arm aside and sent the knife clattering. There were many options, but that knife so near to . . .

For the first time in a long time I felt crippling fear. I couldn't move.

Fitzroy attacked. I acted. I tried to do what I must, but I fumbled my chance to push Henri away. The knife slid, cold as ice, into my side. Then it began to burn. I heard myself scream. I threw myself off the bench, and rolled on my side out of the booth. Then I noticed the blood. I put my hands to my side. 'No,' I heard myself say, 'no, no, no!'

The sounds of the fight continued. I closed my eyes and prayed. I didn't dare move any more. I heard someone come across to me. I opened my eyes and saw Fitzroy above me. He was soaked in blood.

'Where did he hurt you?' he said urgently.

'My side,' I managed to say.

Fitzroy gently touched by my wound. 'I'll telephone for an ambulance. Put pressure on the wound.'

'I can't,' I said.

'Alice, I know it's scary but—'

'You don't understand, I'm pregnant.'

The horrified look on my partner's face was the last thing I remembered.

I woke up in hospital. I ached all over. Fitzroy, red stubble on his chin, cravat askew and still with a fair amount of blood on his clothing, was asleep in a chair beside the bed. A large bruise was forming above one eye, and there was a scrape on his chin. I tried to sit up. Immediately I felt as if I had been thrust through with a sword. I gave an involuntary cry of pain.

Fitzroy snapped awake. He stood up and leant over the bed. 'Alice, don't move. You've had surgery. You must lie still and rest.'

'The baby?' I asked.

Fitzroy shook his head. I stared at him, dry-eyed and uncomprehending. 'I'm so sorry, Alice. It was too early. They couldn't save it.'

At that point I began to scream. I didn't stop until they sedated me.

# Epilogue

Braun proved to be no more than a mathematician in love with a British woman. The police investigated him so thoroughly that Fitzroy said next time we had a suspected spy it might be easiest to simply hand him over to the force and let them do their worst. In consequence Braun was now in the process of becoming of use to the government, and back with Mary.

Henri died. Having an artery cut generally leads to this. Fitzroy said he had been in a hurry to get to me, so he had killed Henri as quickly as possible. Even if it was one of the most gory ways to kill a man. Presumably he sorted the story with Rory. I received a two-line missive from the new Inspector that came via Fitzroy, thanking me for my help, and saying he had closed the case of Rosa's murder with success. The play, of course, never saw the light of day.

I had been in recovery for some weeks and we were now to return to White Orchards. I was staying with Fitzroy and visiting Bertram. He knew I had been in a fight, and was furious with Fitzroy, but he didn't know about the baby.

Fitzroy and I had had several conversations that revolved around the fact he would have pulled me out of the field if he had known. He was careful not to blame me, but he kept returning to his point as if he wasn't sure I wouldn't repeat the mistake.

Other than that he was extraordinarily kind. He did all the reports. Dealt with Morley, and told him I hadn't realised I was pregnant. He let me shout at him about the unfairness of it all. He let me cry over my stupid decisions and not once did he criticise me. Griffin assured me I could have more children. I had not been permanently damaged by the attack. Fitzroy overheard him tell me that. I thanked Griffin without revealing Bertram's situation. I felt it was none of his business.

Dear old Jack barely left my side. Fitzroy joked about getting himself another dog. All the time Fitzroy's eyes seemed to follow me. If we were in a room together he kept watching me. Eventually I called him on it.

'You keep looking at me and looking sad,' I said. 'Am I that pitiful?'

'I keep thinking that I have ruined your life,' he said. 'If I had never come into it, you and Bertram would be happily married, living at White Orchards and,' he swallowed, 'starting your family.'

'I don't blame you,' I said. 'I never have. Not for anything.'

'You should,' he said. 'You would have been so much better off never meeting me.'

'Well, considering Bertram is unlikely to ever make me a mother now, I'm afraid you are stuck with me as a partner for life. If I can't be a mother, I need to have another way for my life to have meaning.'

'You have more than served your nation already.'

'This is all I have left, Eric,' I said quietly. 'Don't let them take it away from me.'

Fitzroy shook his head. 'I won't. I haven't. I knew what you'd say.' He sighed. 'The idea that White Orchards could become a discreet meeting place for dignitaries, diplomats and other interested parties over Christmastide is to go ahead. Of course, you will have the first few days alone, and then—'

'Not alone. I'm not ready for that. You must come too.'

Fitzroy frowned. 'I am far from being Bertram's favourite person.'

'I need your support,' I said. 'I can't tell him about . . . about the baby I lost. It wouldn't be fair.'

Fitzroy came over and knelt down beside my chair. 'Are you sure, Euphemia?' he said. 'That is a very big secret to keep from him.'

I nodded. Tears ran silently down my face. 'It would make him so unhappy to know I lost our only chance.'

'You cannot be sure of that,' urged the spy. 'The doctors are being over-cautious. Bertram always bounces back.'

'I don't think he will this time,' I said.

'If you want me there, of course I will be there,' said Fitzroy. 'But I still think you are making a big mistake not telling him. It will always stand between you.

'It's my mistake to make,' I said. 'Besides, I have you.'

'Always,' said Fitzroy. Then he broke the mood by giving me his cheekiest grin. 'Whether you want me around or not!'